THE DEATH OF IVAN ILYICH
and Other Stories

THE DEATH OF IVAN ILYICH

and Other Stories

◆

Leo Tolstoy

Introduction and Notes by
DR T. C. B. COOK

WORDSWORTH CLASSICS

This edition published 2004 by Wordsworth Editions Limited
8B East Street, Ware, Hertfordshire SG12 9HJ

ISBN 1 84022 453 3

Text © Wordsworth Editions Limited 2004
Introduction and Notes © Tim Cook 2004

Wordsworth ® is a registered trademark of
Wordsworth Editions Limited

2 4 6 8 10 9 7 5 3 1

Typeset by Antony Gray
Printed and bound in Great Britain by
Mackays of Chatham, Chatham, Kent

CONTENTS

GENERAL INTRODUCTION

Wordsworth Classics are inexpensive editions designed to appeal to the general reader and students. We commissioned teachers and specialists to write wide ranging, jargon-free introductions and to provide notes that would assist the understanding of our readers rather than interpret the stories for them. In the same spirit, because the pleasures of reading are inseparable from the surprises, secrets and revelations that all narratives contain, we strongly advise you to enjoy this book before turning to the Introduction.

General Adviser
KEITH CARABINE
Rutherford College
University of Kent at Canterbury

INTRODUCTION

Tolstoy's great novel about married life, *Anna Karenina*, famously begins with a sentence contrasting happy and unhappy families. His own experience of domesticity, as his biographers have shown us, began relatively happily, but degenerated, both for his wife and himself, into nightmare. Some of the psychological processes that were to help create that nightmare are reflected in the novel, which, as his biographers have shown us, is, in the parts dealing with the life of Levin, closely based on Tolstoy's own early married life.

There is in fact ample evidence in Tolstoy's own non-fictional writings and those of members of his family, including his wife, to show how much of his fiction, from the early trilogy *Childhood, Boyhood, Youth* onwards, was semi-autobiographical. Similarly, each of the four stories in this volume can be related either to incidents in the author's life or to a stage in the evolution of his thought based on his own experiences. All of them also deal in a variety of ways with relationships between the sexes and their place in the general context of human life. In writing them he uses, as we shall see, a variety of narrative strategies.

They range from the partly fulfilled hopes of contentment in courtship and marriage explored in 'Family Happiness', published three years before his own marriage in 1862, to the disillusionment and disgust connected with marital and sexual relationships that characterise the four stories from his later years included with it in this volume and written after his two great novels *War and Peace* (1869) and *Anna Karenina* (1877).

The increasing bleakness of Tolstoy's vision of life emerges in the longest and perhaps most remarkable of the stories included here, 'The Death of Ivan Ilyich', in which he focuses all his narrative skills on the situation of a man afflicted with a terminal illness, whose career and social status have been far more important to him than the quality of his marriage and domestic human relationships, and who faces his end in a desert of lovelessness.

In fact from his earliest years Tolstoy's own views on the possibility of genuine love between the sexes and the part which it should play in life were complicated by guilt about his own powerful sexual drive, relieved in the years before his marriage to Sofia Alexandreyevna Behrs by prostitutes, affairs with women in his own social circle and a passionate relationship with a peasant woman, Aksinia, who lived on his own estate at Yasnaya Polyana.

This guilt led him to confess, in a kind of self-purging ritual, the full range of his sexual experiences to his much younger and totally inexperienced bride by making her read his intimate diaries on the eve of their wedding, an episode reprised, almost exactly as it happened, in *Anna Karenina*, Part Four, Chapter 16. It is used again, as we shall see, in 'The Kreutzer Sonata'. Indeed the subsequent strains, suspicions and jealousies that mar the relationship between Tolstoy's alter ego, Levin, in that novel and his young bride Kitty, probably mirror to a great extent the emotional ups and downs that characterised his own marriage at that time. However, as we shall see, even in work published before that marriage, he expresses ideas on male–female relationships that to an enlightened modern reader will seem highly problematic.

Family Happiness

In the first novella in our selection, 'Family Happiness', published in 1859 the narrative voice is that of a seventeen-year-old girl, describing how she fell in love with and ultimately married a family

friend and neighbour, a man in his thirties. The story is split into
two parts, the first dealing with the couple's courtship and wedding,
the second with the early years of their marriage. At its heart is the
conflict between youth and maturity, innocence and experience
and, most importantly, masculine and feminine points of view, here,
uniquely, seen from the latter.

The story was in fact written at a time when Tolstoy was
considering marriage to the young daughter of some neighbours
about three years before he settled finally on Sofia Alexandreyevna.
It anticipates uncannily some of his own future marital problems,
illustrating very clearly his masculist assumptions. Indeed he appears
to have written it as a counterblast to the proto-feminist views
expressed in Chernyshevsky's widely read novel *What Is To Be
Done?*[1]

The girl, Masha, is an orphan, having lost her mother on the eve
of being launched into St Petersburg society. Initially she sees her
mentor as simply a father substitute, since although her dead
mother saw him as a possible husband, he hardly matches her
romantic expectations:

> . . . the hero of my dreams was utterly different. My hero was
> delicate, slender, pale and melancholy. Sergey Mihalovich was a
> man no longer youthful, tall, squarely built, and, as I fancied,
> always cheerful.   [p. 4]

He, on the other hand now sees a 'rose' where six years before he
had seen a 'girl-violet', and begins from the outset to assess her. He
asks her to play the *adagio* of Beethoven's *Moonlight Sonata*, a
movement in tune with her adolescent sensibilities. His apprecia-
tion of her playing begins to change her view of him too, and she
resents the fact that he still regards her as a child.

Tolstoy ends the first chapter, appropriately set in winter, with an
image of the orphaned girl's funereally dark house suddenly being
filled with light. The next chapter is set in spring, and is full of
natural imagery, with extended passages of lyrical writing setting
the scene as seen through a young girl's impressionable eyes, for
instance just before Sergei's next visit:

> We were sitting in the verandah, just going to have tea. The
> garden was already all in green, and among the overgrown
> shrubs the nightingales had been building all through St

---

1 See Eikhenbaum, *Tolstoy in the Seventies*, p. 95.

Peter's fast. The leafy lilac bushes looked as though they had been sprinkled at the top with something white and lilac, where the flowers were just going to come out. The foliage of the birch avenue was all transparent in the setting sun. It was cool and shady in the verandah. There must have been a heavy evening dew on the grass . . . On the white cloth set before us on the verandah stood the brilliantly polished samovar boiling, cream, and biscuits and cakes. Katya, like a careful housewife, was rinsing the cups with her plump hands. I was hungry after bathing; and without waiting for the tea to be ready, I was eating some bread heaped with thick, fresh cream. I had on a linen blouse with open sleeves, and had tied a kerchief over my wet hair.   [p. 89]

Through such paragraphs of intensely evocative descriptive writing Tolstoy slows the narrative down, in this part of the story, and provides a choric background to the developing intimacy of the girl and her potential suitor. She becomes more and more aware of his 'shining eyes', and his sexual interest in her, as he approaches, obliquely, the possibility of marriage. Her response is to try to conform to his expectations and image of her, while noticing, to an extent that foreshadows later difficulties in the relationship, his unwillingness to share with her 'a whole unknown world into which he did not think fit to initiate me'. (p. 13)

Her eagerness to show herself 'worthy' of him and not 'frivolously vain', heightens her awareness of her social environment. She begins to appreciate the self-sacrifice of her ageing companion Katya, and to identify more with the peasants on her estate:

He taught me to look at our people – peasants, house-serfs, and serf-girls – quite differently from how I had done. It sounds an absurd thing to say, but I had grown up to seventeen among these people more remote from them than from people I had never seen. I had never once reflected that these people had their loves, desires, and regrets just as I had.   [p. 15]

In these passages we as readers become increasingly aware of the underlying didactic purpose behind the story. Tolstoy is providing his young feminine readers with a role model in his heroine, indicating the values he would like to see inculcated in them, going on to emphasise how far their own independence and aspirations would be sacrificed in any marriage. We can also see here an early indication of the direction in which Tolstoy's thought would develop, as he came more and more to prefer the philosophy of life of what Lenin called 'the patriarchal naïve peasant'[2] to the values and concerns of the society in which he had been brought up.

With the third chapter we move into autumn, and more vividly detailed scene-setting. The opening paragraphs evoke the hot afternoon and the sights and sounds of the busy estate with the peasants at work on the harvest 'in the scalding sunshine', while Masha, her younger sister Sonya and Katya enjoy the privileges of their social position. When Sergei Mihalovich arrives and Masha overhears him talking to himself about her in a way that confirms his love for her, she realises that now she has some degree of power over him, that he 'was not now like an old uncle, petting and instructing me, but a man equal with me, who loved and feared me, and whom I feared and loved'. (p. 20)

The ensuing moonlit autumn evening and night are described with an intensity and complexity of lyrical, synaesthetic detail that reflect the extreme happiness of Tolstoy's heroine in her knowledge that 'from that day he was mine, and that now I should not lose him'. It is the climactic scene in this part of the story, and is followed by Masha's spiritual preparations for her marital destiny, as she purges herself of minor 'sins' and tries to treat her social 'inferiors' in a way of which her lover would approve. Having remade herself in his image, she looks forward confidently to their life together:

It seemed to me that we should be so endlessly and calmly happy. And I pictured to myself not tours abroad, not society, and a brilliant life, but something quite different, a quiet family life in the country with continual self-sacrifice, continual love for one another, and a continual sense in all things of a kind and beneficent Providence. [p. 28]

So when Sergey Mihalovich reveals, disingenuously, that he plans to go away to avoid greater intimacy, she is all too ready to confess her own feelings and accept a proposal of marriage.

At this stage she feel entirely on equal terms with him, and it is only when he closes the door of their honeymoon carriage that she realises her power has ended. Sudden feelings of pain and humiliation are, however, quickly dissipated.

2 See P. Macherey, *A Theory of Literary Production*, Chapter 19, for a discussion of Lenin's views on Tolstoy, and his Appendix (p. 316) for the passage quoted above.

I felt warm, my eyes sought his in the dusk, and I suddenly felt that I was not afraid of him, that that dread was love, a new and still more tender and passionate love than before. I felt that I was altogether his, and that I was happy in his power over me.

[p. 39]

The second part of the novella finds Masha adjusting to her new life as mistress of an old-fashioned, highly ordered household, previously presided over by her mother-in-law, still a dominant presence in the house. Predictably, the gloom of midwinter brings loneliness and boredom. Her husband is often away on business, and she feels unfulfilled, with no outlet for her energy. As the confining snow piles up around the house she dreams of another life available to people of her class, knowing that 'far away somewhere, in bright light and noise, crowds of people were in movement, were suffering and rejoicing, without a thought of us and our existence as it passed away'. (p. 46)

She also resents being excluded, as a woman, from the public activities which occupy her husband. When, sensing her need for romance and excitement, he takes her to St Petersburg via Moscow, she enters a brave new world of sophisticated city life and is warmly welcomed as a beautiful newcomer, flattered to find herself the centre of attention in an environment he despises. Her social triumph gives her a new sense of power, and she begins to resent his reservations. Soon an invitation to meet a foreign prince sparks off their first real quarrel and evidence of the husband's apprehensive jealousy:

'I have long been expecting this,' I said; 'say it, say it!'

'I don't know what you've been expecting,' he went on. 'I might well have expected the worst, seeing you every day in the uncleanness and idleness and luxury of this silly society, and I've got it too. I've come to feeling ashamed and sick today, as I have never felt for myself. When your friend with her unclean hands pried into my heart and began talking of jealousy, my jealousy – of whom? – a man whom neither I nor you know. And you, on purpose it seems – refuse to understand me and want to sacrifice to me – what? . . . I'm ashamed of you, ashamed of your degradation! . . . Sacrifice!' he repeated.

'Ah, here we have it, the power of the husband,' I thought, 'to insult and humiliate his wife, who is in no way to blame. These are a husband's rights, but I won't submit to it.'

'No, I won't sacrifice anything to you,' I declared, feeling my nostrils dilating unnaturally, and the blood deserting my face. 'I'm going to the *soirée* on Saturday; I shall certainly go!'

[p. 56]

Although they make it up, he now seems 'old and disagreeable' and a gulf opens up between them. He has, in Congreve's words, 'dwindled' into an ordinary husband, while she seeks her satisfactions in a society environment ultimately as constricting as the domestic one she had left. Even when she becomes a mother, she is still, defiantly living a society life, significantly wearing her ball gown when she goes to say good-night to her child, but she is increasingly uneasy about her behaviour and conscious of her husband's stern disapproval. The crisis comes when she finds one of her circle, to her horror, sexually attractive. Recalling her past happiness with her husband, she retreats to the country, where 'every board, every wall, every sofa recalled to me what he had been to me, and what I had lost.' (p. 67)

Spring returns to the old house, but the emotional atmosphere has changed irredeemably. Her husband comes in to find her playing the *andante* of the sonata familiar from their courtship, and the stage is set for a sober restoration of harmony, a redefinition of their love, and her final surrender to his values.

Despite its insights and the lyricism of much of the writing, the didacticism marring much of Tolstoy's later fiction is already present in this story, with the husband providing the moral norm by which we are clearly intended to judge Masha's actions, as she does herself. Although Tolstoy identifies to a considerable extent with the girl's frustrated aspirations, there is no doubt where he thinks power should reside. For him already, the key to successful marriage is the husband's taming of the wife's independent spirit – a process in which childbirth plays an important part. In the remaining stories here, written after the extended analysis of different marriages in *Anna Karenina*, we have variations on this theme and a general darkening of tone.

The Death of Ivan Ilyich

The next story in this volume, 'The Death of Ivan Ilyich', was written in 1886, almost a decade after Tolstoy had finished *Anna Karenina*, and seven years after a remarkable non-fiction work, his *Confession* of 1879, which reveals how much more negative his view of life had become since *Anna Karenina*. He was now in his late fifties and his relationship with his wife had steadily deteriorated.

He had become obsessed with thoughts about death, having compared himself in his *Confession* to a traveller clinging to the weakening branch of life above a pit in which the dragon of death awaits him.[3] Such thoughts and his marital disillusionments engendered in 'The Death of Ivan Ilyich' a story that is Tolstoy's equivalent of a medieval morality play such as *Everyman*.

The *Confession* had signalled the start of the transformation of Tolstoy the admired writer into Tolstoy the revered sage, revealing his increasing concern with religious and spiritual matters. It described how he came to question the doctrines and observances of the Russian Orthodox faith in which he had been brought up and of organised Christianity generally, while always regarding Christ's teachings as paramount. Eventually he would develop a kind of 'religion' of his own, incorporating a rationalisation of his feelings of guilt and disgust at his own and his wife's sexuality. Finally he would come to believe that the ideal life was one of sexual abstinence, and that most human activities and concerns were meaningless when considered in relation to the fact of death.

'The Death of Ivan Ilyich' (originally entitled 'The Death of a Judge'), perhaps the most powerful story ever written about a life approaching its end, marks a stage in the development of these views. We are now in a very different and much darker world from the subjective one of the heroine of 'Family Happiness'. There is a complete absence in it of the vivid, joyous passages of natural description that lighten the tone of the earlier story. Instead of being made privy to the romantic expectations of a young girl approaching marriage, described in her own voice, we have a detached, rather cold-blooded, grimly amused, omniscient narrator charting the accelerated progress of a man through life to his own death. It is a life in which, largely because of the extreme self-centredness of the central figure, marriage becomes a major source of torment amongst other torments.

The narrator begins, in the longest chapter in the story, with what would chronologically be its end: the aftermath of Ilyich's death. He shows us how swiftly the gap left by the ending of an individual life is filled. With black, and all too truthful, humour, he recounts how Ivan's legal colleagues, acquaintances and family react, with most of them immediately calculating how they benefit from the situation. His closest friend Pyotr Ivanovich is, it is true, worried by the death for a while, nervously crossing himself as he

3 L. N. Tolstoy, *My Confession*, p. 19

reluctantly enters the room where the corpse is laid out and sees the dead man's face:

> He was much changed and grown even thinner since Pyotr Ivanovich had last seen him, but, as is always the case with the dead, his face was handsomer and above all more dignified than when he was alive. The expression on the face said that what was necessary had been accomplished, and accomplished rightly. Besides this there was in that expression a reproach and a warning to the living. This warning seemed to Pyotr Ivanovich out of place, or at least not applicable to him. He felt a certain discomfort and so he hurriedly crossed himself once more and turned and went out of the door – too hurriedly and too regardless of propriety, as he himself was aware.   [p. 82]

Ironically, unlike his more determinedly frivolous companion, Shvarts, Pyotr Ivanovich cannot completely shrug off the *memento mori* message of their friend's death, a message that as we shall see Ivan himself neglected until he was compelled to take notice of it. Indeed, as the passage shows, Pyotr Ivanovich's chief concern is with those very 'proprieties' which we shall see ruled Ivan's life almost until its end. The main emotion felt by him and his living friends is, in fact, annoyance at the inconvenience of having to leave the 'unsanctified' candles which light their usual card games for the ones which will illuminate the funeral. This satire of all too recognisable human attitudes is enhanced by comic touches such as the description of the ottoman with 'deranged springs' (p. 83) on which Pyotr Ivanovich sits to talk embarrassedly to the widow before rushing off to that delayed game of cards.

Only in the second chapter, almost equally long, do we move to the dead man himself, whose dying screams, lasting three days, have been described to Pyotr Ivanovich by his shattered wife. We learn that his story is one that is 'most ordinary, and the most awful'. (p. 86)[4] It is 'most ordinary' because it is a familiar one paralleling what happens in a great number of lives, and 'most awful' because all too many of us are likely to face an end similar to that endured by Ivan Ilyich. The story is designed to make us starkly aware of the folly of overvaluing our lifetime achievements and being too worried about external appearances. It demonstrates

---

4 The translation of the Russian here seems rather unfortunate, since 'awful' has lost its original force in colloquial English. 'Terrible' or even 'terrifying' seems more appropriate.

how irrelevant to others, and insignificant in the general scheme of things, individual lives and their concomitant sufferings and concerns ultimately are.

Tolstoy begins with a detailed and fairly leisurely account of Ivan's life, his marriage and his highly respectable and prominent legal career. He is, in fact, a man for whom his domestic life is a poor second to his public position. Marriage is merely a convenience, in that it helps him maintain his status, comforts and sense of self-importance. When his intelligent and attractive wife begins to make emotional demands on him, his reactions are characteristic:

> Very quickly, not more than a year after his wedding, Ivan Ilyich had become aware that conjugal life, though providing certain comforts, was in reality a very intricate and difficult business towards which one must, if one is to do one's duty, that is, lead the decorous life approved by society, work out for oneself a definite line, just as in the government service.
>
> And such a line Ivan Ilyich did work out for himself in his married life. He expected from his home life only those comforts – of dinner at home, of housekeeper and bed – which it could give him, and, above all, that perfect propriety in external observances required by public opinion. For the rest he looked for good-humoured pleasantness, and if he found it he was very thankful. If he met with antagonism and querulousness, he promptly retreated into the separate world he had shut off for himself in his official life, and there he found solace.   [p. 92]

In a third chapter, roughly equivalent in length to the first two, we see Ivan Ilyich rise, overcoming earlier professional setbacks, to a senior level in the judiciary, always ensuring that as far as his image and his public activities are concerned 'perfect propriety' is observed. Because, however, his wife is someone he cannot exercise power over (as the argument implicit in 'Family Happiness' implies he should), he neglects his marriage and its emotional demands in favour of his power and status as a judge, concentrating instead on the face he presents to the outside world, and enjoying the deference of his junior colleagues and the people attending his court.

Eventually he reaches the summit of his career, acquiring a house and furniture to match his status. His wife, whose main concern is now with their material well-being, since she derives no emotional satisfaction from their marriage, is now less hostile than before. However it is at this point that nemesis strikes, in a bourgeois version of its arrival in Greek tragedy. While busying himself with the decoration of his new house he receives the injury which, the story implies, leads ultimately to his death.

These two chapters have dealt with events taking place over many years, but the fourth, almost equally long, lingers over a much shorter period, in which we see Ivan's sinister symptoms developing, along with his anxiety, self-pity and sense of isolation, contributed to by his wife's lack of sympathy[5] and their frequent quarrels.

What light relief there is in the grim and all too predictable narrative is provided by satire of the ignorant knowingness of the various doctors and others who attempt diagnoses right up to the moment when the disease (almost certainly cancer) is recognised as terminal. Ivan is now subjected to their professional power just as the people over whom he exercised his judicial authority had to accept his. At the same time he suddenly realises that death, hitherto an abstract concept only affecting a theoretical Caius in the syllogism 'Caius is a man, men are mortal, therefore Caius is mortal' (p. 110), is about to become the dominant fact in his own life. We see him at work, ravaged by disease but still trying to preserve the appearance of decorous normality in his public duties and trying to fight off the pain.

> He drove away the thought of it, but it still did its work, and then *It* came and stood confronting him and looked at him, and he felt turned to stone, and the light died away in his eyes, and he began to ask himself again, 'Can it be that It is the only truth?'
>
> [p. 111]

From this point on the chapters, with one exception, become very short, as we accelerate, brief stage by brief stage, to the inevitable end, each one recording a further deterioration in the patient's condition and his morale, and as it were hurrying him deathwards. In them Tolstoy gives us a bleakly economical, psychologically penetrating picture of the isolated suffering of an individual human being with a fatal and horribly painful condition, transforming Ivan Ilyich from a successful lawyer into the Everyman figure suggested above, and the story into a mirror into which all of us can look and see our possible fates reflected.

His family, the doctors and his circle of acquaintances are helpless and useless to him in his crisis. His wife, originally dismissing him as

---

5 As Wasiolek points out (*Tolstoy's Major Fiction*, p. 176), Ilyich has previously been indifferent to her pain in pregnancy.

a hypochondriac who is failing to follow medical advice, eventually recognises his plight but can offer little in the way of effective comfort or relief, which is unsurprising, considering the nature of their marriage. By the seventh chapter he has accepted that he is dying and his concern with his official life and public image has begun to take second place to his obsession with his physical condition.

The only person who can alleviate his suffering in any way is the simple practical-minded healthy young peasant Gerasim, who accepts the extreme physical unpleasantness involved in nursing the dying man and discovers a practical method of alleviating his pain. Gerasim embodies Tolstoy's enduring belief that the peasantry's uncomplicated faith and stoical acceptance of whatever life inflicted on them were vastly preferable to the sophisticated insincerities, decadent materialism and 'perfected proprieties' of the society into which he had been born. Ilyich's constricting sense of decorum is such that, though he accepts Gerasim's care and longs 'to be petted, kissed, and wept over' (p. 116), when a colleague comes in he reverts to the severe businesslike persona appropriate to a judge.

From now on Tolstoy dwells on the day-to-day detail of Ivan Ilyich's existence, slowing the action down to make us share his agony hour by hour. At times the narration moves from the past into the present tense to increase the immediacy of our involvement. The next chapter, the eighth, the only one that matches the first four chapters in length concentrates on the extent to which the sick man's relationship with his wife and daughter has deteriorated.

What might, in the case of a less self-centred person, have been a consolation, is merely, another source of torment, while his family, all in vigorous good health and enjoying an active social life, regard his suffering with impatience, worrying instead about the economic consequences for them of his death. The only exception to this, we learn later, is Ivan's small son, whose eyes, dark-ringed with grief over his father's suffering, show how the familial world he has spurned in favour of public success might have offered him the love which could alleviate his pain and loneliness.

The final four chapters, all extremely brief, take us swiftly to the conclusion. In the ninth Tolstoy introduces the terrifying, claustrophobic image of the dark sack into which Ivan feels he is being thrust, struggling helplessly like a trapped animal. Protesting at his treatment by a cruel God he thinks back over his past life. He remembers his childhood and early education and begins at last to question the values he has since come to live by, disgusted even with the marriage he entered into for the wrong reasons. Vivid memories of the distant past flood into his mind in the tenth chapter but he still obstinately refuses to question his values as he tries to find some explanation for his situation:

> 'It could be explained if one were to say that I hadn't lived as I ought. But that can't be alleged,' he said to himself, thinking of all the regularity, correctness, and propriety of his life. 'That really can't be admitted . . . '   [p. 126]

So obsessed is he with this question, with his pain, and with the possibility that the principles he has been living by might have been false ones, that he brutally rebuffs his wife and daughter when they bring him news of the latter's engagement. He, the judge, finds he cannot defend the beliefs that have dictated his behaviour all his life, and consequently he endures still more violent agonies, only briefly relieved by a sacramental visit from a priest invited by his wife, and intensified rather than assuaged by the latter's concern.

The outward sign of these is the scream, lasting for three days, that she described at the beginning of the story. It accompanies his final struggles in the dark sack, as he tries, even at the point of death, to deny that all his life he has been in the wrong. Only at the last minute does he give up fighting, symbolically 'seeing the light', at the moment when his grief-stricken young son's hand touches his. Then, finally aware of the boy's love and his family's distress, he is able to become a complete human being and surrender to his own mortality. His last words to them are a stifled plea for forgiveness as he surrenders to the inevitable and accepts release in death.

The Kreutzer Sonata

In 'The Death of Ivan Ilyich', the protagonist's unsatisfactory domestic life is only one element in a story written to explore far wider issues, though the failure of his marriage is surely intended by Tolstoy to be due to that same self-centredness and failure in personal relationships that make Ivan's death even more terrifying than it might otherwise have been. His self-centredness can be seen as a negative version of the self-sufficiency and self-awareness that John Bayley has identified as important positives in Tolstoy's thought.[6]

The mutual dislike that makes Ivan Ilyich's marriage so bleak becomes homicidal hatred in the next, highly controversial story,

6 J. Bayley, *Tolstoy and the Novel*, p. 50

'The Kreutzer Sonata', published in 1889. It is probably the story in which Tolstoy's writing is closest to Dostoevsky's in its tone and in its exploration of abnormal states of mind.

The story was written at a time when relations between Tolstoy and his wife were disastrously bad. His life was now dominated by his relations with his handsome young assistant Chertkov, which his wife in the end suspected, almost certainly without foundation, of having a sexual basis.[7] (It is possible, however, that the character of Ivan Ilyich's male nurse Gerasim in the earlier story, as well as representing Tolstoy's trust in the peasantry, was partly a covert allusion to Chertkov's moral support in his war with his wife.)

Whereas in 'Family Happiness', Tolstoy uses a deeply involved young first-person female narrator and in 'The Death of Ivan Ilyich' a detached and rather dry commentator of indeterminate sex, in 'The Kreutzer Sonata' he effectively has two first-person narratives, the initial one framing and occasionally interrupting the main autobiographical story told by the murderer Pózdnyshev. The first narration is initially uninvolved and a little amused, later withdrawing into the background, except for a few comments resembling stage directions; the second is urgent and later hysterical in tone. The story was originally circulated in a lithographed version, in which many of Pózdnyshev's arguments are expanded, but they add little of real substance to the revised published version.

The action begins in a railway carriage with a representative group of middle-class passengers discussing contemporary social issues, in particular changing attitudes to marriage. They range from an elderly merchant, who believes in the dying custom of arranged marriages and whose views on marital relationships and duties are firmly based on the Bible, to those who support the more modern 'European' view that one should only marry someone one loves. The most vociferous supporter of the modern position is a woman wearing, significantly, a 'mannish' coat. The debate is listened to by a 'nervous man with glittering eyes', who intervenes in the discussion to question the whole idea of marriage for love, and finally reveals that he has killed his own wife.

He is left with the original narrator when the other passengers leave, driven away by the violence of his tirade against marriage, which he regards as a form of sanctioned prostitution of women, and thereafter tells his own story, only occasionally interrupted by his

---

7 See A. N. Wilson on the relationship, *Tolstoy*, p. 353, and on Sofia's later suspicions, p. 494.

listener, who provides the equivalent of stage directions. Despite the fact that he has murdered one of that gender, he shows a surprising sympathy for women as victims of male repression and exploitation.

The murderer, Pózdnyshev, begins with a self-damning description of his life as a typical young Russian aristocrat of the time in his sexual development and his exploitation of women for pleasure, in a society which regarded it as vital to men's health that they should be sexually active. He denounces the hypocrisy of young men like his earlier self who demanded that their wives should be 'pure' after themselves living sexually active lives. He tells his listener, how he made his own future wife read his diary, a reuse of the episode in *Anna Karenina* based on Tolstoy's own experience.

Pózdnyshev's marriage, however, unlike his creator's, is remarkable for the rapidity of its breakdown. There is total lack of understanding and communication between husband and wife from the first. Pózdnyshev is, of course speaking in his own defence, and in the circumstances is hardly a reliable narrator. Nevertheless, from the first, readers of the story, including Tolstoy's wife, saw how, to a very great extent, the views he puts into Pózdnyshev's mouth replicated his own. Indeed the Afterword (pp. 201–5) Tolstoy added to the story expounds doctrines that seem to confirm this relationship. Moreover, although the grimness of the murderer's tale is from time to time relieved by little touches of stage direction by the narrator and the odd sceptical comment,[8] these do relatively little to distance him or us from its content and arguments. It is left to the violence of the language and the strangeness of Pózdnyshev's behaviour to do that.

By comparison with the work of other writers he is hardly a subtle creation. Although his characterisation may owe a little to Dostoevsky's embittered Underground Man,[9] there is too much of the Tolstoyan propagandist in him to make him the equal of Dostoevsky's studies of minds out of kilter.

His actual story is powerfully told in a series of short chapters each marking a new stage in marital breakdown until we reach the climactic murder. We see in Pózdnyshev's portrayal of his wife how far his obsessions and experience have corrupted his vision. After his considerable premarital experience, in which sexual

8 For instance, in Chapter 9 he protests that sex , called by Pózdnyshev 'vice', is in fact a most natural human function.

9 the central character and first-person narrative voice in Dostoevsky's *Notes From Underground*

relationships have largely been commercial transactions, he has married a suitably 'pure' girl simply on the basis of the curls and tight-fitting jersey which have made her attractive to him, confusing charm of appearance with charm of character. For him 'poetic love' is now seen as an illusion created by a general conspiracy of mothers who know that it

> depends not on moral qualities but on physical nearness and on the *coiffure*, and the colour and cut of the dress. Ask an expert coquette who has set herself the task of captivating a man, which she would prefer to risk: to be convicted in his presence of lying, of cruelty, or even of dissoluteness, or to appear before him in an ugly and badly made dress – she will always prefer the first. She knows that we are continually lying about high sentiments, but really want only her body and will therefore forgive any abomination except an ugly, tasteless costume that is in bad style.   [p. 147]

For Pózdnyshev the excessive consumption of the rich fuels their sensuality, and the repression of men's sexual drive when dealing with women of their own class channels their feelings disastrously into a temporary phenomenon known as 'falling in love'. The disappearance of the arranged marriage which settled a woman's future without the need for someone to 'fall in love' with her was to women's disadvantage, since they now have to compete to be chosen. So they follow the advice of their mothers and set out to deceive potential husbands into thinking them interesting. Yet at the same time, it empowers them and has created an enormous industry designed to satisfy their material needs.

Everything connected with the idea of married love, in his view, is disgusting. His engagement is an unpleasant business in which he found he had nothing in common with his fiancée, his honeymoon an abomination, sexual relations a vice which a husband has to 'cultivate' in his unspoilt and reluctant girl wife in order to enjoy it. Everything is seen in the darkest light (indeed Pózdnyshev dislikes the actual light and draws a shade over the carriage lamp as he is speaking)[10] and described in extreme language.

> I wondered what embittered us against one another, yet it was perfectly simple: that animosity was nothing but the protest of our human nature against the animal nature that overpowered it.

10 'The Kreutzer Sonata', p. 141

I was surprised at our enmity to one another, yet it could not have been otherwise. That hatred was nothing but the mutual hatred of accomplices in a crime – both for the incitement of the crime and for the part taken in it. What was it but a crime, when she, poor thing, became pregnant in the first month and our *swinish* connection continued.   [p. 158]

We as readers can see through his language and readily construct an alternative scenario in which his wife, isolated from her family and faced with such a partner, is depressed almost from the first, with no bond between the couple but their sexual need for each other, and their relationship punctuated by more and more frequent quarrels. So despite his attempt to justify his murder of his wife, Pózdnyshev is constantly making the case for her defence: the lack of common interests, her early depression, his sense that she is his victim when she becomes pregnant, especially as he expects her to go on serving his sexual needs. It is not only his wife for whom he has sympathy:

'My wife, who wanted to nurse, and did nurse the four later children herself, happened to be unwell after the birth of her first child. And those doctors, who cynically undressed her and felt her all over – for which I had to thank them and pay them money – those dear doctors considered that she must not nurse the child; and that first time she was deprived of the only means which might have kept her from coquetry. We engaged a wet nurse, that is, we took advantage of the poverty, the need, and the ignorance of a woman, tempted her away from her own baby to ours, and in return gave her a fine head-dress with gold lace . . .   [p. 162]

Nevertheless, that sympathy is counteracted by the sexual jealousy and possessiveness which is evident in his feelings about the doctors, whom he sees, in any case, as part of the general conspiracy of decadents. (As in 'The Death of Ivan Ilyich', the story reflects a real distrust of doctors in Tolstoy himself.) They are feelings commented upon by his listener, inspiring another torrent of invective. From doctors we move to the children whom society women are reluctant to have in case they fall ill and need care and again Pózdnyshev's attitude is one of sympathy for their dilemma.

Yet his own experience of his wife's attitude to her children, although he acknowledges her qualities as a mother, becomes one more factor in destroying the marriage. Eventually she takes contraceptive measures on her doctors' advice, to preserve her health. In Pózdnyshev's view this is a deeply immoral step that liberates her sexually and, now her children are less in need of her, enables her to pursue the treacherous illusion, as he sees it, of love:

> But love with a husband, *befouled by jealousy and all kinds of anger* [my italics], was no longer the thing she wanted. She had visions of some other, clean, new love; at least I thought she had. And she began to look about her as if expecting something.   [p. 171]

It is at this point, when Pózdnyshev too has begun to 'expect something', that his jealous mind has an object to fasten on: the musician Trukhachévsky whom he has invited into his household and kept inviting despite misgivings, impelled by a mysterious force. It is as though he is in the grip of an evil power he cannot resist.[11] The music which brings Trukhachévsky and Pózdnyshev's wife together is the hectic first movement of Beethoven's *Kreutzer Sonata*. The contrast between this piece and the sonata movement played by Masha at key moments in 'Family Happiness' in itself illustrates how much more tormented the vision of love and marriage explored in Tolstoy's fiction has become.

The name of the musician, Trukhachévsky, suggests, in Russian, 'rottenness'. He is presented in the story as being a very sensual figure, almost feminine, with red lips and a large bottom. This has led to the ingenious suggestion that the story is a study of repressed homosexuality, coupled with misogynistic sadism in Pózdnyshev, with the murder arising from his jealous fantasies about sexual relationships between Trukhachévsky and his wife.[12] If that were the case it would make an interesting parallel with the emotional rejection by Ivan Ilyich of his wife and dependence on Gerasim, whose fresh complexion and healthy body are emphasised in the previous story.

In any case, as we have seen, the relationship between Pózdnyshev and his wife has already deteriorated considerably by the time Trukhachévsky arrives. Pózdnyshev envies the latter's talent, and begins to suspect them of using their music as a cover for other activities, seeing music in his characteristically distorted

11 See Donald Davie's discussion of Tolstoy's intentions in Gifford, *Tolstoy*, pp. 326–7.
12 I. Velikovsky (trans. J. V. Coleman), 'Unconscious Homosexuality in "The Kreutzer Sonata" ', *Psychoanalytic Review*, Vol XXIV, No. 1, 1937

way as yet another of society's devices for furthering immorality. The only element in the story that could indicate the couple's guilt is the sense that Pózdnyshev has that they share some secret pleasure, but as the narration suggests, this could simply be their delight in the music they are playing together. Indeed, if we read between the lines, Tolstoy makes it plain that Pózdnyshev's wife is genuinely puzzled and alarmed by his behaviour. Indeed his wild and irrational rages make her ill.

Up to this point the action has accelerated through the chapters, much as it did in 'The Death of Ivan Ilyich'. After Trukhachévsky's arrival on the scene it slows down, with the conversations dealt with at length, until the final day, the day of the murder. This begins with Pózdnyshev, who has only just been reconciled with his wife, reading a letter from her which tells him that Trukhachévsky has visited his house in his absence. The mere fact that she has told him this is of course an indication that she is guiltless but it is the trigger for her murder.

Thereafter Pózdnyshev describes his actions and feelings as it were in slow motion, with the climactic moment where his dagger enters her body taking three lengthy paragraphs. The lingering sexual relish with which the murder is described is deeply disturbing, and it is small wonder that yet another psychological study[13] has seen it as an expression of Tolstoy's own sadistic hatred of women, caused by his own loss of his mother when he was an infant.

This view does not of course bear too much examination in the light of Tolstoy's earlier work. It is more valuable to see Tolstoy's misogyny as something that evolved through his life, possibly as a result of disappointment with his own marriage and his search for spiritual and intellectual satisfaction elsewhere, driven by his guilt over his own powerful sexual feelings. That guilt comes to be projected more and more on to the women who inspired sexual feelings in him. The name he gives his murderer – Pózdnyshev – is derived from the Russian for 'late', *pózdny*, and much of the story, as the Afterword proves, reflects views he had developed late in life. However, even in 'The Kreutzer Sonata', it is qualified by his idea that patterns of behaviour have been forced on women by the pressures of a sexually corrupt society.

An alternative explanation of Pózdnyshev's behaviour is offered

13 D. Rancour-Laferrière, ' "The Kreutzer Sonata": A Kleinian Approach . . . ', paper read at the 15th International Conference on Literature and Psychology, St Petersburg, 1998

by Andrea Dworkin.[14] This is that he kills his wife because it is the only way in which he can control her sexuality, a theory that links 'The Kreutzer Sonata' with the previous two stories, since it is clear, as we have seen, that Sergey Mihalovich in 'Family Happiness' eventually achieves the power he seeks over his young wife, while Ivan Ilyich, finding that his wife does not conform to his wishes, makes no effort to control her because he can exercise power satisfactorily elsewhere. However, the final story in this volume, 'The Devil', seems to me to support more strongly the explanation offered in the previous paragraph.

The Devil

In this story of 1889, inspired by Tolstoy's own early relationship with the peasant woman Aksinia, referred to at the beginning of this Introduction, we can see his own feelings of guilt about his past re-emerging in a story that is something of a confession. Furthermore he gives the hero Irténev the same surname as he gave his *alter ego* in the early semi-autobiographical *Childhood, Boyhood, Youth*, though John Bayley implies that this has no significance, arguing rather oddly that Tolstoy did not blow out his brains or that of his mistress at Yasnaya Polyana.[15] The whole point, surely, is that the later, *pózdny*, Tolstoy is a very different person from his younger, saner self. Although he covers his tracks a little by giving his hero the mother he himself never had as an adult, the first part of the story closely resembles Tolstoy's account of his own affair.

The third-person narrator begins with a brief account of Irténev's upper-class background and early life, taking us to the point where he leaves the city for the country and starts to look around the locality for a way to satisfy his sexual needs, for the sake of his health. He embodies, of course, the socially approved male assumptions denounced by Pózdnyshev in the previous story. The affair therefore begins with the woman regarded as a medical convenience provided for him by an obliging intermediary.

The descriptions of the peasant Stepanída Pechnikov (the name is linked with the Russian word for 'stove', and hence warmth) as Irténev, despite his guilt feelings, becomes more involved with her than he intends, are economical but erotic. The narrator dwells on her freshness, her 'full breast', and her 'bright, black eyes'. She

14 See Dworkin, *Intercourse*, Chapter 1, *passim*.
15 Bayley, op. cit., pp. 286–7

is repeatedly presented as 'merry and smiling', and the sexual excitement of Irténev is made clear whenever she appears. However, the relationship is regarded by him as no more than a temporary liaison, and he eventually settles on a suitable girl to marry.

The remainder of the story is built round the contrast between his sturdy, ruddy, amoral, highly sexed mistress, who is married to a good-looking peasant, but enjoys a spot of adultery with her employer or other men when he is away on business, and Irténev's wife, Lisa. The latter is pale, thin and apparently undersexed but makes up for this by being obviously deeply in love with her husband, and her more 'spiritual' qualities, supported by her husband's original intention to remain faithful to her, keep the marriage going until pregnancy, an accident and chance encounters with Stepanída revive his own suppressed sexual desires.

In his portrayal of Irténev's devoted and submissive wife, who seems unwilling to think any evil of her husband, Tolstoy seems to be embodying his late vision of what an ideal wife might be, a wife very different from the self-aware, vividly drawn, aspiring girl of 'Family Happiness'. Lisa's reward is to become an innocent victim of her marriage vows. At the same time he gives us, with his stress on Stepanída's physicality, her raised calf-revealing skirts, her high colour, her willing compliance with her master's wishes, a powerful sense of the forces which are to destroy him.

In the final chapters of the story we see how the tension between Irténev's desire to remain faithful and his lust for Stepanída's body gradually increases until it becomes unbearable. Although it is almost never she who makes the advances, he comes to regard her ability to unleash such feelings in him as 'devilish', and it is she rather than Irténev's own desire that Tolstoy seems to have intended us to regard as the 'devil' of the story's title. However, when he came to bring the story to a fitting end, he appears to have had doubts about who was most to blame, the amoral Stepanída, whose animal sexuality leads her to take her pleasures where she can, and for whom her marriage ties are unimportant, or the would-be-moral Irténev, who is only able, finally, to defeat temptation by murder or suicide.

So he leaves us with two possible endings, allowing us to condemn to death whichever of the two lovers we feel is the guiltier, though significantly, if Stepanída is killed, as she is in the longer and more detailed ending, Irténev is let off comparatively lightly by society, as was his murderous predecessor, Pózdnyshev. The innocent and trusting wife, on the other hand is left devastated, and completely unable to understand what has caused her husband's violent action. Whichever ending we choose, Tolstoy's final words are virtually the same:

> And indeed if Eugène Irténev was mentally deranged everyone is in the same case; the most mentally deranged people are certainly those who see in others indications of insanity they do not notice in themselves.   [p. 249]

It is the sexual desire of Irténev and Stepanída for each other that has caused the death of one of them, and in the view of Tolstoy in the last two decades of his life sexual desire has become stripped of all its romantic disguises and is revealed simply as madness, here seen in its most disgusting and devilish form. At the same time the story can be read as yet another example of Tolstoy's dislike of any power, in this case Stepanída's sexuality, exercised by women over men. Yet even as he seems to condemn her to death, there is a suggestion in the language he uses of her that he still retains a lingering admiration for people who have a different, might we say Lawrentian,[16] attitude to sex and life, undarkened by religious dogma.

> She had gone close up to the drum and was raking the corn from under it, and she scorched him with her laughing eyes. That look spoke of a merry, careless love between them, of the fact that she knew he wanted her and had come to her shed, and that she as always was ready to live and be merry with him regardless of all conditions or consequences. Eugène felt himself to be in her power but did not wish to yield.   [p. 250]

Even in this grim late phase, in which, as George Orwell[17] has pointed out, he so resembles King Lear, a character he condemned, in his disgust at sex and his disillusionment with life, he allows a little space for another point of view. He was too great and honest a writer to be contented with a mere moral tract.

In these stories then, one written before and the others after his two great humane novels, we see Tolstoy's views of relations between the sexes gradually changing. Even in the earliest of them, 'Family Happiness', although he seems to understand female aspirations, he

---

16 D. H. Lawrence expressed his strong dislike of Tolstoy's views on sex in an essay reprinted in *Phoenix* (see Bibliography), pp. 246–7.

17 George Orwell, 'Lear, Tolstoy and the Fool', in *Collected Essays* . . . , Vol. IV, pp. 331–48

was a man of his time, holding views about the subordination of women unacceptable in Western society today. In 'The Death of Ivan Ilyich', the least autobiographical and most complex of the stories, he implicitly condemns the protagonist for the failure of his marriage when he abdicates from his responsibilities as a husband in order to exercise power elsewhere. In the last two stories it is women's sexual power that is seen as a deadly moral danger to men, though in fact they may be seen as chronicling Tolstoy's increasing guilt about his own sexuality and marital shortcomings.

At the end of his life he became convinced that sexual abstinence was the only solution and was no longer able to stand the attentions or even presence of his long suffering wife, who had done so much to further his literary career. She had even persuaded the Tsar, temporarily, to allow publication of 'The Kreutzer Sonata', a story which she hated because of Tolstoy's use in it of their own marital unhappiness.[18]

Finally, and famously, he fled from her embraces and died, refusing to see her, on a remote station platform, surrounded by admirers of his uncompromising teachings on a wide range of issues, political (including the doctrine of passive resistance that influenced Gandhi) and religious. Few of them however, may have agreed with views on male–female relationships which, if generally adopted, would have led to the extinction of the human race.

ACKNOWLEDGEMENTS

I would like to thank Keith Carabine, Editor of Wordsworth Classics, for his helpful comments on my drafts and for his patience.

18 See A. N. Wilson, *Tolstoy*, pp. 388–90.

BIBLIOGRAPHY

Works by Tolstoy and His Contemporaries Mentioned Above

Chernyshevsky, *What Is To Be Done?* (trans. B. R. Tucker), Boston 1883

Dostoevsky, F. M., *Notes From Underground*, Penguin, Harmondsworth 1972

Tolstoy, L. N., *Childhood, Boyhood, Youth*, Penguin, Harmondsworth 1964

Tolstoy, L. N., *Anna Karenina*, Penguin, Harmondsworth 1977

Tolstoy, L. N., *My Confession*, with Introduction by R. van de Weyer, London 1995

Tolstoy, L. N., *The Death of Ivan Ilyich* (ed. M. Beresford), Bristol 1992

Tolstoy, S. A., *Autobiography*, London 1922

Critical Works

Bayley, John, *Tolstoy and The Novel*, Oxford 1966; a thoughtful study of the distinctiveness of Tolstoy's achievement as a writer

Christian, R. F., *Tolstoy – A Critical Introduction*, Oxford 1969

Crankshaw, E., *Tolstoy: The Making of a Novelist*, London 1974; a study of the background to Tolstoy's work by a leading expert on Russia and its history

Davie, Donald, *Russian Literature and Modern English Fiction*, Chicago 1965

Dworkin, Andrea, A Polemical Feminist Reading of 'The Kreutzer Sonata', Chapter 1 in *Intercourse*, New York 1997

Edwards, Anne, *Sonya*, London 1981; a lively biography putting the case for Tolstoy's wife and based on her and other writings but written for a popular audience rather than a scholarly one

Gifford, H. (ed.), *Tolstoy*, Penguin, Harmondsworth 1971; a useful collection of extracts from critics writing on different aspects of Tolstoy's works from a variety of perspectives

Greenwood, E. B., *Tolstoy: The Comprehensive Vision*, London 1975; one of the best overall studies of Tolstoy

Jahn, G., *Leo Tolstoy's 'The Death of Ivan Ilyich' – An Interpretation*, New York 1993

Jones, M., *New Essays on Tolstoy*, Cambridge 1978

Knowles, A. V. (ed.), *Tolstoy – The Critical Heritage*, London 1978; a useful compendium of extracts from Tolstoy's early, mainly Russian, critics

Lawrence, D. H., *Phoenix: The Posthumous Papers*, London 1936

Macherey, P., *A Theory of Literary Production*, London 1978; includes a discussion of Tolstoy by this leading Marxist critic and an Appendix containing Lenin's essay on Tolstoy

Maude, A. *The Life of Tolstoy*, Oxford 1929; a classic early life of Tolstoy by a great Tolstoy scholar and translator

Moser, C. A., *The Russian Short Story*, Boston 1986

Nabokov, Vladimir, *Lectures in Russian Literature*, New York 1982

Orwell, George, *Collected Essays*, Penguin, Harmondsworth 1970

Rahv, Philip, *Literature and the Sixth Sense*, Boston 1969

Scott, M., *Beethoven*, London 1951

Simmons, E. J., *Introduction to Tolstoy's Writings*, Chicago 1969

M. Slonim, *The Epic of Russian Literature*, New York 1950

Steiner, George, *Tolstoy or Dostoevsky: An Essay in Contrast*, 1959; a consideration of the differences between the two writers by a major polymath and critic

Velikovsky, I., 'Unconscious Homosexuality in "The Kreutzer Sonata"', *Psychoanalytic Review*, Vol. XXIV, No. 1, 1937

Wasiolek, E., *Tolstoy's Major Fiction*, Chicago 1978

Wilson, A. N., *Tolstoy*, Penguin, Harmondsworth 1989; an extremely well-written and full modern biography, unlikely to be surpassed

FAMILY HAPPINESS

PART ONE

I

WE WERE IN MOURNING for my mother, who had died in the autumn, and we spent the whole winter in the country – Katya, Sonya, and I.

Katya was an old friend of the family, the governess who had brought us up, and whom I had known and loved ever since I had known anything. Sonya was my younger sister. We passed a gloomy and sorrowful winter in our old house at Pokrovskoe. The weather was cold and windy, so that the snowdrifts were heaped up higher than our windows; the windows were almost always frozen over and dimmed; and almost the whole winter we neither walked nor drove out anywhere. It was not often that anyone came to see us, and the few visitors who did come did not add to the gaiety and cheerfulness in our house. They all had mournful faces; they all talked in subdued tones as though afraid of waking someone; never laughed, but sighed, and often shed tears, when they looked at me, and still more at little Sonya, in her black frock. There seemed still a feeling of death in the house; the gloom and horror of death were still in the air. Mamma's room was kept shut up, and a feeling of awe came upon me, and something impelled me to peep into that cold empty room when I passed it on my way up to bed.

I was at that time seventeen; and the very year of her death mamma had intended moving to town for me to come out. The loss of my mother was a great grief to me; but I must confess that behind this grief there was a feeling too that I was young and pretty, as everyone told me, and that here I was wasting a second winter in solitude in the country. Before the end of the winter this sense of depression and loneliness, of boredom, in fact, became so intense that I hardly left my room, did not open the piano, and did not look at a book. When Katya tried to persuade me to take up either occupation, I answered, 'I don't care to, I can't,' while in my soul something said to me, 'What for?' What reason was there to do anything while my best time was being lost, wasted like this? What for? And to the question 'What for?' there was no answer but tears.

They told me I was growing thinner and losing my looks in those days, but even that did not interest me. What did it matter? For whom? ... It seemed to me that all my life was to be passed like this in this remote solitude and helpless dreariness, from which by myself, all alone, I had not the force, nor even the will, to escape. Towards the end of the winter Katya began to be uneasy about me, and made up her mind that come what might she would take me abroad. But to do this we must have money, and we hardly knew what was left us after my mother's death, and every day we were expecting her executor, who was to come and go into our affairs.

In March the executor came.

'Well, thank God!' Katya said to me one day as I wandered aimlessly about like a shadow, with nothing to do, no thought, no wish in my mind. 'Sergey Mihalovich has come home again; he has sent to enquire after us, and is coming to dinner. You must pull yourself together, my little Masha,' she added, 'or what will he think of you? He was so fond of you all.'

Sergey Mihalovich was a near neighbour of ours, and had been a friend of my father's, though he was many years younger. Apart from the effect of his arrival on our plans, and the possibility through it of our getting away from the country, I had been used from a child to love and respect him; and Katya in advising me to rouse myself had guessed rightly that of all my acquaintances I should most dislike to appear to disadvantage before Sergey Mihalovich. Like everyone in the house, from Katya and Sonya, his godchild, down to the humblest coachman, I liked him from habit; but apart from that, he had a peculiar importance in my eyes from a word my mother had once dropped in my presence. She had said that he was the sort of husband she would be glad of for me. At the time this had seemed to me amazing and positively unpleasant; the hero of my dreams was utterly different. My hero was delicate, slender, pale and melancholy. Sergey Mihalovich was a man no longer youthful, tall, squarely built, and, as I fancied, always cheerful. But in spite of that, these words of mamma's had made a deep impression on my imagination; and even six years before, when I was only eleven, and he used to address me by my pet name and play with me, and used to call me 'little-girl-violet', I sometimes wondered, not without dismay, what I should do if he were suddenly to want to marry me.

Before dinner, to which Katya added a cream tart and spinach sauce, Sergey Mihalovich arrived. From the window I saw how he drove up in a little sledge; but as soon as he drove round the corner, I hastened to the drawing-room and tried to pretend that I was not in the least expecting him. But hearing the tramp of feet in the hall, his loud voice and Katya's footsteps, I could not restrain myself, and went out to meet him. He was talking loudly, holding Katya's hand and smiling. Catching sight of me, he stopped short, and for a little while gazed at me, without greeting me. I was disconcerted, and I felt that I was blushing.

'Ah, is it really you?' he said in his unhesitating direct manner, gesticulating with his hands and coming up to me. 'Can anyone change so? How you have grown up! So this is the little violet! You've become quite a rose!'

He took my hand in his big one and squeezed it so warmly, so heartily, that it almost hurt. I expected he would kiss my hand, and was bending towards him, but he pressed my hand once more, and looked me straight in the face with his resolute, good-humoured eyes.

It was six years since I had seen him. He was very much altered; he looked older, darker, and had grown whiskers, which did not suit him at all. But he had just the same direct manner, the same open honest face with large features, the same shrewd, bright eyes and friendly, as it were, childlike smile.

In five minutes he was no longer a visitor; he became like one of the family to all of us, even to the servants, who, as could be seen by their eagerness to please him, were delighted at his arrival. He behaved quite differently from the other neighbours who had called on us since my mother's death, and had thought it necessary to sit in silence or shed tears while they were with us. He was, on the contrary, very talkative and cheerful, and did not say a word about my mother, so that at first such callousness struck me as strange, and even unseemly, in so intimate a friend of the family. But afterwards I felt that it was not callousness, but sincerity, and was grateful for it. In the evening Katya sat down to pour out tea in the old place in the drawing-room, just as she used to do in mamma's lifetime. Sonya and I sat down near her. Old Grigory brought him a pipe he had sought out, that had been papa's, and he fell to walking up and down the room just as in old days.

'What terrible changes there have been in this house when one thinks of it!' he said, stopping short.

'Yes,' said Katya with a sigh, and, putting the lid on the samovar, she looked at him, already on the point of tears.

'You remember your father, I suppose?' he said, turning to me.

'A little,' I answered.

'And how happy you would have been with him now!' he said

softly, and dreamily, gazing at my head above my eyes. 'I was very fond of your father,' he added still more softly, and it seemed to me that his eyes were brighter.

'And now God has taken her too!' said Katya, and immediately she put the dinner napkin down on the teapot, took out her handkerchief, and began to cry.

'Yes, there have been terrible changes in this house,' he repeated, turning away. 'Sonya, show me your playthings,' he added a few instants later, and he went into the parlour. With eyes full of tears I looked at Katya when he had gone out.

'He is such a good friend!' she said. And certainly I felt a sort of warmth and comfort from the sympathy of this good-hearted man from the outside world.

From the drawing-room we could hear Sonya's shrieks and his romping games with her. I sent him some tea into the parlour, and we could hear him sitting down to the piano and striking the keys with Sonya's little hands.

'Marya Alexandrovna!' I heard him call: 'come here and play me something.'

I liked his addressing me so simply in this tone of affectionate peremptoriness; I got up and went to him.

'Here, play this,' he said, opening a volume of Beethoven at the adagio of the sonata *quasi una fantasia*.[1] 'Let me see how you play,' he added, and walked away with his glass of tea to a corner of the parlour.

I somehow felt it impossible with him to refuse and make excuses for playing badly; I seated myself obediently at the piano, and began to play as best I could, though I was afraid of his criticism, knowing that he understood music and loved it. The adagio was in harmony with that feeling of reminiscence that had been called up by the conversation at tea, and I played it, I think, decently. But the scherzo he would not let me play.

'No, that you don't play well,' he said, coming up to me, 'let it be. But the first thing wasn't bad. You've a notion of music, I see.' This measured praise so delighted me that I positively blushed. It was so new and agreeable to me that he, the friend and equal of my father, was talking to me by ourselves seriously, and not treating me as a child, as in old days. Katya went upstairs to put Sonya to bed, and we remained alone together in the parlour.

He talked to me of my father, told me how he had come to know him, and what good times they had had together while I was still busy with my lessons and my playthings. And in what he told me I saw my father for the first time as a simple, lovable man, such as I had never known him till then.

He questioned me too about my tastes, my reading, my plans, and gave me advice. He was not now for me the light-hearted friend, full of jokes, who used to tease me and make playthings for me, but a serious man, frank and affectionate, for whom I felt an instinctive respect and liking. I was at ease and happy, and yet at the same time I could not help feeling a certain constraint as I talked to him. I was apprehensive over every word I uttered; I had such a longing to deserve, on my own account, the love that was bestowed on me now merely as the daughter of my father.

After putting Sonya to bed, Katya joined us and complained to him of my apathy, of which I had said nothing to him.

'The most important thing she didn't tell me,' he said, smiling and shaking his head at me reproachfully.

'What was there to tell?' I said; 'that's very dull, and besides it's passing off.' It actually did seem to me now that my depression was not merely passing away, but had passed away already, or in fact had never been at all.

'It's bad to be unable to stand solitude,' he said; 'surely you're not a young lady.'

'Of course I'm a young lady,' I answered, laughing.

'No, it's a bad sort of young lady who's only alive when she's being admired, and as soon as she's alone lets herself go altogether and finds no charm in anything – who's all for show, and nothing for herself.'

'You've a nice opinion of me,' I said, in order to say something.

'No,' he said after a brief pause, 'it's not for nothing you're so like your father; there's *something in* you,' and his kindly, intent eyes again flattered me and put me to joyful confusion.

Only now I noticed in his face, the first impression of which was cheerfulness, that look in the eyes, peculiar to him, at first bright, then growing more and more intent, and rather mournful.

'You ought not to be and can't be bored,' he said. 'You have music, which you understand, books, and study. You have a whole life before you, for which you can only prepare yourself now so as not to feel regret later. In a year even it will be getting too late.'

He talked to me like a father or an uncle, and I felt that he was continually putting a check on himself so as to keep on my level. I felt both offended at his considering me on a lower level, and pleased that he should think it necessary to try and adapt himself simply on my account.

The rest of the evening he talked about business with Katya.

'Well, goodbye, dear friends,' he said, getting up, and coming up to me, he took my hand.

'When shall we see you again?' asked Katya.

'In the spring,' he answered, still keeping hold of my hand. 'Now I'm going to Danilovka' (our other estate). 'I'll look into things there and arrange what I can, then I'm going on to Moscow to see to my own business, and in the summer we shall meet again.'

'Oh, how is it you are staying such a little while?' I said, with extreme mournfulness; and indeed I had been hoping to see him every day, and I felt suddenly so miserable and afraid that my depression would come back again. This must have been apparent in my eyes and my tone.

'But you must try and work a little more; don't give way to depression,' he said, in a tone, as I thought, too coolly direct, 'and in the spring I shall put you through an examination,' he added, letting go my hand and not looking at me.

In the hall where we stood seeing him off he made haste to put on his fur coat, and again his eyes looked past me. 'He needn't trouble himself,' I thought. 'Does he suppose I'm so pleased at his looking at me? He's a nice man, very nice, but . . . that's all.'

That evening, however, Katya and I sat up talking a long while, not about him, but of how we would spend the summer, and where and how we would stay for the winter. The terrible question – What for? – did not occur to me. It seemed to me very simple and evident that we must live to be happy, and a great deal of happiness seemed lying before me in the future. It seemed as though our dark old house at Pokrovskoe were suddenly full of life and light.

2

Spring had come. My former depression had completely gone, and was replaced by the dreamy spring melancholy of vague hopes and desires. Though I did not spend my time as I had done at the beginning of the winter, but was busily occupied with Sonya and music and reading, I often went off into the garden and spent long, long hours wandering alone about the garden walks or sitting on a garden seat. God only knows what I was dreaming of, what I was hoping and longing for. Sometimes, especially when there was moonlight, I would sit the whole night long till dawn at my bedroom window. Sometimes with nothing on but my dressing-gown I would slip out into the garden, unnoticed by Katya, and run through the dew as far as the pond; once I went as far as the open fields, and alone at night made the round of the whole garden.

I find it hard to recall now the dreams that filled my imagination then. Even when I do remember them, I can hardly believe that those were really my dreams, so strange they were and remote from real life.

At the end of May, Sergey Mihalovich came back, as he had promised, from his travels. The first time he came to see us was in the evening, when we did not at all expect him. We were sitting in the verandah, just going to have tea. The garden was already all in green, and among the overgrown shrubs the nightingales had been building all through St Peter's fast. The leafy lilac bushes looked as though they had been sprinkled at the top with something white and lilac, where the flowers were just going to come out. The foliage of the birch avenue was all transparent in the setting sun. It was cool and shady in the verandah. There must have been a heavy evening dew on the grass. From the yard behind the garden came the last sounds of the day, the noise of the herd being brought home. The half-witted Nikon, passed along the path before the verandah with a water-barrel, and a cool trickle of water from the watering-hose made dark rings on the loose earth round the stems of the dahlias and the sticks that held them up. On the white cloth set before us on the verandah stood the brilliantly polished samovar boiling, cream, and biscuits and cakes. Katya, like a careful house-wife, was rinsing the cups with her plump hands. I was hungry after bathing; and without waiting for the tea to be ready, I was eating some bread heaped with thick, fresh cream. I had on a linen blouse with open sleeves, and had tied a kerchief over my wet hair. Katya was the first to see him from the verandah window.

'Ah, Sergey Mihalovich!' she cried; 'why, we were only just talking about you.'

I got up, and would have retreated to change my dress, but he came upon me just as I was in the doorway.

'Come, why stand on ceremony in the country? Where's the need of being so proper?' he said, looking at my head in the kerchief and smiling. 'Why, you don't mind Grigory, and I'm the same as Grigory to you really.' But precisely at that moment I fancied he was looking at me not at all as Grigory might have done, and I felt awkward.

'I'll be back in a minute,' I said, moving away.

'What's amiss with that?' he called after me. 'You look like a peasant girl.'

'How queerly he looked at me!' I thought, as I hurriedly changed my dress upstairs. Well, thank God, he's come; things will be more lively now.' After looking at myself in the glass I ran gaily downstairs, and not disguising my haste, I went panting out on to the verandah. He was sitting at the table and telling Katya about our affairs. He glanced at me, smiled, and went on talking. Our affairs were, to judge by his account, going very favourably. Now we had only to spend the summer in the country, and then to go either to Petersburg for Sonya's education or abroad.

'Now if only you could come abroad with us,' said Katya. 'We shall be utterly lost there by ourselves.'

'Ah, I should like to go round the world with you!' he said, half in jest, half in earnest.

'Well, do then,' I said; 'let's go round the world.'

He smiled and shook his head.

'What about my mother? and business?' he said. 'Well, that's not the question. Tell me how you've been getting on all this time. Not depressed again, surely?'

When I told him that I had been working hard in his absence and had not been dull, and Katya confirmed my words, he praised me, and in words and looks caressed me like a child, as though he had a right to do so. I felt bound to tell him in detail and with peculiar sincerity all that I had done right, and to acknowledge, as though at confessional, all that he might be displeased at. The evening was so fine that after they had taken away the tea-things we stayed out on the verandah, and the conversation was so interesting to me that I did not notice that gradually all sounds of human life were hushed. The scent of flowers from all round us grew stronger, a thick dew drenched the grass, a nightingale trilled not far off in a lilac bush, and ceased when it heard our voices. The starlit sky seemed sinking over our heads.

I became aware that it was getting dark, because a bat suddenly flew noiselessly under the awning of the verandah and fluttered about my white dress. I shrank back against the wall, and should have liked to scream, but the bat just as swiftly and noiselessly darted out again from under the awning and disappeared in the dusk of the garden.

'How I love your Pokrovskoe,' he said, breaking off from the conversation; 'I could sit all my life here on the verandah.'

'Well, do then, sit still,' said Katya.

'Sit still, indeed,' said he; 'life doesn't sit still.'

'How is it you don't get married?' said Katya. 'You would make such a good husband!'

'Just because I like sitting still,' and he laughed. 'No, Katerina Karlovna, marriage is not for you and me. Everyone's long ago given up looking upon me as a man who might marry. And I've given it up myself for some time past too, and I've felt so comfortable since then really.'

It seemed to me that it was with a sort of unnatural vehemence that he said this.

'What nonsense; thirty-six years old, and done with life already!' said Katya.

'I should think I have done with life!' he went on; 'why, all I want is to sit still. But you want something very different for marriage. You should ask her now,' he added, with a motion of his head towards me. 'It's they who've to think of getting married, while you and I will look on and rejoice in them.'

In his tone there was a suppressed melancholy and constraint which did not escape me. He paused for a while; neither I nor Katya said anything.

'Just imagine,' he went on, turning round on his chair, 'if I were all of a sudden to get married by some unhappy chance to a girl of seventeen like Mash – Marya Alexandrovna. That's an excellent example, I'm very glad it has happened to come up, and it's the best example possible.'

I laughed, and was unable to comprehend what he was glad of, and what it was that had come up.

'Come, tell me the truth, with your hand on your heart,' he said, turning jestingly to me, 'would it not be misery for you to bind your life up with someone elderly, who had lived his life, whose only wish was to sit still, while God only knows what's working in you, what you are longing for?'

I felt uncomfortable; I was silent, not knowing what to answer.

'Oh, it's not an offer I'm making you!' he said, laughing; 'but tell me truly, it's not of such a husband that you dream when you wander about the garden in the evening, and it would be misery for you, wouldn't it?'

'Not misery,' I began.

'Not the right thing, though,' he finished for me.

'Yes; but of course I may be mistaken.'

But again he interrupted me.

'There, you see, and she's perfectly right, and I'm grateful to her for her sincerity, and very glad we have had this conversation! And what's more, it would be the greatest calamity for me too,' he added.

'What a queer fellow you are, you're not changed a bit!' said Katya, and she went in from the verandah to order supper.

We were both silent after Katya had gone, and all was still around us. Only the nightingale was flooding all the garden with melody, not now the jerky faltering notes of evening, but the serene, unhurried song of the night. And another nightingale, from the ravine below, for the first time that evening answered him in the distance. The nearer one ceased, seemed listening for a moment, and then still more shrilly, more intensely, poured out drop by drop his melodious trill. And with sovereign calm these voices rang out in their night world, so remote from us. The gardener went by on his way to sleep in the greenhouse; his steps in thick boots echoed retreating along the path. Twice someone uttered a shrill whistle at the bottom of the hill, and all was silence again. Scarcely audibly the leaves rustled, the curtain of the verandah fluttered, and some sweet fragrance hovering in the air was wafted into the verandah and flooded it. I felt awkward at being silent after what had been said, but what to say I did not know. I looked at him. His shining eyes in the dusk looked round at me.

'It's good to be alive!' he said.

For some reason I sighed.

'Eh?'

'It's good to be alive!' I repeated.

And again we were silent, and again I felt ill at ease. I was haunted by the thought that I had wounded him by agreeing with him that he was elderly, and I wanted to soothe him, but I didn't know how to do it.

'I must say goodbye, though,' he said, getting up, 'mother expects me back to supper. I've hardly seen her today.'

'And I wanted to play you a new sonata,' I said.

'Another time,' he said, coldly I thought. 'Goodbye.'

It seemed to me now more than ever that I had wounded him, and I felt sorry. Katya and I went with him as far as the steps, and stood in the courtyard looking down the road along which he had vanished. When the thud of his horse's hoofs had died away, I went round to the verandah, and again I fell to gazing into the garden; and in the dewy darkness, where the night sounds now were still, for a long while yet I saw and heard all that I longed to see and hear.

He came a second time and a third, and the awkwardness arising from the strange conversation that had passed between us had completely disappeared, and was never renewed again. During the whole summer he used to come two or three times a week to see us;

and I became so used to him, that when he did not come for some time I felt it strange to be going on with life by myself, and I was angry with him, and considered he was behaving badly in deserting me. He treated me like some favourite young comrade, asked me questions, drew me into frankness on the deepest subjects, gave me advice and encouragement, sometimes scolded me and checked me. But in spite of his continual efforts to put himself on my level, I felt that behind what I understood in him there remained a whole unknown world into which he did not think fit to initiate me, and this somehow more than anything increased my respect for him and attracted me to him. I knew from Katya and from the neighbours that besides his care of his old mother, with whom he lived, besides looking after his property and ours, he had a great deal to do with the public affairs of the provincial nobility, and that he had much vexatious opposition to encounter in it. But what was his attitude to all this, what were his convictions, his plans, his hopes, I could never find out from him. Whenever I turned the conversation on his affairs, he wrinkled his brows in his peculiar way that seemed to say, 'Stop that, please, what's that to do with you?' and changed the subject. At first this used to offend me, but later on I got so used to our always talking only of what concerned me that I thought it quite natural.

What I disliked too at first, though afterwards it pleased me, was his complete indifference and, as it were, contempt for my appearance. Never by a glance or a word did he hint that he thought me pretty; on the contrary, he wrinkled his brows and laughed when people called me pretty before him. He took a positive pleasure in finding defects in my appearance and teasing me about them. The fashionable dresses and elaborate coiffure in which Katya liked to make me elegant on festive occasions only called forth jeers from him, mortifying kind-hearted Katya, and at first disconcerting me. Katya, who had made up her mind that he thought me attractive, could never make out his not liking to see the girl he admired shown off to the best advantage. I soon saw what he wanted. He was eager to feel sure that I had no frivolous vanity. And as soon as I saw that, there actually was not left in me a trace of vanity in regard to what I wore, how I did my hair, and how I moved. But in place of that there was transparently obvious an affectation of simplicity, just at the moment when I had ceased to be able to be simple. I knew that he loved me; but how, whether as a child or as a woman, I had not as yet asked myself. I prized his love; and feeling that he considered me the best girl in the world, I could not help wishing to keep up this delusion in him. And involuntarily I deceived him. But while deceiving him, I did myself become better. I felt how much better and more dignified it was for me to show off the finer side of my soul than of my body. My hair, my hands, my face, my ways, whatever they might be, bad or good, it seemed to me that he had summed up once for all, and knew so well that I could add nothing – except a desire to deceive – to his estimate by attention to my looks. My soul he did not know, because he loved it, because at this very time it was growing and developing, and there I could deceive him, and I did deceive him. And how safe I felt with him when I clearly perceived this! All my causeless bashfulness, my awkwardness in moving, disappeared completely. I felt that whether he saw me full face, or in profile, sitting or standing, with my hair done up high or hanging low, he knew all of me, and I fancied was satisfied with me as I was. I think that if, contrary to his practice, he had suddenly told me, as others did, that I had a fine face, I should really have been anything but pleased. But, on the other hand, what comfort and gladness there was in my soul when, after some word I had uttered, he gazed intently at me, and in a voice of emotion, to which he tried to give a jesting tone, said – 'Yes, yes, there's *something* in you . . . You're a splendid girl, that I must tell you.' And what was it for which I received such a reward, filling my heart with pride and gladness? For saying that I felt so for old Grigory's love for his little grandchild, or for being moved to tears by some poem or story I had read, or for preferring Mozart to Schulhoff.[2] And it's marvellous, when I think of it, the extraordinary instinct by which I guessed at that time what was fine and what I ought to like, though in those days I had not really the least notion of what was fine and what was to be liked. The greater number of my old habits and tastes were not to his liking; and he had but by the twitching of an eyebrow, by a glance, to show that he did not like what I was going to say, to make his peculiar grimace of commiseration and faint contempt, and it seemed to me already that I didn't care for what I had liked till then. Sometimes when he had hardly begun to give me some piece of advice, it seemed to me that I knew already what he was saying. He would question me, looking into my eyes, and his eyes drew from me the thought he wanted to find in me. All my ideas at that time, all my feelings were not mine; but his ideas and feelings, which had suddenly become mine, passed into my life and lighted it up. Quite unconsciously I had come to look at everything with different eyes – at Katya, at our servants, and at Sonya and at

myself and my pursuits. Books which I used to read simply to
escape from ennui suddenly became one of the greatest pleasures of
my life; and all simply because we talked together about books,
read them together, and he brought them to me. Before this time
looking after Sonya and giving her lessons had been a burdensome
task which I forced myself to perform simply from a sense of duty.
He sat by during the lessons, and to watch over Sonya's progress
became a delight to me. To learn a piece of music all through
thoroughly had seemed to me hitherto an impossible feat; but now,
knowing that he would hear and perhaps praise it, I would play the
same passage forty times over, till poor Katya stuffed her ears up
with cotton wool, while I was still unwearied. The same old sonatas
were played somehow quite differently now, and sounded quite
different and far finer. Even Katya, whom I knew and loved like
another self – even she was transformed in my eyes. Only now I
understood for the first time that she was under no compulsion to
be the mother, the friend, the slave that she was to us. I grasped all
the self-sacrifice and devotion of this loving nature, felt all that I
owed to her, and learned to love her more than ever. He taught me
to look at our people – peasants, house-serfs, and serf-girls – quite
differently from how I had done. It sounds an absurd thing to say,
but I had grown up to seventeen among these people more remote
from them than from people I had never seen. I had never once
reflected that these people had their loves, desires, and regrets just
as I had. Our garden, our copses, our fields, which I had known so
long, had suddenly become new and beautiful in my eyes. It was
not for nothing that he said that in life there is only one certain
happiness – living for others. At the time this seemed to me
strange, I did not understand it; but this conviction without
conscious thought had already come into my heart. He opened to
me a whole world of pleasures in the present, without changing
anything in my daily existence, without adding anything except
himself to any impression. Everything that from my childhood had
been voiceless around suddenly blossomed into life. He had but to
come into it for all to become speaking, rushing headlong into my
soul and flooding it with happiness.

Often during that summer I would go upstairs to my own room,
lie down on my bed; and instead of the melancholy of spring, the
hopes and longings for the future that had absorbed me, a thrill of
happiness in the present took possession of me. I could not sleep,
got up, sat on Katya's bed, and told her that I was perfectly happy,
which, as now I recall, it was utterly unnecessary to tell her – she

could see it for herself. But she told me that she too had nothing to wish for, and that she too was very happy, and kissed me. I believed her – it seemed so right and inevitable that everyone should be happy. But Katya could think of sleep too, and even pretending to be angry, sometimes drove me away from her bed and fell asleep, while I would spend long hours going over all that made me so happy. Sometimes I got up and said my prayers a second time, praying in my own words to thank God for all the happiness He had given me.

And in the room all was still; only Katya breathed drowsily and evenly, the clock ticked by her side, and I turned from side to side, murmuring words, or crossing myself and kissing the cross on my neck. The doors were closed, the shutters were on the windows, some fly or gnat buzzed, stirring continually in the same spot. And I would have liked never to leave this room; I did not want morning to come, I did not want the spiritual atmosphere that enfolded me ever to be dissipated. It seemed to me that my dreams, my thoughts, and prayers were live things, living with me in the darkness, flying about my bed, hovering over me. And every idea was his idea, and every feeling was his feeling. I did not know then that this was love – I thought that this might always be so, that of itself, for no other end, this feeling had come to me.

3

One day during harvest-time Katya and Sonya and I had gone after dinner out into the garden to our favourite seat in the shade of the lime trees above the ravine, beyond which stretched a view of forest and fields. Sergey Mihalovich had not been to see us for three days, and that day we were expecting him, especially as our bailiff told us he had promised to come to the fields. About two o'clock we saw him on horseback riding towards the ryefield. Katya, glancing with a smile at me, sent for some peaches and cherries, of which he was very fond, lay down on the seat, and began to doze. I tore off a flat, crooked branch of lime tree with juicy leaves and sappy bark that moistened my hand; and waving it over Katya, I went on reading, breaking off continually to look towards the field track by which he would come. Sonya was rigging up an arbour for her dolls at the root of an old lime tree. The day was hot, windless, steamy, the clouds kept packing closer and growing blacker, a storm had been brewing since the morning. I was excited, as always before a storm. But after midday the clouds began to break up at the edges, the sun

floated out into clear sky, and only on one edge there was grumbling
thunder; and from a lowering storm-cloud that hung over the
horizon and melted into the dust of the fields, pale zigzags of
lightning now and then cleft their way through to the earth. It was
evident that the storm had passed off for that day, from us at least.
Along the road that could be seen in parts beyond the garden there
was a continual slow string of high creaking waggons laden with
sheaves, and rapidly rattling to meet them a line of the unladen carts
returning, with legs swinging and skirts fluttering in them. The
thick dust did not fly away nor settle, but hung in the air behind the
hedge between the transparent foliage of the garden trees. Further
away at the threshing-floor the same voices could be heard and the
same creaking of wheels; and the same yellow sheaves, after slowly
making their way past the fence, were there flying in the air, and
before my eyes the oval stacks were growing up, the pointed roofs
were taking shape, and the figures of peasants swarmed bustling
about them. In front, too, in the dusty fields, carts were moving and
yellow sheaves were to be seen, and the sounds of carts, of voices,
and of singing floated across from far away. On one side the stubble
was growing more and more bare, with lines of hedge overgrown
with wormwood. More to the right, below, all about the cut field
that lay in unseemly confusion, were dotted the bright gowns of the
peasant women tying sheaves, bending down and spreading out their
arms, and the untidy field was being put in order, and handsome
sheaves were ranged close about it. It was as though straightway
before my eyes summer was turning into autumn. The dust and the
sultry heat hung over all except our favourite nook in the garden.
On every side in this dust and sultry heat, in the scalding sunshine,
the labouring peasants were talking, noisily working and moving.

But Katya was so sweetly snoring under her white cambric
handkerchief, on our cool garden seat, the cherries glistened with
such juicy blackness on the plate, our dresses were so cool and fresh,
the water in the jug sparkled with such rainbow-coloured brightness
in the sun, and all was so well with me. 'I can't help it,' I thought;
'am I to blame for being happy? But how share my happiness, how
and to whom am I to give up all myself and all my happiness? . . .'

The sun had already gone down behind the tree-tops of the birch
avenue, the dust was settling in the fields, the distance showed
clearer and more distinct in the slanting sunshine, the storm-clouds
had quite disappeared, at the threshing-floor behind the trees three
new stacks could be seen, and the peasants had gone away from
them. Carts went trotting by with loud shouts, clearly making their

last journey; peasant women with rakes on their shoulders and sheaf-ties stuck in their girdles were strolling homewards singing loudly, and still Sergey Mihalovich did not come, although I had long ago seen him ride off under the hill. Suddenly his figure appeared in the avenue, from the direction in which I had not at all looked for him (he had gone round the ravine). Taking off his hat, with a good-humoured beaming face, he was coming with rapid steps towards me. Seeing that Katya was asleep, he bit his lip, shut his eyes, and advanced on tiptoe. I saw at once that he was in that characteristic mood of irrational gaiety which I liked extremely in him, and we used to call 'wild delight'. He was like a schoolboy playing truant; the whole of him, from his face down to his feet, was radiant with content, happiness, and childlike frolic.

'Well, good-day, young violet! How are you? quite well?' he said in a whisper, coming up to me and pressing my hand. 'Oh, I'm first-rate!' he said in answer to my enquiry; 'today I'm thirteen; should like to play horses and climb trees.'

'Wild delight!' I said, looking at his laughing eyes, and feeling that this *wild delight* was infecting me too.

'Yes,' he answered, winking and keeping back a smile. 'But why beat Katerina Karlovna on the nose?'

I had not noticed as I looked at him, and went on waving the branch, that I had twitched the handkerchief off Katya and was stroking her face with the leaves. I laughed.

'And she will say she has not been asleep,' I whispered, as though to avoid waking Katya; but really not for that – it was simply that I enjoyed whispering with him.

He moved his lips, mimicking me, pretending I had spoken so softly that he could hear nothing. Seeing the plate of cherries, he snatched it, as it were, slily, walked off to Sonya under the lime tree, and sat on her dolls. Sonya was angry at first, but he soon made peace with her, starting a game in which he was to race her in eating the cherries.

'Would you like me to send for some more?' I said. 'Or shall we go and get some ourselves?'

He took the plate, sat the dolls in it, and we all three walked to the walled-in garden. Sonya ran laughing after us, tugging at his coat to make him give up the dolls. He gave her them and turned seriously to me.

'Yes, there is no doubt you are a violet,' he said to me still as softly, though there was no one here to be afraid of waking; 'as I came near you, after all that dust and heat and work, there was the scent of violets. Not the scented violet, but you know . . . that early, dark, little one that smells of the thawing snow and the spring grass.'

'Oh, and is everything going well in the fields?' I asked him, to disguise the blissful confusion produced by his words.

'Splendidly! The peasants are everywhere so splendid . . . The more one knows of them, the better one likes them.'

'Yes,' I said, 'today, before you came, I looked from the garden at their work, and I felt all at once so ashamed that they should be working, while I was so comfortable, that – '

'No affectation on that subject, my dear!' he interrupted me, with sudden seriousness, but glancing affectionately into my face, 'that's a holy thing. God forbid you should trifle with that.'

'But it's only to you I say it.'

'Oh yes, I know. Well, how about the cherries?'

The walled-in garden was shut up, and there were no gardeners about (they had all been sent off to the harvest). Sonya ran off to get the key; but without waiting for her to come back, he climbed up at a corner, lifted the netting, and jumped down on the other side.

'Like some?' I heard him asking from there; 'pass the plate.'

'No, I want to pick them myself too; I'll go for the key,' I said. 'Sonya won't find it.'

But at the same time I longed to look at what he was doing there, how he was looking, how he was moving, supposing that no one could see him. It simply was that at that time I did not want to lose sight of him for a minute. I ran on tiptoe through the nettles round the enclosure to the other side where the wall was lower, and standing on an empty barrel, so that the wall did not reach to my bosom, I leant over. I scanned the enclosure with its old gnarled trees and its broad saw-edged leaves, behind which the heavy juicy black fruit hung down straight; and poking my head under the net, I saw Sergey Mihalovich under the knotted branches of an old cherry tree. He undoubtedly thought I had gone away, and that no one was seeing him. With his hat off and his eyes closed, he was sitting on a broken-down old cherry tree, carefully rolling a bit of cherry gum into a ball. Suddenly he shrugged his shoulders, opened his eyes, and saying something, he smiled. So unlike him was that word and that smile that I felt ashamed of having spied on him. I fancied the word was 'Masha'. 'It can't be!' I thought. 'Darling Masha!' he repeated, still more softly and tenderly. But this time I distinctly heard those two words. My heart throbbed so violently, and such an agitating, as it were forbidden, joy suddenly took possession of me, that I clutched at the wall with both hands that I might not fall and betray myself. He heard my movement, looked round in alarm, and suddenly looking down, he flushed, crimsoned like a child. He tried to say something to me, but could not, and more and more hotly his face flamed. He smiled, though, looking at me. I smiled too. His whole face beamed with delight. He was not now like an old uncle, petting and instructing me, but a man equal with me, who loved and feared me, and whom I feared and loved. We said nothing, and simply gazed at each other. But suddenly he frowned, the smile and the light in his eyes died away, and coldly, in his fatherly way again, he addressed me, as though we were doing something wrong, and he had come to his senses and advised me to do the same.

'Get down, you'll hurt yourself,' he said. 'And put your hair straight. What do you look like?'

'Why is he pretending? Why does he want to hurt me?' I thought with vexation. And at the same instant I felt an irresistible desire to confuse him once more and to try my power over him.

'No, I want to pick some myself,' I said, and clutching hold of the nearest branch, I swung my feet up on to the wall. Before he had time to assist me, I had jumped down on to the ground inside the enclosure.

'What silly things you do!' he said, flushing again, and trying to conceal his confusion under the guise of anger. 'Why, you might have hurt yourself. And how are you to get out from here?'

He was even more confused than before, but now this confusion did not rejoice, but dismayed me. It infected me; I blushed, and avoiding him and not knowing what to say, I began picking cherries though I had nowhere to put them. I blamed myself, I felt remorseful and frightened, and it seemed to me that I had ruined myself for ever in his esteem. We were both mute, and both were wretched. Sonya running up with the key rescued us from this painful position. For long after this we said nothing to one another, but both addressed Sonya. When we got back to Katya, who declared she had not been asleep, but had heard all we said, I regained my composure. He tried to drop back into his fatherly, patronising tone, but he did not quite succeed with it, and did not impose on me. I vividly recalled now a conversation that had taken place between us a few days before.

Katya was saying how much easier it was for a man to love and to express his love than for a woman.

'A man can say that he loves, but a woman can't,' she said.

'But it seems to me that a man cannot and ought not to say that he loves,' he said.

'Why not?' I asked.

'Because it will always be a lie. As though it were a strange sort of discovery that someone is in love! Just as if, as soon as he says that, something went snap-bang – he loves. Just as if, when he utters that word, something extraordinary is bound to happen, with signs and portents, and all the cannons firing at once. It seems to me,' he went on, 'that people who solemnly utter those words, "I love you," either deceive themselves, or what's still worse, deceive others.'

'Then how is a woman to find out that she is loved when she's not told it?' asked Katya.

'That I can't say,' he answered. 'Every man has his own way of telling things. And where there's feeling it finds expression. When I read novels I always fancy the perplexed countenance that Lieutenant Strelsky or Alfred must have when he says, "I love thee, Eleonora!"[3] imagining that something extraordinary will suddenly happen; and nothing is changed in either her or him – the same eyes and nose and everything!'

Even at the time I felt instinctively in this jesting saying something serious relating to me, but Katya could not tolerate such irreverent treatment of the heroines of romance.

'Your everlasting paradoxes!' she said. 'Come, tell us the truth, do you mean to say you have never told a woman that you loved her?'

'I never said such a thing, and never fell on one knee,' he answered, laughing, 'and I'm not going to.'

'Yes, he has no need to tell me he loves me,' I thought now, vividly recalling that conversation. 'He loves me, I know it, and his efforts to seem indifferent will not alter my conviction.'

All that evening he spoke little to me, but in every word he said to Katya and to Sonya, in every gesture and glance of his, I saw love, and had no doubt of it. I only felt sore and angry with him for thinking it necessary to go on being reserved and affecting coldness, when everything was now so clear, and when it might have been so easy and simple to be so incredibly happy. But what tormented me like a crime was my having jumped down into the cherry garden to him. I was continually thinking that through this he had lost all respect for me and was angry with me.

After tea I went towards the piano, and he followed me.

'Play something; it's a long while since I've heard you,' he said, overtaking me in the drawing-room.

'Yes, I wanted to . . . Sergey Mihalovich!' I said suddenly, looking him straight in the face. 'You are not angry with me?'

'What for?' he asked.

'For not minding what you said this afternoon,' I said, reddening.

He understood, shook his head, and smiled. His face said that he ought to scold me, but he could not find it in his heart to do so.

'It didn't matter, we're friends again?' I said, sitting down to the piano.

'I should hope so!' he said.

In the big lofty hall there were only two candles on the piano; the rest of the room was in half-darkness. The clear summer night looked in at the open windows. Everything was still except Katya's footsteps creaking at intervals in the dark drawing-room; and his horse, tied up under the window, snorting and stamping his hoofs on the burdocks. He was sitting behind me so that I could not see him; but everywhere – in the half-dark of this room, in the sounds of the night, in myself – I felt his presence. Every glance, every movement of his, though I did not see them, was echoed in my heart. I played a sonata fantasia of Mozart's, which he had brought me, and I had practised in his presence and for him. I was not thinking at all of what I was playing, but I fancy I played it well, and it seemed to me that he liked it. I felt the pleasure he was feeling in it; and without looking at him, I felt his eyes fastened on me from behind. Quite involuntarily, while still moving my fingers unconsciously, I looked round at him. His head stood out against the light background of the clear night. He was sitting leaning on his elbow with his head in his hands, and looking intently at me with shining eyes. I smiled, seeing the look on his face, and stopped playing. He smiled too, and shook his head reproachfully at the music for me to go on. When I had finished the moon was higher and shone brightly, and now besides the dim light of the candles a different silvery light came in at the window and was cast on the floor. Katya said that it was beyond everything, how I had stopped in the finest passage, and how badly I had played. But he said, on the contrary, I had never played so well as today, and began walking up and down the rooms, across the hall into the dark drawing-room, and back again into the hall, every time looking round at me and smiling. And I smiled, I wanted to laugh indeed for no reason – so glad I was at something that was happening today, just now. As soon as he had disappeared through the doorway I embraced Katya, with whom I was standing at the piano, and began kissing her in my favourite spot, in the plump neck under her chin. As soon as he returned, I put on a serious face, and with difficulty kept myself from laughing.

'What has come to her today?' Katya said to him.

But he did not answer, he simply looked at me and laughed. He knew what had come to me.

'Look what a night!' he said from the drawing-room, stopping before the balcony window that opened on to the garden.

We went up to him, and truly it was a night such as I have never seen since. The full moon stood over the house behind us so that it could not be seen; and half the shadow of the roof, of the columns and the verandah awning, lay slanting *en raccourci* on the sandy path and the circular lawn. All the rest was light, and bathed in silver dew and moonlight. The broad flowery path, all bright and cold, with shadows of the dahlias and their sticks lying slanting on one edge, and its rough gravel glistening, ran into the mist in the distance. Behind the trees there gleamed the roof of the conservatory, and below the ravine rose the gathering mist. The lilac bushes, already beginning to lose their leaves, were bright all over in every twig. The flowers, all drenched with dew, could be distinguished from one another. In the avenues the light and shade were so mingled that they seemed not trees and little paths between, but transparent, quivering, and trembling houses. To the right of the house all was black, indistinct, and weird. All the more brilliant rising up out of this darkness was the fantastically-shaped top of the poplar, which seemed as though, for some strange inexplicable cause, it had halted near the house, in the dazzling brightness above it, instead of flying far, far away into the distant dark-blue sky.

'Let us go for a walk,' said I.

Katya agreed, but said I must put on my goloshes.

'Oh no, Katya,' I said. 'Sergey Mihalovich will give me his arm.'

As though that could save me from getting my feet wet! But at the time, that was to all three of us quite intelligible and not at all strange. He never did offer me his arm, but now I took it of myself, and he did not think it strange. We all three went out of the verandah. All that world, that sky, that garden, that air, were not the same as I had known.

When I looked ahead down the avenue, along which we were walking, it seemed to me continually that over there further we could not go; that there the world of the possible ended, that it must all be crystallised for ever in its beauty. But we moved on, and the magic wall of beauty parted, admitted us, and there too it seemed was our old familiar garden with the trees and paths and dry leaves. And we did actually walk along the paths, stepped into the rings of light and shadow, and there were real dry leaves that rustled under our feet, and a real fresh twig that struck me in the face. And this was really he, walking gently and smoothly beside me, carefully supporting my arm, and it was really Katya who walked with creaking shoes beside us. And doubtless that was the moon in the sky that gleamed at us through the motionless twigs.

But at every step the magic wall closed up again before us and behind us, and I could not believe that it was possible to walk further, could not believe in all as it really was.

'Ah, a frog!' said Katya.

'Who's saying that, what for?' I thought. But then I recollected that it was Katya, that she was afraid of frogs, and I looked down at my feet. A little frog hopped and stopped motionless before me, and its little shadow could be seen in the light on the clay of the path.

'But you're not afraid,' he said.

I looked round at him. One lime tree was missing in the part of the avenue we were passing – I could see his face clearly. It was so handsome and happy.

He said, 'You're not afraid'; but I heard him saying, 'I love you, sweet girl! I love you, I love you!' repeated his eyes, his arm; and the light and the shadow and the air, everything repeated the same.

We walked round the whole garden. Katya walked beside us with her little steps, breathing heavily from fatigue. She said it was time to turn back, and I felt sorry, so sorry for her, poor thing. 'Why isn't she feeling the same as we?' I thought. 'Why isn't everyone young and everyone happy like this night, and me and him?'

We went home, but for a long while yet he stayed on though the cocks were crowing, everyone in the house was asleep, and his horse more and more often stamped on the weeds and snorted under the window. Katya did not remind us that it was late, and we sat on chatting of the most trivial things, unaware of the time till past two o'clock. The cocks were crowing for the third time, and the dawn was beginning when he went away. He said goodbye as usual, saying nothing special; but I knew that from that day he was mine, and that now I should not lose him. As soon as I had owned to myself that I loved him, I told Katya too all about it. She was glad and touched by my telling her, though she, poor thing, could go to sleep that night; but I, for a long, long while yet, walked up and down the verandah, and out into the garden, and recalling every word, every gesture, I walked along the garden paths along which I had walked with him. I did not sleep all that night, and for the first time in my life I saw the sun rise and the early morning. And such a night and such a morning

I have never seen again. 'Only why doesn't he tell me simply that he loves me?' I mused. 'Why does he invent some sort of difficulties, and call himself old, when it's all so simple and so splendid? Why does he waste the precious time which maybe will never return? Only let him say, "I love," say it in words; let him take my hand in his, bend his head over it, and say, "I love you." Let him blush and drop his eyes before me, and then I will tell him all. Not tell him even, but embrace him, clasp him to me, and weep. But what if I'm mistaken, if he does not love me?' suddenly occurred to me.

I was frightened at my own feeling. God knows what lengths it might lead me to, and his and my confusion in the orchard when I had jumped over to him came back to my mind, and my heart ached and ached. Tears streamed from my eyes, and I began to pray. And there came to me a strange reassuring thought and hope. I resolved to fast and prepare myself from that day to take the sacrament on my birthday and the same day to be betrothed.

By what means, in what way, how this could come to pass, I knew not, but from that minute I believed and knew it would be so. It was broad daylight, and the peasants had begun getting up when I went back to my room.

4

It was the time of the Fast of the Assumption,[4] so no one in the house was surprised at my intention of fasting during these days.

During the whole of that week he did not once come to see us; and far from wondering, being disturbed and angry with him, I was glad he did not come, and looked for him only on my birthday. All that week I got up early every day; and while they were putting the horses in, I walked alone about the garden, going over in my mind the sins of the previous day, and considering what I had to do today to be satisfied with the day and not once to fall into sin. It seemed to me at that time so easy to be perfectly sinless – it only needed trying a little, it seemed. The horses were brought round, and with Katya or the maid I got into the trap and drove three miles to the church. As I entered church I always recalled the prayer for all 'who enter in the fear of God', and tried with that feeling in my heart to mount the two steps of the porch overgrown with grass. In the church there were usually at that time not more than some ten persons, peasant women and house-serfs, keeping the fast. With studied meekness I tried to respond to their low bows, and walked myself – it seemed to me a great achievement – to the candle drawer to take candles from the old elder, a soldier, and placed them myself in the sockets. Through the doors could be seen the altar cover, embroidered by mamma; above the holy picture-stand were two angels with stars, who used to seem to me so huge when I was little, and a dove with a yellow halo which used to attract my attention in early days. Behind the choir one could see the font where I had assisted at the christening of so many children of our house-serfs and had been christened myself. The old priest came out wearing a stole made out of my father's pall, and officiated in the same voice in which ever since I remember anything I had heard the church service in our house, and Sonya's christening and the last mass for my father and my mother's burial service. And the same jarring voice of the deacon rang out in the choir, and the same old woman whom I always remember in church at every service stood bent over at the wall, gazed with tearful eyes at the holy picture in the choir, pressed her cramped fingers to her faded kerchief, and mumbled something in her toothless mouth. And all this seemed no longer curious, nor through a single memory familiar to me; it was all now grand and holy in my eyes, and seemed to me full of profound significance. I listened to every word of the prayer, tried to respond in feeling to it; and if I could not understand it, I prayed inwardly to God to enlighten me, or made a prayer of my own in place of the one I could not follow. When the Confessions were read, I thought of my past, and that childish innocent past seemed to me so black in comparison with the pure condition of my soul now that I wept and was horrified at myself. But at the same time I felt that it would all be forgiven, and that if there had been even more sin in me, sweeter still would have been my repentance. When the priest at the end of the service said, 'The blessing of God be with you,' it seemed to me that I felt instantly passing into me a physical sensation of wellbeing, as though a sort of light and warmth had rushed into my heart. The service was over, the good father came up to me and enquired should he not come to us for the all-night service and when; but I touchingly thanked him for what he wished, as I imagined, to do for my sake, and said that I would myself walk or drive over.

'You want to put yourself to that trouble?' he said.

And I did not know what to answer for fear of falling into the sin of pride.

I always let the horses go back from the service if I were without Katya, and walked home alone, bowing low and meekly to all who met me, and trying to find opportunities to help, to advise, to sacrifice myself for someone, to assist in lifting a load, to dandle a baby, to make way by stepping into the mud. One evening I heard the bailiff, in giving his account to Katya, say that the peasant Semyon had come to beg some planks for his daughter's coffin and a rouble for the funeral service, and that he'd given it him.

'Are they really so poor?' I asked.

'Very poor, madam, not a pinch of salt in the house,' answered the bailiff.

I felt a pang at my heart, and at the same time I felt a sort of joy at hearing this. Deluding Katya with the pretext that I was going for a walk, I ran upstairs, and got out all my money (it was very little, but all that I had). Crossing myself, I went alone through the verandah and the garden to the village to Semyon's hut. It was at the edge of the village, and unseen by anyone I ran up to the window, laid the money in the window, and tapped on it. A door creaked, someone came out of the hut and called after me. Shaking and chill with panic like a guilty creature, I ran home. Katya asked me where I had been, what was the matter with me, but I did not even understand what she said to me, and made no answer. Everything seemed all at once so worthless and petty to me. I locked myself in my own room and walked up and down a long while alone, unable to do anything, unable to think, to get a clear idea of my own feelings. I thought of the joy of all the family, of the words they would say of the person who had brought the money, and I felt sorry too that I had not given it myself. I thought of what Sergey Mihalovich would say when he heard of it, and at the same time rejoiced that no one would ever hear of it. And I was full of joy, and all people and I myself seemed so bad to me, and so tenderly I looked on myself and everyone that the thought of death came to me like a dream of bliss. I smiled and prayed and wept; and with such passionate fervour I loved everyone in the world, and myself too at that moment. Between the services I read the gospel, and more and more comprehensible it had become to me, and more and more touching and simple the history of that divine life, and more awful and inconceivable the depths of feeling and thought I found in its teaching. But, on the other hand, how clear and simple everything seemed to me when getting up from that book I looked into my heart and pondered on the life surrounding me. It seemed so difficult to be bad, and so simple to love everyone and be loved by them. Everyone was so kind and gentle with me; even Sonya, whose lessons I still went on with, was quite different, tried to understand, to please me and not to vex me. As I was, so were all of them to me. Going over my enemies, of whom I had to beg forgiveness before making my confession, I could only remember one young lady, whom I had a year ago made ridiculous in the presence of guests, and who had given up coming to see us. I wrote a letter to her, confessing my fault, and begging her forgiveness. She answered with a letter, in which she too begged my forgiveness, and forgave me. I wept with joy, reading those simple lines, in which at that time I saw such deep and touching feeling. My old nurse cried when I begged her forgiveness. 'Why were they all so good to me? How had I deserved such love?' I asked myself. And I could not help thinking of Sergey Mihalovich, and for a long while I thought of him. I could not help it, and did not even look on it as a sin. But I thought of him now not at all as I had done on the night when I first knew that I loved him. I thought of him as of myself, unconsciously associating him with every thought of my future. The overwhelming influence of which I was conscious in his presence had entirely disappeared in my imagination. I felt myself now his equal, and from the height of my present spiritual condition I completely understood him. What had hitherto seemed strange in him was quite clear to me now. Only now I understood why he had said that happiness is only to be found in living for others, and now I perfectly agreed with him. It seemed to me that we should be so endlessly and calmly happy. And I pictured to myself not tours abroad, not society, and a brilliant life, but something quite different, a quiet family life in the country with continual self-sacrifice, continual love for one another, and a continual sense in all things of a kind and beneficent Providence.

I took the sacrament, as I had intended, on my birthday. In my heart there was such complete happiness when I came home that day from church that I was afraid of life, afraid of every impression, of anything that could disturb that happiness. But we had hardly got out of the trap at the steps when a familiar vehicle rattled on the bridge, and I caught sight of Sergey Mihalovich. He congratulated me, and we went together into the drawing-room. Never since I had known him had I been as calm and self-possessed as that morning. I felt that there was a whole new world in me which he did not understand, which was above him. I did not feel the slightest embarrassment with him. He must have understood what this was due to, and there was a peculiar tender gentleness and reverent consideration in his manner to me. I was going to the piano, but he locked it and put the key in his pocket.

'Don't spoil your mood,' he said. 'There is music now in your soul, better than any in the world.'

I was grateful to him for this, and at the same time I rather disliked his so easily and clearly understanding all that should have been hidden from all in my soul. At dinner he said he had come to congratulate me on my birthday, and at the same time to say goodbye, as he was going next day to Moscow. As he said this he looked at Katya, but then glanced stealthily at me, and I saw that he was afraid he would detect emotion in my face. But I was not surprised nor agitated. I did not even ask whether he were going for long. I knew he would say this, and I knew he would not go. How I knew it I cannot explain to this day; but on that memorable day it seemed to me that I knew everything that had been and would be. I was as though in a happy dream when whatever happens seems as though it has been already, and that one has known it long ago, and it all seems, too, as though it were to come, and one knows that it will come.

He had meant to leave soon after dinner; but Katya, tired after the service, had gone to lie down, and he was obliged to wait till she waked up to say goodbye to her. The hall was hot with the sun on it. We went out into the verandah. As soon as we had sat down, I began with perfect composure speaking of what was bound to decide the fate of my love. And I began to speak neither too soon nor too late, but the very moment we were seated, before anything had been said, before there had been a conversation of some tone or character that might have hindered what I wanted to say. I can't understand how I came by such composure, such decision, and such exactness in my phrases. It was as though it were not I, but something apart from my own will was speaking in me. He sat opposite me, his elbow leaning on the rail, and drawing a branch of lilac to him, he was stripping off its leaves. When I began to speak, he let the branch go, and leaned his head on his hand. It might be the attitude of a man in perfect repose or in great agitation.

'What are you going away for?' I asked deliberately and significantly, looking him straight in the face.

He did not at once answer.

'Business!' he said, dropping his eyes.

I saw that it was not easy for him to lie to me, and in answer to a question put to him so frankly.

'Listen,' I said. 'You know what today is for me. For many reasons this day is very important to me. If I ask you this, it is not to show my interest (you know how well I know you, and how I care for you), I ask because I must know . . . What are you going for?'

'It's very difficult for me to tell you the true reason why I am going away,' he said. 'During this week I have been thinking a great deal about you and myself, and have decided that I ought to go. You understand why, and if you care for me you will not ask.' He passed his hand over his forehead, and covered his eyes with it. 'It's painful to me . . . And easy for you to understand.'

My heart began to beat violently.

'I can't understand,' I said; '*I can't*; but you – do tell me, for God's sake, for the sake of today, tell me – I can hear anything calmly,' I said.

He shifted his position, glanced at me, and again drew the branch to him.

'Well,' he said, after a brief pause, in a voice that tried in vain to be steady, 'though it's absurd and impossible to put it into words, though it's painful even, I will try and explain to you . . . ' he added, pausing as though in physical pain.

'Well?' said I.

'Imagine that there was a certain Monsieur A., let us say,' he said, 'elderly and *blasé*, and a Mademoiselle B., young and happy, knowing nothing of men or of life. Through various family circumstances he loved her as a daughter, and was not afraid of loving her in any other way.'

He paused, but I did not interrupt.

'But he forgot that B. was so young, that life was still a plaything for her,' he went on, with sudden swiftness and determination, not looking at me, 'and that it was easy to love her in a different way, and that that would be an amusement to her. And he made a mistake, and suddenly was aware that another feeling, as bitter as remorse, had forced its way into his soul, and he was afraid. He was afraid of destroying their old affectionate relations, and resolved to go away rather than destroy those relations.' As he said this, again as it were carelessly, he passed his hand over his eyes and hid them.

'Why was he afraid of loving in another way?' I said, scarcely audibly, suppressing my emotion, and my voice was steady; to him it probably seemed playful. He answered in a tone, as it were, of offence.

'You are young,' he said. 'I am not young. You want to amuse yourself, but I want something else. Amuse yourself, only not with me, or I shall believe in it, and it will do me harm, and you will be sorry for it. That was what A. said,' he added. 'Oh, well, that's all nonsense, but you understand why I'm going. And we won't talk any more about it. Please don't.'

'No, no, we will talk about it,' I said, and there was a quiver of tears in my voice. 'Did he love her, or not?'

He did not answer.

'And if he didn't love her, why did he play with her as if she were a baby?' I said.

'Yes, yes, A. was to blame,' he answered, hurriedly interrupting me, 'but it was all over, and they parted . . . friends.'

'But that's awful! And could there be no other ending? . . . ' I uttered faintly, and was terrified at what I had said.

'Yes, there is,' he said, uncovering his agitated face and looking straight at me. 'There are two different endings. Only, for God's sake, don't interrupt, and listen to me quietly. Some say,' he began, standing up and smiling a sickly, bitter smile, 'some say that A. went out of his mind, fell madly in love with B., and told her so. And she only laughed. For her it was a jest, but for him it was the question of his whole life.'

I started, and would have interrupted him to say that he must not speak for me, but he laid his hand on mine, restraining me.

'Wait a minute,' he said in a shaking voice. 'Others say that she took pity on him; fancied, poor girl, having seen no one else, that she really could love him, and consented to become his wife. And he in his madness believed it – believed that life would begin over again for him – but she saw herself that she had deceived him, and that he was deceiving her . . . We won't talk any more about it,' he concluded, apparently unable to go on, and he began walking up and down facing me.

He had said, 'We won't talk of it,' but I saw that with all the strength of his soul he was waiting for my words. I tried to speak, but couldn't – something ached poignantly in my bosom. I glanced at him; he was pale, and his lower lip was quivering. I felt sorry for him. I made an effort, and suddenly, bursting through the spell of silence that seemed enchaining me, I began speaking in a subdued inner voice, which I feared every second would break.

'There's a third ending,' I said, and stopped, but he did not speak, 'a third ending, that he did not love her, but he hurt her, hurt her, and thought he was right, and went away, and seemed proud too for some reason. It's you, not I, you, that it's a jest to; from the first day I've loved you – loved!' I repeated, and at that word 'loved' my voice involuntarily passed from a soft murmur into a wild shriek that frightened me myself.

He stood facing me, his lips quivering more and more, and two tears stood out on his pale cheeks.

'It's a shame!' I almost screamed, feeling that I was choking with angry, unshed tears. 'What's it for?' I articulated, and stood up to get away from him.

But he did not let me go. His head lay on my knees, his lips were kissing my trembling hands, and his tears wetted them.

'My God! if I had known,' he said.

'What for? what for?' I was still repeating, but my soul was full of happiness, happiness that seemed to have gone for ever and was coming back to me.

Five minutes later Sonya was running upstairs to Katya and shouting to all the household that Masha was going to marry Sergey Mihalovich.

5

There was no reason for delaying our marriage, and neither of us desired to do so. Katya would indeed have liked us to go to Moscow to purchase and order the trousseau, and his mother urged his providing himself with a new carriage and furniture, and having the house repapered, before he was married. But we both insisted that all this should be done afterwards if it really were so necessary, and that we should be married a fortnight after my birthday, quite quietly, without a trousseau, without guests and bridesmen, without a wedding supper, champagne, and all the conventional accompaniments of a wedding. He told me how disappointed his mother was that his wedding was to take place without music, without mountains of boxes, and without the complete redecoration of the whole house (like her own wedding, which had cost thirty thousand roubles), and how seriously and surreptitiously she was turning out her chest of stores and consulting with her housekeeper, Maryushka, about certain rugs, curtains, and tea-trays essential to our happiness. Katya too, on my behalf, was busy in the same way with my old nurse, Kuzminishna, and it did not do to speak lightly of it to her. She was firmly persuaded that when we were talking of our future together we were simply babbling the lovers' nonsense peculiar to persons in our position; but that our real future happiness would depend entirely on the correct cutting and careful stitching of chemises and the hemming of tablecloths and dinner-napkins. Mysterious communications on the progress of the preparations passed several times a day between Nikolskoe and Pokrovskoe; and though the relations between Katya and his mother appeared on the surface to be of the tenderest, one had a sense of a somewhat antagonistic but most delicate diplomacy in their intercourse. Tatyana Semyonovna, his mother, with whom

I now became more intimately acquainted, was a ceremonious, old-fashioned lady, very correct in the management of her household. He loved her not simply as a son, from duty, but as a man, from feeling, considering her as the best, the wisest, the kindest, and most loving woman in the world. Tatyana Semyonovna was always kind to us, to me particularly so, and she was glad her son should marry; but when I was with her as her future daughter-in-law, it seemed to me that she tried to make me feel that as a match for her son I might have been better, and that it would not be amiss for me to keep that in mind, and I perfectly understood her and agreed with her.

During that fortnight we saw each other every day. He used to come to dinner and to stay on till midnight; but although he said – and I knew he spoke the truth – that he had no life apart from me, he never spent the whole day with me, and tried to go on with his usual work. Our external relations remained the same as before right up to our wedding. We still addressed each other formally by our full names; he did not kiss even my hand; and far from seeking opportunities of being alone with me, seemed positively to avoid them. It was as though he feared the too violent, disquieting tenderness that was within him. I don't know whether he or I had changed, but now I felt completely on an equality with him, saw no trace in him of that effort after simplicity that I had once disliked in him; and often, to my satisfaction, I seemed to see before me, instead of a man inspiring respect and awe, a soft-hearted child dazed with happiness. 'So that was all there was in him,' I often thought. 'He's just the same sort of person as I am, nothing more.' Now it seemed to me that the whole of him was before my eyes, and that I had learned to know him fully, and all that I had learned was so simple and so perfectly in harmony with me. Even his plans for our life together in the future were just my plans, only better and more clearly defined in his words.

The weather was bad during those days, and the greater part of the time we spent indoors. Our best, most intimate talks took place in the corner between the piano and the little window. The light of the candles was reflected on the black window close by, and on the glistening pane there was often the patter and drip of raindrops. On the roof the rain beat, and in the pool below there was the splash of water; there was a damp draught from the window under the eaves, and it made it seem all the brighter, warmer, and more joyful in our corner.

'Do you know, I've long been wanting to say one thing to you,' he said late one evening when we were sitting alone together in our corner. 'When you were playing, I thought of it.'

'You need not tell me; I know all about it,' I said.

'Yes, that's true. We won't talk of it.'

'No, tell me, what is it?' I asked.

'Why, do you remember when I told you the story of A. and B.?'

'I should think you'd better not recall that silly story! It's a good thing it ended as it did.'

'Yes, a little more, and all my happiness would have been shattered by my own hand. You saved me. But the thing is, I was always telling lies then, and it's on my conscience. I want to speak out now.'

'Oh, please, you needn't.'

'Don't be afraid,' he said, smiling. 'I only want to justify myself. When I began to speak I was trying to be reasonable.'

'Why be reasonable?' I said. 'You never ought to.'

'Yes, I was wrong in my reasoning. After all my disappointments and mistakes in life, when I came this year into the country I said to myself so resolutely that love was over for me; that all that was left me was the duties of the decline of life; that for a long while I failed to recognise what my feeling for you was, and what it might lead me to. I hoped and did not hope. At one time it seemed to me you were flirting, at another I had faith – and I didn't know myself what I was going to do. But after that evening – do you remember, when we walked in the garden at night? – I was frightened; my present happiness seemed too great and impossible. Think what it would have been if I had let myself hope and in vain? But, of course, I thought only of myself, because I'm a sickening egoist.'

He paused, looking at me.

'But still you know it was not altogether nonsense that I talked then. I might well, and ought to, feel afraid. I am taking so much from you, and I can give so little. You are a child still; you are a bud not yet fully out, which will blossom more fully later; you love for the first time; while I – '

'Yes, tell me truly,' I said, but all at once I felt frightened of his answer. 'No, I don't want you to,' I added.

'Whether I have been in love before, eh?' he said, at once guessing my thought; 'that I can tell you. No, I haven't. Never anything like this feeling.' But suddenly it seemed as though some bitter recollection had flashed into his mind. 'No, and now I ought to have your heart to have the right to love you,' he said mournfully. 'So hadn't I good reason to think twice before saying that I loved you? What do I give you? Love, it is true.'

'Is that so little?' I said, looking into his eyes.

'Little, my dear, little for you,' he went on. 'You have beauty and youth. Often now I can't sleep at night for happiness, and all the time I'm thinking of how we will live our life together. I have lived through a great deal, and it seems to me that I have found what one wants to be happy – a quiet, secluded life in our remote countryside, with the power of doing good to people, to whom it's so easy to do good, who are so little used to it; then work, work which seems to be bringing forth fruit; then leisure, nature, books, music, love for one's neighbours; that is my happiness, and I dreamed of none higher. And now to crown all that, such a friend as you, a family perhaps, and all that a man can desire.'

'Yes,' I said.

'For me, who have outlived my youth, yes, but not for you,' he went on. 'You have seen nothing of life; you may perhaps want to seek happiness in something else, and perhaps you may find it in something else. You fancy now that this is happiness because you love me.'

'No, I have always loved this quiet home life, and wished for nothing else,' I said. 'And you are only saying what I have thought.'

He smiled.

'That only seems so to you, my dear. But it's little for you. You have beauty and youth,' he repeated musingly.

But I was irritated at his not believing me, and as it were reproaching me with my beauty and my youth.

'Then what do you love me for?' I said angrily – 'for my youth or for myself?'

'I don't know, but I love you,' he answered, looking at me with his intent gaze that fascinated me.

I made no answer, and involuntarily I looked into his eyes. All at once something strange happened to me. At first I ceased to see what was around me, then his face vanished before my eyes, only his eyes shone it seemed just opposite my eyes, then it seemed to me that his eyes were piercing into me, everything was a blur, I saw nothing, and had to shut my eyes to tear myself away from the sensation of delight and terror produced in me by that gaze.

On the eve of the day fixed for our wedding the weather cleared. It had been summer when the rains had begun, now after they had ceased came the first cold fine evening of autumn. Everything was wet and cold and bright, and in the garden one observed for the first time the openness, the bright tints, and bareness of autumn. The sky was clear and chill and pale. I went to bed happy in the thought that the next day, the day of my wedding, would be fine. On the day I waked with the sun, and the thought that it was today . . . as it were, scared and amazed me. I went out into the garden. The sun had only just risen, and its light filtered in patches through the lime trees of the avenue, which were losing their yellow leaves. The path was strewn with rustling leaves. The wrinkled bright red bunches of berries on the mountain ash gleamed on the branches among the few frost-bitten, curling leaves. The dahlias were withered and blackened. Frost lay for the first time like silver on the pale green of the grass and the trampled burdocks round the house. In the clear cold sky there was not, and could not be, a single cloud. 'Can it really be today?' I asked myself, not believing in my own happiness. 'Shall I really tomorrow wake up not here, but in the unfamiliar Nikolskoe house with colonnades? Shall I never any more meet him in the evenings and talk of him at night with Katya? Shall I never sit with him at the piano in the Pokrovskoe drawing-room, nor see him off and tremble for his safety in the dark night?' But I remembered that he had said yesterday that he should come for the last time, and Katya had made me try on my wedding dress, and had said, 'For tomorrow'; and for an instant I believed in it, and then doubted again. 'Can I truly be going from today to live there with my mother-in-law, without Nadyozha, without old Grigory, without Katya? Shall I go to bed without kissing my old nurse and hearing her say in her old way as she crosses me, "Good-night, miss"? Shall I give Sonya no more lessons, nor play with her, nor knock through the wall to her in the morning, and hear her ringing laugh? Can it be that today I shall become someone that I don't know myself, and a new life, the realisation of my hopes and wishes, is opening before me? Will that new life be for always?'

Impatiently I awaited his arrival. I was unhappy alone with these thoughts. He came early, and it was only with him that I fully believed that I should be his wife today, and that thought lost its terrors for me.

Before dinner we walked to our church to attend a memorial service for my father.

'If only he could have been living now!' I thought, as we returned home, and without speaking I clung to the arm of the man who had been his dearest friend. During the prayers, kneeling with my head bowed down to the cold stone of the chapel floor, I so thoroughly believed that his soul was understanding me and blessing my choice, that even now it seemed to me that his spirit was hovering about us, and that I felt his blessing upon me. And memories and hopes and happiness and sorrow all melted together into one sweet and solemn feeling in harmony with the still keen air, the quietness, the bareness of the fields, and the pale sky, shedding on everything a bright but feeble sunshine that tried in vain to burn my cheek. I fancied that the man at my side understood and shared my feeling. He was walking slowly and in silence, and in his face, into which I peeped from time to time, showed the same grave emotion between sorrow and joy that was to be seen in nature, and was in my heart. All at once he turned to me. I saw he was going to say something. 'What if he speaks of something else, not what I am thinking of?' flashed into my mind. But he began speaking of my father without even mentioning his name.

'Once he said to me jokingly: "You had better marry my Masha!"' he said.

'How happy he would have been now!' I said, squeezing the arm on which mine was lying.

'Yes, you were a child then,' he went on, looking into my eyes. 'I used to kiss those eyes then, and loved them only because they were like his, and never dreamed they would be so dear to me on their own account. I used to call you Masha then.'

'Call me "thee", ' I said.

'I was just meaning to call thee so,' he said; 'it's only now that I feel thee quite mine.' And a serene and happy gaze that drew my eyes to him rested upon me.

And we went on walking slowly along the indistinct field-path through the trampled, broken stubble, and our steps and our voices were all that we could hear. On one side across the ravine as far as the distant, bare-looking copse stretched the brownish stubble, on which on the side away from us a peasant was noiselessly at work with a wooden plough making wider and wider the black strip of earth. A drove of horses scattered over the hillside below seemed quite close. On the other side, and in front right up to the garden and our house, which could be seen beyond it, stretched the dark thawing field, with here and there strips of green winter-corn. The sun was shining on it all, bright but not hot, and on everything lay the long threads of spider webs. They were floating in the air about us, lying on the stubble where the frost had dried, falling into our eyes, on to our hair and our clothes. When we talked our voices resounded and seemed to hang in the still air above us, as though we were the only creatures in the midst of the whole world, and were alone under that blue dome, in which the mild sunshine played flashing and quivering.

I too longed to call him 'thee', but I was ashamed to.

'Why art thou walking so fast?' I said hurriedly, almost in a whisper, and I could not help blushing. He walked more slowly and looked still more fondly, still more gladly and happily at me.

When we got home his mother was already there with the guests, whom we had not been able to avoid having, and up to the moment when we came out of church and got into the carriage to drive to Nikolskoe I was not alone with him.

The church was almost empty; at a glance I saw only his mother, standing on a rug in the choir, Katya in a cap with lilac ribbons, and two or three of our servants looking inquisitively at me. At him I did not look, but I felt his presence beside me. I listened intently to the words of the service and repeated them, but there was no response to them in my soul. I could not pray, and gazed blankly at the holy pictures, at the lights, at the embroidered cross on the back of the priest's stole, at the picture-stand, at the church window, and understood nothing. I only felt that something extraordinary was being performed on me. When the priest turned to me with the cross, congratulated me, and said that he had christened, and now, by God's blessing, he had married me, and Katya and his mother kissed us, and I heard Grigory's voice calling the carriage, I wondered and was dismayed that everything was over, with no extraordinary feeling in my soul to correspond with the mysterious ceremony I had passed through. We kissed each other, and that kiss was so strange and remote from my feeling. 'And is that all?' I thought. We came out into the porch; the rumbling of the wheels resounded with a deeper note under the church roof; the fresh air blew into our faces; he put on his hat and gave me his arm to the carriage. From the carriage window I had a glimpse of a frosty moon with a ring round it. He sat down beside me and closed the door after him. Something seemed to stab me to the heart. It was as though I felt insulted by the assurance with which he did this. Katya's voice called for me to cover my head, the wheels rattled over the pavement, and then along the soft road, and we had driven off. Huddled up in a corner, I looked out of the window at the far-away moonlit fields, and at the road flying by in the chill light of the moon. And without looking at him, I felt him here beside me. 'Why, is this all from this minute of which I expected so much?' I thought, and it still seemed somehow degrading and humiliating to be sitting alone so close to him. I turned to him with the intention of saying something. But the words would not be uttered; it seemed as though there were no trace of my former feeling of tenderness in me, but a feeling of humiliation and dread had taken its place.

'Till this minute I could not believe that it was possible,' he said softly in response to my glance.

'Yes, but I'm somehow afraid,' I said.

'Afraid of me, my darling?' he said, taking my hand and letting his hand drop into it.

My hand lay lifeless in his hand, and my heart ached with cold.

'Yes,' I whispered.

But at that moment my heart suddenly began to beat more violently, my hand trembled and squeezed his hand; I felt warm, my eyes sought his in the dusk, and I suddenly felt that I was not afraid of him, that that dread was love, a new and still more tender and passionate love than before. I felt that I was altogether his, and that I was happy in his power over me.

PART TWO

I

DAYS, WEEKS, TWO MONTHS of solitary country life had slipped by, imperceptibly it seemed at the time; but meanwhile there had been feeling, emotion, and happiness for a whole lifetime in those two months. My dreams and his of the ordering of our lives together in the country were fulfilled not at all as we had expected. But our life did not fall short of our dreams. There was none of that hard work, doing one's duty and sacrificing one's life for one's neighbour, that I had pictured to myself when I was engaged. There was, on the contrary, simply the egoistic feeling of love for each other, the desire to be loved, and a causeless, continual gaiety and forgetfulness of all else in the world. He did, it is true, go off at times to his study to do some sort of work; at times he did drive to the town on business, and superintend the management of the land. But I saw what an effort it was to him to tear himself away from me. And he would acknowledge himself, later, that everything in the world in which I had no share seemed to him so absurd that he could not understand how one could be interested in it. It was just the same with me. I used to read, and to interest myself with music, with his mother, and with the village school; but it was all simply because each of those pursuits was associated with him and won his approbation. But as soon as there was no idea of him associated with my pursuit, my hands dropped at my side, and it seemed to me quite amusing to think there was anything in the world besides him. Possibly this was a bad, selfish feeling, but this feeling gave me happiness, and lifted me high above the whole world. He was the only person existing on earth for me, and I regarded him as the best, the most faultless, man in the world. Consequently I could have no other object in life than him – than being in his eyes what he believed me to be. And he considered me the first and best woman in the world, endowed with every possible virtue; and I tried to be that woman in the eyes of the first and best man in the whole world.

One day he came into the room just as I was saying my prayers. I looked round at him and went on with my prayers. He sat down at the table so as not to disturb me, and opened a book. But I fancied he was watching me, and I looked round. He smiled, I laughed outright, and could not go on praying.

'Have you said your prayers already?' I asked.

'Yes; but you go on, I'll go away.'

'But you do say prayers, I hope?'

He would have gone out without answering; but I stopped him.

'My love, please, for my sake, read the prayers with me!'

He stood beside me, and letting his hands drop awkwardly, with a serious face he began hesitatingly to read. From time to time he turned to me and sought approval and encouragement in my face.

When he had finished, I laughed and hugged him.

'It's all you, all you! It's as though I were ten years old again,' he said, blushing and kissing my hands.

Our house was one of those old country houses in which several generations of a family have passed their lives, respecting and loving one another. Everything breathed of good, honourable, family memories which at once when I entered that house seemed to become my memories. The arrangement and the management of the house were all ordered by Tatyana Semyonovna in the old style. I cannot say that everything was elegant and beautiful; but from the servants, down to the furniture and the food, all was plentiful, all was neat, solid, and orderly, inspiring respect. In symmetrical arrangement the furniture stood in the drawing-room, and the portraits hung on the walls, and the home-made rugs and strips of matting were laid on the floors. In the divan-room there was an old harpsichord, two chiffoniers of different patterns, sofas, and little tables with lattice-work and raised ornaments. In my boudoir, decorated by Tatyana Semyonovna with special care, stood the best furniture of different ages and patterns, and among other things an old pier-glass, at which at first I could not look without feeling shy, though later on it became dear to me as an old friend. Tatyana Semyonovna's voice was never heard, but everything in the house went as though by clockwork. Though there were many superfluous servants, all those servants wearing soft boots without heels (Tatyana Semyonovna considered creaking shoes and clacking heels as the most disagreeable things in the world), all those servants seemed proud of their position, stood in awe of their old mistress, looked on my husband and me with patronising affection, and seemed to take a particular pleasure in doing their work.

Every Saturday regularly all the floors in the house were scrubbed and the carpets were beaten; on the first day of each month a service was held with sprinkling of holy water; always on Tatyana

Semyonovna's name-day and her son's (mine, too, for the first time, that autumn) a banquet was given to the whole neighbourhood. And all this had been done without change for as long as Tatyana Semyonovna could remember. My husband took no part in the management of the house; he confined himself to looking after the land and the peasants, and a great deal of work that gave him. He used to get up even in the winter very early, so that when I waked up I did not find him. He usually came back to morning tea, which we drank alone together; and almost always at that time, after the exertions and worries of his work on the estate, he was in that particularly cheerful state of mind which we used to call *wild delight*. Often I used to ask him to tell me what he had been doing in the morning, and he would tell me such nonsense that we went into fits of laughter. Sometimes I insisted on a serious account, and he would restrain a smile and tell me. I looked at his eyes, at his moving lips, and did not understand a word, but simply enjoyed seeing him and hearing his voice.

'Come, what did I say, repeat it?' he would ask. But I could never repeat anything, so ludicrous it seemed that *he* should talk to *me*, not of himself or me, but of something else, as though it mattered what happened outside us. Only much later I began to have some slight understanding of his cares and to be interested in them. Tatyana Semyonovna did not make her appearance till dinner-time; she drank her tea alone in the morning, and only sent greetings to us by messengers. In our private world of frantic happiness a voice from her staid, decorous nook, so different, sounded so strange that often I could not restrain myself, and simply giggled in response to the maid who, standing with folded hands, announced sedately that 'Tatyana Semyonovna desired me to enquire how you slept after yesterday's walk, and about herself desired me to inform you that all night long she had a pain in her side, and a stupid dog in the village barked so and prevented her sleeping. And I was desired to enquire also how you liked today's baking, and to beg you to observe that Taras did not do the baking today, but Nikolasha for the first time as an experiment, and very fairly well, she says, he has done, especially the dough-rings, but he has over-baked the tea-rusks.' Till dinner-time we were not much together. I played the piano and read alone, while he was writing and going his rounds on the land again. But at dinner-time, at four o'clock, we met together in the dining-room; mamma sailed out of her room; and the poor ladies, of whom there were always two or three staying in the house, appeared on the scene. Regularly every day my husband gave his arm in the old fashion to his mother to take her in to dinner. But she insisted on his offering me the other, and regularly every day we were squeezed and got in each other's way at the door. At dinner my mother-in-law presided, and a conversation was maintained decorously reasonable and rather solemn in tone. The simple phrases that passed between my husband and me made an agreeable break in the solemnity of these ceremonious dinners. Sometimes disputes would spring up between mother and son, and they mocked at each other. I particularly loved these disputes and their mockery of one another, because the tender and enduring love that bound them together was never more strongly expressed than on these occasions. After dinner mamma settled herself in a big armchair in the drawing-room, and powdered snuff, or cut the leaves of some newly-purchased book, while we read aloud, or went off to the divan-room to the harpsichord. We read a great deal together at that time, but music was our best and favourite pleasure, every time touching new chords in our hearts, and as it were revealing us to each other anew. When I played his favourite pieces, he sat on a sofa at some distance where I could scarcely see him, and from a sort of shame at his emotion tried to conceal the impression the music made on him. But often when he was not expecting it, I got up from the piano, ran to him, and tried to catch on his face traces of his emotion, an unnatural brightness and moisture in his eyes, which he tried in vain to conceal from me. Mamma often wanted to look at us in the divan-room, but no doubt she sometimes was afraid of being a constraint to us, and she would pass through the room with a serious and indifferent face, pretending not to look at us. But I knew she had no reason really for going so often to her room and returning again. Evening tea was poured out by me in the big drawing-room, and again all the family circle gathered round the table. This duty of solemnly presiding before the sacred shrine of the samovar and the array of glasses and cups was for a long while a source of confusion to me. I always felt that I was not yet worthy of this honour; that I was too young and frivolous to turn the tap of such a big samovar, to set the glasses on the tray for Nikita, and to say as I did so, 'For Pyotr Ivanovich, for Marya Minichna'; to enquire, 'Is it sweet?' and to leave pieces of sugar for the old nurse and other deserving persons.

'Capital! capital!' my husband would often say, 'quite like a grown-up person;' and that only increased my confusion.

After tea mamma played patience or listened to Marya Minichna fortune-telling with the cards; then she kissed us both and made the sign of the cross on us, and we went to our own room. For the most part though, we used to sit up together till midnight, and this was our best and pleasantest time. He talked to me about his past; we made plans, philosophised sometimes, and tried to speak very softly all the time, so that we should not be heard upstairs and reported to Tatyana Semyonovna,9 who expected us to go to bed early. Sometimes getting hungry, we would steal quietly to the sideboard, procure a cold supper through the good offices of Nikita, and eat it by the light of one candle in my boudoir. We lived like strangers in that big, old house in which the stern spirit of the old world and of Tatyana Semyonovna held sway over all. Not she only, but the house-serfs, the old maidservants, the furniture, the pictures, aroused in me respect, a sort of awe and a sense that he and I were a little out of our element, that we must live here very circumspectly and discreetly. Looking back now, I can see that many things, that fettering, unvarying routine, and that mass of idle, inquisitive people in our house, were inconvenient and burdensome, but at the time the very constraint added a zest to our love. He was as far as I was from showing any sign that anything was not to his liking. On the contrary, he positively shut his eyes as it were to what was amiss. Mamma's footman, Dmitry Sidorov, who was very fond of the pipe, used regularly, every day after dinner, when we were in the divan-room, to go into my husband's study and take his tobacco out of the drawer. And it was worth seeing the good-humoured consternation with which Sergey Mihalovich would come up to me on tiptoe, and holding up his finger and winking, point to Dmitry Sidorov, who had not the slightest suspicion that he was seen. And when Dmitry Sidorov had retreated without noticing us, my husband, delighted that everything had ended so satisfactorily, would declare, as at every other opportunity, that I was 'a darling', and kiss me. Sometimes I did not like this easy-going readiness to forgive everything, this sort of disregard of everything, and without noticing that it was just the same with me, I considered it a weakness, 'Like a child who dare not show his will!' I thought.

'Ah, my dear,' he answered, when I said to him one day that I was surprised at his weakness, 'how can one be displeased at anything when one is as happy as I am? It's easier to give way oneself than to overrule others – of that I have long been convinced – and there is no position in which one cannot be happy. And we are so happy, I cannot be angry; for me now there is nothing wrong, it is all only pitiful or amusing. And above all – *le mieux est l'ennemi du bien.* Would you believe it, when I hear the bell ring, when I receive a letter, when I simply wake up, I'm in terror – terror at having to go on with life, at some change coming in it; for better than the present there can never be?'

I believed him, but I did not understand him; I was happy, but it seemed to me that this was always so and could not be otherwise, and was always so with everyone, and that somewhere ahead there was another happiness, not greater, but different.

So passed two months. Winter had come with its frosts and its storms, and I had begun, in spite of his being with me, to feel lonely. I had begun to feel that life was a repetition of the same thing; that there was nothing new either in me or in him; and that, on the contrary, we kept going back as it were on what was old. He began to give himself up to his work apart from me more than before, and I began to feel again that he had in his soul a sort of private world of his own into which he did not wish to admit me. His everlasting serenity irritated me. I loved him no less than before, and was as happy as before in his love. But my love had come to a standstill, and was not growing greater, and besides my love a sort of new feeling of restlessness had begun to steal into my soul. Loving was not enough for me after the happiness I had known in learning to love him. I longed for activity, not for a peaceful evenly flowing life. I longed for excitement, danger, and sacrifice for my feeling. I had a surplus of energy that found no outlet in our quiet life. I had attacks of depression, which I tried to hide from him, as something wrong, and attacks of frenzied gaiety and passion that alarmed him. He was aware of my state of mind before I was, and suggested our going to town. But I begged him not to go, not to change our mode of life, not to break up our happiness. And I really was happy; but my torment was that this happiness cost me no sort of effort, no sort of sacrifice, while energy for effort, for sacrifice, was fretting me. I loved him, and saw that I was everything to him; but I longed for everyone to see our love, for people to try and hinder my loving him, so that I could love him in spite of everything. My mind, and even my feelings, were occupied, but there was another feeling – the feeling of youth, the need of activity, which found no satisfaction in our quiet life. Why had he suggested that we might go to town when that was all I desired? If he had not said that, may be I should have seen that the feeling that made me miserable was harmful nonsense, was my fault; that the sacrifice I was looking for was here before me in the conquering of that feeling. The idea that I could escape from my depression simply by moving to town had involuntarily occurred to me; and at the same time I should have been ashamed and sorry to tear him away from all he loved for my sake. But time went by, the snow drifted higher and higher against the walls of the house, and we were still alone and alone, and were still the same to one another; while far away somewhere, in bright light and noise, crowds of people were in movement, were suffering and rejoicing, without a thought of us and our existence as it passed away. What was worst of all to me was the feeling that every day the routine of our life was nailing our life down into one definite shape; that our feeling was becoming not spontaneous, but was affected by bondage to the monotonous, passionless action of time. In the morning we were cheerful, at dinner polite, in the evening tender. 'Good! . . . ' I said to myself, 'that's all very well, to do good and lead an upright life, as he says, but we've plenty of time for that, and there is something else for which I only have the energy now.' That was not what I needed, I needed strife; I wanted feeling to guide us in life, and not life to be the guide to feeling. I longed to go with him to the edge of a precipice and to say, 'Another step, and I fling myself down! another movement and I am lost!' and for him, pale at the edge of the abyss, to snatch me up in his strong arms, hold me over it, so that my heart would stand still, and bear me away whither he would.

My state of mind positively affected my health, and my nerves began to suffer. One morning – I was worse than usual – he came back from his counting-house out of humour, which was rare with him. I noticed it at once, and asked him what was the matter; but he would not tell me, saying it was of no consequence. As I found out later, the captain of the district police had summoned our peasants, and from ill-will to my husband had made illegal exactions from them, and had used threats to them. My husband had not yet been able to stomach all this so as to feel it all simply pitiful and absurd; he was irritated, and so did not want to speak of it to me. But I fancied that he did not care to tell me about it because he regarded me as a child who could not understand what interested him. I turned away from him, was silent, and then sent to Marya Minichna, who was staying with us, to ask her to come to tea. After tea, which I finished unusually quickly, I took Marya Minichna off to the divan-room and began a loud conversation with her about some nonsense which was utterly uninteresting to me. He walked about the room, glancing now and then at us. Those glances for some reason or other had the effect on me of making me want to talk and even laugh more and more. Everything I said seemed funny to me, and everything Marya Minichna said. Without saying anything to me he went away into his study and closed the door after him. As soon as he was not there to hear, all my gaiety suddenly vanished, so that Marya Minichna wondered and asked me what was the matter . . . I did not answer, but sat down on a sofa and felt inclined to cry. 'And what is he inventing to worry over?' I thought. 'Some nonsense which he thinks important; but if he will only tell me, I'll show him it's all rubbish. No; he must needs suppose I shouldn't understand, must needs humiliate me with his stately composure, and always be in the right with me. But I'm right too when I'm bored and dreary, when I want to live, to move about,' I thought, 'and not to stick in the same place and feel that time is passing over me. I want to go forward, and every day, every hour, I want novelty; while he wants to stop still and to keep me stopping still with him. And how easy it would be for him! There's no need for this to take me to town; all he needs to do is to be as I am, not to school himself away from his nature, not to hold himself in, but to live simply. That's the very thing he tells me to do, but he's not simple himself. So there!' I felt that tears were gathering, and that I was angry with him. I was dismayed at this anger, and went in to him. He was sitting in his study writing. Hearing my footsteps, he looked round for an instant, carelessly and calmly, and went on writing. That glance displeased me; instead of going up to him I stood at the table at which he was writing, and opening a book began looking at it. He broke off once more and looked at me.

'Masha, are you cross?' he said.

I responded by a cold glance, which said, 'You needn't ask – why this politeness?' He shook his head and smiled timidly and tenderly, but for the first time my smile did not respond to his smile.

'What happened today?' I asked. 'Why wouldn't you tell me?'

'Nothing of consequence, a trifling annoyance!' he answered. 'I can tell you now, though. Two peasants had gone to the town . . . '

But I did not let him finish his tale.

'Why was it you wouldn't tell me when I asked you at tea?'

'I should have said something stupid; I was angry then.'

'It was then I wanted you to.'

'What for?'

'Why do you imagine that I can never be any help to you in anything?'

'What do I imagine?' he said, flinging down his pen. 'I imagine that I can't live without you. In everything, everything you're not merely a help to me, but you do everything. So that's the discovery you've been making!' he laughed. 'I only live through you. It seems to me that all is well simply because you are here, because you . . . '

'Yes, I know all that; I'm a dear child who must be tranquillised!' I said, in such a tone that he looked at me in wonder, as though he was seeing me for the first time. 'I don't want tranquillity, there's enough of it in you, quite enough,' I added.

'Well, do you see this was what was the matter,' he began hurriedly, interrupting me, evidently afraid to let me give utterance to all I was feeling. 'What would you say about it?'

'I don't care to hear it now!' I answered. Though I did want to hear him, it was so agreeable to me to trouble his tranquillity of mind. 'I don't want to play at life, I want to live,' I said, 'just as you do.'

On his face, which always reflected every feeling so quickly and so vividly, there was a look of pain and of intense attention.

'I want to live with you on equal terms.' But I could not go on; such sadness, such profound sadness, was apparent in his face. He was silent for a little.

'But in what way are you not on equal terms with me?' he said. 'Is it because I, and not you, have to deal with the police captain and drunken peasants?'

'Oh, not only that,' I said.

'For God's sake, understand me, my dear,' he went on. 'I know that we are always hurt by shocks; I have lived and learned that. I love you, and consequently I can't help wanting to save you from shocks. That's my life, my love for you, so don't you hinder my living either.'

'You are always right!' I said, not looking at him.

It annoyed me that again in his soul all was clear and calm, while I was full of vexation and a feeling like remorse.

'Masha! what is the matter with you?' he said. 'The point is not whether I am right or you are right, but of something quite different. What have you against me? Don't speak at once, think a little, and tell me all you are thinking about. You are vexed with me, and you're probably right, but do let me know what I've done wrong?'

But how could I tell him all that was in my heart? The fact that he understood me at once; that again I was a child before him; that I could do nothing that he would not understand and have foreseen, exasperated me more than ever.

'I have nothing against you,' I said; 'it's simply that I'm dull, and I don't want to be dull. But you say it must be so, and again you are right!'

I said this and glanced at him. I had attained my aim; his tranquillity had gone, alarm and pain were visible in his face.

'Masha,' he began in a gentle, troubled voice, 'this is no jesting matter what we are doing now. It is our fate that is being decided now. I beg you to make no answer, but to listen to me. Why do you want to make me suffer?'

But I interrupted him.

'I know you will be right. You'd better not speak – you are right!' I said coldly, as though not I, but some evil spirit in me were speaking.

'If you only knew what you are doing!' he said in a shaking voice.

I burst into tears, and I felt better. He sat down beside me and kept silence. I felt sorry for him and ashamed of myself, and vexed at what I had done. I did not look at him. It seemed to me that he must be looking at me either severely or in perplexity at that moment. I looked round; a soft tender glance was fixed upon me as though asking forgiveness. I took him by the hand and said, 'Forgive me – I don't know what I said myself.'

'No; but I know what you said, and you said what is true.'

'What?' I asked.

'That we must go to Petersburg,' he said; 'there's nothing for us to do here now.'

'As you wish,' I said.

He put his arms round me and kissed me.

'You forgive me,' he said; 'I have acted wrongly towards you.'

That evening I played to him a long while, and he walked about the room murmuring something. He had the habit of murmuring to himself, and I often used to ask him what he was whispering, and he would always after a moment's thought tell me exactly what he had been saying; generally, lines of verse, and sometimes fearful nonsense, but always of a kind which showed me his humour at the time.

'What are you whispering today?' I asked.

He stopped, thought a little, and with a smile quoted the two lines of Lermontov[5] – 'And in his madness prays for storms, As though in storms he might find peace.'

'No, he's more than a man, he knows everything!' I thought. 'How can one help loving him?'

I got up, took him by the arm, and began walking with him, trying to keep step with him.

'Yes?' he asked smiling, and watching me.

'Yes,' I said in a whisper, and a sort of mood of mirth came upon us both, our eyes laughed, and we made our strides longer and longer, and rose more and more upon tiptoe. And with this stride, to the great horror of Grigory and the amazement of mamma, who was playing patience in the drawing-room, we pranced through all the rooms as far as the dining-room, and there stopped, looked at each other, and went off into a roar of laughter.

A fortnight later, before Christmas, we were in Petersburg.

2

Our journey to Petersburg, the week in Moscow, my relations and his, settling into a new home, the road, the new places and persons – all this passed like a dream. It was all so varied, so new, so gay; it was all so warmly and brightly lighted up by his presence, his love, that our quiet country life seemed to me something long past and of no importance. To my great astonishment, instead of the worldly haughtiness and frigidity I had expected to find in people, everyone met me with such unfeigned cordiality and pleasure (not only our kinsfolk, but strangers too), that it seemed as though they had been thinking of nothing but me, had only been waiting for me to be happy themselves. It was also something quite unexpected by me that in the circle of society, which seemed to me the very best, my husband had, as it appeared, many acquaintances of whom he had never talked to me. And often it seemed strange and unpleasant to me to hear from him severe criticisms of some of those people who seemed to me so nice. I could not understand why he was so reserved with them, and tried to avoid making many acquaintances which seemed to me flattering. It seemed to me that the more nice people one knew the better, and that all were nice.

'This is how we will manage, do you see,' he had said to me just before we left the country: 'here I am a little Croesus,[6] but there we shall be people of very modest means, and so we must only stay in town till Easter, and not go into society, or else we shall get into difficulties; and besides, I shouldn't care to for your sake.'

'Why go into society?' I answered; 'we'll only see the theatres and our relations, hear the opera and some good music, and even before Easter will go back to the country.'

But as soon as we had arrived in Petersburg these plans were forgotten. I found myself all of a sudden in such a new happy world, so many delights encompassed me, such new interests opened out before me, that at once, though unconsciously, I renounced all my past and all the plans of that past. 'That was after all mere trifling; it hadn't begun, but this is the thing! And what will come next?'

I thought. The restlessness and the fits of depression that had worried me in the country had all at once, as though by magic, completely vanished. My love for my husband had become calmer, and it never occurred to me here to wonder whether he loved me less. And indeed I could not doubt his love; every thought I had was instantly understood, every feeling was shared, every desire fulfilled. His tranquillity disappeared here or no longer irritated me. Besides I felt that here, besides his former love for me, he was admiring me too. Often after paying a call, on being introduced to some new acquaintance, or entertaining a party of friends in the evening, when I had performed the duties of hostess, trembling inwardly in fear of making some blunder, he would say: 'Ah! bravo, little girl, capital, don't be frightened! That's capital, really!' And I was highly delighted. Soon after our arrival he wrote a letter to his mother; and when he called me to add a word from myself, he would not let me read what he had written, which led me of course to insist, and I read: 'You would not know Masha,' he wrote, 'indeed, I hardly know her myself. Where can she have picked up this charming, gracious composure, affability, social tact, and high breeding, in fact. And it's all so simple, charming, sweet. Everyone's in ecstasies over her, and I myself am never tired of admiring her, and, if it were possible, I should love her more than before.'

'Oh! so that's what I am like!' I thought. And I was so gay and happy, I even fancied that I loved him more than ever. My success with all our acquaintances was a complete surprise to me. I was continually being told on all hands that there I had made a particularly good impression on an uncle; that here an aunt had been quite bewitched by me; here a man declared that there were no women like me in Petersburg; and there a lady assures me that I have but to wish it in order to become the woman most sought after in society. A cousin of my husband's, in particular, a Princess D., a society woman no longer young, who had impetuously fallen in love with me, used more than anyone to say flattering things to me that turned my head. When this cousin invited me for the first time to go to a ball, and asked my husband about it, he turned to me, and with a scarcely perceptible sly smile, asked, 'Did I want to go?' I bent my head in token of assent, and felt that I blushed.

'She's like a criminal confessing what she wants,' he said, laughing good-humouredly.

'But, you know, you said that we couldn't go into society, and besides, you don't like it,' I answered, smiling, and looking with imploring eyes at him.

'If you want to very much, we'll go,' he said.

'We had better not, really.'

'Do you want to . . . very much?' he asked again.

I did not answer.

'Society is no great calamity so far,' he went on; 'but an unsatisfied craving for society, that's bad, and ugly too. We certainly must go, and we will go,' he wound up resolutely.

'To tell you the truth,' I said, 'I never longed for anything in the world so much as this ball.'

We went to the ball, and my enjoyment of it surpassed all my expectations. At the ball, even more than before, it seemed to me that I was the centre round which everything was moving; that it was only for me that the great hall was lighted up, the music was playing, and that crowd of people, ecstatically admiring me, had come together. Everyone, from the hairdresser and the lady's maid, to my partners and the old gentlemen walking about the hall, told me, or gave me to understand, that they loved me. The general criticism passed upon me at that ball, and reported to me afterwards by our cousin, was that I was utterly unlike other women, that there was something individual in me, the charm of the country, simple and exquisite. This success so flattered me that I frankly told my husband how I should like that year to go to two or three more balls, 'so as to have had quite enough of them,' I added hypocritically.

My husband readily agreed, and at first accompanied me with evident pleasure, enjoying my triumph, and apparently quite forgetting or giving up the decision he had expressed before.

Later on he became obviously bored and weary of the life we were leading. But I had no thoughts for that; if I did sometimes notice his intent, serious gaze, fixed inquiringly upon me, I refused to understand its significance. I was so blinded by that devotion to me I seemed to see suddenly aroused in all outsiders, that atmosphere of luxury, pleasure, and novelty, which I was breathing here for the first time, his moral influence that had repressed me had so quickly vanished here. It was so pleasant for me in this world to feel not merely on a level with him, but superior to him, and for that to love him even more and more independently than before, that I could not imagine what drawbacks he could see for me in fashionable life. I had a feeling of pride and self-satisfaction quite new to me when, as we entered a ballroom, all eyes were turned upon me; while he, as though ashamed to claim his ownership of me before the crowd, made haste to leave me and obliterate himself in the throng of black coats.

'Wait a little!' I often thought while my eyes sought him, an inconspicuous, often weary-looking figure at the further end of the hall. 'Wait a little!' I thought: 'we shall go home, and you will see and understand for whose sake I tried to be beautiful and brilliant, and what it is I love out of all that surrounds me this evening.' I quite sincerely fancied, indeed, that my triumphs only delighted me by enabling me to sacrifice them to him. The only way in which fashionable life might be harmful to me was, I thought, the possibility of being attracted by one of the men I met in society, of arousing my husband's jealousy. But he had such trust in me, he seemed so tranquil and indifferent, and all the young men I met seemed so unimportant in comparison with him, that the sole danger of society, as I considered it, did not frighten me. But, all the same, the attentions of many men in society afforded me gratification, flattered my vanity, led me to imagine that there was a sort of merit in my love for my husband, and made my behaviour with him more self-confident and, as it were, more casual.

'Oh, I saw how eagerly you were talking with N. N.,' I said one evening on the way home from a ball, shaking my finger at him, and mentioning a well-known Petersburg lady with whom he had been talking that evening. I said this to rouse him – he was particularly silent and bored.

'Oh, why talk like that? And you it is talking like that, Masha!' he murmured through his teeth, knitting his brow as though in physical pain. 'How unsuitable it is with you and me! Leave that to others; these false relations may spoil our real ones, and I still hope the real will come back.'

I felt ashamed, and I did not speak.

'Will they come back, Masha? What do you think?' he asked.

'They have never been spoilt, and will not be spoilt,' I said. And at the time I really thought so.

'God grant it may be so,' he commented, 'or else it would be high time for us to be back in the country.'

But it was only once that he spoke like this, the rest of the time it seemed to me that he was as well content as I was, and I was so delighted and happy. If he really were dull sometimes, I comforted myself by reflecting I too had been dull for his sake in the country. If our relations really had altered somewhat, it would all come back again as soon as we were by ourselves again in the summer with Tatyana Semyonovna in our house at Nikolskoe.

So the winter slipped away without my noticing it, and, regardless of our plans, we spent Holy Week too in Petersburg. On Low

Sunday, when we were making preparations for our departure, everything had been packed, and my husband, who had already made purchases of presents, flowers, and various things for our country life, was in a particularly warm and cheerful state of mind, his cousin arrived unexpectedly, and began begging me to stay till Saturday so as to go to a *soirée* at Countess R.'s. She said that Countess R. was most pressing in her invitation; that a certain foreign Prince M. had been eager to make my acquaintance ever since the last ball; that it was simply with that object that he was coming to the *soirée*, and that he said that I was the prettiest woman in Russia. All Petersburg was to be there, and in fact it would be simply monstrous if I were not to go.

My husband was at the other end of the drawing-room talking to someone.

'Well, so you'll come, Marie, eh?' said his cousin.

'We meant to go into the country the day after tomorrow,' I answered irresolutely, glancing at my husband. Our eyes met; he hurriedly turned away.

'I will persuade him to stay,' said his cousin, 'and we'll go on Saturday to break hearts, eh?'

'That would upset our plans, and we've packed,' I answered, beginning to yield.

'Why, she'd better drive round this evening and pay her respects to the prince,' my husband said from the other end of the room, in a tone of repressed anger, such as I had never heard from him.

'Oh, he's jealous; why, it's the first time I've seen it!' laughed his cousin. 'Why, it's not for the prince's sake, Sergey Mihalovich, but for all of us, I'm trying to persuade her. How Countess R. did entreat her to come!'

'It rests with her,' my husband commented frigidly, and he went out of the room.

I saw that he was moved beyond his wont. This distressed me, and I made no promise to his cousin. As soon as she had gone, I went in to my husband. He was walking up and down absorbed in thought, and neither saw nor heard me come into the room on tiptoe.

'He's picturing his dear Nikolskoe,' I thought, looking at him, 'and his morning coffee in the light drawing-room, and his fields and the peasants, and the evenings in the divan-room, and our secret suppers in the night . . . No,' I decided inwardly, 'I'd give up all the balls in the world, and the flattery of all the princes in the world, for his glad confusion, his gentle caress.' I was going to tell him that I wouldn't go to the *soirée*, and didn't want to go, when he suddenly looked round, and seeing me, frowned, and the gently dreamy expression of his face changed. Again penetration, sagacity, and patronising composure were expressed in his eyes. He did not care for me to see him as a plain man; he wanted always to be a demigod standing on a pedestal before me.

'What is it, my dear?' he asked, turning carelessly and calmly to me.

I did not answer. It annoyed me that he was reserved with me, would not remain as I loved him.

'You want to go on Saturday to the *soirée*?' he queried.

'I did want to,' I answered, 'but you dislike it. Besides, everything's packed,' I added.

Never had he looked at me so coldly, never had he spoken so coldly to me.

'I won't go till Tuesday, and will order the things to be unpacked,' he said, 'so that you can go if you are disposed. As a favour to me, do go. I'm not going away.'

He began, as he always did when he was troubled, to walk jerkily up and down the room, without looking at me.

'I positively don't understand you,' I said, standing still and following him with my eyes: 'you say you are always so calm.' He never had said so. 'Why do you talk to me so strangely? I am ready to sacrifice this pleasure for your sake, and in a sort of ironical way in which you've never spoken to me before you insist on my going.'

'Well! you make *sacrifices*' (he laid special stress on this word), 'and I make sacrifices – what can be better? It's a conflict of generosity. Isn't that what you call domestic happiness?'

It was the first time I had heard from him such bitterly sneering words. And the sneer did not put me to shame, but offended me; and the bitterness did not alarm me, but infected me. Did he say this, he who had always shunned phrases in our relations, he always genuine and direct? And in return for what? For my really having wanted to sacrifice for him a pleasure in which I could see nothing wrong, and for my having so well understood and loved him a minute before. Our parts were changed; he avoided direct and simple statements, while I sought them.

'You are very much changed,' I said, sighing; 'in what way have I been in fault? It's not the *soirée*, but something before that that you have in your heart against me. Why this want of straightforwardness? Didn't you feel such dread of it yourself once? Tell me straight out what you have against me?' 'What can he say?' I wondered, reflecting complacently that there had been nothing he could reproach me with all that winter.

I came forward into the middle of the room, so that he was obliged to pass close by me, and looked at him. He would come up, embrace me, and all would be over, was the thought that occurred to me, and I felt positively sorry I should not have the chance of showing him how wrong he was. But he stopped at the end of the room and started at me.

'Do you still not understand?' he said.

'No.'

'Well, then, I will tell you. It's loathsome to me, for the first time what I feel and cannot help feeling is loathsome to me . . . ' He stopped, evidently shocked at the harsh sound of his own voice.

'But what is it?' I asked, with tears of indignation in my eyes.

'It's loathsome that the prince thought you pretty, and that consequently you are rushing to meet him, forgetting your husband and yourself and womanly dignity, and refuse to understand what your husband must feel about you, if you've no feeling of dignity in yourself. On the contrary, you come to tell your husband that you will *sacrifice* it, that is, "to exhibit myself to His Highness, would have been a great happiness, but I *sacrifice* it".'

The longer he spoke, the more furious he grew with the sound of his own voice, and that voice had a cruel, malignant, coarse note in it. I had never seen, had never expected to see him like this. The blood rushed to my heart, I was frightened, but a feeling of undeserved shame and wounded vanity excited me, and I longed to revenge myself on him.

'I have long been expecting this,' I said; 'say it, say it!'

'I don't know what you've been expecting,' he went on. 'I might well have expected the worst, seeing you every day in the uncleanness and idleness and luxury of this silly society, and I've got it too. I've come to feeling ashamed and sick today, as I have never felt for myself. When your friend with her unclean hands pried into my heart and began talking of jealousy, my jealousy – of whom? – a man whom neither I nor you know. And you, on purpose it seems – refuse to understand me and want to sacrifice to me – what? . . . I'm ashamed of you, ashamed of your degradation! . . . Sacrifice!' he repeated.

'Ah, here we have it, the power of the husband,' I thought, 'to insult and humiliate his wife, who is in no way to blame. These are a husband's rights, but I won't submit to it.'

'No, I won't sacrifice anything to you,' I declared, feeling my nostrils dilating unnaturally and the blood deserting my face. 'I'm going to the *soirée* on Saturday; I shall certainly go!'

'And God grant you may enjoy it, only everything's over between us!' he shouted in a fit of ungovernable fury. 'But you will never torture me any more. I was a fool to . . .' he began again, but his lips quivered, and with a visible effort he refrained from finishing what he was saying.

I feared and hated him at that moment. I wanted to say a great deal to him and to revenge all his insults. But if I had opened my mouth, I should have cried and lowered myself before him. I walked out of the room without a word. But as soon as I ceased to hear his steps, I was at once aghast at what we had done. I was in terror that the tie which made up my whole happiness would be severed for ever, and I wanted to go back. 'But has he sufficiently recovered his composure to understand me when I mutely hold out my hand to him and look at him?' I wondered. 'Will he understand my generosity? What if he calls my sorrow hypocrisy? Or with a sense of his rectitude and haughty composure, accepts my repentance and forgives me? And why, why has he, whom I loved so much, so cruelly insulted me?'

I went not to him, but to my own room, where I sat a long while alone, and wept with terror, going over every word of the conversation between us, substituting for those words others, adding other kind words, and again with horror and a feeling of humiliation remembering what had happened. When I went in to tea in the evening, and in the presence of S., who had called, met my husband, I felt that from that day a gulf had opened between us. S. asked me when we were going? Before I had time to answer, my husband replied, 'On Tuesday; we're going to the *soirée* at Countess R.'s? You're going, of course?' he said, turning to me.

I was frightened at the sound of this direct speech, and looked timidly at my husband. His eyes were looking straight at me, their expression was vindictive and sneering, his voice was cold and steady.

'Yes,' I answered.

In the evening when we were alone, he came up to me and held out his hand.

'Please forget what I said to you!' he said. I took his hand, a faltering smile was on my face, and tears were ready to gush from my eyes, but he drew back his hand; and as though dreading a sentimental scene, sat down in a low chair at some distance from me. 'Can he possibly still consider himself in the right?' I wondered, and the words of reconciliation and the entreaty not to go to the *soirée* that were on the tip of my tongue were never uttered.

'We must write to mother that we've put off leaving,' he said, 'or else she'll be uneasy.'

'But when are you thinking of going?' I asked.

'On Tuesday, after the *soirée*,' he answered.

'I hope that's not on my account?' I said, looking into his eyes. But his eyes looked blankly at me and told me nothing, as though they were hidden by a cloud from me. His face struck me suddenly as old and disagreeable.

We went to the *soirée*, and good, friendly relations seemed re-established between us; but these relations were quite different from what had been once.

At the *soirée* I was sitting among some ladies when the prince came up to me in such a way that I had to get up to talk to him. As I got up, I could not help looking for my husband, and I saw him look at me from the other end of the room and turn away. I felt suddenly so ashamed and sick that I was miserably confused, and blushed all over my face and neck under the prince's eyes. But I was obliged to stand up and listen to what he said to me, as he scanned me, looking down at me. Our conversation did not last long – there was nowhere for him to sit down beside me, and he probably felt that I was very uncomfortable with him. We talked of the last ball, of where I was to spend the summer, and so on. On leaving me, he expressed a desire to be introduced to my husband, and I saw them brought together and talking at the other end of the room. The prince probably said something about me, for in the middle of the conversation he looked with a smile in my direction.

My husband all at once flushed hotly, made a low bow, and walked away from the prince. I blushed too; I was ashamed to think what an impression the prince must have received of me, and still more of my husband. It seemed to me that everyone noticed my awkward embarrassment while I was talking to the prince and my husband's strange behaviour in leaving his side. There was no knowing what interpretation they would put on it. Didn't they know by now of my talk with my husband about the prince? His cousin took me home, and on the way I talked to her about my husband. I could not restrain myself, and told her all that had passed between us in regard to this luckless *soirée*. She comforted me, assuring me that it was just an ordinary tiff, of no importance, and leaving no traces. She explained to me my husband's character from her point of view, saying that he had grown very haughty and unsociable. I agreed with her, and it seemed to me that I myself understood him better and more sensibly now.

But afterwards, when I was alone with my husband, this criticism of him lay on my conscience like a crime, and I felt that the gulf that separated us had grown wider.

<h1 style="text-align:center">3</h1>

From that day our life and our relations were completely changed. We were not so happy by ourselves as before. There were questions we avoided touching upon, and conversation came easier to us before a third person than face to face. Whenever the conversation turned on life in the country or touched on the ball, we were both as it were a little dizzy, and had an awkwardness in looking at one another. It was as though we were both aware where the gulf lay that parted us, and dreaded going near it. I was persuaded that he was proud and hot-tempered, and that I must be on my guard not to irritate him on his weak points. He was convinced that I could not live without society, that the country was distasteful to me, and that he must submit to this unfortunate taste; and we both avoided plain speech about these subjects, and both judged each other falsely. We had long ceased to be the most perfect creatures in the world in each other's eyes; now we made comparisons with others, and secretly judged each other. I fell ill just before we were to leave town; and instead of going back to the country, we moved to a summer villa in the outskirts, and from there my husband went home alone to see his mother. When he left me, I had recovered sufficiently to have gone with him, but he persuaded me to stay where I was, on the pretext of anxiety about my health. I felt that he was not afraid for my health, but of our not getting on well in the country; I did not insist very warmly, and was left behind. Without him I felt dull and solitary; but when he came back, I saw that he did not add to my life what he had added once. Our old relations – when any thought, any impression, not shared with him, weighed on me like a crime, when every act, every word of his, seemed to me the pattern of perfection, when we wanted to laugh for glee, looking at each other – these relations had so imperceptibly passed into others that we had not discovered that they were no more. Each of us had found our separate interests, which we did not now attempt to share. It had even ceased to trouble us that each had a separate private world, shut off from the other. We had grown used to that idea, and a year later we no longer felt awkward when we looked at each other. Utterly vanished were his moods of wild gaiety with me, his boyishness, his readiness to forgive everything, and carelessness of everything, which had once worried me; there was no more that deep gaze that had once troubled and rejoiced me, no more prayers and ecstasies together. We did not often see each other even. He was continually absent on journeys, and did not dread, did not regret leaving me, while I was continually in society where I had no need of him.

There were no more scenes and quarrels between us; I tried to satisfy him; he did everything I wished, and we loved one another in a way.

When we were left alone, which rarely happened, I felt no joy, no emotion, no confusion, in being with him; it was as though I were by myself. I knew very well that this was my husband – not any new, unknown person, but a good man – my husband, whom I knew as I knew myself. I was certain that I knew everything he would do, what he would say, and how he would look; and if he acted or looked not as I had expected, it seemed to me indeed that it was by mistake. I expected nothing from him. In fact, he was my husband and nothing more. It seemed to me that this was as it should be indeed, and that any other relations do not generally exist, and, indeed, between us never had existed. When he was away, particularly at first, I had felt lonely, nervous; in his absence, I recognised more keenly the value of his support to me. When he returned, I flung myself on his neck in delight, though two hours later I had completely forgotten this delight, and I had nothing to say to him. Only in the moments of quiet, sober tenderness, which did occur between us, it seemed to me that something was wrong, that I had an ache at my heart, and in his eyes it seemed to me I read the same thing. I was conscious of that limit of feeling beyond which he, it seemed, would not and I could not step. Sometimes this was a grief to me, but I had no time for brooding over anything, and I tried to forget this grief at the vaguely felt change in diversions which were always in readiness for me. Society life, which at first had dazzled me by its brilliance and the flattery of my vanity, soon had a complete hold on my inclinations, became a habit, laid its shackles upon me, and occupied in my heart all the space there was for feeling. I never remained alone, and dreaded brooding over my position. All my time, from late in the morning to late at night, was occupied and did not belong to me, even if I did not go out anywhere. This was now neither pleasing nor boring to me, but it seemed that so and not otherwise it must always have been.

So passed three years, during which our relations remained the same, came as it were to a full stop, crystallised, and could become neither worse nor better. In these three years two events of importance occurred in our family life, but neither of them affected my life. They were the birth of my first baby and the death of Tatyana Semyonovna. At first the feeling of motherhood came upon me with such force, and produced such unexpected ecstasy in me, that I thought a new life was beginning for me; but two months later, when I began to go out into society again, this feeling, growing less and less, passed into habit and coldly doing my duty. My husband, on the contrary, from the time of the birth of our first child, became the gentle, tranquil man he had been in the past, always in his own home, and the same tenderness and gaiety he had shown in the past was now devoted to the child. Often when I went into the nursery in a ball dress to sign my child with the cross[7] for the night, and found my husband in the nursery, I caught his eyes fixed on me, as it were reproachfully and sternly scrutinising, and I felt ashamed. I was suddenly horrified at my indifference to my child, and asked myself, 'Can I be worse than other women? But what can I do?' I thought. 'I love my son, but I can't sit for days at a time with him; it bores me, and I'm not going to sham feeling for anything.' His mother's death was a great grief to him. It was painful to him, as he said, to be at Nikolskoe after her loss; but for me, though I was sorry for her and sympathised with my husband's grief, it was pleasanter and more comfortable now in the country. The greater part of all these three years we spent in town. I was only once for two months in the country, and in the third year we went abroad.

We spent the summer at a watering-place. I was then twenty-one. Our circumstances were, I supposed, in a flourishing condition; from my home life I demanded nothing more than it gave. Everyone I knew, it seemed to me, loved me; my health was good, my dresses were the smartest at the springs; I knew that I was handsome. The weather was magnificent; a peculiar atmosphere of beauty and elegance surrounded me, and I was very happy. I was not happy as I used to be at Nikolskoe, when I felt that I was happy in myself, that I deserved that happiness, that my happiness was great, but that it must be even greater because one longed for more and more happiness. Then it was different, but this summer, too, I was well content. I wanted nothing; I hoped for nothing; I feared nothing. My life, it seemed to me, was full, and my conscience, it seemed, was at rest. Of all the young men I met that season, there was not one whom I distinguished in any way from the rest, or even from old Prince K., our ambassador, who was very attentive to me. One was young, another was old; one was a light-haired Englishman, another a Frenchman with a beard; all were alike to me, but all were indispensable. It was all these equally indistinguishable persons that made up the joyous atmosphere of life about me. Only one of them, an Italian, Marchese D., drew my attention more than the rest by the boldness with which he expressed his adoration to me. He never let slip a chance of being with me, of dancing, riding, being at the casino and so on with me, and of telling me that I was beautiful. Sometimes I saw him out of window near our house, and often the unpleasant intent stare of his brilliant eyes made me blush and look round. He was young, handsome, elegant, and, above all, in his smile and the expression of his brow he resembled my husband, though he was far better looking. This likeness struck me in him, although in general, in his lips, in his eyes, in his long chin, instead of the exquisite expression of kindliness and idealistic serenity of my husband, there was something coarse and animal. I imagined at the time that he loved me passionately, and sometimes thought of him with proud commiseration. I sometimes tried to pacify him, to lead him into a tone of gentle, half-affectionate confidence, but he abruptly repelled those attempts and continued to disturb me disagreeably by his unexpressed passion, that threatened every moment to find expression. Though I did not own it to myself, I was afraid of this man, and against my will I often thought of him. My husband was acquainted with him, and he behaved even more coldly and superciliously with him than with our other acquaintances, to whom he existed only as the husband of his wife. Towards the end of the season I was ill, and did not leave the house for a fortnight. When, for the first time after my illness, I went out in the evening to listen to the music, I found out that a certain Lady S., a famous beauty, who had long been expected, had arrived during this interval. A circle gathered round me, people met me with delight; but an even better circle had gathered around the celebrated beauty. Everyone about me was talking of nothing but her and her beauty. She was pointed out to me, and she certainly was charming; but what struck me disagreeably was the conceited expression of her face, and I said so. That day everything seemed to me dull that had before seemed so agreeable. Next day Lady S. got up a party to visit the castle, which I declined to join. Scarcely anyone remained with me, and everything was utterly transformed in my eyes. Everything and everyone seemed to me stupid and dull; I wanted to cry, to make haste and finish our cure, and to return to Russia. In my soul there was a sort of evil feeling, but I had not yet acknowledged it to myself. I declared myself still not strong, and gave up showing myself in society, merely going out now and then in the morning alone to drink the waters, or taking drives into the neighbouring country with L. M., a Russian lady of my acquaintance. My husband was not there at that time; he had gone away for a few days to Heidelberg, while waiting for the end of my cure to return to Russia, and he only came over to see me from time to time.

One day Lady S. carried off all the fashionable society of the place to a hunt, and L. M. and I drove after dinner to the castle. While we were driving slowly in our carriage up the winding road under the venerable chestnut trees through which the pretty, elegant environs of Baden[8] lay before us in the distance lighted up by the setting sun, we talked seriously, as we had not talked before. L. M., whom I had known for a long while, struck me now for the first time as a good intelligent woman, to whom one could say anything, and with whom it was pleasant to be friends. We talked of home and children, and the emptiness of the life here; we longed to be in Russia, in the country, and felt a sort of pleasant melancholy. Under the influence of this serious feeling we went into the castle. Within the walls it was cool and shady, overhead the sun played about the ruins, steps and voices were audible. Framed as it were by the doorway, we saw that view of Baden, exquisite, though frigid to our Russian eyes. We sat down to rest, and gazed in silence at the setting sun. The voices reached us more distinctly, and it seemed to me that my surname was mentioned. I began listening, and unconsciously we heard every word. The voices I knew; it was Marchese D. and the Frenchman, a friend of his, whom I knew too. They were talking about me and Lady S. The Frenchman compared her with me, and analysed the beauty of each. He said nothing insulting, but the blood rushed to my heart when I heard his words. He enumerated minutely the good points in me and in Lady S. I had already had a child, while Lady S. was only nineteen. My hair was better, but Lady S. had a more graceful figure; Lady S. was a grand lady; 'while yours,' said he, 'is only middling, one of those little Russian princesses who so often turn up here nowadays.' He wound up by saying that I did well not to fight it out with Lady S., and that I was as good as buried in Baden.

'I'm sorry for her.'

'If only she doesn't want to console herself with you . . . ' he added with a cruel laugh of amusement.

'If she goes away, I go after her!' a voice declared coarsely in an Italian accent.

'Happy mortal, he can still love!' laughed the Frenchman.

'Love!' said the voice, and paused. 'I can't not love – there's no life without it. To make a romance of life is the one thing worth while. And my romance never stops in the middle, and this I will carry through to the end.'

'*Bonne chance, mon ami,*' said the Frenchman.

We heard no further, for they had gone round the corner, and we heard their steps on the other side. They came down the stairs, and a few minutes later came out of a side door, and were much surprised to see us. I blushed when Marchese D. approached me, and felt frightened when, on leaving the castle, he gave me his arm. I could not refuse, and we walked together to our carriage behind L. M., who was walking with his friend. I was mortified by what the Frenchman had said about me, though I secretly owned that he only put into words what I had myself been feeling. But the Marchese's words had astounded and shocked me by their coarseness. I was miserable at the thought that I had heard his words, and in spite of that he was not afraid of me. I was disgusted at feeling him so close to me; and without looking at him, without answering him, I tried to hold my arm so as not to hear what he said while I walked hurriedly after L. M. and the Frenchman. The Marchese said something about the fine view, about the unexpected happiness of meeting me, and something more, but I did not hear him. I was thinking just then of my husband, my child, Russia; I felt ashamed of something, regretted something, longed for something; and I was in a hurry to get home to my solitary room in the Hôtel de Bade so as to ponder at my leisure over all that had only just begun to stir in my heart. But L. M. walked slowly; it was still some distance to the carriage; my escort, as I fancied, obstinately slackened his pace, as though trying to keep me. 'Impossible!' I thought, and resolutely walked faster. But he positively detained me, and even squeezed my arm. L. M. turned the corner of the road, and we were completely alone. I felt frightened. 'Excuse me!' I said coldly, and tried to get my hand free, but the lace of my sleeve caught in his button. Bending down with his chest towards me, he began to disentangle it, and his ungloved fingers touched my hand. A feeling new to me – half terror, half pleasure – ran like a shiver down my back. I glanced at him to show by a cold look all the contempt I felt for him. But my glance expressed not that – it expressed alarm and excitement. His glowing, moist eyes, close up to my very face, stared passionately at me, at my neck, at my bosom, both his hands fingered my arm above the wrist, his open lips said something – said that he loved me, that I was everything to him – and those lips were approaching me, and those hands squeezed mine more tightly, and seemed to burn me. A flame ran through my veins, a mist was before my eyes, I shuddered, and the words with which I tried to stop him died away in my throat. Suddenly I felt a kiss on my cheek, and all chill and shivering I stopped and looked at him. Incapable of either speaking or moving, I stood in terror, expecting and desiring something. It all lasted for one moment. But that moment was awful! I saw the whole of him so completely at that moment. I understood his face so thoroughly; under the straw hat, that steep, low brow, so like my husband's, that handsome straight nose with dilated nostrils, those long moustaches and little beard waxed into points, those smooth shaven cheeks and sunburnt neck. I hated, I feared him – he belonged to a different world. But at that moment something in me responded so intensely to the excitement and passion of that hated alien man. Such an insuperable longing was in me to abandon myself to the kisses of that coarse and handsome mouth, to the embraces of those white hands with delicate veins and rings on their fingers. Such a craving possessed me to fling myself headlong into the inviting abyss of forbidden pleasures that had suddenly opened at my feet.

'I'm so miserable,' I thought; 'let more and more misery gather about me.'

He put one arm about me, and bent down to my face.

'Let more and more shame and sin be heaped up on my head.'

'Je vous aime,' he whispered, in the voice which was so like my husband's voice. It brought back to me my husband and child, beings so long precious to me, with whom now all was over. But suddenly at that moment L. M., out of sight round the turn in the road, called to me. I came to myself, tore my hand away, and not looking at him almost ran after L. M. We got into the carriage, and only then I glanced at him. He took off his hat and asked me something, smiling. He had no notion of the unutterable loathing I was feeling for him at that instant.

My life seemed to me so miserable, the future so hopeless, the past so black. L. M. talked to me, but I did not take in what she said. It seemed to me that she was talking to me simply from pity, to conceal the contempt I aroused in her. In every word, in every look, I seemed to detect that contempt and insulting pity. The kiss burnt my cheek with shame, and the thought of my husband and child was more than I could bear. I had hoped to think over my position when I was alone in my room, but I was afraid to be alone. I did not drink the tea they brought me; and, not knowing why I did so, began at once with feverish haste to get ready for the evening train to go to Heidelberg to my husband. When I was sitting with my maid in an empty carriage, when the engine had started and the fresh air blew on me from the window, I began to recover my self-possession, and to picture my past and my future more clearly. All my married life from the day when we moved to Petersburg suddenly presented itself to me in a new light, and lay like a reproach on my conscience. For the first time I vividly recalled our early days together in the country, our plans; for the first time it occurred to me to ask, What had been his joys all this time? And I felt that I had wronged him. 'But why didn't he stop me? Why was he hypocritical with me? Why did he avoid frank discussion? Why did he humiliate me?' I asked myself. 'Why did he not use all the power love gave him over me? Or did he not love me?' But however he might be to blame, a stranger's kiss lay on my cheek, and I felt it. The nearer I got to Heidelberg, the more definitely I imagined my husband, and the more terrible did the approaching interview with him seem to me. 'I will tell him all, all; I will wipe out all with tears of repentance,' I thought, 'and he will forgive me.' But I could not have said what was the 'all' I would tell him, and I did not believe myself that he would forgive me.

But as soon as I went into the room to my husband, and saw his tranquil, though surprised, face, I felt that I had nothing to tell him, nothing to confess, and nothing to ask his forgiveness for. My grief and remorse must remain locked up within me.

'What fancy is this?' he said. 'Why, I meant to come to you tomorrow.' But looking more closely into my face, he seemed alarmed. 'What is it? what's the matter?' he said.

'Nothing,' I answered, hardly able to restrain my tears. 'I've come for good. Let's start tomorrow for Russia.'

He bent a rather long, silent, and intent look upon me.

'But tell me what has happened to you?' he said.

I could not help blushing and dropping my eyes. In his eyes there was a gleam of mortification and anger. I was dismayed at the ideas that might occur to him; and with a ready hypocrisy I had never expected of myself, I said – 'Nothing has happened, simply I felt dull and depressed alone, and I have been thinking a great deal of our life and of you. For such a long time I have been to blame towards you! Why should you come out here with me, where you've no wish to be? I've long been to blame in my behaviour to you,' I repeated, and again tears came into my eyes. 'Let us go back to the country and stay there for ever.'

'Oh, my dear, spare me sentimental scenes,' he said coldly. 'So far as wanting to go back to the country goes, it's a good thing indeed, for our money's running short; but your "for ever's" a dream. I know you won't stay long. Now drink some tea, and you'll feel better,' he concluded, getting up to ring for the waiter.

I imagined all he might be thinking of me, and I was humiliated at the fearful thought I ascribed to him, as I met his incredulous, and, as it were, shame-stricken eyes fixed upon me. No, he cannot and will not understand me! I said I would go and have a look at the baby, and went out of the room. I longed to be alone and to weep and weep and weep.

4

The Nikolskoe house, so long empty and unwarmed, was full of life again, but not so those who lived in it. My mother-in-law was no more, and we were alone face to face with each other. But now we were far from wanting solitude; it was a constraint to us indeed. The winter was all the worse for me from my being unwell; and I only recovered my health, indeed, after the birth of my second son. My relations with my husband continued to be the same cold, friendly relations as during our life in town. But in the country every board, every wall, every sofa recalled to me what he had been to me, and what I had lost. It was as if an unforgiven injury lay between us, as though he were punishing me for something, and affecting to be himself unaware of it. There was nothing to beg forgiveness for, nothing to ask for mercy from; he punished me simply by not giving me up all himself, all his soul as before. But to no one, to nothing did he give it, as though he had it not. Sometimes it occurred to me that he was only pretending to be like this to torment me; that the old feeling was still living in him, and I tried to evoke it. But every time he seemed to shun frankness, as though he suspected me of affectation and dreaded all sentiment as ludicrous. His look and tone said: 'I know it all; I know it all – no need to talk about it; and all you want to say I know too. And I know, too, that you say one thing and do another.' At first I was offended by this avoidance of openness, but afterward I got used to think that it was not the fear of openness, but the absence of the desire for openness. I could not easily bring my tongue now to tell him that I loved him, or to ask him to read the prayers with me, or to invite him to listen while I played. One could feel the existence of certain settled stipulations of propriety between us now. We lived each our separate life; he with his pursuits, in which I had no need and no desire now to share; I with my idleness, which did not vex or grieve him now as before. The children were too little, and could not as yet be a bond between us.

But spring came. Katya and Sonya had come for the summer to the country, alterations were to be made in the house at Nikolskoe, and we removed to Pokrovskoe. The old house was just the same, with its verandah, its folding table and piano in the bright hall, and my old room, with its white curtains and dreams of girlhood, that seemed left forgotten in that house. In that room there were two beds – one, in old days mine, in which my fat little Kokosha lay when I made the sign of the cross over him in the evenings, while in the other, a little one, Vanya's little face peeped out of his nightclothes. After signing them with the cross, I often used to stand still in the middle of the quiet room; and all at once, from every corner, from the walls, from the curtains, there rose up the old forgotten visions of youth. The old voices of the songs of girlhood began singing again. And where were those visions? What had become of those sweet, tender songs? All had come to pass that I had scarcely dared to hope for. The vague dreams melting into one another had become reality, and the reality had become a dreary, difficult, and joyless life. And everything was the same; the same garden one could see from the window, the same path, the same seat out there above the ravine, the same nightingale's songs floating in from near the pond, the same lilac in full flower, and the same moon over our house – and yet all so terribly, so incredibly changed! Everything so cold that might be so precious and so near one's heart! Just as in old days, sitting in the drawing-room, Katya and I, we talk softly together, and we talk of him. But Katya is yellow and wrinkled, her eyes do not sparkle with joy and hope, but express sympathetic distress and commiseration. We do not sing his praises as we did of old, we criticise him; we don't wonder what we have done to be so happy; nor long, as of old, to tell all the world what we think. Like conspirators, we whisper to one another, and ask each other for the hundredth time, Why has it all changed so sadly? And he is still the same, except that the line is deeper between his brows, and there is more grey hair about his temples; but the profound, intense look in his eyes is clouded over for ever from me. I, too, am still the same, but I have no love nor the desire of love, no longing for work, nor content with myself. And so remote and impossible seemed to me now my old religious ecstasies, my old love for him, and my old intense life, I could not have understood now what had once seemed so dear and right to me – the happiness of living for others. Why for others, when one did not care even to live for oneself?

I had completely given up music ever since we moved to Petersburg; but now the old piano, the old music-books were a refuge for me again.

One day I was not well, I stopped at home alone; Katya and Sonya had driven with him to Nikolskoe to look at the new building there. The table was set for tea, I went down, and while waiting for them sat down to the piano. I opened the sonata *quasi una fantasia*, and began playing it. No one was within sight or hearing, the windows were open into the garden, and the familiar, majestically melancholy music resounded in the room. I finished the first part, and quite unconsciously, from old habit, looked round to the corner in which he used once to sit listening to me. But he was not there. The chair, long unmoved, stood in the corner; and past the open window I could see the lilac in the bright sunset, and the evening freshness flowed into the room. I leaned my elbows on the piano, hid my face in both hands, and pondered. I sat a long while so, with a heartache recalling all the past that could not come back, and timidly considering what was to come. But before me it seemed that there was nothing; it seemed that I desired nothing and hoped for nothing. 'Can I have lived out my life?' I thought with horror; and lifting my head, I tried to forget myself, to escape thinking by playing again, and began again the same andante. 'My God!' I thought, 'forgive me, if I am in fault, or restore me what was once so good in my soul, and teach me what to do, how to live now!' The sound of wheels over the grass and at the entrance reached me, and familiar steps could be heard stepping cautiously in the verandah and ceasing. But the old feeling did not stir in response to those familiar footsteps. When I had finished, I heard the steps behind me, and a hand was laid on my shoulder.

'What a clever girl you are to play that sonata!' he said.

I did not speak.

'Have you had tea?'

I shook my head, and did not look round at him for fear of betraying the traces of emotion left on my face.

'They'll be here directly; the horse was too fresh, and they've come on foot from the highroad,' he said.

'Let's wait for them,' I said, and went out into the verandah, hoping he would come after me; but he asked after the children and went up to them. Again his presence, his simple, kindly voice made me doubt whether anything had been lost by me. 'What more could I desire? He's kind and gentle, he's a good father, and I don't know myself what more I want.' I went out on the balcony and sat under the verandah awning on the very seat on which I had sat on the day of our avowal of love to one another. The sun had set now; it was beginning to get dusk; and one of the dark rainclouds of springtime was hanging over the house and garden. Only through the trees could be seen the clear rim of the sky with the fading glow and the evening star beginning to shine. Over all hung the shadow of a transparent cloud, and everything seemed waiting for a gentle spring shower. The wind had dropped; not one leaf, not one blade of grass was stirring; the scent of the lilac and the wild cherry, strong as though all the air were in flower, hovered over the garden and verandah suddenly in gusts growing fainter, and intenser, so that one wanted to close one's eyes and see nothing, hear nothing, shutting out everything but this sweet fragrance. The dahlias and the rose-bushes, not yet in flower, stood immovably erect on their well-dug black bed as though they were slowly growing upwards on their white-shaved sticks. In piercing chorus the frogs croaked with all their might from the ravine, as though for the last time before the rain which would drive them to the water. The single continuous sound of water rose above their harsh croak. The nightingales called at intervals, and one could hear them flitting in alarm from spot to spot. Again this spring a nightingale was building in a bush under the window; and when I came out, I heard him fly away to the avenue, and there utter one note; then he ceased, waiting too.

In vain I tried to be calm, and waited and grieved for something. He came back from upstairs and sat down beside me.

'I think they'll get wet,' he said.

'Yes,' I assented, and we were both for a long while silent.

The cloud sank lower and lower in the windless sky; everything became more hushed, more fragrant, and more still; and all at once a drop fell and, as it were, leaped up again on the sailcloth awning of the verandah, another splashed on the gravel of the path, there was a patter on the burdocks, and the fresh rain began falling more heavily in big drops. The nightingales and the frogs were quite silent, only the thin sound of water, though it seemed further off through the rain, still persisted; and some bird hidden in the dry leaves, probably near the verandah, repeated regularly its monotonous two notes. He got up, and was about to go away.

'Where are you going?' I asked, detaining him. 'It's so nice here.'

'I meant to send them an umbrella and goloshes,' he said.

'There's no need; it will soon be over.' He agreed with me, and we remained together by the verandah balustrade. I rested my arm on the slippery, wet rail and put my head out. The fresh rain pattered unevenly on my hair and neck. The cloud, getting lighter and thinner, was passing over us; the even patter of the rain changed into drops, dripping irregularly from above and from the leaves. Again the frogs began croaking below, again the nightingales began to stir, and from the wet bushes called to one another from one side and then from the other. All the sky was clear again in front of us.

'How nice it is!' he said, sitting near me on the balustrade, and passing his hand over my wet hair.

This simple caress affected me like a reproach. I wanted to cry.

'And what more can a man want?' he said. 'I am so contented now that I want nothing; perfectly happy!'

'That was not how you used once to speak of your happiness!' I thought. 'However great it was, you used to say that you always wanted more and more. But now you are satisfied and content, while my heart is full as it were of unuttered repentance and unshed tears.'

'And I feel it's nice,' I said; 'but I'm sad just from it's all being so nice before my eyes. It's all so disconnected, so incomplete in me, there's a continual longing for something, though it's so peaceful and happy here. Surely you too have a sort of melancholy mingling in your enjoyment of nature, as though you longed for something of the past?'

He took his hand from my head and was silent for a while.

'Yes, it used to be so with me, particularly in the spring,' he said, as though recalling it. 'And I used to sit up the whole night too, longing and hoping, and happy nights they were! ... But then everything was in the future, and now it's all behind; now what is, is enough for me, and I find it splendid,' he concluded, with such convincing carelessness, that painful as it was to hear it, the belief forced itself on me that he was speaking the truth.

'And is there nothing you wish for?' I asked.

'Nothing impossible,' he answered, guessing my feeling. 'See, you're getting your head wet,' he added, once more passing his hand over my hair as though caressing a child; 'you envy the leaves and the grass for the rain wetting them; you would like to be the grass and the leaves and the rain; while I merely rejoice in them, as I do in everything in the world that is good and young and happy.'

'And do you regret nothing of the past?' I went on questioning, feeling that my heart was growing heavier and heavier.

He pondered and was silent again. I saw that he wanted to answer quite sincerely.

'No!' he answered briefly.

'Not true, not true!' I said, turning to him and looking into his eyes. 'You don't regret the past?'

'No,' he repeated once more. 'I am thankful for it, but I don't regret the past.'

'Do you mean to say you would not desire to have it back?' I said.

He turned and began looking into the garden.

'I don't desire it, as I don't desire to have wings,' he said. 'It's impossible!'

'And would you not correct the past; don't you reproach yourself or me?'

'Never! All has been for the best.'

'Listen!' I said, touching his arm to make him look round at me. 'Listen: why did you never tell me that you wanted me to live just as you did want me to? Why did you give me a freedom I did not know how to use? Why did you give up teaching me? If you had cared, if you had managed me differently, nothing, nothing would have happened!' I said in a voice more and more intensely expressive of cold anger and reproach, and not the love of old days.

'What wouldn't have happened?' he said in surprise, turning to me; 'why nothing did, as it is. All's well. Very well!' he added, smiling.

'Can it be he does not understand, or, worse still, doesn't want to understand?' I thought, and tears came into my eyes.

'It wouldn't have happened that though I have done you no wrong, I am punished by your indifference, your contempt even!' I burst out suddenly. 'It wouldn't have happened that for no fault of mine you took away from me all that was precious to me.'

'What do you mean, my dear?' he said, as though not understanding what I was saying.

'No, let me speak . . . You took away from me your confidence, your love, your respect even, because I don't believe that you love me now after what it was in old days. No; I want to have out once for all what has been making me miserable a long while,' I said, preventing his speaking again. 'Was it my fault that I knew nothing of life, and you left me to find it out alone? . . . Is it my fault that now when of myself I have come to see what is essential, when for nearly a year I've been struggling to get back to you – you repel me as though not understanding what I want, and all in such a way that it's impossible to reproach you while I'm either to blame or unhappy? Yes, you want to fling me back into that life, which might well make the misery of us both.'

'But in what way have I shown you that?' he asked, in genuine dismay and surprise.

'Didn't you only yesterday say, and you're for ever saying that I can't stand being here, and that we shall have to go back for the winter to Petersburg, which is hateful to me?' I went on. 'Instead of being a support to me, you avoid all frank speech, any sincere tender word with me. And then when I fall utterly, you will reproach me and rejoice at my fall.'

'Stop, stop!' he said sternly and coldly; 'that's wrong what you're saying now. That only proves that you feel ill-will against me, that you do not – '

'That I don't love you? . . . Say it, say it!' I completed his sentence, and tears streamed from my eyes. I sat down on the seat and hid my face in my handkerchief.

'This is how he understands me!' I thought, trying to restrain the sobs that choked me. 'Our old love is over, over!' a voice said in my heart. He did not come to me, did not comfort me. He was offended by what I had said. His voice was dry and composed.

'I don't know what it is you reproach me with,' he began; 'if it is that I don't love you as once I did . . . '

'Did love!' I exclaimed in the handkerchief, and the bitter tears streamed more violently into it.

'Time is to blame for that and we ourselves. Each stage has its love.' He paused. 'And shall I tell you the whole truth if you desire frank speech? . . . Just as that year when I got to know you I spent sleepless nights thinking of you and created my love for myself, and that love grew and grew in my heart, in the same way in Petersburg and abroad I spent awful nights without sleep, and crushed, tore to shreds, that love that was my torture. I did not crush it, but only what tortured me. I found peace, and still I love you, but with a different love.'

'Yes, you call it love, but it's a torture!' I said. 'Why did you let me go into society if you thought it so harmful that you lost your love for me on account of it?'

'It was not society, my dear!' he said.

'Why didn't you use your authority?' I went on. 'Why didn't you tie me up, kill me? It would have been better for me now than to be deprived of all that made my happiness. I should be happy, I shouldn't be ashamed.'

I sobbed again, and hid my face.

At that moment Katya and Sonya, wet and good-humoured, came

into the verandah, loudly chattering and laughing; but seeing us, they were quiet, and at once went in.

We sat a long while silent when they had gone; I wept away my tears, and felt better. I glanced at him. He was sitting with his head propped in his hands, and he wanted to say something in response to my look, but he only sighed heavily, and again leaned on his elbow. I went up to him and took away his hand. His eyes rested dreamily upon me.

'Yes,' he began, as though going on with his thoughts. 'All of us, especially you women, have to go for themselves through all the nonsense of life to come back to life itself; they can't believe anyone else. You were far then from having got through all that sweet charming nonsense, which I used to admire as I watched you, and I left you to get through it, and felt that I had no right to hinder you, though for me that time had long gone by.'

'Why did you live through it with me and let me live through that nonsense if you loved me?' I said.

'Because you would have tried, but would not have been able, to believe me; you had to find out for yourself . . . and you have found it out.'

'You reasoned, you reasoned much,' said I. 'You loved little.'

Again we were silent.

'That's cruel what you said just now, but it's the truth!' he said suddenly, getting up and walking about the verandah. 'Yes, it's the truth. I was to blame,' he added, stopping opposite me. 'Either I ought not to have let myself love you at all, or I ought to have loved you more simply, yes!'

'Let us forget it all . . . ' I said timidly.

'No, what's past will not come back, one can never bring it back!' and his voice softened as he said this.

'Everything has returned now . . . ' I said, laying my hand on his shoulder.

He took my hand away and pressed it.

'No; it was not true when I said I did not regret the past. No, I do regret it, I weep for our past love – love which is no more, and can never come again. Who is to blame for it, I don't know. Love is left, but not the same; its place is left, but it is all wasted away; there is no strength and substance in it, there are left memories and gratitude, but – '

'Don't say so!' I interrupted. 'Let it all be again as it was before . . . It can be, can't it?' I asked, looking into his eyes. But his eyes were clear and untroubled, and they did not look deeply into mine. At the moment I was saying it, I felt that what I desired and asked him about was impossible. He smiled a quiet, gentle, as it seemed to me, elderly smile.

'How young you are still, and I am so old!' he said. 'There is not in me what you are looking for . . . Why deceive ourselves?' he added, still with the same smile.

I stood mutely beside him, and there was greater peace in my heart.

'Don't let us try to repeat life,' he went on; 'we won't lie to ourselves. And that we are rid of the heartaches and emotions of old days, thank God indeed! We have no need to seek and be troubled. We have found what we sought, and happiness enough has fallen to our lot. It's time now for us to stand aside and make way, see, for this person!' he said, pointing to Vanya, in the arms of the nurse, who was standing at the verandah doors. 'That's so, dear one,' he ended, drawing my head to him and kissing it. It was not a lover, but an old friend kissing me. And from the garden the fragrant freshness of the night rose sweeter and stronger, the night sounds and stillness grew more and more solemn, and the stars thronged more thickly in the sky. I looked at him, and there was a sudden sense of ease in my soul, as though that sick moral nerve which made me suffer had been removed. All at once I felt clearly and calmly that the feeling of that time had gone never to return, like the time itself, and that to bring it back now would be not only impossible, but painful and forced. And indeed was that time so good which seemed to me so happy? And it was all so long, so long ago!

'It's time for tea, though!' he said, and we went together into the drawing-room. At the door we met again the nurse and Vanya. I took the baby into my arms, covered his bare red little toes, hugged him to me and kissed him, just touching him with my lips. He moved his little hand with outspread wrinkled fingers, as though in his sleep, and opened vague eyes, as though seeking or recalling something. Suddenly those little eyes rested on me, a spark of intelligence flashed in them, the full pouting lips began to work, and parted in a smile. 'Mine, mine, mine!' I thought, with a blissful tension in all my limbs, pressing him to my bosom, and with an effort restraining myself from hurting him.

And I began kissing his little cold feet, his little stomach, his hand and his little head, scarcely covered with soft hair. My husband came up to me; I quickly covered the child's face and uncovered it again.

'Ivan Sergeich!' said my husband, chucking him under the chin. But quickly I hid Ivan Sergeich again. No one but I was to look at him for long. I glanced at my husband, his eyes laughed as he watched me, and for the first time for a long while it was easy and sweet to me to look into them.

With that day ended my love-story with my husband, the old feeling became a precious memory never to return; but the new feeling of love for my children and the father of my children laid the foundation of another life, happy in quite a different way, which I am still living up to the present moment.

THE DEATH OF IVAN ILYICH

Inside the great building of the Law Courts, during the interval in the hearing of the Melvinsky case, the members of the judicial council and the public prosecutor were gathered together in the private room of Ivan Yegorovich Shebek, and the conversation turned upon the celebrated Krasovsky case. Fyodor Vassilievich hotly maintained that the case was not in the jurisdiction of the court. Yegor Ivanovich stood up for his own view; but from the first Pyotr Ivanovich, who had not entered into the discussion, took no interest in it, but was looking through the newspapers which had just been brought in.

'Gentlemen!' he said, 'Ivan Ilyich is dead!'

'You don't say so!'

'Here, read it,' he said to Fyodor Vassilievich, handing him the fresh still damp-smelling paper.

Within a black margin was printed: 'Praskovya Fyodorovna Golovin[9] with heartfelt affliction informs friends and relatives of the decease of her beloved husband, member of the Court of Justice, Ivan Ilyich Golovin, who passed away on the 4th of February. The funeral will take place on Thursday at one o'clock.'

Ivan Ilyich was a colleague of the gentlemen present, and all liked him. It was some weeks now since he had been taken ill; his illness had been said to be incurable. His post had been kept open for him, but it had been thought that in case of his death Alexyeev might receive his appointment, and either Vinnikov or Shtabel would succeed to Alexyeev's. So that on hearing of Ivan Ilyich's death, the first thought of each of the gentlemen in the room was of the effect this death might have on the transfer or promotion of themselves or their friends.

'Now I am sure of getting Shtabel's place or Vinnikov's,' thought Fyodor Vassilievich. 'It was promised me long ago, and the promotion means eight hundred roubles additional income, besides the grants for office expenses.'

'Now I shall have to petition for my brother-in-law to be transferred from Kaluga,' thought Pyotr Ivanovich. 'My wife will be very glad. She won't be able to say now that I've never done anything for her family.'

'I thought somehow that he'd never get up from his bed again,' Pyotr Ivanovich said aloud. 'I'm sorry!'

'But what was it exactly that was wrong with him?'

'The doctors could not decide. That's to say, they did decide, but differently. When I saw him last, I thought he would get over it.'

'Well, I positively haven't called there ever since the holidays. I've kept meaning to go.'

'Had he any property?'

'I think there's something, very small, of his wife's. But something quite trifling.'

'Yes, one will have to go and call. They live such a terribly long way off.'

'A long way from you, you mean. Everything's a long way from your place.'

'There, he can never forgive me for living the other side of the river,' said Pyotr Ivanovich, smiling at Shebek. And they began to talk of the great distances between different parts of the town, and went back into the court.

Besides the reflections upon the changes and promotions in the service likely to ensue from this death, the very fact of the death of an intimate acquaintance excited in everyone who heard of it, as such a fact always does, a feeling of relief that 'it is he that is dead, and not I.'

'Only think! he is dead, but here am I all right,' each one thought or felt. The more intimate acquaintances, the so-called friends of Ivan Ilyich, could not help thinking too that now they had the exceedingly tiresome social duties to perform of going to the funeral service and paying the widow a visit of condolence.

The most intimately acquainted with their late colleague were Fyodor Vassilievich and Pyotr Ivanovich.

Pyotr Ivanovich had been a comrade of his at the school of jurisprudence, and considered himself under obligations to Ivan Ilyich.

Telling his wife at dinner of the news of Ivan Ilyich's death and his reflections as to the possibility of getting her brother transferred into their circuit, Pyotr Ivanovich, without lying down for his usual nap, put on his frockcoat and drove to Ivan Ilyich's.

At the entrance before Ivan Ilyich's flat stood a carriage and two hired flies. Downstairs in the entry near the hat-stand there was leaning against the wall a coffin-lid with tassels and braiding freshly rubbed up with pipeclay. Two ladies were taking off their cloaks. One of them he knew, the sister of Ivan Ilyich; the other was a lady he did not know. Pyotr Ivanovich's colleague, Shvarts, was coming down; and from the top stair, seeing who it was coming in, he stopped and winked at him, as though to say: 'Ivan Ilyich has made a mess of it; it's a very different matter with you and me.'

Shvarts's face, with his English whiskers and all his thin figure in his frockcoat, had, as it always had, an air of elegant solemnity; and this solemnity, always such a contrast to Shvarts's playful character, had a special piquancy here. So thought Pyotr Ivanovich.

Pyotr Ivanovich allowed the ladies to precede him and slowly followed them upstairs. Shvarts did not come down but remained where he was, and Pyotr Ivanovich understood that he wanted to arrange where they should play bridge that evening. The ladies went upstairs to the widow's room, and Shvarts with seriously compressed lips but a playful look in his eyes, indicated by a twist of his eyebrows the room to the right where the body lay.

Pyotr Ivanovich, like everyone else on such occasions, entered feeling uncertain what he would have to do. All he knew was that at such times it is always safe to cross oneself. But he was not quite sure whether one should make obeisances while doing so. He therefore adopted a middle course. On entering the room he began crossing himself and made a slight movement resembling a bow. At the same time, as far as the motion of his head and arm allowed, he surveyed the room. Two young men – apparently nephews, one of whom was a high-school pupil – were leaving the room, crossing themselves as they did so. An old woman was standing motionless, and a lady with strangely arched eyebrows was saying something to her in a whisper. A vigorous, resolute Church Reader, in a frockcoat, was reading something in a loud voice with an expression that precluded any contradiction. The butler's assistant, Gerasim, stepping lightly in front of Pyotr Ivanovich, was strewing something on the floor. Noticing this, Pyotr Ivanovich was immediately aware of a faint odour of a decomposing body.

The last time he had called on Ivan Ilyich, Peter Ivanovich had seen Gerasim in the study. Ivan Ilyich had been particularly fond of him and he was performing the duty of a sick nurse.

Pyotr Ivanovich continued to make the sign of the cross slightly inclining his head in an intermediate direction between the coffin, the Reader, and the icons on the table in a corner of the room. Afterwards, when it seemed to him that this movement of his arm in crossing himself had gone on too long, he stopped and began to look at the corpse.

The dead man lay, as dead men always lie, in a specially heavy way, his rigid limbs sunk in the soft cushions of the coffin, with the head forever bowed on the pillow. His yellow waxen brow with bald patches over his sunken temples was thrust up in the way peculiar to the dead, the protruding nose seeming to press on the upper lip. He was much changed and grown even thinner since Pyotr Ivanovich had last seen him, but, as is always the case with the dead, his face was handsomer and above all more dignified than when he was alive. The expression on the face said that what was necessary had been accomplished, and accomplished rightly. Besides this there was in that expression a reproach and a warning to the living. This warning seemed to Pyotr Ivanovich out of place, or at least not applicable to him. He felt a certain discomfort and so he hurriedly crossed himself once more and turned and went out of the door – too hurriedly and too regardless of propriety, as he himself was aware.

Shvarts was waiting for him in the adjoining room with legs spread wide apart and both hands toying with his top-hat behind his back. The mere sight of that playful, well-groomed, and elegant figure refreshed Peter Ivanovich. He felt that Shvarts was above all these happenings and would not surrender to any depressing influences. His very look said that this incident of a church service for Ivan Ilyich could not be a sufficient reason for infringing the order of the session – in other words, that it would certainly not prevent his unwrapping a new pack of cards and shuffling them that evening while a footman placed fresh candles on the table: in fact, that there was no reason for supposing that this incident would hinder their spending the evening agreeably. Indeed he said this in a whisper as Peter Ivanovich passed him, proposing that they should meet for a game at Fyodor Vassilievich's. But apparently Peter Ivanovich was not destined to play bridge that evening. Fyodor Vassilievich (a short, fat woman who despite all efforts to the contrary had continued to broaden steadily from her shoulders downwards and who had the same extraordinarily arched eyebrows as the lady who had been standing by the coffin), dressed all in black, her head covered with lace, came out of her own room with some other ladies, conducted them to the room where the dead body lay, and said: 'The service will begin immediately. Please go in.'

Shvarts, making an indefinite bow, stood still, obviously neither accepting nor declining this invitation. Praskovya Fyodorovna, recognising Pyotr Ivanovich, sighed, went right up to him, took his hand, and said, 'I know that you were a true friend of Ivan Ilyich's . . .' and looked at him, expecting from him the suitable action in response to these words. Pyotr Ivanovich knew that, just as before he had to cross himself, now what he had to do was to press her hand, to sigh and to say, 'Ah, I was indeed!' And he did so. And as he did so, he felt that the desired result had been attained; that he was touched, and she was touched.

'Come, since it's not begun yet, I have something I want to say to you,' said the widow. 'Give me your arm.'

Pyotr Ivanovich gave her his arm, and they moved towards the inner rooms, passing Shvarts, who winked gloomily at Pyotr Ivanovich.

'So much for our "screw"! Don't complain if we find another partner. You can make a fifth when you do get away,' said his humorous glance.

Pyotr Ivanovich sighed still more deeply and despondently, and Praskovya Fyodorovna pressed his hand gratefully. Going into her drawing-room, that was upholstered with pink cretonne and lighted by a dismal-looking lamp, they sat down at the table, she on a sofa and Pyotr Ivanovich on a low ottoman with deranged springs which yielded spasmodically under his weight. Praskovya Fyodorovna was about to warn him to sit on another seat, but felt such a recommendation out of keeping with her position, and changed her mind. Sitting down on the ottoman, Pyotr Ivanovich remembered how Ivan Ilyich had arranged this drawing-room, and had consulted him about this very pink cretonne with green leaves. Seating herself on the sofa, and pushing by the table (the whole drawing-room was crowded with furniture and things), the widow caught the lace of her black fichu in the carving of the table. Pyotr Ivanovich got up to disentangle it for her; and the ottoman, freed from his weight, began bobbing up spasmodically under him. The widow began unhooking her lace herself, and Pyotr Ivanovich again sat down, suppressing the mutinous ottoman springs under him. But the widow could not quite free herself, and Pyotr Ivanovich rose again, and again the ottoman became mutinous and popped up with a positive snap. When this was all over, she took out a clean cambric handkerchief and began weeping. Pyotr Ivanovich had been chilled off by the incident with the lace and the struggle with the ottoman springs, and he sat looking sullen. This awkward position was cut short by the entrance of Sokolov, Ivan Ilyich's butler, who came in to announce that the place in the cemetery fixed on by Praskovya Fyodorovna would cost two hundred roubles. She left off weeping, and with the air of a victim glancing at Pyotr Ivanovich, said in French that it was very terrible for her. Pyotr Ivanovich made a silent gesture signifying his unhesitating conviction that it must indeed be so.

'Please, smoke,' she said in a magnanimous, and at the same time, crushed voice, and she began discussing with Sokolov the question of the price of the site for the grave.

Pyotr Ivanovich, lighting a cigarette, listened to her very circumstantial enquiries as to the various prices of sites and her decision as to the one to be selected. Having settled on the site for the grave, she made arrangements also about the choristers. Sokolov went away.

'I see to everything myself,' she said to Pyotr Ivanovich, moving on one side the albums that lay on the table; and noticing that the table was in danger from the cigarette-ash, she promptly passed an ashtray to Pyotr Ivanovich, and said: 'I consider it affectation to pretend that my grief prevents me from looking after practical matters. On the contrary, if anything could – not console me . . . but distract me, it is seeing after everything for him.' She took out her handkerchief again, as though preparing to weep again; and suddenly, as though struggling with herself, she shook herself, and began speaking calmly: 'But I've business to talk about with you.'

Pyotr Ivanovich bowed, carefully keeping in check the springs of the ottoman, which had at once begun quivering under him.

'The last few days his sufferings were awful.'

'Did he suffer very much?' asked Pyotr Ivanovich.

'Oh, awfully! For the last moments, hours indeed, he never left off screaming. For three days and nights in succession he screamed incessantly. It was insufferable. I can't understand how I bore it; one could hear it through three closed doors. Ah, what I suffered!'

'And was he really conscious?' asked Pyotr Ivanovich.

'Yes,' she whispered, 'up to the last minute. He said goodbye to us a quarter of an hour before his death, and asked Volodya to be taken away too.'

The thought of the sufferings of a man he had known so intimately, at first as a light-hearted boy, a schoolboy, then grown up as a partner at whist, in spite of the unpleasant consciousness of his own and this woman's hypocrisy, suddenly horrified Pyotr Ivanovich. He saw again that forehead, the nose that seemed squeezing the lip, and he felt frightened for himself. 'Three days and nights of awful suffering and death. Why, that may at once, any minute, come upon me too,' he thought, and he felt for an instant terrified. But immediately, he could not himself have said how, there came to his support the customary reflection that this had happened to Ivan Ilyich and not to him, and that to him this must not and could not happen; that in thinking thus he was giving way to depression, which was not the right thing to do, as was evident from Shvarts's expression of face. And making these reflections, Pyotr Ivanovich felt reassured, and began with interest enquiring details about Ivan Ilyich's end, as though death were a mischance peculiar to Ivan Ilyich, but not at all incidental to himself.

After various observations about the details of the truly awful physical sufferings endured by Ivan Ilyich (these details Pyotr Ivanovich learned only through the effect Ivan Ilyich's agonies had had on the nerves of Praskovya Fyodorovna), the widow apparently thought it time to get to business.

'Ah, Pyotr Ivanovich, how hard it is, how awfully, awfully hard!' and she began to cry again.

Pyotr Ivanovich sighed, and waited for her to blow her nose. When she had done so, he said, 'Indeed it is,' and again she began to talk, and brought out what was evidently the business she wished to discuss with him; that business consisted in the enquiry as to how on the occasion of her husband's death she was to obtain a grant from the government. She made a show of asking Pyotr Ivanovich's advice about a pension. But he perceived that she knew already to the minutest details, what he did not know himself indeed, every-thing that could be got out of the government on the ground of this death; but that what she wanted to find out was, whether there were not any means of obtaining a little more? Pyotr Ivanovich tried to imagine such means; but after pondering a little, and out of politeness abusing the government for its stinginess, he said that he believed that it was impossible to obtain more. Then she sighed and began unmistakably looking about for an excuse for getting rid of her visitor. He perceived this, put out his cigarette, got up, pressed her hand, and went out into the passage.

In the dining-room, where was the bric-à-brac clock that Ivan Ilyich had been so delighted at buying, Pyotr Ivanovich met the priest and several people he knew who had come to the service for the dead, and saw too Ivan Ilyich's daughter, a handsome young lady. She was all in black. Her very slender figure looked even slenderer than usual. She had a gloomy, determined, almost wrathful expression. She bowed to Pyotr Ivanovich as though he were to blame in some way. Behind the daughter, with the same offended air on his face, stood a rich young man, whom Pyotr Ivanovich knew too, an examining magistrate, the young lady's fiancé, as he had heard. He bowed dejectedly to him, and would have gone on into the dead man's room, when from the staircase there appeared the figure of the son, the high-school boy, extra-ordinarily like Ivan Ilyich. He was the little Ivan Ilyich over again as Pyotr Ivanovich remembered him at school. His eyes were red with crying, and had that look often seen in unclean boys of thirteen or fourteen. The boy, seeing Pyotr Ivanovich, scowled morosely and bashfully. Pyotr Ivanovich nodded to him and went into the dead man's room. The service for the dead began – candles, groans, incense, tears, sobs. Pyotr Ivanovich stood frowning, staring at his feet in front of him. He did not once glance at the dead man, and right through to the end did not once give way to depressing influences, and was one of the first to walk out. In the hall there was no one. Gerasim, the young peasant, darted out of the dead man's room, tossed over with his strong hand all the fur cloaks to find Pyotr Ivanovich's, and gave it him.

'Well, Gerasim, my boy?' said Pyotr Ivanovich, so as to say something. 'A sad business, isn't it?'

'It's God's will. We shall come to the same,' said Gerasim, showing his white, even, peasant teeth in a smile, and, like a man in a rush of extra work, he briskly opened the door, called up the coachman, saw Pyotr Ivanovich into the carriage, and darted back to the steps as though bethinking himself of what he had to do next.

Pyotr Ivanovich had a special pleasure in the fresh air after the smell of incense, of the corpse, and of carbolic acid.

'Where to?' asked the coachman.

'It's not too late. I'll still go round to Fyodor Vassilievich's.'

And Pyotr Ivanovich drove there. And he did, in fact, find them just finishing the first rubber, so that he came just at the right time to take a hand.

2

The previous history of Ivan Ilyich was the simplest, the most ordinary, and the most awful.

Ivan Ilyich died at the age of forty-five, a member of the Judicial Council. He was the son of an official, whose career in Petersburg through various ministries and departments had been such as leads people into that position in which, though it is distinctly obvious that they are unfit to perform any kind of real duty, they yet cannot, owing to their long past service and their official rank, be dismissed; and they therefore receive a specially created fictitious post, and by no means fictitious thousands – from six to ten – on which they go on living till extreme old age. Such was the privy councillor, the superfluous member of various superfluous institutions, Ilya Efimovich Golovin.

He had three sons. Ivan Ilyich was the second son. The eldest son's career was exactly like his father's, only in a different department, and he was by now close upon that stage in the service in which the same sinecure would be reached. The third son was the unsuccessful one. He had in various positions always made a mess of things, and was now employed in the railway department. And his father and his brothers, and still more their wives, did not merely dislike meeting him, but avoided, except in extreme necessity, recollecting his existence. His sister had married Baron Greff, a Petersburg official of the same stamp as his father-in-law. Ivan Ilyich was *le phénix de la famille*,[10] as people said. He was not so frigid and precise as the eldest son, nor so wild as the youngest. He was the happy mean between them – a shrewd, lively, pleasant, and well-bred man. He had been educated with his younger brother at the school of jurisprudence. The younger brother had not finished the school course, but was expelled when in the fifth class. Ivan Ilyich completed the course successfully. At school he was just the same as he was later on all his life – an intelligent fellow, highly good-humoured and sociable, but strict in doing what he considered to be his duty. His duty he considered whatever was so considered by those persons who were set in authority over him. He was not a toady as a boy, nor later on as a grown-up person; but from his earliest years he was attracted, as a fly to the light, to persons of good standing in the world, assimilated their manners and their views of life, and established friendly relations with them. All the enthusiasms of childhood and youth passed, leaving no great traces in him; he gave way to sensuality and to vanity, and latterly when in the higher classes at school to liberalism, but always keeping within certain limits which were unfailingly marked out for him by his instincts.

At school he had committed actions which had struck him beforehand as great vileness, and gave him a feeling of loathing for himself at the very time he was committing them. But later on, perceiving that such actions were committed also by men of good position, and were not regarded by them as base, he was able, not to regard them as good, but to forget about them completely, and was never mortified by recollections of them.

Leaving the school of jurisprudence in the tenth class, and receiving from his father a sum of money for his outfit, Ivan Ilyich ordered his clothes at Sharmer's, hung on his watch-chain a medallion inscribed *respice finem*,[11] said goodbye to the prince who was the principal of his school, had a farewell dinner with his comrades at Donon's, and with all his new fashionable belongings – travelling trunk, linen, suits of clothes, shaving and toilet appurtenances, and travelling rug, all ordered and purchased at the very best shops – set off to take the post of secretary on special commissions for the governor of a province, a post which had been obtained for him by his father.

In the province Ivan Ilyich without loss of time made himself a position as easy and agreeable as his position had been in the school of jurisprudence. He did his work, made his career, and at the same time led a life of well-bred social gaiety. Occasionally he visited various districts on official duty, behaved with dignity both with his superiors and his inferiors; and with exactitude and an incorruptible honesty of which he could not help feeling proud, performed the duties with which he was entrusted, principally having to do with the dissenters. When engaged in official work he was, in spite of his youth and taste for frivolous amusements, exceedingly reserved, official, and even severe. But in social life he was often amusing and witty, and always good-natured, well bred, and *bon enfant*, as was said of him by his chief and his chief's wife, with whom he was like one of the family.

In the province there was, too, a connection with one of the ladies who obtruded their charms on the stylish young lawyer. There was a dressmaker, too, and there were drinking bouts with smart officers visiting the neighbourhood, and visits to a certain outlying street after supper; there was a rather cringing obsequiousness in his behaviour, too, with his chief, and even his chief's wife. But all this was accompanied with such a tone of the highest breeding, that it could not be called by harsh names; it all came under the rubric of the French saying, *Il faut que la jeunesse se passe.*[12] Everything was done with clean hands, in clean shirts, with French phrases, and, what was of most importance, in the highest society, and consequently with the approval of people of rank.

Such was Ivan Ilyich's career for five years, and then came a change in his official life. New methods of judicial procedure were established; new men were wanted to carry them out. And Ivan Ilyich became such a new man. Ivan Ilyich was offered the post of examining magistrate, and he accepted it in spite of the fact that this post was in another province, and he would have to break off all the ties he had formed and form new ones. Ivan Ilyich's friends met together to see him off, had their photographs taken in a group, presented him with a silver cigarette-case, and he set off to his new post.

As an examining magistrate, Ivan Ilyich was as *comme il faut*,[13] as well bred, as adroit in keeping official duties apart from private life, and as successful in gaining universal respect, as he had been as secretary of private commissions. The duties of his new office were in themselves of far greater interest and attractiveness for Ivan Ilyich. In his former post it had been pleasant to pass in his smart uniform from Sharmer's through the crowd of petitioners and officials waiting timorously and envying him, and to march with his easy swagger straight into the governor's private room, there to sit down with him to tea and cigarettes. But the persons directly subject to his authority were few. The only such persons were the district police superintendents and the dissenters, when he was serving on special commissions. And he liked treating such persons affably, almost like comrades; liked to make them feel that he, able to annihilate them, was behaving in this simple, friendly way with them. But such people were then few in number. Now as an examining magistrate Ivan Ilyich felt that everyone – everyone without exception – the most dignified, the most self-satisfied people, all were in his hands, and that he had but to write certain words on a sheet of paper with a printed heading, and this dignified self-satisfied person would be brought before him in the capacity of a defendant or a witness; and if he did not care to make him sit down, he would have to stand up before him and answer his questions. Ivan Ilyich never abused this authority of his; on the contrary, he tried to soften the expression of it. But the consciousness of this power and the possibility of softening its effect constituted for him the chief interest and attractiveness of his new position. In the work itself, in the preliminary enquiries, that is, Ivan Ilyich very rapidly acquired the art of setting aside every consideration irrelevant to the official aspect of the case, and of reducing every case, however complex, to that form in which it could in a purely external fashion be put on paper, completely excluding his personal view of the matter, and what was of paramount importance, observing all the necessary formalities. All this work was new. And he was one of the first men who put into practical working the reforms in judicial procedure enacted in 1864.[14]

On settling in a new town in his position as examining magistrate, Ivan Ilyich made new acquaintances, formed new ties, took up a new line, and adopted a rather different attitude. He took up an attitude of somewhat dignified aloofness towards the provincial authorities, while he picked out the best circle among the legal gentlemen and wealthy gentry living in the town, and adopted a tone of slight dissatisfaction with the government, moderate liberalism, and lofty civic virtue. With this, while making no change in the elegance of his get-up, Ivan Ilyich in his new office gave up shaving, and left his beard free to grow as it liked. Ivan Ilyich's existence in the new town proved to be very agreeable; the society which took the line of opposition to the governor was friendly and good; his income was larger, and he found a source of increased enjoyment in whist, at which he began to play at this time; and having a faculty for playing cards good-humouredly, and being rapid and exact in his calculations, he was as a rule on the winning side.

After living two years in the new town, Ivan Ilyich met his future wife. Praskovya Fyodorovna Mihel was the most attractive, clever, and brilliant girl in the set in which Ivan Ilyich moved. Among other amusements and recreations after his labours as a magistrate, Ivan Ilyich started a light, playful flirtation with Praskovya Fyodorovna.

Ivan Ilyich when he was an assistant secretary had danced as a rule; as an examining magistrate he danced only as an exception. He danced now as it were under protest, as though to show 'that though I am serving on the new reformed legal code, and am of the fifth class in official rank, still if it comes to a question of dancing, in that line too I can do better than others'. In this spirit he danced now and then towards the end of the evening with Praskovya Fyodorovna, and it was principally during these dances that he won the heart of Praskovya Fyodorovna. She fell in love with him. Ivan Ilyich had no clearly defined intention of marrying; but when the girl fell in love with him, he put the question to himself: 'After all, why not get married?' he said to himself.

The young lady, Praskovya Fyodorovna, was of good family, nice-looking. There was a little bit of property. Ivan Ilyich might have reckoned on a more brilliant match, but this was a good match. Ivan Ilyich had his salary; she, he hoped, would have as much of her own. It was a good family; she was a sweet, pretty, and perfectly *comme il faut* young woman. To say that Ivan Ilyich got married because he fell in love with his wife and found in her sympathy with his views of life, would be as untrue as to say that he got married because the people of his world approved of the match. Ivan Ilyich was influenced by both considerations; he was doing what was agreeable to himself in securing such a wife, and at the same time doing what persons of higher standing looked upon as the correct thing.

And Ivan Ilyich got married.

The process itself of getting married and the early period of married life, with the conjugal caresses, the new furniture, the new crockery, the new house linen, all up to the time of his wife's pregnancy, went off very well; so that Ivan Ilyich had already begun to think that so far from marriage breaking up that kind of frivolous, agreeable, light-hearted life, always decorous and always approved by society, which he regarded as the normal life, it would even increase its agreeableness. But at that point, in the early months of his wife's pregnancy, there came in a new element, unexpected, unpleasant, tiresome and unseemly, which could never have been anticipated, and from which there was no escape.

His wife, without any kind of reason, it seemed to Ivan Ilyich, *de gaité de coeur*,[15] as he expressed it, began to disturb the agreeableness and decorum of their life. She began without any sort of justification to be jealous, exacting in her demands on his attention, squabbled over everything, and treated him to the coarsest and most unpleasant scenes.

At first Ivan Ilyich hoped to escape from the unpleasantness of this position by taking up the same frivolous and well-bred line that had served him well on other occasions of difficulty. He endeavoured to ignore his wife's ill-humour, went on living light-heartedly and agreeably as before, invited friends to play cards, tried to get away himself to the club or to his friends. But his wife began on one occasion with such energy, abusing him in such coarse language, and so obstinately persisted in her abuse of him every time he failed in carrying out her demands, obviously having made up her mind firmly to persist till he gave way, that is, stayed at home and was as dull as she was, that Ivan Ilyich took alarm. He perceived that matrimony, at least with his wife, was not invariably conducive to the pleasures and proprieties of life; but, on the contrary, often destructive of them, and that it was therefore essential to erect some barrier to protect himself from these disturbances. And Ivan Ilyich began to look about for such means of protecting himself. His official duties were the only thing that impressed Praskovya Fyodorovna, and Ivan Ilyich began to use his official position and the duties arising from it in his struggle with his wife to fence off his own independent world apart.

With the birth of the baby, the attempts at nursing it, and the various unsuccessful experiments with foods, with the illnesses, real and imaginary, of the infant and its mother, in which Ivan Ilyich was expected to sympathise, though he never had the slightest idea about them, the need for him to fence off a world apart for himself outside his family life became still more imperative. As his wife grew more irritable and exacting, so did Ivan Ilyich more and more transfer the centre of gravity of his life to his official work. He became fonder and fonder of official life, and more ambitious than he had been.

Very quickly, not more than a year after his wedding, Ivan Ilyich had become aware that conjugal life, though providing certain comforts, was in reality a very intricate and difficult business towards which one must, if one is to do one's duty, that is, lead the decorous life approved by society, work out for oneself a definite line, just as in the government service.

And such a line Ivan Ilyich did work out for himself in his married life. He expected from his home life only those comforts – of dinner at home, of housekeeper and bed – which it could give him, and, above all, that perfect propriety in external observances required by public opinion. For the rest, he looked for good-humoured pleasantness, and if he found it he was very thankful. If he met with antagonism and querulousness, he promptly retreated into the separate world he had shut off for himself in his official life, and there he found solace.

Ivan Ilyich was prized as a good official, and three years later he was made assistant public prosecutor. The new duties of this position, their dignity, the possibility of bringing anyone to trial and putting anyone in prison, the publicity of the speeches and the success Ivan Ilyich had in that part of his work – all this made his official work still more attractive to him.

Children were born to him. His wife became steadily more querulous and ill-tempered, but the line Ivan Ilyich had taken up for himself in home life put him almost out of reach of her grumbling.

After seven years of service in the same town, Ivan Ilyich was transferred to another province with the post of public prosecutor. They moved, money was short, and his wife did not like the place they had moved to. The salary was indeed a little higher than before, but their expenses were larger. Besides, a couple of children died, and home life consequently became even less agreeable for Ivan Ilyich.

For every mischance that occurred in their new place of residence, Praskovya Fyodorovna blamed her husband. The greater number of subjects of conversation between husband and wife, especially the education of the children, led to questions which were associated with previous quarrels, and quarrels were ready to break out at every instant. There remained only those rare periods of being in love which did indeed come upon them, but never lasted long. These were the islands at which they put in for a time, but they soon set off again upon the ocean of concealed hostility, that was made manifest in their aloofness from one another. This aloofness might have distressed Ivan Ilyich if he had believed that this ought not to be so, but by now he regarded this position as perfectly normal, and it was indeed the goal towards which he worked in his home life. His aim was to make himself more and more free from the unpleasant aspects of domestic life and to render them harmless and decorous. And he attained this aim by spending less and less time with his family; and when he was forced to be at home, he endeavoured to secure his tranquillity by the presence of outsiders. The great thing for Ivan Ilyich was having his office. In the official world all the interest of life was concentrated for him. And this interest absorbed him. The sense of his own power, the consciousness of being able to ruin anyone he wanted to ruin, even the external dignity of his office, when he made his entry into the court or met subordinate officials, his success in the eyes of his superiors and his subordinates, and, above all, his masterly handling of cases, of which he was conscious, – all this delighted him and, together with chat with his colleagues, dining out, and whist, filled his life. So that, on the whole, Ivan Ilyich's life still went on in the way he thought it should go – agreeably and decorously.

So he lived for another seven years. His eldest daughter was already sixteen, another child had died, and there was left only one other, a boy at the high school, a subject of dissension. Ivan Ilyich wanted to send him to the school of jurisprudence, while Praskovya Fyodorovna to spite him sent him to the high school. The daughter had been educated at home, and had turned out well; the boy too did fairly well at his lessons.

3

Such was Ivan Ilyich's life for seventeen years after his marriage. He had been by now a long while prosecutor, and had refused several appointments offered him, looking out for a more desirable post, when there occurred an unexpected incident which utterly destroyed his peace of mind. Ivan Ilyich had been expecting to be appointed presiding judge in a university town, but a certain Goppe somehow stole a march on him and secured the appointment. Ivan Ilyich took offence, began upbraiding him, and quarrelled with him and with his own superiors. A coolness was felt towards him, and on the next appointment that was made he was again passed over.

This was in the year 1880. That year was the most painful one in Ivan Ilyich's life. During that year it became evident on the one hand that his pay was insufficient for his expenses; on the other hand, that he had been forgotten by everyone, and that what seemed to him the most monstrous, the cruelest injustice, appeared to other people as a quite commonplace fact. Even his father felt no obligation to assist him. He felt that everyone had deserted him, and that everyone regarded his position with an income of three thousand five hundred roubles as a quite normal and even fortunate one. He alone, with a sense of the injustice done him, and the everlasting nagging of his wife and the debts he had begun to accumulate, living beyond his means, knew that his position was far from being normal.

The summer of that year, to cut down his expenses, he took a holiday and went with his wife to spend the summer in the country at her brother's.

In the country, with no official duties to occupy him, Ivan Ilyich was for the first time a prey not to simple boredom, but to intolerable depression; and he made up his mind that things could not go on like that, and that it was absolutely necessary to take some decisive steps.

After a sleepless night spent by Ivan Ilyich walking up and down the terrace, he determined to go to Petersburg to take active steps and to get transferred to some other department, so as to revenge himself on *them*, the people, that is, who had not known how to appreciate him.

Next day, in spite of all the efforts of his wife and his mother-in-law to dissuade him, he set off to Petersburg.

He went with a single object before him – to obtain a post with an income of five thousand. He was ready now to be satisfied with a post in any department, of any tendency, with any kind of work. He must only have a post – a post with five thousand, in the executive department, the banks, the railways, the Empress Marya's institutions,[16] even in the customs duties – what was essential was five thousand, and essential it was, too, to get out of the department in which they had failed to appreciate his value.

And, behold, this quest of Ivan Ilyich's was crowned with wonderful, unexpected success. At Kursk there got into the same first-class carriage F. S. Ilyin, an acquaintance, who told him of a telegram just received by the governor of Kursk, announcing a change about to take place in the ministry – Pyotr Ivanovich was to be superseded by Ivan Semyonovich.

The proposed change, apart from its significance for Russia, had special significance for Ivan Ilyich from the fact that by bringing to the front a new person, Pyotr Petrovich, and obviously, therefore, his friend Zahar Ivanovich, it was in the highest degree propitious to Ivan Ilyich's own plans. Zahar Ivanovich was a friend and schoolfellow of Ivan Ilyich's.

At Moscow the news was confirmed. On arriving at Petersburg, Ivan Ilyich looked up Zahar Ivanovich, and received a positive promise of an appointment in his former department – that of justice.

A week later he telegraphed to his wife: 'Zahar Miller's place. At first report I receive appointment.'

Thanks to these changes, Ivan Ilyich unexpectedly obtained, in the same department as before, an appointment which placed him two stages higher than his former colleagues, and gave him an income of five thousand, together with the official allowance of three thousand five hundred for travelling expenses. All his ill-humour with his former enemies and the whole department was forgotten, and Ivan Ilyich was completely happy.

Ivan Ilyich went back to the country more light-hearted and good-tempered than he had been for a very long while. Praskovya Fyodorovna was in better spirits, too, and peace was patched up between them. Ivan Ilyich described what respect everyone had shown him in Petersburg; how all those who had been his enemies had been put to shame, and were cringing now before him; how envious they were of his appointment, and still more of the high favour in which he stood at Petersburg.

Praskovya Fyodorovna listened to this, and pretended to believe it, and did not contradict him in anything, but confined herself to making plans for her new arrangements in the town to which they would be moving. And Ivan Ilyich saw with delight that these plans were his plans; that they were agreed; and that his life after this disturbing hitch in its progress was about to regain its true, normal character of light-hearted agreeableness and propriety.

Ivan Ilyich had come back to the country for a short stay only. He had to enter upon the duties of his new office on the 10th of September; and besides, he needed some time to settle in a new place, to move all his belongings from the other province, to purchase and order many things in addition; in short, to arrange things as settled in his own mind, and almost exactly as settled in the heart too of Praskovya Fyodorovna.

And now when everything was so successfully arranged, and when he and his wife were agreed in their aim, and were, besides, so little together, they got on with one another as they had not got on together since the early years of their married life. Ivan Ilyich had thought of taking his family away with him at once; but his sister and his brother-in-law, who had suddenly become extremely cordial and intimate with him and his family, were so pressing in urging them to stay that he set off alone.

Ivan Ilyich started off; and the light-hearted temper produced by his success, and his good understanding with his wife, one thing backing up another, did not desert him all the time. He found a charming set of apartments, the very thing both husband and wife had dreamed of. Spacious, lofty reception-rooms in the old style, a comfortable, dignified-looking study for him, rooms for his wife and daughter, a school-room for his son, everything as though planned on purpose for them. Ivan Ilyich himself looked after the furnishing of them, chose the wallpapers, bought furniture, by preference antique furniture, which had a peculiar *comme-il-faut* style to his mind, and it all grew up and grew up, and really attained the ideal he had set before himself. When he had half finished arranging the house, his arrangement surpassed his own expectations. He saw the *comme-il-faut* character, elegant and free from vulgarity, that the whole would have when it was all ready. As she fell asleep he pictured to himself the reception-room as it would be. Looking at the drawing-room, not yet finished, he could see the hearth, the screen, the *étagère*,[17] and the little chairs dotted here and there, the plates and dishes on the wall, and the bronzes as they would be when they were all put in their places. He was delighted with the thought of how he would impress Praskovya and Lizanka, who had taste too in this line. They would never expect anything like it. He was particularly successful in coming across and buying cheap old pieces of furniture, which gave a peculiarly aristocratic air to the whole. In his letters he purposely disparaged everything so as to surprise them. All this so absorbed him that the duties of his new office, though he was so fond of his official work, interested him less than he had expected. During sittings of the court he had moments of inattention; he pondered the question which sort of cornices to have on the window-blinds, straight or fluted. He was so interested in this business that he often set to work with his own hands, moved a piece of furniture, or hung up curtains himself. One day he went up a ladder to show a workman, who did not understand, how he wanted some hangings draped, made a false step and slipped; but, like a strong and nimble person, he clung on, and only knocked his side against the corner of a frame. The bruised place ached, but it soon passed off. Ivan Ilyich felt all this time particularly good-humoured and well. He wrote: 'I feel fifteen years younger.' He thought his house-furnishing would be finished in September, but it dragged on to the middle of October. But then the effect was charming; not he only said so, but everyone who saw it told him so too.

In reality, it was all just what is commonly seen in the houses of people who are not exactly wealthy but want to look like wealthy people, and so succeed only in being like one another – hangings, dark wood, flowers, rugs and bronzes, everything dark and highly polished, everything that all people of a certain class have so as to be like all people of a certain class. And in his case it was all so like that it made no impression at all; but it all seemed to him somehow special. When he met his family at the railway station and brought them to his newly furnished rooms, all lighted up in readiness, and a footman in a white tie opened the door into an entry decorated with flowers, and then they walked into the drawing-room and the study, uttering cries of delight, he was very happy, conducted them everywhere, eagerly drinking in their praises, and beaming with satisfaction. The same evening, while they talked about various things at tea, Praskovya Fyodorovna enquired about his fall, and he laughed and showed them how he had gone flying, and how he had frightened the upholsterer.

'It's as well I'm something of an athlete. Another man might have been killed, and I got nothing worse than a blow here; when it's touched it hurts, but it's going off already; nothing but a bruise.'

And they began to live in their new abode, which, as is always the case, when they had got thoroughly settled in they found to be short of just one room, and with their new income, which, as always, was only a little – some five hundred roubles – too little, and everything went very well. Things went particularly well at first, before everything was quite finally arranged, and there was still something to do to the place – something to buy, something to order, something to move, something to make to fit. Though there were indeed several disputes between husband and wife, both were so well satisfied, and there was so much to do, that it all went off without serious quarrels. When there was nothing left to arrange, it became a little dull, and something seemed to be lacking, but by then they were making acquaintances and forming habits, and life was filled up again.

Ivan Ilyich, after spending the morning in the court, returned home to dinner, and at first he was generally in a good humour, although this was apt to be upset a little, and precisely on account of the new abode. Every spot on the tablecloth, on the hangings, the string of a window blind broken, irritated him. He had devoted so much trouble to the arrangement of the rooms that any disturbance of their order distressed him. But, on the whole, the life of Ivan Ilyich ran its course as, according to his conviction, life ought to do – easily, agreeably, and decorously. He got up at nine, drank his coffee, read the newspaper, then put on his official uniform, and went to the court. There the routine of the daily work was ready mapped out for him, and he stepped into it at once. People with petitions, enquiries in the office, the office itself, the sittings – public and preliminary. In all this the great thing necessary was to exclude everything with the sap of life in it, which always disturbs the regular course of official business, not to admit any sort of relations with people except the official relations; the motive of all intercourse had to be simply the official motive, and the intercourse itself to be only official. A man would come, for instance, anxious for certain information. Ivan Ilyich, not being the functionary on duty, would have nothing whatever to do with such a man. But if this man's relation to him as a member of the court is such as can be formulated on official stamped paper – within the limits of such a relation Ivan Ilyich would do everything, positively everything he could, and in doing so would observe the semblance of human friendly relations, that is, the courtesies of social life. But where the official relation ended, there everything else stopped too. This art of keeping the official aspect of things apart from his real life, Ivan Ilyich possessed in the highest degree; and through long practice and natural aptitude, he had brought it to such a pitch of perfection that he even permitted himself at times, like a skilled specialist as it were in jest, to let the human and official relations mingle. He allowed himself this liberty just because he felt he had the power at any moment if he wished it to take up the purely official line again and to drop the human relation. This thing was not simply easy, agreeable, and decorous; in Ivan Ilyich's hands it attained a positively artistic character. In the intervals of business he smoked, drank tea, chatted a little about politics, a little about public affairs, a little about cards, but most of all about appointments in the service. And tired, but feeling like some artist who has skilfully played his part in the performance, one of the first violins in the orchestra, he returned home. At home his daughter and her mother had been paying calls somewhere, or else someone had been calling on them; the son had been at school, had been preparing his lessons with his teachers, and duly learning correctly what was taught at the high school. Everything was as it should be. After dinner, if there were no visitors, Ivan Ilyich sometimes read some book of which people were talking, and in the evening sat down to work, that is, read official papers, compared them with the laws, sorted depositions, and put them under the laws. This he found neither tiresome nor entertaining. It was tiresome when he might have been playing 'screw'; but if there were no 'screw' going on, it was anyway better than sitting alone or with his wife. Ivan Ilyich's pleasures were little dinners, to which he invited ladies and gentlemen of good social position, and such methods of passing the time with them as were usual with such persons, so that his drawing-room might be like all other drawing-rooms.

Once they even gave a party – a dance. And Ivan Ilyich enjoyed it, and everything was very successful, except that it led to a violent quarrel with his wife over the tarts and sweetmeats. Praskovya Fyodorovna had her own plan; while Ivan Ilyich insisted on getting everything from an expensive pastry-cook, and ordered a great many tarts, and the quarrel was because these tarts were left over and the pastry-cook's bill came to forty-five roubles. The quarrel was a violent and unpleasant one, so much so that Praskovya Fyodorovna called him, 'Fool, imbecile'. And he clutched at his head, and in his anger made some allusion to a divorce. But the party itself was enjoyable. There were all the best people, and Ivan Ilyich danced with Princess Trufonov, the sister of the one so well known in connection with the charitable association called, 'Bear my Burden'. His official pleasures lay in the gratification of his pride; his social pleasures lay in the gratification of his vanity. But Ivan Ilyich's most real pleasure was the pleasure of playing 'screw', the Russian equivalent for 'poker'. He admitted to himself that after all, after whatever unpleasant incidents there had been in his life, the pleasure which burned like a candle before all others was sitting with good players, and not noisy partners, at 'screw'; and, of course, a four-hand game (playing with five was never a success, though one pretends to like it particularly), and with good cards, to play a shrewd, serious game, then supper and a glass of wine. And after 'screw', especially after winning some small stakes (winning large sums was unpleasant), Ivan Ilyich went to bed in a particularly happy frame of mind.

So they lived. They moved in the very best circle, and were visited by people of consequence and young people.

In their views of their circle of acquaintances, the husband, the wife, and the daughter were in complete accord; and without any expressed agreement on the subject, they all acted alike in dropping and shaking off various friends and relations, shabby persons who swooped down upon them in their drawing-room with Japanese plates on the walls, and pressed their civilities on them. Soon these shabby persons ceased fluttering about them, and none but the very best society was seen at the Golovins. Young men began to pay attention to Lizanka; and Petrishtchev, the son of Dmitry Ivanovich Petrishtchev, and the sole heir of his fortune, an examining magistrate, began to be so attentive to Lizanka, that Ivan Ilyich had raised the question with his wife whether it would not be as well to arrange a sledge drive for them, or to get up some theatricals. So they lived. And everything went on in this way without change, and everything was very nice.

4

All were in good health. One could not use the word ill-health in connection with the symptoms Ivan Ilyich sometimes complained of, namely, a queer taste in his mouth and a sort of uncomfortable feeling on the left side of the stomach.

But it came to pass that this uncomfortable feeling kept increasing, and became not exactly a pain, but a continual sense of weight in his side and irritable temper. This irritable temper continually growing and growing, began at last to mar the agreeable easiness and decorum that had reigned in the Golovin household. Quarrels between the husband and wife became more and more frequent, and soon all the easiness and amenity of life had fallen away, and mere propriety was maintained with difficulty. Scenes became again more frequent. Again there were only islands in the sea of contention – and but few of these – at which the husband and wife could meet without an outbreak. And Praskovya Fyodorovna said now, not without grounds, that her husband had a trying temper. With her characteristic exaggeration, she said he had always had this awful temper, and she had needed all her sweetness to put up with it for twenty years. It was true that it was he now who began the quarrels. His gusts of temper always broke out just before dinner, and often just as he was beginning to eat, at the soup. He would notice that some piece of the crockery had been chipped, or that the food was not nice, or that his son put his elbow on the table, or his daughter's hair was not arranged as he liked it. And whatever it was, he laid the blame of it on Praskovya Fyodorovna. Praskovya Fyodorovna had at first retorted in the same strain, and said all sorts of horrid things to him; but on two occasions, just at the beginning of dinner, he had flown into such a frenzy that she perceived that it was due to physical derangement, and was brought on by taking food, and she controlled herself; she did not reply, but simply made haste to get dinner over. Praskovya Fyodorovna took great credit to herself for this exercise of self-control. Making up her mind that her husband had a fearful temper, and made her life miserable, she began to feel sorry for herself. And the more she felt for herself, the more she hated her husband. She began to wish he were dead; yet could not wish it, because then there would be no income. And this exasperated her against him even more. She considered herself dreadfully unfortunate, precisely because even his death could not save her, and she felt irritated and concealed it, and this hidden irritation on her side increased his irritability.

After one violent scene, in which Ivan Ilyich had been particularly unjust, and after which he had said in explanation that he certainly was irritable, but that it was due to illness, she said that if he were ill he ought to take steps, and insisted on his going to see a celebrated doctor.

He went. Everything was as he had expected; everything was as it always is. The waiting and the assumption of dignity, that professional dignity he knew so well, exactly as he assumed it himself in court, and the sounding and listening and questions that called for answers that were foregone conclusions and obviously superfluous, and the significant air that seemed to insinuate – you only leave it all to us, and we will arrange everything, for us it is certain and incontestable how to arrange everything, everything in one way for every man of every sort. It was all exactly as in his court of justice. Exactly the same air as he put on in dealing with a man brought up for judgment, the doctor put on for him.

The doctor said: This and that proves that you have such-and-such a thing wrong inside you; but if that is not confirmed by analysis of this and that, then we must assume this and that. If we assume this and that, then – and so on. To Ivan Ilyich there was only one question of consequence, Was his condition dangerous or not? But the doctor ignored that irrelevant enquiry. From the doctor's point of view this was a side issue, not the subject under consideration; the only real question was the balance of probabilities between a loose kidney, chronic catarrh, and appendicitis. It was not a question of the life of Ivan Ilyich, but the question between the loose kidney and the intestinal appendix. And this question, as it seemed to Ivan Ilyich, the doctor solved in a brilliant manner in favour of the appendix, with the reservation that analysis of the water might give a fresh clue, and that then the aspect of the case would be altered. All this was point for point identical with what Ivan Ilyich had himself done in brilliant fashion a thousand times over in dealing with some man on his trial. Just as brilliantly the doctor made his summing-up, and triumphantly, gaily even, glanced over his spectacles at the prisoner in the dock. From the doctor's summing-up Ivan Ilyich deduced the conclusion – that things looked bad, and that he, the doctor, and most likely everyone else, did not care, but that things looked bad for him. And this conclusion impressed Ivan Ilyich morbidly, arousing in him a great feeling of pity for himself, of great anger against this doctor who could be unconcerned about a matter of such importance.

But he said nothing of that. He got up, and, laying the fee on the table, he said, with a sigh, 'We sick people probably often ask inconvenient questions. Tell me, is this generally a dangerous illness or not?'

The doctor glanced severely at him with one eye through his spectacles, as though to say: 'Prisoner at the bar, if you will not keep within the limits of the questions allowed you, I shall be compelled to take measures for your removal from the precincts of the court.' 'I have told you what I thought necessary and suitable already,' said the doctor; 'the analysis will show anything further.' And the doctor bowed him out.

Ivan Ilyich went out slowly and dejectedly, got into his sledge, and drove home. All the way home he was incessantly going over all the doctor had said, trying to translate all these complicated, obscure, scientific phrases into simple language, and to read in them an answer to the question, It's bad – is it very bad, or nothing much as yet? And it seemed to him that the upshot of all the doctor had said was that it was very bad. Everything seemed dismal to Ivan Ilyich in the streets. The sledge-drivers were dismal, the houses were dismal, the people passing, and the shops were dismal. This ache, this dull gnawing ache, that never ceased for a second, seemed, when connected with the doctor's obscure utterances, to have gained a new, more serious significance. With a new sense of misery Ivan Ilyich kept watch on it now.

He reached home and began to tell his wife about it. His wife listened; but in the middle of his account his daughter came in with her hat on, ready to go out with her mother. Reluctantly she half sat down to listen to these tedious details, but she could not stand it for long, and her mother did not hear his story to the end.

'Well, I'm very glad,' said his wife; 'now you must be sure and take the medicine regularly. Give me the prescription; I'll send Gerasim to the chemist's!' And she went to get ready to go out.

He had not taken breath while she was in the room, and he heaved a deep sigh when she was gone.

'Well,' he said, 'may be it really is nothing as yet.'

He began to take the medicine, to carry out the doctor's directions, which were changed after the analysis of the water. But it was just at this point that some confusion arose, either in the analysis or in what ought to have followed from it. The doctor himself, of course, could not be blamed for it, but it turned out that things had not gone as the doctor had told him. Either he had forgotten or told a lie, or was hiding something from him.

But Ivan Ilyich still went on just as exactly carrying out the doctor's direction, and in doing so he found comfort at first.

From the time of his visit to the doctor Ivan Ilyich's principal occupation became the exact observance of the doctor's prescriptions as regards hygiene and medicine and the careful observation of his ailment in all the functions of his organism. Ivan Ilyich's principal interest came to be people's ailments and people's health. When anything was said in his presence about sick people, about deaths and recoveries, especially in the case of an illness resembling his own, he listened, trying to conceal his excitement, asked questions, and applied what he heard to his own trouble.

The ache did not grow less; but Ivan Ilyich made great efforts to force himself to believe that he was better. And he succeeded in deceiving himself so long as nothing happened to disturb him. But as soon as he had a mischance, some unpleasant words with his wife, a failure in his official work, an unlucky hand at 'screw', he was at once acutely sensible of his illness. In former days he had borne with such mishaps, hoping soon to retrieve the mistake, to make a struggle, to reach success later, to have a lucky hand. But now he was cast down by every mischance and reduced to despair. He would say to himself: 'Here I'm only just beginning to get better, and the medicine has begun to take effect, and now this mischance or disappointment.' And he was furious against the mischance or the people who were causing him the disappointment and killing him, and he felt that this fury was killing him, but could not check it. One would have thought that it should have been clear to him that this exasperation against circumstances and people was aggravating his disease, and that therefore he ought not to pay attention to the unpleasant incidents. But his reasoning took quite the opposite direction. He said that he needed peace, and was on the watch for everything that disturbed his peace, and at the slightest disturbance of it he flew into a rage. What made his position worse was that he read medical books and consulted doctors. He got worse so gradually that he might have deceived himself, comparing one day with another, the difference was so slight. But when he consulted the doctors, then it seemed to him that he was getting worse, and very rapidly so indeed. And in spite of this, he was continually consulting the doctors.

That month he called on another celebrated doctor. The second celebrity said almost the same as the first, but put his questions differently; and the interview with this celebrity only redoubled the doubts and terrors of Ivan Ilyich. A friend of a friend of his, a very good doctor, diagnosed the disease quite differently; and in spite of the fact that he guaranteed recovery, by his questions and his suppositions he confused Ivan Ilyich even more and strengthened his suspicions. A homoeopath gave yet another diagnosis of the complaint, and prescribed medicine, which Ivan Ilyich took secretly for a week; but after a week of the homoeopathic medicine he felt no relief, and losing faith both in the other doctor's treatment and in this, he fell into even deeper depression. One day a lady of his acquaintance talked to him of the healing wrought by the holy pictures. Ivan Ilyich caught himself listening attentively and believing in the reality of the facts alleged. This incident alarmed him. 'Can I have degenerated to such a point of intellectual feebleness?' he said to himself. 'Nonsense! it's all rubbish. I must not give way to nervous fears, but fixing on one doctor, adhere strictly to his treatment. That's what I will do. Now it's settled. I won't think about it, but till next summer I will stick to the treatment, and then I shall see. Now I'll put a stop to this wavering!' It was easy to say this, but impossible to carry it out. The pain in his side was always dragging at him, seeming to grow more acute and ever more incessant; it seemed to him that the taste in his mouth was queerer, and there was a loathsome smell even from his breath, and his appetite and strength kept dwindling. There was no deceiving himself; something terrible, new, and so important that nothing more important had ever been in Ivan Ilyich's life, was taking place in him, and he alone knew of it. All about him did not or would not understand, and believed that everything in the world was going on as before. This was what tortured Ivan Ilyich more than anything. Those of his own household, most of all his wife and daughter, who were absorbed in a perfect whirl of visits, did not, he saw, comprehend it at all, and were annoyed that he was so depressed and exacting, as though he were to blame for it. Though they tried indeed to disguise it, he saw he was a nuisance to them; but that his wife had taken up a definite line of her own in regard to his illness, and stuck to it regardless of what he might say and do. This line was expressed thus: 'You know,' she would say to acquaintances, 'Ivan Ilyich cannot, like all other simple-hearted folks, keep to the treatment prescribed him. One day he'll take his drops and eat what he's ordered, and go to bed in good time; the next day, if I don't see to it, he'll suddenly forget to take his medicine, eat sturgeon (which is forbidden by the doctors), yes, and sit up at "screw" till past midnight.'

'Why, when did I do that?' Ivan Ilyich asked in vexation one day at Pyotr Ivanovich's.

'Why, yesterday, with Shebek.'

'It makes no difference. I couldn't sleep for pain.'

'Well, it doesn't matter what you do it for, only you'll never get well like that, and you make us wretched.'

Praskovya Fyodorovna's external attitude to her husband's illness, openly expressed to others and to himself, was that Ivan Ilyich was to blame in the matter of his illness, and that the whole illness was another injury he was doing to his wife. Ivan Ilyich felt that the expression of this dropped from her unconsciously, but that made it no easier for him.

In his official life, too, Ivan Ilyich noticed, or fancied he noticed, a strange attitude to him. At one time it seemed to him that people were looking inquisitively at him, as a man who would shortly have to vacate his position; at another time his friends would suddenly begin chaffing him in a friendly way over his nervous fears, as though that awful and horrible, unheard-of thing that was going on within him, incessantly gnawing at him, and irresistibly dragging him away somewhere, were the most agreeable subject for joking. Shvarts especially, with his jocoseness, his liveliness, and his *comme-il-faut* tone, exasperated Ivan Ilyich by reminding him of himself ten years ago.

Friends came sometimes to play cards. They sat down to the card-table; they shuffled and dealt the new cards. Diamonds were led and followed by diamonds, the seven. His partner said, 'Can't trump,' and played the two of diamonds. What then? Why, delightful, capital, it should have been – he had a trump hand. And suddenly Ivan Ilyich feels that gnawing ache, that taste in his mouth, and it strikes him as something grotesque that with that he could be glad of a trump hand.

He looks at Mihail Mihailovich, his partner, how he taps on the table with his red hand, and affably and indulgently abstains from snatching up the trick, and pushes the cards towards Ivan Ilyich so as to give him the pleasure of taking them up, without any trouble, without even stretching out his hand. 'What, does he suppose that I'm so weak that I can't stretch out my hand?' thinks Ivan Ilyich, and he forgets the trumps, and trumps his partner's cards, and plays his trump hand without making three tricks; and what's the most awful thing of all is that he sees how upset Mihail Mihailovich is about it, while he doesn't care a bit, and it's awful for him to think why he doesn't care.

They all see that he's in pain, and say to him, 'We can stop if you're tired. You go and lie down.' Lie down? No, he's not in the least tired; they will play the rubber. All are gloomy and silent. Ivan Ilyich feels that it is he who has brought this gloom upon them, and he cannot disperse it. They have supper, and the party breaks up, and Ivan Ilyich is left alone with the consciousness that his life is poisoned for him and poisons the life of others, and that this poison is not losing its force, but is continually penetrating more and more deeply into his whole existence.

And with the consciousness of this, and with the physical pain in addition, and the terror in addition to that, he must lie in his bed, often not able to sleep for pain the greater part of the night; and in the morning he must get up again, dress, go to the law-court, speak, write, or, if he does not go out, stay at home for all the four-and-twenty hours of the day and night, of which each one is a torture. And he had to live thus on the edge of the precipice alone, without one man who would understand and feel for him.

5

In this way one month, then a second, passed by. Just before the New Year his brother-in-law arrived in the town on a visit to them. Ivan Ilyich was at the court when he arrived. Praskovya Fyodorovna had gone out shopping. Coming home and going into his study, he found there his brother-in-law, a healthy, florid man, engaged in unpacking his trunk. He raised his head, hearing Ivan Ilyich's step, and for a second stared at him without a word. That stare told Ivan Ilyich everything. His brother-in-law opened his mouth to utter an 'Oh!' of surprise, but checked himself. That confirmed it all.

'What! have I changed?'

'Yes, there is a change.'

And all Ivan Ilyich's efforts to draw him into talking of his appearance his brother-in-law met with obstinate silence. Praskovya Fyodorovna came in; the brother-in-law went to see her. Ivan Ilyich locked his door, and began gazing at himself in the looking-glass, first full face, then in profile. He took up his photograph, taken with his wife, and compared the portrait with what he saw in the looking-glass. The change was immense. Then he bared his arm to the elbow, looked at it, pulled the sleeve down again, sat down on an ottoman, and felt blacker than night.

'I mustn't, I mustn't,' he said to himself, jumped up, went to the table, opened some official paper, tried to read it, but could not. He opened the door, went into the drawing-room. The door into the drawing-room was closed. He went up to it on tiptoe and listened.

'No, you're exaggerating,' Praskovya Fyodorovna was saying.

'Exaggerating? You can't see it. Why, he's a dead man. Look at his eyes – there's no light in them. But what's wrong with him?'

'No one can tell. Nikolaev' (that was another doctor) 'said something, but I don't know. Leshtchetitsky' (this was the celebrated doctor) 'said the opposite.'

Ivan Ilyich walked away, went to his own room, lay down, and fell to musing. 'A kidney – a loose kidney.' He remembered all the doctors had told him, how it had been detached, and how it was loose; and by an effort of imagination he tried to catch that kidney and to stop it, to strengthen it. So little was needed, he fancied. 'No, I'll go again to Pyotr Ivanovich' (this was the friend who had a friend a doctor). He rang, ordered the horse to be put in, and got ready to go out.

'Where are you off to, Jean?' asked his wife with a peculiarly melancholy and exceptionally kind expression.

This exceptionally kind expression exasperated him. He looked darkly at her.

'I want to see Pyotr Ivanovich.'

He went to the friend who had a friend a doctor. And with him to the doctor's. He found him in, and had a long conversation with him.

Reviewing the anatomical and physiological details of what, according to the doctor's view, was taking place within him, he understood it all. It was just one thing – a little thing wrong with the intestinal appendix. It might all come right. Only strengthen one sluggish organ, and decrease the undue activity of another, and absorption would take place, and all would be set right. He was a little late for dinner. He ate his dinner, talked cheerfully, but it was a long while before he could go to his own room to work. At last he went to his study, and at once sat down to work. He read his legal documents and did his work, but the consciousness never left him of having a matter of importance very near to his heart which he had put off, but would look into later. When he had finished his work, he remembered that the matter near his heart was thinking about the intestinal appendix. But he did not give himself up to it; he went into the drawing-room to tea. There were visitors; and there was talking, playing on the piano, and singing; there was the young examining magistrate, the desirable match for the daughter. Ivan Ilyich spent the evening, as Praskovya Fyodorovna observed, in better spirits than any of them; but he never forgot for an instant that he had the important matter of the intestinal appendix put off for consideration later. At eleven o'clock he said good-night and went to his own room. He had slept alone since his illness in a little room adjoining his study. He went in, undressed, and took up a novel of Zola, but did not read it; he fell to thinking. And in his imagination the desired recovery of the intestinal appendix had taken place. There had been absorption, rejection, re-establishment of the regular action.

'Why, it's all simply that,' he said to himself. 'One only wants to assist nature.' He remembered the medicine, got up, took it, lay down on his back, watching for the medicine to act beneficially and overcome the pain. 'It's only to take it regularly and avoid injurious influences; why, already I feel rather better, much better.' He began to feel his side; it was not painful to the touch. 'Yes, I don't feel it – really, much better already.' He put out the candle and lay on his side. 'The appendix is getting better, absorption.' Suddenly he felt the familiar, old, dull, gnawing ache, persistent, quiet, in earnest. In his mouth the same familiar loathsome taste. His heart sank, his brain felt dim, misty. 'My God, my God!' he said, 'again, again, and it will never cease.' And suddenly the whole thing rose before him in quite a different aspect. 'Intestinal appendix! kidney!' he said to himself. 'It's not a question of the appendix, not a question of the kidney, but of life and . . . death. Yes, life has been and now it's going, going away, and I cannot stop it. Yes. Why deceive myself? Isn't it obvious to everyone, except me, that I'm dying, and it's only a question of weeks, of days – at once perhaps. There was light, and now there is darkness. I was here, and now I am going! Where?' A cold chill ran over him, his breath stopped. He heard nothing but the throbbing of his heart.

'I shall be no more, then what will there be? There'll be nothing. Where then shall I be when I'm no more? Can this be dying? No; I don't want to!' He jumped up, tried to light the candle; and fumbling with trembling hands, he dropped the candle and the candlestick on the floor and fell back again on the pillow. 'Why trouble? it doesn't matter,' he said to himself, staring with open eyes into the darkness. 'Death. Yes, death. And they – all of them – don't understand, and don't want to understand, and feel no pity. They are playing.' (He caught through the closed doors the faraway cadence of a voice and the accompaniment.) 'They don't care, but they will die too. Fools! Me sooner and them later; but it will be the same for them. And they are merry. The beasts!' Anger stifled him. And he was agonisingly, insufferably miserable. 'It cannot be that all men always have been doomed to this awful horror!' He raised himself.

'There is something wrong in it; I must be calm, I must think it all over from the beginning.' And then he began to consider. 'Yes, the beginning of my illness. I knocked my side, and I was just the same, that day and the days after; it ached a little, then more, then doctors, then depression, misery, and again doctors; and I've gone on getting closer and closer to the abyss. Strength growing less. Nearer and nearer. And here I am, wasting away, no light in my eyes. I think of how to cure the appendix, but this is death. Can it be death?' Again a horror came over him; gasping for breath, he bent over, began feeling for the matches, and knocked his elbow against the bedside table. It was in his way and hurt him; he felt furious with it, in his anger knocked against it more violently, and upset it. And in despair, breathless, he fell back on his spine waiting for death to come that instant.

The visitors were leaving at that time. Praskovya Fyodorovna was seeing them out. She heard something fall, and came in.

'What is it?'

'Nothing. I dropped something by accident.'

She went out, brought a candle. He was lying, breathing hard and fast, like a man who has run a mile, and staring with fixed eyes at her.

'What is it, Jean?'

'No–othing, I say. I dropped something.' – 'Why speak? She won't understand,' he thought.

She certainly did not understand. She picked up the candle, lighted it for him, and went out hastily. She had to say goodbye to a departing guest. When she came back, he was lying in the same position on his back, looking upwards.

'How are you – worse?'

'Yes.'

She shook her head, sat down.

'Do you know what, Jean? I wonder if we hadn't better send for Leshtchetitsky to see you here?'

This meant calling in the celebrated doctor, regardless of expense. He smiled malignantly, and said no. She sat a moment longer, went up to him, and kissed him on the forehead.

He hated her with all the force of his soul when she was kissing him, and had to make an effort not to push her away.

'Good-night. Please God, you'll sleep.'

'Yes.'

6

Ivan Ilyich saw that he was dying, and was in continual despair.

At the bottom of his heart Ivan Ilyich knew that he was dying; but so far from growing used to this idea, he simply did not grasp it – he was utterly unable to grasp it.

The example of the syllogism that he had learned in Kiseveter's logic – Caius is a man, men are mortal, therefore Caius is mortal – had seemed to him all his life correct only as regards Caius, but not at all as regards himself. In that case it was a question of Caius, a man, an abstract man, and it was perfectly true, but he was not Caius, and was not an abstract man; he had always been a creature quite, quite different from all others; he had been little Vanya with a mamma and papa, and Mitya and Volodya, with playthings and a coachman and a nurse; afterwards with Katenka, with all the joys and griefs and ecstasies of childhood, boyhood, and youth. What did Caius know of the smell of the leathern ball Vanya had been so fond of? Had Caius kissed his mother's hand like that? Caius had not heard the silk rustle of his mother's skirts. He had not made a riot at school over the pudding. Had Caius been in love like that? Could Caius preside over the sittings of the court?

And Caius certainly was mortal, and it was right for him to die; but for me, little Vanya, Ivan Ilyich, with all my feelings and ideas – for me it's a different matter. And it cannot be that I ought to die. That would be too awful.

That was his feeling.

'If I had to die like Caius, I should have known it was so, some inner voice would have told me so. But there was nothing of the sort in me. And I and all my friends, we felt that it was not at all the same as with Caius. And now here it is!' he said to himself. 'It can't be! It can't be, but it is! How is it? How's one to understand it?' And he could not conceive it, and tried to drive away this idea as false, incorrect, and morbid, and to supplant it by other, correct, healthy ideas. But this idea, not as an idea merely, but as it were an actual fact, came back again and stood confronting him.

And to replace this thought he called up other thoughts, one after another, in the hope of finding support in them. He tried to get back into former trains of thought, which in old days had screened off the thought of death. But, strange to say, all that had in old days covered up, obliterated the sense of death, could not now produce the same effect. Latterly, Ivan Ilyich spent the greater part of his time in these efforts to restore his old trains of thought which had shut off death. At one time he would say to himself, 'I'll put myself into my official work; why, I used to live in it.' And he would go to the law-courts, banishing every doubt. He would enter into conversation with his colleagues, and would sit carelessly, as his old habit was, scanning the crowd below dreamily, and with both his wasted hands he would lean on the arms of the oak armchair just as he always did; and bending over to a colleague, pass the papers to him and whisper to him, then suddenly dropping his eyes and sitting up straight, he would pronounce the familiar words that opened the proceedings. But suddenly in the middle, the pain in his side, utterly regardless of the stage he had reached in his conduct of the case, began its work. It riveted Ivan Ilyich's attention. He drove away the thought of it, but it still did its work, and then It came and stood confronting him and looked at him, and he felt turned to stone, and the light died away in his eyes, and he began to ask himself again, 'Can it be that It is the only truth?' And his colleagues and his subordinates saw with surprise and distress that he, the brilliant, subtle judge, was losing the thread of his speech, was making blunders. He shook himself, tried to regain his self-control, and got somehow to the end of the sitting, and went home with the painful sense that his judicial labours could not as of old hide from him what he wanted to hide; that he could not by means of his official work escape from It. And the worst of it was that It drew him to itself not for him to do anything in particular, but simply for him to look at It straight in the face, to look at It and, doing nothing, suffer unspeakably.

And to save himself from this, Ivan Ilyich sought amusements, other screens, and these screens he found, and for a little while they did seem to save him; but soon again they were not so much broken down as let the light through, as though It pierced through everything, and there was nothing that could shut It off.

Sometimes during those days he would go into the drawing-room he had furnished, that drawing-room where he had fallen, for which – how bitterly ludicrous it was for him to think of it! – for the decoration of which he had sacrificed his life, for he knew that it was that bruise that had started his illness. He went in and saw that the polished table had been scratched by something. He looked for the cause, and found it in the bronze clasps of the album, which had been twisted on one side. He took up the album, a costly one, which he had himself arranged with loving care, and was vexed at the carelessness of his daughter and her friends. Here a page was torn, here the photographs had been shifted out of their places. He carefully put it to rights again and bent the clasp back.

Then the idea occurred to him to move all this *établissement* of the albums to another corner where the flowers stood. He called the footman; or his daughter or his wife came to help him. They did not agree with him, contradicted him; he argued, got angry. But all that was very well, since he did not think of It; It was not in sight.

But then his wife would say, as he moved something himself, 'Do let the servants do it, you'll hurt yourself again,' and all at once It peeped through the screen; he caught a glimpse of It. He caught a glimpse of It, but still he hoped It would hide itself. Involuntarily though, he kept watch on his side; there it is just the same still, aching still, and now he cannot forget it, and *It* is staring openly at him from behind the flowers. What's the use of it all?

'And it's the fact that here, at that curtain, as if it had been storming a fort, I lost my life. Is it possible? How awful and how silly! It cannot be! It cannot be, and it is.'

He went into his own room, lay down, and was again alone with It. Face to face with It, and nothing to be done with It. Nothing but to look at It and shiver.

7

How it came to pass during the third month of Ivan Ilyich's illness, it would be impossible to say, for it happened little by little, imperceptibly, but it had come to pass that his wife and his daughter and his son and their servants and their acquaintances, and the doctors, and, most of all, he himself – all were aware that all interest in him for other people consisted now in the question how soon he would leave his place empty, free the living from the constraint of his presence, and be set free himself from his sufferings.

He slept less and less; they gave him opium, and began to inject morphine. But this did not relieve him. The dull pain he experienced in the half-asleep condition at first only relieved him as a change, but then it became as bad, or even more agonising, than the open pain. He had special things to eat prepared for him according to the doctors' prescriptions; but these dishes became more and more distasteful, more and more revolting to him.

Special arrangements, too, had to be made for his other physical needs, and this was a continual misery to him. Misery from the uncleanliness, the unseemliness, and the stench, from the feeling of another person having to assist in it.

But just from this most unpleasant side of his illness there came comfort to Ivan Ilyich. There always came into his room on these occasions to clear up for him the peasant who waited at table, Gerasim.

Gerasim was a clean, fresh, young peasant, who had grown stout and hearty on the good fare in town. Always cheerful and bright. At first the sight of this lad, always cleanly dressed in the Russian style, engaged in this revolting task, embarrassed Ivan Ilyich.

One day, getting up from the night-stool, too weak to replace his clothes, he dropped on to a soft low chair and looked with horror at his bare, powerless thighs, with the muscles so sharply standing out on them.

Then there came in with light, strong steps Gerasim, in his thick boots, diffusing a pleasant smell of tar from his boots, and bringing in the freshness of the winter air. Wearing a clean hempen apron, and a clean cotton shirt, with his sleeves tucked up on his strong, bare young arms, without looking at Ivan Ilyich, obviously trying to check the radiant happiness in his face so as not to hurt the sick man, he went up to the night-stool.

'Gerasim,' said Ivan Ilyich faintly.

Gerasim started, clearly afraid that he had done something amiss, and with a rapid movement turned towards the sick man his fresh, good-natured, simple young face, just beginning to be downy with the first growth of beard.

'Yes, your honour.'

'I'm afraid this is very disagreeable for you. You must excuse me. I can't help it.'

'Why, upon my word, sir!' And Gerasim's eyes beamed, and he showed his white young teeth in a smile. 'What's a little trouble? It's a case of illness with you, sir.'

And with his deft, strong arms he performed his habitual task, and went out, stepping lightly. And five minutes later, treading just as lightly, he came back.

Ivan Ilyich was still sitting in the same way in the armchair.

'Gerasim,' he said, when the latter had replaced the night-stool all sweet and clean, 'please help me; come here.' Gerasim went up to him. 'Lift me up. It's difficult for me alone, and I've sent Dmitry away.'

Gerasim went up to him; as lightly as he stepped he put his strong arms round him, deftly and gently lifted and supported him, with the other hand pulled up his trousers, and would have set him down again. But Ivan Ilyich asked him to carry him to the sofa. Gerasim, without effort, carefully not squeezing him, led him, almost carrying him, to the sofa, and settled him there.

'Thank you; how neatly and well . . . you do everything.'

Gerasim smiled again, and would have gone away. But Ivan Ilyich felt his presence such a comfort that he was reluctant to let him go.

'Oh, move that chair near me, please. No, that one, under my legs. I feel easier when my legs are higher.'

Gerasim picked up the chair, and without letting it knock, set it gently down on the ground just at the right place, and lifted Ivan Ilyich's legs on to it. It seemed to Ivan Ilyich that he was easier just at the moment when Gerasim lifted his legs higher.

'I'm better when my legs are higher,' said Ivan Ilyich. 'Put that cushion under me.'

Gerasim did so. Again he lifted his legs to put the cushion under them. Again it seemed to Ivan Ilyich that he was easier at that moment when Gerasim held his legs raised. When he laid them down again, he felt worse.

'Gerasim,' he said to him, 'are you busy just now?'

'Not at all, sir,' said Gerasim, who had learned among the town-bred servants how to speak to gentlefolks.

'What have you left to do?'

'Why, what have I to do? I've done everything, there's only the wood to chop for tomorrow.'

'Then hold my legs up like that – can you?'

'To be sure, I can.' Gerasim lifted the legs up. And it seemed to Ivan Ilyich that in that position he did not feel the pain at all.

'But how about the wood?'

'Don't you trouble about that, sir. We shall have time enough.'

Ivan Ilyich made Gerasim sit and hold his legs, and began to talk to him. And, strange to say, he fancied he felt better while Gerasim had hold of his legs.

From that time forward Ivan Ilyich would sometimes call Gerasim, and get him to hold his legs on his shoulders, and he liked talking with him. Gerasim did this easily, readily, simply, and with a good-nature that touched Ivan Ilyich. Health, strength, and heartiness in all other people were offensive to Ivan Ilyich; but the strength and heartiness of Gerasim did not mortify him, but soothed him.

Ivan Ilyich's great misery was due to the deception that for some reason or other everyone kept up with him – that he was simply ill, and not dying, and that he need only keep quiet and follow the doctor's orders, and then some great change for the better would be the result. He knew that whatever they might do, there would be no result except more agonising sufferings and death. And he was made miserable by this lie, made miserable at their refusing to acknowledge what they all knew and he knew, by their persisting in lying over him about his awful position, and in forcing him too to take part in this lie. Lying, lying, this lying carried on over him on the eve of his death, and destined to bring that terrible, solemn act of his death down to the level of all their visits, curtains, sturgeons for dinner . . . was a horrible agony for Ivan Ilyich. And, strange to say, many times when they had been going through the regular performance over him, he had been within a hair's breadth of screaming at them: 'Cease your lying! You know, and I know, that I'm dying; so do, at least, give over lying!' But he had never had the spirit to do this. The terrible, awful act of his dying was, he saw, by all those about him, brought down to the level of a casual, unpleasant, and to some extent indecorous, incident (somewhat as they would behave with a person who should enter a drawing-room smelling unpleasant). It was brought down to this level by that very decorum to which he had been enslaved all his life. He saw that no one felt for him, because no one would even grasp his position. Gerasim was the only person who recognised the position, and felt sorry for him. And that was why Ivan Ilyich was only at ease with Gerasim. He felt comforted when Gerasim sometimes supported his legs for whole nights at a stretch, and would not go away to bed, saying, 'Don't you worry yourself, Ivan Ilyich, I'll get sleep enough yet,' or when suddenly dropping into the familiar peasant forms of speech, he added: 'If thou weren't sick, but as 'tis, 'twould be strange if I didn't wait on thee.' Gerasim alone did not lie; everything showed clearly that he alone understood what it meant, and saw no necessity to disguise it, and simply felt sorry for his sick, wasting master. He even said this once straight out, when Ivan Ilyich was sending him away.

'We shall all die. So what's a little trouble?' he said, meaning by this to express that he did not complain of the trouble just because he was taking this trouble for a dying man, and he hoped that for him too someone would be willing to take the same trouble when his time came.

Apart from this deception, or in consequence of it, what made the greatest misery for Ivan Ilyich was that no one felt for him as he would have liked them to feel for him. At certain moments, after prolonged suffering, Ivan Ilyich, ashamed as he would have been to own it, longed more than anything for someone to feel sorry for him, as for a sick child. He longed to be petted, kissed, and wept over, as children are petted and comforted. He knew that he was an important member of the law-courts, that he had a beard turning grey, and that therefore it was impossible. But still he longed for it. And in his relations with Gerasim there was something approaching to that. And that was why being with Gerasim was a comfort to him. Ivan Ilyich longs to weep, longs to be petted and wept over, and then there comes in a colleague, Shebek; and instead of weeping and being petted, Ivan Ilyich puts on his serious, severe, earnest face, and from mere inertia gives his views on the effect of the last decision in the Court of Appeal, and obstinately insists upon them. This falsity around him and within him did more than anything to poison Ivan Ilyich's last days.

8

It was morning. All that made it morning for Ivan Ilyich was that Gerasim had gone away, and Pyotr the footman had come in; he had put out the candles, opened one of the curtains, and begun surreptitiously setting the room to rights. Whether it were morning or evening, Friday or Sunday, it all made no difference; it was always just the same thing. Gnawing, agonising pain never ceasing for an instant; the hopeless sense of life always ebbing away, but still not yet gone; always swooping down on him that fearful, hated death, which was the only reality, and always the same falsity. What were days, or weeks, or hours of the day to him?

'Will you have tea, sir?'

'He wants things done in their regular order. In the morning the family should have tea,' he thought, and only said – 'No.'

'Would you care to move on to the sofa?'

'He wants to make the room tidy, and I'm in his way. I'm uncleanness, disorder,' he thought, and only said – 'No, leave me alone.'

The servant still moved busily about his work. Ivan Ilyich stretched out his hand. Pyotr went up to offer his services.

'What can I get you?'

'My watch.'

Pyotr got out the watch, which lay just under his hand, and gave it him.

'Half-past eight. Are they up?'

'Not yet, sir. Vladimir Ivanovich' (that was his son) 'has gone to the high school, and Praskovya Fyodorovna gave orders that she was to be waked if you asked for her. Shall I send word?'

'No, no need. Should I try some tea?' he thought. 'Yes, tea . . . bring it.'

Pyotr was on his way out. Ivan Ilyich felt frightened of being left alone. How to keep him? Oh, the medicine. 'Pyotr, give me my medicine.' Oh well, maybe, medicine may still be some good. He took the spoon, drank it. 'No, it does no good. It's all rubbish, deception,' he decided, as soon as he tasted the familiar, mawkish, hopeless taste. 'No, I can't believe it now. But the pain, why this pain; if it would only cease for a minute.' And he groaned. Pyotr turned round. 'No, go on. Bring the tea.'

Pyotr went away. Ivan Ilyich, left alone, moaned, not so much from the pain, awful as it was, as from misery. 'Always the same thing again and again, all these endless days and nights. If it would only be quicker. Quicker to what? Death, darkness. No, no. Anything better than death!'

When Pyotr came in with the tea on a tray, Ivan Ilyich stared for some time absent-mindedly at him, not grasping who he was and what he wanted. Pyotr was disconcerted by this stare. And when he showed he was disconcerted, Ivan Ilyich came to himself.

'Oh yes,' he said, 'tea, good, set it down. Only help me to wash and put on a clean shirt.'

And Ivan Ilyich began his washing. He washed his hands slowly, and then his face, cleaned his teeth, combed his hair, and looked in the looking-glass. He felt frightened at what he saw, especially at the way his hair clung limply to his pale forehead. When his shirt was being changed, he knew he would be still more terrified if he glanced at his body, and he avoided looking at himself. But at last it was all over. He put on his dressing-gown, covered himself with a rug, and sat in the armchair to drink his tea. For one moment he felt refreshed; but as soon as he began to drink the tea, again there was the same taste, the same pain. He forced himself to finish it, and lay down, stretching out his legs. He lay down and dismissed Pyotr.

Always the same. A gleam of hope flashes for a moment, then again the sea of despair roars about him again, and always pain, always pain, always heartache, and always the same thing. Alone it is awfully dreary; he longs to call someone, but he knows beforehand that with others present it will be worse. 'Morphine again – only to forget again. I'll tell him, the doctor, that he must think of something else. It can't go on; it can't go on like this.'

One hour, two hours pass like this. Then there is a ring at the front door. The doctor, perhaps. Yes, it is the doctor, fresh, hearty, fat, and cheerful, wearing that expression that seems to say, 'You there are in a panic about something, but we'll soon set things right for you.' The doctor is aware that this expression is hardly fitting here, but he has put it on once and for all, and can't take it off, like a man who has put on a frockcoat to pay a round of calls.

In a hearty, reassuring manner the doctor rubs his hands.

'I'm cold. It's a sharp frost. Just let me warm myself,' he says with an expression, as though it's only a matter of waiting a little till he's warm, and as soon as he's warm he'll set everything to rights.

'Well, now, how are you?'

Ivan Ilyich feels that the doctor would like to say, 'How's the little trouble?' but that he feels that he can't talk like that, and says, 'How did you pass the night?'

Ivan Ilyich looks at the doctor with an expression that asks – 'Is it possible you're never ashamed of lying?'

But the doctor does not care to understand this look.

And Ivan Ilyich says – 'It's always just as awful. The pain never leaves me, never ceases. If only there were something!'

'Ah, you're all like that, all sick people say that. Come, now I do believe I'm thawed; even Praskovya Fyodorovna, who's so particular, could find no fault with my temperature. Well, now I can say good-morning.' And the doctor shakes hands.

And dropping his former levity, the doctor, with a serious face, proceeds to examine the patient, feeling his pulse, to take his temperature, and then the tappings and soundings begin.

Ivan Ilyich knows positively and indubitably that it's all nonsense and empty deception; but when the doctor, kneeling down, stretches over him, putting his ear first higher, then lower, and goes through various gymnastic evolutions over him with a serious face, Ivan Ilyich is affected by this, as he used sometimes to be affected by the speeches of the lawyers in court, though he was perfectly well aware that they were telling lies all the while and why they were telling lies.

The doctor, kneeling on the sofa, was still sounding him, when there was the rustle of Praskovya Fyodorovna's silk dress in the doorway, and she was heard scolding Pyotr for not having let her know that the doctor had come.

She comes in, kisses her husband, and at once begins to explain that she has been up a long while, and that it was only through a misunderstanding that she was not there when the doctor came.

Ivan Ilyich looks at her, scans her all over, and sets down against her her whiteness and plumpness, and the cleanness of her hands and neck, and the glossiness of her hair, and the gleam full of life in her eyes. With all the force of his soul he hates her. And when she touches him it makes him suffer from the thrill of hatred he feels for her.

Her attitude to him and his illness is still the same. Just as the doctor had taken up a certain line with the patient which he was not now able to drop, so she too had taken up a line with him – that he was not doing something he ought to do, and was himself to blame, and she was lovingly reproaching him for his neglect, and she could not now get out of this attitude.

'Why, you know, he won't listen to me; he doesn't take his medicine at the right times. And what's worse still, he insists on lying in a position that surely must be bad for him – with his legs in the air.'

She described how he made Gerasim hold his legs up.

The doctor smiled with kindly condescension that said, 'Oh well, it can't be helped, these sick people do take up such foolish fancies; but we must forgive them.'

When the examination was over, the doctor looked at his watch, and then Praskovya Fyodorovna informed Ivan Ilyich that it must of course be as he liked, but she had sent today for a celebrated doctor, and that he would examine him, and have a consultation with Mihail Danilovich (that was the name of their regular doctor).

'Don't oppose it now, please. This I'm doing entirely for my own sake,' she said ironically, meaning it to be understood that she was doing it all for his sake, and was only saying this to give him no right to refuse her request. He lay silent, knitting his brows. He felt that he was hemmed in by such a tangle of falsity that it was hard to disentangle anything from it.

Everything she did for him was entirely for her own sake, and she told him she was doing for her own sake what she actually was doing for her own sake as something so incredible that he would take it as meaning the opposite.

At half-past eleven the celebrated doctor came. Again came the sounding, and then grave conversation in his presence and in the other room about the kidney and the appendix, and questions and answers, with such an air of significance, that again, instead of the real question of life and death, which was now the only one that confronted him, the question that came uppermost was of the kidney and the appendix, which were doing something not as they ought to do, and were for that reason being attacked by Mihail Danilovich and the celebrated doctor, and forced to mend their ways.

The celebrated doctor took leave of him with a serious, but not a hopeless face. And to the timid question that Ivan Ilyich addressed to him while he lifted his eyes, shining with terror and hope, up towards him, Was there a chance of recovery? he answered that he could not answer for it, but that there was a chance. The look of hope with which Ivan Ilyich watched the doctor out was so piteous that, seeing it, Praskovya Fyodorovna positively burst into tears, as she went out of the door to hand the celebrated doctor his fee in the next room.

The gleam of hope kindled by the doctor's assurance did not last long. Again the same room, the same pictures, the curtains, the wallpaper, the medicine-bottles, and ever the same, his aching suffering body. And Ivan Ilyich began to moan; they gave him injections, and he sank into oblivion. When he waked up it was getting dark; they brought him his dinner. He forced himself to eat some broth; and again everything the same, and again the coming night.

After dinner at seven o'clock, Praskovya Fyodorovna came into his room, dressed as though to go to a *soirée*, with her full bosom laced in tight, and traces of powder on her face. She had in the morning mentioned to him that they were going to the theatre. Sarah Bernhardt was visiting the town, and they had a box, which he had insisted on their taking. By now he had forgotten about it, and her smart attire was an offence to him. But he concealed this feeling when he recollected that he had himself insisted on their taking a box and going, because it was an aesthetic pleasure, beneficial and instructive for the children.

Praskovya Fyodorovna came in satisfied with herself, but yet with something of a guilty air. She sat down, asked how he was, as he saw, simply for the sake of asking, and not for the sake of learning anything, knowing indeed that there was nothing to learn, and began telling him how absolutely necessary it was; how she would not have gone for anything, but the box had been taken, and Ellen, their daughter, and Petrishtchev (the examining lawyer, the daughter's suitor) were going, and that it was out of the question to let them go alone. But that she would have liked much better to stay with him. If only he would be sure to follow the doctor's prescription while she was away.

'Oh, and Fyodor Dmitryevich' (the suitor) 'would like to come in. May he? And Liza?'

'Yes, let them come in.'

The daughter came in, in full dress, her fresh young body bare, while his body made him suffer so. But she made a show of it; she was strong, healthy, obviously in love, and impatient of the illness, suffering, and death that hindered her happiness.

Fyodor Dmitryevich came in too in evening dress, his hair curled *à la Capoul*,[18] with his long sinewy neck tightly fenced round by a white collar, with his vast expanse of white chest and strong thighs displayed in narrow black trousers, with one white glove in his hand and a crush opera hat.

Behind him crept in unnoticed the little high-school boy in his new uniform, poor fellow, in gloves, and with that awful blue ring under his eyes that Ivan Ilyich knew the meaning of.

He always felt sorry for his son. And pitiable indeed was his scared face of sympathetic suffering. Except Gerasim, Ivan Ilyich fancied that Volodya was the only one that understood and was sorry.

They all sat down; again they asked how he was. A silence followed. Liza asked her mother about the opera-glass. An altercation ensued between the mother and daughter as to who had taken it, and where it had been put. It turned into an unpleasant squabble.

Fyodor Dmitryevich asked Ivan Ilyich whether he had seen Sarah Bernhardt?[19] Ivan Ilyich could not at first catch the question that was asked him, but then he said, 'No, have you seen her before?'

'Yes, in *Adrienne Lecouvreur*.'[20]

Praskovya Fyodorovna observed that she was particularly good in that part. The daughter made some reply. A conversation sprang up about the art and naturalness of her acting, that conversation that is continually repeated and always the same.

In the middle of the conversation Fyodor Dmitryevich glanced at Ivan Ilyich and relapsed into silence. The others looked at him and became mute too. Ivan Ilyich was staring with glittering eyes straight before him, obviously furious with them. This had to be set right, but it could not anyhow be set right. This silence had somehow to be broken. No one would venture on breaking it, and all began to feel alarmed that the decorous deception was somehow breaking down, and the facts would be exposed to all. Liza was the first to pluck up courage. She broke the silence. She tried to cover up what they were all feeling, but inadvertently she gave it utterance.

'*If we are going*, though, it's time to start,' she said, glancing at her watch, a gift from her father; and with a scarcely perceptible meaning smile to the young man, referring to something only known to themselves, she got up with a rustle of her skirts.

They all got up, said goodbye, and went away. When they were gone, Ivan Ilyich fancied he was easier; there was no falsity – that had gone away with them, but the pain remained. That continual pain, that continual terror, made nothing harder, nothing easier. It was always worse.

Again came minute after minute, hour after hour, still the same and still no end, and ever more terrible the inevitable end.

'Yes, send Gerasim,' he said in answer to Pyotr's question.

9

Late at night his wife came back. She came in on tiptoe, but he heard her, opened his eyes, and made haste to close them again. She wanted to send away Gerasim and sit up with him herself instead. He opened his eyes and said, 'No, go away.'

'Are you in great pain?'

'Always the same.'

'Take some opium.'

He agreed, and drank it. She went away.

Till three o'clock he slept a miserable sleep. It seemed to him that he and his pain were being thrust somewhere into a narrow, deep, black sack, and they kept pushing him further and further in, and still could not thrust him to the bottom. And this operation was awful to him, and was accompanied with agony. And he was afraid, and yet wanted to fall into it, and struggled and yet tried to get into it. And all of a sudden he slipped and fell and woke up. Gerasim, still the same, is sitting at the foot of the bed half-dozing peacefully, patient. And he is lying with his wasted legs clad in stockings, raised on Gerasim's shoulders, the same candle burning in the alcove, and the same interminable pain.

'Go away, Gerasim,' he whispered.

'It's all right, sir. I'll stay a bit longer.'

'No, go away.'

He took his legs down, lay sideways on his arm, and he felt very sorry for himself. He only waited till Gerasim had gone away into the next room; he could restrain himself no longer, and cried like a child. He cried at his own helplessness, at his awful loneliness, at the cruelty of people, at the cruelty of God, at the absence of God.

'Why hast Thou done all this? What brought me to this? Why, why torture me so horribly?'

He did not expect an answer, and wept indeed that there was and could be no answer. The pain grew more acute again, but he did not stir, did not call.

He said to himself, 'Come, more then; come, strike me! But what for? What have I done to Thee? what for?'

Then he was still, ceased weeping, held his breath, and was all attention; he listened, as it were, not to a voice uttering sounds, but to the voice of his soul, to the current of thoughts that rose up within him.

'What is it you want?' was the first clear idea able to be put into words that he grasped.

'What? Not to suffer, to live,' he answered.

And again he was utterly plunged into attention so intense that even the pain did not distract him.

'To live? Live how?' the voice of his soul was asking.

'Why, live as I used to live before – happily and pleasantly.'

'As you used to live before – happily and pleasantly?' queried the voice. And he began going over in his imagination the best moments of his pleasant life. But, strange to say, all these best moments of his pleasant life seemed now not at all what they had seemed then. All – except the first memories of childhood – there, in his childhood there had been something really pleasant in which one could have lived if it had come back. But the creature who had this pleasant experience was no more; it was like a memory of someone else.

As soon as he reached the beginning of what had resulted in him as he was now, Ivan Ilyich, all that had seemed joys to him then now melted away before his eyes and were transformed into something trivial, and often disgusting.

And the further he went from childhood, the nearer to the actual present, the more worthless and uncertain were the joys. It began with life at the school of jurisprudence. Then there had still been something genuinely good; then there had been gaiety; then there had been friendship; then there had been hopes. But in the higher classes these good moments were already becoming rarer. Later on, during the first period of his official life, at the governor's, good moments appeared; but it was all mixed, and less and less of it was good. And further on even less was good, and the further he went the less good there was.

His marriage . . . as gratuitous as the disillusion of it and the smell of his wife's breath and the sensuality, the hypocrisy! And that deadly official life, and anxiety about money, and so for one year, and two, and ten, and twenty, and always the same thing. And the further he went, the more deadly it became. 'As though I had been going steadily downhill, imagining that I was going uphill. So it was in fact. In public opinion I was going uphill, and steadily as I got up it life was ebbing away from me . . . And now the work's done, there's only to die.'

'But what is this? What for? It cannot be! It cannot be that life has been so senseless, so loathsome? And if it really was so loathsome and senseless, then why die, and die in agony? There's something wrong.'

'Can it be I have not lived as one ought?' suddenly came into his head. 'But how not so, when I've done everything as it should be done?' he said, and at once dismissed this only solution of all the enigma of life and death as something utterly out of the question.

'What do you want now? To live? Live how? Live as you live at the courts when the usher booms out: "The judge is coming!" . . . The judge is coming, the judge is coming,' he repeated to himself. 'Here he is, the judge! But I'm not to blame!' he shrieked in fury. 'What's it for?' And he left off crying, and turning with his face to the wall, fell to pondering always on the same question, 'What for, why all this horror?'

But however much he pondered, he could not find an answer. And whenever the idea struck him, as it often did, that it all came of his never having lived as he ought, he thought of all the correctness of his life and dismissed this strange idea.

10

Another fortnight had passed. Ivan Ilyich could not now get up from the sofa. He did not like lying in bed, and lay on the sofa. And lying almost all the time facing the wall, in loneliness he suffered all the inexplicable agonies, and in loneliness pondered always that inexplicable question, What is it? Can it be true that it's death? And an inner voice answered, 'Yes, it is true.' 'Why these agonies?' and a voice answered, 'For no reason.' Beyond and besides this there was nothing.

From the very beginning of his illness, ever since Ivan Ilyich first went to the doctor's, his life had been split up into two contradictory moods, which were continually alternating – one was despair and the anticipation of an uncomprehended and awful death; the other was hope and an absorbed watching over the actual condition of his body. First there was nothing confronting him but a kidney or intestine which had temporarily declined to perform their duties, then there was nothing but unknown awful death, which there was no escaping.

These two moods had alternated from the very beginning of the illness; but the further the illness progressed, the more doubtful and fantastic became the conception of the kidney, and the more real the sense of approaching death.

He had but to reflect on what he had been three months before and what he was now, to reflect how steadily he had been going downhill, for every possibility of hope to be shattered.

Of late, in the loneliness in which he found himself, lying with his face to the back of the sofa, a loneliness in the middle of a populous town and of his numerous acquaintances and his family, a loneliness than which none more complete could be found anywhere – not at the bottom of the sea, not deep down in the earth; – of late in this fearful loneliness Ivan Ilyich had lived only in imagination in the past. One by one the pictures of his past rose up before him. It always began from what was nearest in time and went back to the most remote, to childhood, and rested there. If Ivan Ilyich thought of the stewed prunes that had been offered him for dinner that day, his mind went back to the damp, wrinkled French plum of his childhood, of its peculiar taste and the flow of saliva when the stone was sucked; and along with this memory of a taste there rose up a whole series of memories of that period – his nurse, his brother, his playthings. 'I mustn't . . . it's too painful,' Ivan Ilyich said to himself, and he brought himself back to the present. The button on the back of the sofa and the creases in the morocco. 'Morocco's dear, and doesn't wear well; there was a quarrel over it. But the morocco was different, and different too the quarrel when we tore father's portfolio and were punished, and mamma bought us the tarts.' And again his mind rested on his childhood, and again it was painful, and he tried to drive it away and think of something else.

And again at that point, together with that chain of associations, quite another chain of memories came into his heart, of how his illness had grown up and become more acute. It was the same there, the further back the more life there had been. There had been both more that was good in life and more of life itself. And the two began to melt into one. 'Just as the pain goes on getting worse and worse, so has my whole life gone on getting worse and worse,' he thought. One light spot was there at the back, at the beginning of life, and then it kept getting blacker and blacker, and going faster and faster. 'In inverse ratio to the square of the distance from death,' thought Ivan Ilyich. And the image of a stone falling downwards with increasing velocity sank into his soul. Life, a series of increasing sufferings, falls more and more swiftly to the end, the most fearful sufferings. 'I am falling.' He shuddered, shifted himself, would have resisted, but he knew beforehand that he could not resist; and again, with eyes weary with gazing at it, but unable not to gaze at what was before him, he stared at the back of the sofa and waited, waited expecting that fearful fall and shock and dissolution. 'Resistance is impossible,' he said to himself. 'But if one could at least comprehend what it's for? Even that's impossible. It could be explained if one were to say that I hadn't lived as I ought. But that can't be alleged,' he said to himself, thinking of all the regularity, correctness, and propriety of his life. 'That really can't be admitted,' he said to himself, his lips smiling ironically as though someone could see his smile and be deceived by it. 'No explanation! Agony, death . . . What for?'

II

So passed a fortnight. During that fortnight an event occurred that had been desired by Ivan Ilyich and his wife. Petrishtchev made a formal proposal. This took place in the evening. Next day Praskovya Fyodorovna went in to her husband, revolving in her mind how to inform him of Fyodor Dmitryevich's proposal, but that night there had been a change for the worse in Ivan Ilyich. Praskovya Fyodorovna found him on the same sofa, but in a different position. He was lying on his face, groaning, and staring straight before him with a fixed gaze.

She began talking of remedies. He turned his stare on her. She did not finish what she had begun saying; such hatred of her in particular was expressed in that stare.

'For Christ's sake, let me die in peace,' he said.

She would have gone away, but at that moment the daughter came in and went up to say good-morning to him. He looked at his daughter just as at his wife, and to her enquiries how he was, he told her drily that they would soon all be rid of him. Both were silent, sat a little while, and went out.

'How are we to blame?' said Liza to her mother. 'As though we had done it! I'm sorry for papa, but why punish us?'

At the usual hour the doctor came. Ivan Ilyich answered, 'Yes, no,' never taking his exasperated stare from him, and towards the end he said, 'Why, you know that you can do nothing, so let me be.'

'We can relieve your suffering,' said the doctor.

'Even that you can't do; let me be.'

The doctor went into the drawing-room and told Praskovya Fyodorovna that it was very serious, and that the only resource left them was opium to relieve his sufferings, which must be terrible. The doctor said his physical sufferings were terrible, and that was true; but even more terrible than his physical sufferings were his mental sufferings, and in that lay his chief misery.

His moral sufferings were due to the fact that during that night, as he looked at the sleepy, good-natured, broad-cheeked face of Gerasim, the thought had suddenly come into his head, 'What if in reality all my life, my conscious life, has been not the right thing?' The thought struck him that what he had regarded before as an utter impossibility, that he had spent his life not as he ought, might be the truth. It struck him that those scarcely detected impulses of struggle within him against what was considered good by persons of higher position, scarcely detected impulses which he had dismissed, that they might be the real thing, and everything else might be not the right thing. And his official work, and his ordering of his daily life and of his family, and these social and official interests, – all that might be not the right thing. He tried to defend it all to himself. And suddenly he felt all the weakness of what he was defending. And it was useless to defend it.

'But if it's so,' he said to himself, 'and I am leaving life with the consciousness that I have lost all that was given me, and there's no correcting it, then what?' He lay on his back and began going over his whole life entirely anew. When he saw the footman in the morning, then his wife, then his daughter, then the doctor, every movement they made, every word they uttered, confirmed for him the terrible truth that had been revealed to him in the night. In them he saw himself, saw all in which he had lived, and saw distinctly that it was all not the right thing; it was a horrible, vast deception that concealed both life and death. This consciousness intensified his physical agonies, multiplied them tenfold. He groaned and tossed from side to side and pulled at the covering over him. It seemed to him that it was stifling him and weighing him down. And for that he hated them.

They gave him a big dose of opium; he sank into unconsciousness; but at dinner-time the same thing began again. He drove them all away, and tossed from side to side.

His wife came to him and said, 'Jean, darling, do this for my sake' (for my sake?). 'It can't do harm, and it often does good. Why, it's nothing. And often in health people – '

He opened his eyes wide.

'What? Take the sacrament? What for? No. Besides . . . '

She began to cry.

'Yes, my dear? I'll send for our priest, he's so nice.'

'All right, very well,' he said.

When the priest came and confessed him he was softened, felt as it were a relief from his doubts, and consequently from his sufferings, and there came a moment of hope. He began once more thinking of the intestinal appendix and the possibility of curing it. He took the sacrament with tears in his eyes.

When they laid him down again after the sacrament for a minute, he felt comfortable, and again the hope of life sprang up. He began to think about the operation which had been suggested to him. 'To live, I want to live,' he said to himself. His wife came in to congratulate him; she uttered the customary words and added – 'It's quite true, isn't it, that you're better?'

Without looking at her, he said, 'Yes.'

Her dress, her figure, the expression of her face, the tone of her voice, – all told him the same: 'Not the right thing. All that in which you lived and are living is lying, deceit, hiding life and death away from you.' And as soon as he had formed that thought, hatred sprang up in him, and with that hatred agonising physical sufferings, and with these sufferings the sense of inevitable, approaching ruin. Something new was happening; there were screwing and shooting pains, and a tightness in his breathing.

The expression of his face as he uttered that 'Yes' was terrible. After uttering that 'Yes,' looking her straight in the face, he turned on to his face, with a rapidity extraordinary in his weakness, and shrieked – 'Go away, go away, let me be!'

12

From that moment there began the scream that never ceased for three days, and was so awful that through two closed doors one could not hear it without horror. At the moment when he answered his wife he grasped that he had fallen, that there was no return, that the end had come, quite the end, while doubt was still as unsolved, still remained doubt.

'Oo! Oo–o! Oo!' he screamed in varying intonations. He had

begun screaming, 'I don't want to!' and so had gone on screaming on the same vowel sound – oo!

All those three days, during which time did not exist for him, he was struggling in that black sack into which he was being thrust by an unseen resistless force. He struggled as the man condemned to death struggles in the hands of the executioner, knowing that he cannot save himself. And every moment he felt that in spite of all his efforts to struggle against it, he was getting nearer and nearer to what terrified him. He felt that his agony was due both to his being thrust into this black hole and still more to his not being able to get right into it. What hindered him from getting into it was the claim that his life had been good. That justification of his life held him fast and would not let him get forward, and it caused him more agony than all.

All at once some force struck him in the chest, in the side, and stifled his breathing more than ever; he rolled forward into the hole, and there at the end there was some sort of light. It had happened with him, as it had sometimes happened to him in a railway carriage, when he had thought he was going forward while he was going back, and all of a sudden recognised his real direction.

'Yes, it has all been not the right thing,' he said to himself, 'but that's no matter.' He could, he could do the right thing. 'What is the right thing?' he asked himself, and suddenly he became quiet.

This was at the end of the third day, two hours before his death. At that very moment the schoolboy had stealthily crept into his father's room and gone up to his bedside. The dying man was screaming and waving his arms. His hand fell on the schoolboy's head. The boy snatched it, pressed it to his lips, and burst into tears.

At that very moment Ivan Ilyich had rolled into the hole, and caught sight of the light, and it was revealed to him that his life had not been what it ought to have been, but that that could still be set right. He asked himself, 'What is the right thing?' – and became quiet, listening. Then he felt someone was kissing his hand. He opened his eyes and glanced at his son. He felt sorry for him. His wife went up to him. He glanced at her. She was gazing at him with open mouth, the tears unwiped streaming over her nose and cheeks, a look of despair on her face. He felt sorry for her.

'Yes, I'm making them miserable,' he thought. 'They're sorry, but it will be better for them when I die.' He would have said this, but had not the strength to utter it. 'Besides, why speak? I must act,' he thought. With a glance to his wife he pointed to his son and said – 'Take away . . . sorry for him . . . And you too . . . ' He tried to say 'forgive', but said 'forgo' . . . and too weak to correct himself, shook his hand, knowing that He would understand whose understanding mattered.

And all at once it became clear to him that what had tortured him and would not leave him was suddenly dropping away all at once on both sides and on ten sides and on all sides. He was sorry for them, must act so that they might not suffer. Set them free and be free himself of those agonies. 'How right and how simple!' he thought. 'And the pain?' he asked himself. 'Where's it gone? Eh, where are you, pain?'

He began to watch for it.

'Yes, here it is. Well what of it, let the pain be.'

'And death. Where is it?'

He looked for his old accustomed terror of death, and did not find it. 'Where is it? What death?' There was no terror, because death was not either.

In the place of death there was light.

'So this is it!' he suddenly exclaimed aloud. 'What joy!'

To him all this passed in a single instant, and the meaning of that instant suffered no change after. For those present his agony lasted another two hours. There was a rattle in his throat, a twitching in his wasted body. Then the rattle and the gasping came at longer and longer intervals.

'It is over!' someone said over him.

He caught those words and repeated them in his soul.

'Death is over,' he said to himself. 'It's no more.'

He drew in a breath, stopped midway in the breath, stretched and died.

THE KREUTZER SONATA

But I say unto you, that everyone that looketh on a woman to lust after her hath committed adultery with her already in his heart.

Matthew 5:28

The disciples say unto him, If the case of the man is so with his wife, it is not expedient to marry. But he said unto them, All men cannot receive this saying, but they to whom it is given.

Ibid. 19:10–11

I

IT WAS EARLY SPRING, and the second day of our journey. Passengers going short distances entered and left our carriage, but three others, like myself, had come all the way with the train. One was a lady, plain and no longer young, who smoked, had a harassed look, and wore a mannish coat and cap; another was an acquaintance of hers, a talkative man of about forty, whose things looked neat and new; the third was a rather short man who kept himself apart. He was not old, but his curly hair had gone prematurely grey. His movements were abrupt and his unusually glittering eyes moved rapidly from one object to another. He wore an old overcoat, evidently from a first-rate tailor, with an astrakhan collar, and a tall astrakhan cap. When he unbuttoned his overcoat a sleeveless Russian coat and embroidered shirt showed beneath it. A peculiarity of this man was a strange sound he emitted, something like a clearing of his throat, or a laugh begun and sharply broken off.

All the way this man had carefully avoided making acquaintance or having any intercourse with his fellow passengers. When spoken to by those near him he gave short and abrupt answers, and at other times read, looked out of the window, smoked, or drank tea and ate something he took out of an old bag.

It seemed to me that his loneliness depressed him, and I made several attempts to converse with him, but whenever our eyes met, which happened often as he sat nearly opposite me, he turned away and took up his book or looked out of the window.

Towards the second evening, when our train stopped at a large station, this nervous man fetched himself some boiling water and made tea. The man with the neat new things – a lawyer as I found out later – and his neighbour, the smoking lady with the mannish coat, went to the refreshment-room to drink tea.

During their absence several new passengers entered the carriage, among them a tall, shaven, wrinkled old man, evidently a trades-man, in a coat lined with skunk fur, and a cloth cap with an enormous peak. The tradesman sat down opposite the seats of the lady and the lawyer, and immediately started a conversation with a young man who had also entered at that station and, judging by his appearance, was a tradesman's clerk.

I was sitting the other side of the gangway and as the train was standing still I could hear snatches of their conversation when nobody was passing between us. The tradesman began by saying that he was going to his estate which was only one station farther on; then as usual the conversation turned to prices and trade, and they spoke of the state of business in Moscow and then of the Nízhni-Nóvgorod Fair. The clerk began to relate how a wealthy merchant, known to both of them, had gone on the spree at the fair, but the old man interrupted him by telling of the orgies he had been at in former times at Kunávin Fair. He evidently prided himself on the part he had played in them, and recounted with pleasure how he and some acquaintances, together with the merchant they had been speaking of, had once got drunk at Kunávin and played such a trick that he had to tell of it in a whisper. The clerk's roar of laughter filled the whole carriage; the old man laughed also, exposing two yellow teeth.

Not expecting to hear anything interesting, I got up to stroll about the platform till the train should start. At the carriage door I met the lawyer and the lady who were talking with animation as they approached.

'You won't have time,' said the sociable lawyer, 'the second bell[21] will ring in a moment.'

And the bell did ring before I had gone the length of the train. When I returned, the animated conversation between the lady and the lawyer was proceeding. The old tradesman sat silent opposite to them, looking sternly before him, and occasionally mumbled disapprovingly as if chewing something.

'Then she plainly informed her husband,' the lawyer was smilingly saying as I passed him, 'that she was not able, and did not wish, to live with him since . . .'

He went on to say something I could not hear. Several other passengers came in after me. The guard passed, a porter hurried in, and for some time the noise made their voices inaudible. When all was quiet again the conversation had evidently turned from the particular case to general considerations.

The lawyer was saying that public opinion in Europe was occupied with the question of divorce, and that cases of 'that kind' were occurring more and more often in Russia. Noticing that his was the only voice audible, he stopped his discourse and turned to the old man.

'Those things did not happen in the old days, did they?' he said, smiling pleasantly.

The old man was about to reply, but the train moved and he took off his cap, crossed himself, and whispered a prayer. The lawyer turned away his eyes and waited politely. Having finished his prayer and crossed himself three times the old man set his cap straight, pulled it well down over his forehead, changed his position, and began to speak.

'They used to happen even then, sir, but less often,' he said. 'As times are now they can't help happening. People have got too educated.'

The train moved faster and faster and jolted over the joints of the rails, making it difficult to hear, but being interested I moved nearer. The nervous man with the glittering eyes opposite me, evidently also interested, listened without changing his place.

'What is wrong with education?' said the lady, with a scarcely perceptible smile. 'Surely it can't be better to marry as they used to in the old days when the bride and bridegroom did not even see one another before the wedding,' she continued, answering not what her interlocutor had said but what she thought he would say, in the way many ladies have. 'Without knowing whether they loved, or whether they could love, they married just anybody, and were wretched all their lives. And you think that was better?' she said, evidently addressing me and the lawyer chiefly and least of all the old man with whom she was talking.

'They've got so very educated,' the tradesman reiterated, looking contemptuously at the lady and leaving her question unanswered.

'It would be interesting to know how you explain the connection between education and matrimonial discord,' said the lawyer, with a scarcely perceptible smile.

The tradesman was about to speak, but the lady interrupted him.

'No,' she said, 'those times have passed.' But the lawyer stopped her.

'Yes, but allow the gentleman to express his views.'

'Foolishness comes from education,' the old man said categorically.

'They make people who don't love one another marry, and then wonder that they live in discord,' the lady hastened to say, turning to look at the lawyer, at me, and even at the clerk, who had got up and, leaning on the back of the seat, was smilingly listening to the conversation. 'It's only animals, you know, that can be paired off as their master likes; but human beings have their own inclinations and attachments,' said the lady, with an evident desire to annoy the tradesman.

'You should not talk like that, madam,' said the old man, 'animals are cattle, but human beings have a law given them.'

'Yes, but how is one to live with a man when there is no love?' the lady again hastened to express her argument, which probably seemed very new to her.

'They used not to go into that,' said the old man in an impressive tone, 'it is only now that all this has sprung up. The least thing makes them say: "I will leave you!" The fashion has spread even to the peasants. "Here you are!" she says, "Here, take your shirts and trousers and I will go with Vánka; his head is curlier than yours." What can you say? The first thing that should be required of a woman is fear!'

The clerk glanced at the lawyer, at the lady, and at me, apparently suppressing a smile and prepared to ridicule or to approve of the tradesman's words according to the reception they met with.

'Fear of what?' asked the lady.

'Why this: Let her fear her husband! That fear!'

'Oh, the time for that, sir, has passed,' said the lady with a certain viciousness.

'No, madam, that time cannot pass. As she, Eve, was made from the rib of a man, so it will remain to the end of time,' said the old man, jerking his head with such sternness and such a victorious look that the clerk at once concluded that victory was on his side, and laughed loudly.

'Ah yes, that's the way you men argue,' said the lady unyieldingly, and turned to us. 'You have given yourselves freedom but want to shut women up in a tower.[22] You no doubt permit yourselves everything.'

'No one is permitting anything, but a man does not bring offspring into the home; while a woman – a wife – is a leaky vessel,' the tradesman continued insistently. His tone was so impressive that it evidently vanquished his hearers, and even the lady felt crushed but still did not give in.

'Yes, but I think you will agree that a woman is a human being and has feelings as a man has. What is she to do then, if she does not love her husband?'

'Does not love!' said the tradesman severely, moving his brows and lips. 'She'll love, no fear!' This unexpected argument particularly pleased the clerk, and he emitted a sound of approval.

'Oh, no, she won't!' the lady began, 'and when there is no love you can't enforce it.'

'Well, and supposing the wife is unfaithful, what then?' asked the lawyer.

'That is not admissible,' said the old man. 'One has to see to that.'

'But if it happens, what then? You know it does occur.'

'It happens among some, but not among us,' said the old man.

All were silent. The clerk moved, came still nearer, and, evidently unwilling to be behindhand, began with a smile.

'Yes, a young fellow of ours had a scandal. It was a difficult case to deal with. It too was a case of a woman who was a bad lot. She began to play the devil, and the young fellow is respectable and cultured. At first it was with one of the office-clerks. The husband tried to persuade her with kindness. She would not stop, but played all sorts of dirty tricks. Then she began to steal his money. He beat her, but she only grew worse. Carried on intrigues, if I may mention it, with an unchristened Jew. What was he to do? He turned her out altogether and lives as a bachelor, while she gads about.'

'Because he is a fool,' said the old man. 'If he'd pulled her up properly from the first and not let her have her way, she'd be living with him, no fear! It's giving way at first that counts. Don't trust your horse in the field, or your wife in the house.'

At that moment the guard entered to collect the tickets for the next station. The old man gave up his.

'Yes, the female sex must be curbed in time or else all is lost!'

'Yes, but you yourself just now were speaking about the way married men amuse themselves at the Kunávin fair,' I could not help saying.

'That's a different matter,' said the old man and relapsed into silence.

When the whistle sounded the tradesman rose, got out his bag from under the seat, buttoned up his coat, and slightly lifting his cap went out of the carriage.

2

As soon as the old man had gone several voices were raised.

'A daddy of the old style!' remarked the clerk.

'A living Domostróy!'[23] said the lady. 'What barbarous views of women and marriage!'

'Yes, we are far from the European understanding of marriage,' said the lawyer.

'The chief thing such people do not understand,' continued the lady, 'is that marriage without love is not marriage; that love alone sanctifies marriage, and that real marriage is only such as is sanctified by love.'

The clerk listened smilingly, trying to store up for future use all he could of the clever conversation.

In the midst of the lady's remarks we heard, behind me, a sound like that of a broken laugh or sob; and on turning round we saw my neighbour, the lonely grey-haired man with the glittering eyes, who had approached unnoticed during our conversation, which evidently interested him. He stood with his arms on the back of the seat, evidently much excited; his face was red and a muscle twitched in his cheek.

'What kind of love . . . love . . . is it that sanctifies marriage?' he asked hesitatingly.

Noticing the speaker's agitation, the lady tried to answer him as gently and fully as possible.

'True love . . . When such love exists between a man and a woman, then marriage is possible,' she said.

'Yes, but how is one to understand what is meant by "true love"?' said the gentleman with the glittering eyes timidly and with an awkward smile.

'Everybody knows what love is,' replied the lady, evidently wishing to break off her conversation with him.

'But I don't,' said the man. 'You must define what you understand . . . '

'Why? It's very simple,' she said, but stopped to consider. 'Love? Love is an exclusive preference for one above everybody else,' said the lady.

'Preference for how long? A month, two days, or half an hour?' said the grey-haired man and began to laugh.

'Excuse me, we are evidently not speaking of the same thing.'

'Oh, yes! Exactly the same.'

'She means,' interposed the lawyer, pointing to the lady, 'that in the first place marriage must be the outcome of attachment – or love, if you please – and only where that exists is marriage sacred, so to speak. Secondly, that marriage when not based on natural attachment – love, if you prefer the word – lacks the element that makes it morally binding. Do I understand you rightly?' he added, addressing the lady.

The lady indicated her approval of his explanation by a nod of her head.

'It follows . . . ' the lawyer continued – but the nervous man whose eyes now glowed as if aflame and who had evidently restrained himself with difficulty, began without letting the lawyer finish: 'Yes, I mean exactly the same thing, a preference for one person over everybody else, and I am only asking: a preference for how long?'

'For how long? For a long time; for life sometimes,' replied the lady, shrugging her shoulders.

'Oh, but that happens only in novels and never in real life. In real life this preference for one may last for years (that happens very rarely), more often for months, or perhaps for weeks, days, or hours,' he said, evidently aware that he was astonishing everybody by his views and pleased that it was so.

'Oh, what are you saying?' 'But no . . . ' 'No, allow me . . . ' we all three began at once. Even the clerk uttered an indefinite sound of disapproval.

'Yes, I know,' the grey-haired man shouted above our voices, 'you are talking about what is supposed to be, but I am speaking of what is. Every man experiences what you call love for every pretty woman.'

'Oh, what you say is awful! But the feeling that is called love does exist among people, and is given not for months or years, but for a lifetime!'

'No, it does not! Even if we should grant that a man might prefer a certain woman all his life, the woman in all probability would prefer someone else; and so it always has been and still is in the world,' he said, and taking out his cigarette-case he began to smoke.

'But the feeling may be reciprocal,' said the lawyer.

'No, sir, it can't!' rejoined the other. 'Just as it cannot be that in a cartload of peas, two marked peas will lie side by side. Besides, it is not merely this impossibility, but the inevitable satiety. To love one person for a whole lifetime is like saying that one candle will burn a whole life,' he said, greedily inhaling the smoke.

'But you are talking all the time about physical love. Don't you acknowledge love based on identity of ideals, on spiritual affinity?' asked the lady.

'Spiritual affinity! Identity of ideals!' he repeated, emitting his peculiar sound. 'But in that case why go to bed together? (Excuse my coarseness!) Or do people go to bed together because of the identity of their ideals?' he said, bursting into a nervous laugh.

'But permit me,' said the lawyer. 'Facts contradict you. We do see that matrimony exists, that all mankind, or the greater part of it, lives in wedlock, and many people honourably live long married lives.'

The grey-haired man again laughed.

'First you say that marriage is based on love, and when I express a doubt as to the existence of a love other than sensual, you prove the existence of love by the fact that marriages exist. But marriages in our days are mere deception!'

'No, allow me!' said the lawyer. 'I only say that marriages have existed and do exist.'

'They do! But why? They have existed and do exist among people who see in marriage something sacramental, a mystery binding them in the sight of God. Among them marriages do exist. Among us, people marry regarding marriage as nothing but copulation, and the result is either deception or coercion. When it is deception it is easier to bear. The husband and wife merely deceive people by pretending to be monogamists, while living polygamously. That is bad, but still bearable. But when, as most frequently happens, the husband and wife have undertaken the external duty of living together all their lives, and begin to hate each other after a month, and wish to part but still continue to live together, it leads to that terrible hell which makes people take to drink, shoot themselves, and kill or poison themselves or one another,' he went on, speaking more and more rapidly, not allowing anyone to put in a word and becoming more and more excited. We all felt embarrassed.

'Yes, undoubtedly there are critical episodes in married life,' said the lawyer, wishing to end this disturbingly heated conversation.

'I see you have found out who I am!' said the grey-haired man softly, and with apparent calm.

'No, I have not that pleasure.'

'It is no great pleasure. I am that Pózdnyshev in whose life that critical episode occurred to which you alluded; the episode when he killed his wife,' he said, rapidly glancing at each of us.

No one knew what to say and all remained silent.

'Well, never mind,' he said with that peculiar sound of his. 'However, pardon me. Ah! . . . I won't intrude on you.'

'Oh, no, if you please . . . ' said the lawyer, himself not knowing 'if you please' what.

But Pózdnyshev, without listening to him, rapidly turned away and went back to his seat. The lawyer and the lady whispered together. I sat down beside Pózdnyshev in silence, unable to think of anything to say. It was too dark to read, so I shut my eyes pretending that I wished to go to sleep. So we travelled in silence to the next station.

At that station the lawyer and the lady moved into another car, having some time previously consulted the guard about it. The clerk lay down on the seat and fell asleep. Pózdnyshev kept smoking and drinking tea which he had made at the last station.

When I opened my eyes and looked at him he suddenly addressed me resolutely and irritably: 'Perhaps it is unpleasant for you to sit with me, knowing who I am? In that case I will go away.'

'Oh no, not at all.'

'Well then, won't you have some? Only it's very strong.'

He poured out some tea for me.

'They talk . . . and they always lie . . . ' he remarked.

'What are you speaking about?' I asked.

'Always about the same thing. About that love of theirs and what it is! Don't you want to sleep?'

'Not at all.'

'Then would you like me to tell you how that love led to what happened to me?'

'Yes, if it will not be painful for you.'

'No, it is painful for me to be silent. Drink the tea . . . or is it too strong?'

The tea was really like beer, but I drank a glass of it. Just then the guard entered. Pózdnyshev followed him with angry eyes, and only began to speak after he had left.

3

'Well then, I'll tell you. But do you really want to hear it?'

I repeated that I wished it very much. He paused, rubbed his face with his hands, and began: 'If I am to tell it, I must tell everything from the beginning: I must tell how and why I married, and the kind of man I was before my marriage.

'Till my marriage I lived as everybody does, that is, everybody in our class. I am a landowner and a graduate of the university, and was a marshal of the gentry. Before my marriage I lived as everyone does, that is, dissolutely; and while living dissolutely I was convinced, like everybody in our class, that I was living as one has to. I thought I was a charming fellow and quite a moral man. I was not a seducer, had no unnatural tastes, did not make that the chief purpose of my life as many of my associates did, but I practised debauchery in a steady, decent way for health's sake. I avoided women who might tie my hands by having a child or by attachment for me. However, there may have been children and attachments, but I acted as if there were not. And this I not only considered moral, but I was even proud of it.'

He paused and gave vent to his peculiar sound, as he evidently did whenever a new idea occurred to him.

'And you know, that is the chief abomination!' he exclaimed. 'Dissoluteness does not lie in anything physical – no kind of physical misconduct is debauchery; real debauchery lies precisely in freeing oneself from moral relations with a woman with whom you have physical intimacy. And such emancipation I regarded as a merit. I remember how I once worried because I had not had an opportunity to pay a woman who gave herself to me (having probably taken a fancy to me) and how I only became tranquil after having sent her some money – thereby intimating that I did not consider myself in any way morally bound to her ... Don't nod as if you agreed with me,' he suddenly shouted at me. 'Don't I know these things? We all, and you too unless you are a rare exception, hold those same views, just as I used to. Never mind, I beg your pardon, but the fact is that it's terrible, terrible, terrible!'

'What is terrible?' I asked.

'That abyss of error in which we live regarding women and our relations with them. No, I can't speak calmly about it, not because of that "episode", as he called it, in my life, but because since that "episode" occurred my eyes have been opened and I have seen everything in quite a different light. Everything reversed, everything reversed!'

He lit a cigarette and began to speak, leaning his elbows on his knees.

It was too dark to see his face, but, above the jolting of the train, I could hear his impressive and pleasant voice.

4

'Yes, only after such torments as I have endured, only by their means, have I understood where the root of the matter lies – understood what ought to be, and therefore seen all the horror of what is.

'So you will see how and when that which led up to my "episode" began. It began when I was not quite sixteen. It happened when I still went to the grammar school and my elder brother was a first-year student at the university. I had not yet known any woman, but, like all the unfortunate children of our class, I was no longer an innocent boy. I had been depraved two years before that by other boys. Already woman, not some particular woman but woman as something to be desired, woman, every woman, woman's nudity, tormented me. My solitude was not pure. I was tormented, as ninety-nine per cent of our boys are. I was horrified, I suffered, I prayed, and I fell. I was already depraved in imagination and in fact, but I had not yet taken the last step. I was perishing, but I had not yet laid hands on another human being. But one day a comrade of my brother's, a jolly student, a so-called good fellow, that is, the worst kind of good-for-nothing, who had taught us to drink and to play cards, persuaded us after a carousal to go *there*. We went. My brother was also still innocent, and he fell that same night. And I, a fifteen-year-old boy, defiled myself and took part in defiling a woman, without at all understanding what I was doing. I had never heard from any of my elders that what I was doing was wrong, you know. And indeed no one hears it now. It is true it is in the Commandments, but then the Commandments are only needed to answer the priest at Scripture examination, and even then they are not very necessary, not nearly as necessary as the commandment about the use of *ut* in conditional sentences in Latin.

'And so I never heard those older persons whose opinions I respected say that it was an evil. On the contrary, I heard people I respected say it was good. I had heard that my struggles and sufferings would be eased after that. I heard this and read it, and heard my elders say it would be good for my health, while from my comrades I heard that it was rather a fine, spirited thing to do. So in general I expected nothing but good from it. The risk of disease? But that too had been foreseen. A paternal government saw to that. It sees to the correct working of the brothels,[24] and makes profligacy safe for schoolboys. Doctors too deal with it for a consideration.

That is proper. They assert that debauchery is good for the health, and they organise proper well-regulated debauchery. I know some mothers who attend to their sons' health in that sense. And science sends them to the brothels.'

'Why do you say "science"?' I asked.

'Why, who are the doctors? The priests of science. Who deprave youths by maintaining that this is necessary for their health? They do.

'Yet if a one-hundredth part of the efforts devoted to the cure of syphilis were devoted to the eradication of debauchery, there would long ago not have been a trace of syphilis left. But as it is, efforts are made not to eradicate debauchery but to encourage it and to make debauchery safe. That is not the point however. The point is that with me – and with nine-tenths, if not more, not of our class only but of all classes, even the peasants – this terrible thing happens that happened to me; I fell not because I succumbed to the natural temptation of a particular woman's charm – no, I was not seduced by a woman – but I fell because, in the set around me, what was really a fall was regarded by some as a most legitimate function good for one's health, and by others as a very natural and not only excusable but even innocent amusement for a young man. I did not understand that it was a fall, but simply indulged in that half-pleasure, half-need, which, as was suggested to me, was natural at a certain age. I began to indulge in debauchery as I began to drink and to smoke. Yet in that first fall there was something special and pathetic. I remember that at once, on the spot before I left the room, I felt sad, so sad that I wanted to cry – to cry for the loss of my innocence and for my relationship with women, now sullied for ever. Yes, my natural, simple relationship with women was spoilt for ever. From that time I have not had, and could not have, pure relations with women. I had become what is called a libertine. To be a libertine is a physical condition like that of a morphinist, a drunkard, or a smoker. As a morphinist, a drunkard, or a smoker is no longer normal, so too a man who has known several women for his pleasure is not normal but is a man perverted for ever, a libertine. As a drunkard or a morphinist can be recognised at once by his face and manner, so it is with a libertine. A libertine may restrain himself, may struggle, but he will never have those pure, simple, clear, brotherly relations with a woman. By the way he looks at a young woman and examines her, a libertine can always be recognised. And I had become and I remained a libertine, and it was this that brought me to ruin.'

5

'Ah, yes! After that things went from bad to worse, and there were all sorts of deviations. Oh, God! When I recall the abominations I committed in this respect I am seized with horror! And that is true of me, whom my companions, I remember, ridiculed for my so-called innocence. And when one hears of the "gilded youths", of officers, of the Parisians . . . ! And when all these gentlemen, and I – who have on our souls hundreds of the most varied and horrible crimes against women – when we thirty-year-old profligates, very carefully washed, shaved, perfumed, in clean linen and in evening dress or uniform, enter a drawing-room or ballroom, we are emblems of purity, charming!

'Only think of what ought to be, and of what is! When in society such a gentleman comes up to my sister or daughter, I, knowing his life, ought to go up to him, take him aside, and say quietly, "My dear fellow, I know the life you lead, and how and with whom you pass your nights. This is no place for you. There are pure, innocent girls here. Be off!" That is what ought to be; but what happens is that when such a gentleman comes and dances, embracing our sister or daughter, we are jubilant, if he is rich and well-connected. Maybe after Rigulboche[25] he will honour my daughter! Even if traces of disease remain, no matter! They are clever at curing that nowadays. Oh, yes, I know several girls in the best society whom their parents enthusiastically gave in marriage to men suffering from a certain disease. Oh, oh . . . the abomination of it! But a time will come when this abomination and falsehood will be exposed!'

He made his strange noise several times and again drank tea. It was fearfully strong and there was no water with which to dilute it. I felt that I was much excited by the two glasses I had drunk. Probably the tea affected him too, for he became more and more excited. His voice grew increasingly mellow and expressive. He continually changed his position, now taking off his cap and now putting it on again, and his face changed strangely in the semi-darkness in which we were sitting.

'Well, so I lived till I was thirty, not abandoning for a moment the intention of marrying and arranging for myself a most elevated and pure family life. With that purpose I observed the girls suitable for that end,' he continued. 'I weltered in a mire of debauchery and at the same time was on the lookout for a girl pure enough to be worthy of me.

'I rejected many just because they were not pure enough to suit me, but at last I found one whom I considered worthy. She was one of two daughters of a once-wealthy Pénza landowner who had been ruined.

'One evening after we had been out in a boat and had returned by moonlight, and I was sitting beside her admiring her curls and her shapely figure in a tight-fitting jersey, I suddenly decided that it was she! It seemed to me that evening that she understood all that I felt and thought, and that what I felt and thought was very lofty. In reality it was only that the jersey and the curls were particularly becoming to her and that after a day spent near her I wanted to be still closer.

'It is amazing how complete is the delusion that beauty is goodness. A handsome woman talks nonsense, you listen and hear not nonsense but cleverness. She says and does horrid things, and you see only charm. And if a handsome woman does not say stupid or horrid things, you at once persuade yourself that she is wonderfully clever and moral.

'I returned home in rapture, decided that she was the acme of moral perfection, and that therefore she was worthy to be my wife, and I proposed to her next day.

'What a muddle it is! Out of a thousand men who marry (not only among us but unfortunately also among the masses) there is hardly one who has not already been married ten, a hundred, or even, like Don Juan, a thousand times, before his wedding.

'It is true as I have heard and have myself observed that there are nowadays some chaste young men who feel and know that this thing is not a joke but an important matter.

'God help them! But in my time there was not one such in ten thousand. And everybody knows this and pretends not to know it. In all the novels they describe in detail the heroes' feelings and the ponds and bushes beside which they walk, but when their great love for some maiden is described, nothing is said about what has happened to these interesting heroes before: not a word about their frequenting certain houses, or about the servant-girls, cooks, and other people's wives! If there are such improper novels they are not put into the hands of those who most need this information – the unmarried girls.

'We first pretend to these girls that the profligacy which fills half the life of our towns, and even of the villages, does not exist at all.

'Then we get so accustomed to this pretence that at last, like the English, we ourselves really begin to believe that we are all moral people and live in a moral world. The girls, poor things, believe this quite seriously. So too did my unfortunate wife. I remember how, when we were engaged, I showed her my diary, from which she could learn something, if but a little, of my past, especially about my last *liaison*, of which she might hear from others, and about which I therefore felt it necessary to inform her. I remember her horror, despair, and confusion, when she learnt of it and understood it. I saw that she then wanted to give me up. And why did she not do so? ... '

He again made that sound, swallowed another mouthful of tea, and remained silent for a while.

6

'No, after all, it is better, better so!' he exclaimed. 'It serves me right! But that's not to the point – I meant to say that it is only the unfortunate girls who are deceived.

'The mothers know it, especially mothers educated by their own husbands – they know it very well. While pretending to believe in the purity of men, they act quite differently. They know with what sort of bait to catch men for themselves and for their daughters.

'You see it is only we men who don't know (because we don't wish to know) what women know very well, that the most exalted poetic love, as we call it, depends not on moral qualities but on physical nearness and on the *coiffure*, and the colour and cut of the dress. Ask an expert coquette who has set herself the task of captivating a man, which she would prefer to risk: to be convicted in his presence of lying, of cruelty, or even of dissoluteness, or to appear before him in an ugly and badly made dress – she will always prefer the first. She knows that we are continually lying about high sentiments, but really only want her body and will therefore forgive any abomination except an ugly, tasteless costume that is in bad style.

'A coquette knows that consciously, and every innocent girl knows it unconsciously just as animals do.

'That is why there are those detestable jerseys, bustles, and naked shoulders, arms, almost breasts. A woman, especially if she has passed the male school, knows very well that all the talk about elevated subjects is just talk, but that what a man wants is her body and all that presents it in the most deceptive but alluring light; and she acts accordingly. If we only throw aside our familiarity with this indecency, which has become a second nature to us, and look at the life of our upper classes as it is, in all its shamelessness – why, it is simply a brothel . . . You don't agree? Allow me, I'll prove it,' he said, interrupting me. 'You say that the women of our society have other interests in life than prostitutes have, but I say no, and will prove it. If people differ in the aims of their lives, by the inner content of their lives, this difference will necessarily be reflected in externals and their externals will be different. But look at those unfortunate despised women and at the highest society ladies: the same costumes, the same fashions, the same perfumes, the same exposure of arms, shoulders, and breasts, the same tight skirts over prominent bustles, the same passion for little stones, for costly, glittering objects, the same amusements, dances, music, and singing. As the former employ all means to allure, so do these others.

7

'Well, so these jerseys and curls and bustles caught me!

'It was very easy to catch me for I was brought up in the conditions in which amorous young people are forced like cucumbers in a hot-bed. You see our stimulating superabundance of food, together with complete physical idleness, is nothing but a systematic excitement of desire. Whether this astonishes you or not, it is so. Why, till quite recently I did not see anything of this myself, but now I have seen it. That is why it torments me that nobody knows this, and people talk such nonsense as that lady did.

'Yes, last spring some peasants were working in our neighbourhood on a railway embankment. The usual food of a young peasant is rye-bread, kvas, and onions; he keeps alive and is vigorous and healthy; his work is light agricultural work. When he goes to railway-work his rations are buckwheat porridge and a pound of meat a day. But he works off that pound of meat during his sixteen hours' work wheeling barrow-loads of half a ton weight, so it is just enough for him. But we who everyday consume two pounds of meat, and game, and fish and all sorts of heating foods and drinks – where does that go to? Into excesses of sensuality. And if it goes there and the safety-valve is open, all is well; but try and close the safety-valve, as I closed it temporarily, and at once a stimulus arises which, passing through the prism of our artificial life, expresses itself in utter infatuation, sometimes even platonic. And I fell in love as they all do.

'Everything was there to hand: raptures, tenderness, and poetry. In reality that love of mine was the result, on the one hand of her mamma's and the dressmakers' activity, and on the other of the superabundance of food consumed by me while living an idle life. If on the one hand there had been no boating, no dressmaker with her waists and so forth, and had my wife been sitting at home in a shapeless dressing-gown, and had I on the other hand been in circumstances normal to man – consuming just enough food to suffice for the work I did, and had the safety-valve been open – it happened to be closed at the time – I should not have fallen in love and nothing of all this would have happened.

8

'Well, and now it so chanced that everything combined – my condition, her becoming dress, and the satisfactory boating. It had failed twenty times but now it succeeded. Just like a trap! I am not joking. You see nowadays marriages are arranged that way – like traps. What is the natural way? The lass is ripe, she must be given in marriage. It seems very simple if the girl is not a fright and there are men wanting to marry. That is how it was done in olden times. The lass was grown up and her parents arranged the marriage. So it was done, and is done, among all mankind – Chinese, Hindus, Mohammedans, and among our own working classes; so it is done among at least ninety-nine per cent of the human race. Only among one per cent or less, among us libertines, has it been discovered that that is not right, and something new has been invented. And what is this novelty? It is that the maidens sit round and the men walk about, as at a bazaar, choosing. And the maidens wait and think, but dare not say: "Me, please!" "No, me!" "Not her, but me!" "Look what shoulders and other things I have!" And we men stroll around and look, and are very pleased. "Yes, I know! I won't be caught!" They stroll about and look, and are very pleased that everything is arranged like that for them. And then in an unguarded moment – snap! He is caught!'

'Then how ought it to be done?' I asked. 'Should the woman propose?'

'Oh, I don't know how; only if there's to be equality, let it be equality. If they have discovered that prearranged matches are degrading, why this is a thousand times worse! Then the rights and chances were equal, but here the woman is a slave in a bazaar or the bait in a trap. Tell any mother, or the girl herself, the truth, that she is only occupied in catching a husband . . . oh dear! what an insult! Yet they all do it and have nothing else to do. What is so terrible is to see sometimes quite innocent poor young girls engaged on it. And again, if it were but done openly – but it is always done deceitfully.

"Ah, the origin of species, how interesting!" "Oh, Lily takes such an interest in painting! And will you be going to the exhibition? How instructive!" And the troyka-drives, and shows, and symphonies! "Oh! how remarkable! My Lily is mad on music." "And why don't you share these convictions?" And boating . . . But their one thought is: "Take me, take me!" "Take my Lily!" "Or try – at least!" Oh, what an abomination! What falsehood!' he concluded, finishing his tea and beginning to put away the tea-things.

9

'You know,' he began while packing the tea and sugar into his bag. 'The domination of women from which the world suffers all arises from this.'

'What "domination of women"?' I asked. 'The rights, the legal privileges, are on the man's side.'

'Yes, yes! That's just it,' he interrupted me. 'That's just what I want to say. It explains the extraordinary phenomenon that on the one hand woman is reduced to the lowest stage of humiliation, while on the other she dominates. Just like the Jews: as they pay us back for their oppression by a financial domination, so it is with women. "Ah, you want us to be traders only, – all right, as traders we will dominate you!" say the Jews. "Ah, you want us to be merely objects of sensuality – all right, as objects of sensuality we will enslave you," say the women. Woman's lack of rights arises not from the fact that she must not vote or be a judge – to be occupied with such affairs is no privilege – but from the fact that she is not man's equal in sexual intercourse and has not the right to use a man or abstain from him as she likes – is not allowed to choose a man at her pleasure instead of being chosen by him. You say that is monstrous. Very well! Then a man must not have those rights either. As it is at present, a woman is deprived of that right while a man has it. And to make up for that right she acts on man's sensuality, and through his sensuality subdues him so that he only chooses formally, while in reality it is she who chooses. And once she has obtained these means she abuses them and acquires a terrible power over people.'

'But where is this special power?' I enquired.

'Where is it? Why everywhere, in everything! Go round the shops in any big town. There are goods worth millions and you cannot estimate the human labour expended on them, and look whether in nine-tenths of these shops there is anything for the use of men. All the luxuries of life are demanded and maintained by women.

'Count all the factories. An enormous proportion of them produce useless ornaments, carriages, furniture, and trinkets, for women. Millions of people, generations of slaves, perish at hard labour in factories merely to satisfy woman's caprice. Women, like queens, keep nine-tenths of mankind in bondage to heavy labour. And all because they have been abased and deprived of equal rights with men. And they revenge themselves by acting on our sensuality and catch us in their nets. Yes, it all comes of that.

'Women have made of themselves such an instrument for acting upon our sensuality that a man cannot quietly consort with a woman. As soon as a man approaches a woman he succumbs to her stupefying influence and becomes intoxicated and crazy. I used formerly to feel uncomfortable and uneasy when I saw a lady dressed up for a ball, but now I am simply frightened and plainly see her as something dangerous and illicit. I want to call a policeman and ask for protection from the peril, and demand that the dangerous object be removed and put away.

'Ah, you are laughing!' he shouted at me, 'but it is not at all a joke. I am sure a time will come, and perhaps very soon, when people will understand this and will wonder how a society could exist in which actions were permitted which so disturb social tranquillity as those adornments of the body directly evoking sensuality, which we tolerate for women in our society. Why, it's like setting all sorts of traps along the paths and promenades – it is even worse! Why is gambling forbidden while women in costumes which evoke sensuality are not forbidden? They are a thousand times more dangerous!

10

'Well, you see, I was caught that way. I was what is called in love. I not only imagined her to be the height of perfection, but during the time of our engagement I regarded myself also as the height of perfection. You know there is no rascal who cannot, if he tries, find rascals in some respects worse than himself, and who consequently cannot find reasons for pride and self-satisfaction. So it was with me: I was not marrying for money – covetousness had nothing to do with it – unlike the majority of my acquaintances who married for money or connections – I was rich, she was poor. That was one thing. Another thing I prided myself on was that while others married intending to continue in future the same polygamous life they had lived before marriage, I was firmly resolved to be monogamous after marriage, and there was no limit to my pride on that score. Yes, I was a dreadful pig and imagined myself to be an angel.

'Our engagement did not last long. I cannot now think of that time without shame! What nastiness! Love is supposed to be spiritual and not sensual. Well, if the love is spiritual, a spiritual communion, then that spiritual communion should find expression in words, in conversations, in discourse. There was nothing of the kind. It used to be dreadfully difficult to talk when we were left alone. It was the labour of Sisyphus.[26] As soon as we thought of something to say and said it, we had again to be silent, devising something else. There was nothing to talk about. All that could be said about the life that awaited us, our arrangements and plans, had been said, and what was there more? Now if we had been animals we should have known that speech was unnecessary; but here on the contrary it was necessary to speak, and there was nothing to say, because we were not occupied with what finds vent in speech. And moreover there was that ridiculous custom of giving sweets, of coarse gormandising on sweets, and all those abominable preparations for the wedding: remarks about the house, the bedroom, beds, wraps, dressing-gowns, underclothing, costumes. You must remember that if one married according to the injunctions of Domostróy, as that old fellow was saying, then the feather-beds, the trousseau, and the bedstead – are all but details appropriate to the sacrament. But among us, when of ten who marry there are certainly nine who not only do not believe in the sacrament, but do not even believe that what they are doing entails certain obligations – where scarcely one man out of a hundred has not been married before, and of fifty scarcely one is not preparing in advance to be unfaithful to his wife at every convenient opportunity – when the majority regard the going to church as only a special condition for obtaining possession of a certain woman – think what a dreadful significance all these details acquire. They show that the whole business is only that; they show that it is a kind of sale. An innocent girl is sold to a profligate, and the sale is accompanied by certain formalities.

11

'That is how everybody marries and that is how I married, and the much vaunted honeymoon began. Why, its very name is vile!' he hissed viciously. 'In Paris I once went to see the sights, and noticing a bearded woman and a water-dog on a signboard, I entered the show. It turned out to be nothing but a man in a woman's low-necked dress, and a dog done up in walrus skin and swimming in a bath. It was very far from being interesting; but as I was leaving, the showman politely saw me out and, addressing the public at the entrance, pointed to me and said, "Ask the gentleman whether it is not worth seeing! Come in, come in, one franc apiece!" I felt ashamed to say it was not worth seeing, and the showman had probably counted on that. It must be the same with those who have experienced the abomination of a honeymoon and who do not disillusion others. Neither did I disillusion anyone, but I do not now see why I should not tell the truth. Indeed, I think it needful to tell the truth about it. One felt awkward, ashamed, repelled, sorry, and above all dull, intolerably dull! It was something like what I felt when I learnt to smoke – when I felt sick and the saliva gathered in my mouth and I swallowed it and pretended that it was very pleasant. Pleasure from smoking, just as from that, if it comes at all, comes later. The husband must cultivate that vice in his wife in order to derive pleasure from it.'

'Why vice?' I said. 'You are speaking of the most natural human functions.'

'Natural?' he said. 'Natural? No, I may tell you that I have come to the conclusion that it is, on the contrary, *un*natural. Yes, quite *un*natural. Ask a child, ask an unperverted girl.

'Natural, you say!

'It is natural to eat. And to eat is, from the very beginning, enjoyable, easy, pleasant, and not shameful; but this is horrid, shameful, and painful. No, it is unnatural! And an unspoilt girl, as I have convinced myself, always hates it.'

'But how,' I asked, 'would the human race continue?'

'Yes, would not the human race perish?' he said, irritably and ironically, as if he had expected this familiar and insincere objection. 'Teach abstention from child-bearing so that English lords may always gorge themselves – that is all right. Preach it for the sake of greater pleasure – that is all right; but just hint at abstention from child-bearing in the name of morality – and, my goodness, what a rumpus . . . ! Isn't there a danger that the human race may die out because they want to cease to be swine? But forgive me! This light is unpleasant, may I shade it?' he said, pointing to the lamp. I said I did not mind; and with the haste with which he did everything, he got up on the seat and drew the woollen shade over the lamp.

'All the same,' I said, 'if everyone thought this the right thing to do, the human race would cease to exist.'

He did not reply at once.

'You ask how the human race will continue to exist,' he said, having again sat down in front of me, and spreading his legs far apart he leant his elbows on his knees. 'Why should it continue?'

'Why? If not, we should not exist.'

'And why should we exist?'

'Why? In order to live, of course.'

'But why live? If life has no aim, if life is given us for life's sake, there is no reason for living. And if it is so, then the Schopenhauers, the Hartmanns, and all the Buddhists as well,[27] are quite right. But if life has an aim, it is clear that it ought to come to an end when that aim is reached. And so it turns out,' he said with noticeable agitation, evidently prizing his thought very highly. 'So it turns out. Just think: if the aim of humanity is goodness, righteousness, love – call it what you will – if it is what the prophets have said, that all mankind should be united together in love, that the spears should be beaten into pruning-hooks and so forth, what is it that hinders the attainment of this aim? The passions hinder it. Of all the passions the strongest, cruellest, and most stubborn is the sex-passion, physical love; and therefore if the passions are destroyed, including the strongest of them – physical love – the prophecies will be fulfilled, mankind will be brought into a unity, the aim of human existence will be attained, and there will be nothing further to live for. As long as mankind exists the ideal is before it, and of course not the rabbits' and pigs' ideal of breeding as fast as possible, nor that of monkeys or Parisians – to enjoy sex-passion in the most refined manner, but the ideal of goodness attained by continence and purity. Towards that people have always striven and still strive. You see what follows.

'It follows that physical love is a safety-valve. If the present generation has not attained its aim, it has not done so because of its passions, of which the sex-passion is the strongest. And if the sex-passion endures there will be a new generation and consequently the possibility of attaining the aim in the next generation. If the next one does not attain it, then the next after that may, and so on, till the aim is attained, the prophecies fulfilled, and mankind attains unity. If not, what would result? If one admits that God created men for the attainment of a certain aim, and created them mortal but sexless, or created them immortal, what would be the result? Why, if they were mortal but without the sex-passion, and died without attaining the aim, God would have had to create new people to attain his aim. If they were immortal, let us grant that (though it would be more difficult for the same people to correct their mistakes and approach perfection than for those of another generation) they might attain that aim after many thousands of years, but then what use would they be afterwards? What could be done with them? It is best as it is . . . But perhaps you don't like that way of putting it? Perhaps you are an evolutionist? It comes to the same thing. The highest race of animals, the human race, in order to maintain itself in the struggle with other animals ought to unite into one whole like a swarm of bees, and not breed continually; it should bring up sexless members as the bees do; that is, again, it should strive towards continence and not towards inflaming desire – to which the whole system of our life is now directed.' He paused. 'The human race will cease? But can anyone doubt it, whatever his outlook on life may be? Why, it is as certain as death. According to all the teaching of the Church the end of the world will come, and according to all the teaching of science the same result is inevitable.

12

'In our world it is just the reverse: even if a man does think of continence while he is a bachelor, once married he is sure to think continence no longer necessary. You know those wedding tours – the seclusion into which, with their parents' consent, the young couple go – are nothing but licensed debauchery. But a moral law avenges itself when it is violated. Hard as I tried to make a success of my honeymoon, nothing came of it. It was horrid, shameful, and dull, the whole time. And very soon I began also to experience a painful, oppressive feeling. That began very quickly. I think it was on the third or fourth day that I found my wife depressed. I began asking her the reason and embracing her, which in my view was all she could want, but she removed my arm and began to cry. What about? She could not say. But she felt sad and distressed. Probably her exhausted nerves suggested to her the truth as to the vileness of our relation but she did not know how to express it. I began to question her, and she said something about feeling sad without her mother. It seemed to me that this was untrue, and I began comforting her without alluding to her mother. I did not understand that she was simply depressed and her mother was merely an excuse. But she immediately took offence because I had not mentioned her mother, as though I did not believe her. She told me she saw that I did not love her. I reproached her with being capricious, and suddenly her face changed entirely and instead of sadness it expressed irritation, and with the most venomous words she began accusing me of selfishness and cruelty. I gazed at her. Her whole face showed complete coldness and hostility, almost hatred. I remember how horror-struck I was when I saw this. 'How? What?' I thought. 'Love is a union of souls – and instead of that there is this! Impossible, this is not she!' I tried to soften her, but encountered such an insuperable wall of cold virulent hostility that before I had time to turn round I too was seized with irritation and we said a great many unpleasant things to one another. The impression of that first quarrel was dreadful. I call it a quarrel, but it was not a quarrel but only the disclosure of the abyss that really existed between us. Amorousness was exhausted by the satisfaction of sensuality and we were left confronting one another in our true relation: that is, as two egotists quite alien to each other who wished to get as much pleasure as possible each from the other. I call what took place between us a quarrel, but it was not a quarrel, only the consequence of the cessation of sensuality – revealing our real relations to one another. I did not understand that this cold and hostile relation was our normal state, I did not understand it because at first this hostile attitude was very soon concealed from us by a renewal of redistilled sensuality, that is by love-making.

'I thought we had quarrelled and made it up again, and that it would not recur. But during that same first month of honeymoon a period of satiety soon returned, we again ceased to need one another, and another quarrel supervened. This second quarrel struck me even more painfully than the first. "So the first one was not an accident but was bound to happen and will happen again," I thought. I was all the more staggered by that second quarrel because it arose from such an impossible pretext. It had something to do with money, which I never grudged and could certainly not have grudged to my wife. I only remember that she gave the matter such a twist that some remark of mine appeared to be an expression of a desire on my part to dominate over her by means of money, to which I was supposed to assert an exclusive right – it was something impossibly stupid, mean, and not natural either to me or to her. I became exasperated, and upbraided her with lack of consideration for me. She accused me of the same thing, and it all began again. In her words and in the expression of her face and eyes I again noticed the cruel cold hostility that had so staggered me before. I had formerly quarrelled with my brother, my friends, and my father, but there had never, I remember, been the special venomous malice which there was here. But after a while this mutual hatred was screened by amorousness, that is sensuality, and I still consoled myself with the thought that these two quarrels had been mistakes and could be remedied. But then a third and a fourth quarrel followed and I realised that it was not accidental, but that it was bound to happen and would happen so, and I was horrified at the prospect before me. At the same time I was tormented by the terrible thought that I alone lived on such bad terms with my wife, so unlike what I had expected, whereas this did not happen between other married couples. I did not know then that it is our common fate, but that everybody imagines, just as I did, that it is their peculiar misfortune, and everyone conceals this exceptional and shameful misfortune not only from others but even from himself and does not acknowledge it to himself.

'It began during the first days and continued all the time, ever increasing and growing more obdurate. In the depths of my soul I felt from the first weeks that I was lost, that things had not turned out as I expected, that marriage was not only no happiness but a very heavy burden; but like everybody else I did not wish to acknowledge this to myself (I should not have acknowledged it even now but for the end that followed) and I concealed it not only from others but from myself too. Now I am astonished that I failed to see my real position. It might have been seen from the fact that the quarrels began on pretexts it was impossible to remember when they were over. Our reason was not quick enough to *devise* sufficient excuses for the animosity that always existed between us. But more striking still was the insufficiency of the excuses for our reconciliations. Sometimes there were words, explanations, even tears, but sometimes . . . oh! it is disgusting even now to think of it – after the most cruel words to one another, came sudden silent glances, smiles, kisses, embraces . . . Faugh, how horrid! How is it I did not then see all the vileness of it?'

13

Two fresh passengers entered and settled down on the farthest seats. He was silent while they were seating themselves but as soon as they had settled down continued, evidently not for a moment losing the thread of his idea.

'You know, what is vilest about it,' he began, 'is that in theory love is something ideal and exalted, but in practice it is something abominable, swinish, which it is horrid and shameful to mention or remember. It is not for nothing that nature has made it disgusting and shameful. And if it is disgusting and shameful one must understand that it is so. But here, on the contrary, people pretend that what is disgusting and shameful is beautiful and lofty. What were the first symptoms of my love? Why that I gave way to animal excesses, not only without shame but being somehow even proud of the possibility of these physical excesses, and without in the least considering either her spiritual or even her physical life. I wondered what embittered us against one another, yet it was perfectly simple: that animosity was nothing but the protest of our human nature against the animal nature that overpowered it.

'I was surprised at our enmity to one another; yet it could not have been otherwise. That hatred was nothing but the mutual hatred of accomplices in a crime – both for the incitement to the crime and for the part taken in it. What was it but a crime when she, poor thing, became pregnant in the first month and our *swinish* connection continued? You think I am straying from my subject? Not at all! I am telling you *how* I killed my wife. They asked me at the trial with what and how I killed her. Fools! They thought I killed her with a knife, on the 5th of October. It was not then I killed her, but much earlier. Just as they are all now killing, all, all . . . '

'But with what?' I asked.

'That is just what is so surprising, that nobody wants to see what is so clear and evident, what doctors ought to know and preach, but are silent about. Yet the matter is very simple. Men and women are created like the animals so that physical love is followed by pregnancy and then by suckling – conditions under which physical love is bad for the woman and for her child. There are an equal number of men and women. What follows from this? It seems clear, and no great wisdom is needed to draw the conclusion that animals do, namely, the need of continence. But no. Science has been able to discover some kind of leucocytes that run about in the blood, and all sorts of useless nonsense, but cannot understand that. At least one does not hear of science teaching it!

'And so a woman has only two ways out: one is to make a monster of herself, to destroy and go on destroying within herself to such degree as may be necessary the capacity of being a woman, that is, a mother, in order that a man may quietly and continuously get his enjoyment; the other way out – and it is not even a way out but a simple, coarse, and direct violation of the laws of nature – practised in all so-called decent families – is that, contrary to her nature, the woman must be her husband's mistress even while she is pregnant or nursing – must be what not even an animal descends to, and for which her strength is insufficient. That is what causes nerve troubles and hysteria in our class, and among the peasants causes what they call being "possessed by the devil" – epilepsy. You will notice that no pure maidens are ever "possessed", but only married women living with their husbands. That is so here, and it is just the same in Europe. All the hospitals for hysterical women are full of those who have violated nature's law. The epileptics and Charcot's patients are complete wrecks you know, but the world is full of half-crippled women. Just think of it, what a great work goes on within a woman when she conceives or when she is nursing an infant. That is growing which will continue us and replace us. And this sacred work is violated – by what? It is terrible to think of it! And they prate about the freedom and the rights of women! It is as if cannibals fattened their captives to be eaten, and at the same time declared that they were concerned about their prisoners' rights and freedom.'

All this was new to me and startled me.

'What is one to do? If that is so,' I said, 'it means that one may love one's wife once in two years, yet men . . . '

'Men must!' he interrupted me. 'It is again those precious priests of science who have persuaded everybody of that. Imbue a man with the idea that he requires vodka, tobacco, or opium, and all these things will be indispensable to him. It seems that God did not understand what was necessary and therefore, omitting to consult those wizards, arranged things badly. You see matters do not tally. They have decided that it is essential for a man to satisfy his desires, and the bearing and nursing of children comes and interferes with it and hinders the satisfaction of that need. What is one to do then? Consult the wizards! They will arrange it. And they have devised something. Oh! when will those wizards with their deceptions be

dethroned? It is high time! It has come to such a point that people
go mad and shoot themselves and all because of this. How could it
be otherwise? The animals seem to know that their progeny
continue their race, and they keep to a certain law in this matter.
Man alone neither knows it nor wishes to know, but is concerned
only to get all the pleasure he can. And who is doing that? The lord
of nature – man! Animals, you see, only come together at times
when they are capable of producing progeny, but the filthy lord of
nature is at it any time if only it pleases him! And as if that were not
sufficient, he exalts this apish occupation into the most precious
pearl of creation, into love. In the name of this love, that is, this
filth, he destroys – what? Why, half the human race! All the women
who might help the progress of mankind towards truth and
goodness he converts, for the sake of his pleasure, into enemies
instead of helpmates. See what it is that everywhere impedes the
forward movement of mankind. Women! And why are they what
they are? Only because of that. Yes, yes . . . ' he repeated several
times, and began to move about, and to get out his cigarettes and to
smoke, evidently trying to calm himself.

14

'I too lived like a pig of that sort,' he continued in his former tone.
'The worst thing about it was that while living that horrid life I
imagined that, because I did not go after other women, I was living
an honest family life, that I was a moral man and in no way
blameworthy, and if quarrels occurred it was her fault and resulted
from her character.

'Of course the fault was not hers. She was like everybody else –
like the majority of women. She had been brought up as the
position of women in our society requires, and as therefore all
women of the leisured classes without exception are brought up and
cannot help being brought up. People talk about some new kind of
education for women. It is all empty words: their education is
exactly what it has to be in view of our unfeigned, real, general
opinion about women.

'The education of women will always correspond to men's opinion
about them. Don't we know how men regard women: *Wein, Weib,
und Gesang*,[28] and what the poets say in their verses? Take all poetry,
all pictures and sculpture, beginning with love poems and the nude
Venuses and Phrynes,[29] and you will see that woman is an instrument
of enjoyment; she is so on the Trubá and the Grachévka,[30] and also

at the Court balls. And note the devil's cunning: if they are here for enjoyment and pleasure, let it be known that it is pleasure and that woman is a sweet morsel. But no, first the knights-errant declare that they worship women (worship her, and yet regard her as an instrument of enjoyment), and now people assure us that they respect women. Some give up their places to her, pick up her handkerchief; others acknowledge her right to occupy all positions and to take part in the government, and so on. They do all that, but their outlook on her remains the same. She is a means of enjoyment. Her body is a means of enjoyment. And she knows this. It is just as it is with slavery. Slavery, you know, is nothing else than the exploitation by some of the unwilling labour of many. Therefore to get rid of slavery it is necessary that people should not wish to profit by the forced labour of others and should consider it a sin and a shame. But they go and abolish the external form of slavery and arrange so that one can no longer buy and sell slaves, and they imagine and assure themselves that slavery no longer exists, and do not see or wish to see that it does, because people still want and consider it good and right to exploit the labour of others. And as long as they consider that good, there will always be people stronger or more cunning than others who will succeed in doing it. So it is with the emancipation of woman: the enslavement of woman lies simply in the fact that people desire, and think it good, to avail themselves of her as a tool of enjoyment. Well, and they liberate woman, give her all sorts of rights equal to man, but continue to regard her as an instrument of enjoyment, and so educate her in childhood and afterwards by public opinion. And there she is, still the same humiliated and depraved slave, and the man still a depraved slave-owner.

'They emancipate women in universities and in law courts, but continue to regard her as an object of enjoyment. Teach her, as she is taught among us, to regard herself as such, and she will always remain an inferior being. Either with the help of those scoundrels the doctors she will prevent the conception of offspring – that is, will be a complete prostitute, lowering herself not to the level of an animal but to the level of a thing – or she will be what the majority of women are, mentally diseased, hysterical, unhappy, and lacking capacity for spiritual development. High schools and universities cannot alter that. It can only be changed by a change in men's outlook on women and women's way of regarding themselves. It will change only when woman regards virginity as the highest state, and does not, as at present, consider the highest state of a human being a shame and a disgrace. While that is not so, the ideal of every girl, whatever her education may be, will continue to be to attract as many men as possible, as many males as possible, so as to have the possibility of choosing.

'But the fact that one of them knows more mathematics, and another can play the harp, makes no difference. A woman is happy and attains all she can desire when she has bewitched man. Therefore the chief aim of a woman is to be able to bewitch him. So it has been and will be. So it is in her maiden life in our society, and so it continues to be in her married life. For a maiden this is necessary in order to have a choice, for the married woman in order to have power over her husband.

'The one thing that stops this or at any rate suppresses it for a time, is children, and then only if the mother is not a monster, that is, if she nurses them herself. But here the doctors again come in.

'My wife, who wanted to nurse, and did nurse the four later children herself, happened to be unwell after the birth of her first child. And those doctors, who cynically undressed her and felt her all over – for which I had to thank them and pay them money – those dear doctors considered that she must not nurse the child; and that first time she was deprived of the only means which might have kept her from coquetry. We engaged a wet nurse, that is, we took advantage of the poverty, the need, and the ignorance of a woman, tempted her away from her own baby to ours, and in return gave her a fine head-dress[31] with gold lace. But that is not the point. The point is that during that time when my wife was free from pregnancy and from suckling, the feminine coquetry which had lain dormant within her manifested itself with particular force. And coinciding with this the torments of jealousy rose up in me with special force. They tortured me all my married life, as they cannot but torture all husbands who live with their wives as I did with mine, that is, immorally.

15

'During the whole of my married life I never ceased to be tormented by jealousy, but there were periods when I specially suffered from it. One of these periods was when, after the birth of our first child, the doctors forbade my wife to nurse it. I was particularly jealous at that time, in the first place because my wife was experiencing that unrest natural to a mother which is sure to be aroused when the natural course of life is needlessly violated; and secondly, because seeing how easily she abandoned her moral obligations as a mother, I rightly though unconsciously concluded that it would be equally easy for her to disregard her duty as a wife, especially as she was quite well and in spite of the precious doctors' prohibition was able to nurse her later children admirably.'

'I see you don't like doctors,'[32] I said, noticing a peculiarly malevolent tone in his voice whenever he alluded to them.

'It is not a case of liking or disliking. They have ruined my life as they have ruined and are ruining the lives of thousands and hundreds of thousands of human beings, and I cannot help connecting the effect with the cause. I understand that they want to earn money like lawyers and others, and I would willingly give them half my income, and all who realise what they are doing would willingly give them half of their possessions, if only they would not interfere with our family life and would never come near us. I have not collected evidence, but I know dozens of cases (there are any number of them!) where they have killed a child in its mother's womb asserting that she could not give it birth, though she has had children quite safely later on; or they have killed the mother on the pretext of performing some operation. No one reckons these murders any more than they reckoned the murders of the Inquisition, because it is supposed that it is done for the good of mankind. It is impossible to number all the crimes they commit. But all those crimes are as nothing compared to the moral corruption of materialism they introduce into the world, especially through women.

'I don't lay stress on the fact that if one is to follow their instructions, then on account of the infection which exists everywhere and in everything, people would not progress towards greater unity but towards separation; for according to their teaching we ought all to sit apart and not remove the carbolic atomiser from our mouths (though now they have discovered that even that is of no avail). But that does not matter either. The principal poison lies in the demoralisation of the world, especially of women.

'Today one can no longer say: "You are not living rightly, live better." One can't say that, either to oneself or to anyone else. If you live a bad life it is caused by the abnormal functioning of your nerves, & c. So you must go to them, and they will prescribe eight penn'orth of medicine from a chemist, which you must take!

'You get still worse: then more medicine and the doctor again. An excellent trick!

'That however is not the point. All I wish to say is that she nursed her babies perfectly well and that only her pregnancy and the nursing of her babies saved me from the torments of jealousy. Had it not been for that it would all have happened sooner. The children saved me and her. In eight years she had five children and nursed all except the first herself.'

'And where are your children now?' I asked.

'The children?' he repeated in a frightened voice.

'Forgive me, perhaps it is painful for you to be reminded of them.'

'No, it does not matter. My wife's sister and brother have taken them. They would not let me have them. I gave them my estate, but they did not give them up to me. You know I am a sort of lunatic. I have left them now and am going away. I have seen them, but they won't let me have them because I might bring them up so that they would not be like their parents, and they have to be just like them. Oh well, what is to be done? Of course they won't let me have them and won't trust me. Besides, I do not know whether I should be able to bring them up. I think not. I am a ruin, a cripple. Still I have one thing in me. I know! Yes, that is true, I know what others are far from knowing.

'Yes, my children are living and growing up just such savages as everybody around them. I saw them, saw them three times. I can do nothing for them, nothing. I am now going to my place in the south. I have a little house and a small garden there.

'Yes, it will be a long time before people learn what I know. How much of iron and other metal there is in the sun and the stars is easy to find out, but anything that exposes our swinishness is difficult, terribly difficult!

'You at least listen to me, and I am grateful for that.

16

'You mentioned my children. There again, what terrible lies are told about children! Children a blessing from God, a joy! That is all a lie. It was so once upon a time, but now it is not so at all. Children are a torment and nothing else. Most mothers feel this quite plainly, and sometimes inadvertently say so. Ask most mothers of our propertied classes and they will tell you that they do not want to have children for fear of their falling ill and dying. They don't want to nurse them if they do have them, for fear of becoming too much attached to them and having to suffer. The pleasure a baby gives them by its loveliness, its little hands and feet, and its whole body, is not as great as the suffering caused by the very fear of its possibly falling ill and dying, not to speak of its actual illness or death. After weighing the advantages and disadvantages it seems disadvantageous, and therefore undesirable, to have children. They say this quite frankly and boldly, imagining that these feelings of theirs arise from their love of children, a good and laudable feeling of which they are proud. They do not notice that by this reflection they plainly repudiate love, and only affirm their own selfishness. They get less pleasure from a baby's loveliness than suffering from fear on its account, and therefore the baby they would love is not wanted. They do not sacrifice themselves for a beloved being, but sacrifice a being whom they might love, for their own sakes.

'It is clear that this is not love but selfishness. But one has not the heart to blame them – the mothers in well-to-do families – for that selfishness, when one remembers how dreadfully they suffer on account of their children's health, again thanks to the influence of those same doctors among our well-to-do classes. Even now, when I do but remember my wife's life and the condition she was in during the first years when we had three or four children and she was absorbed in them, I am seized with horror! We led no life at all, but were in a state of constant danger, of escape from it, recurring danger, again followed by a desperate struggle and another escape – always as if we were on a sinking ship. Sometimes it seemed to me that this was done on purpose and that she pretended to be anxious about the children in order to subdue me. It solved all questions in her favour with such tempting simplicity. It sometimes seemed as if all she did and said on these occasions was pretence. But no! She herself suffered terribly, and continually tormented herself about the children and their health and illnesses. It was torture for her and for me too; and it was impossible for her not to suffer. After all, the attachment to her children, the animal need of feeding, caressing, and protecting them, was there as with most women, but there was not the lack of imagination and reason that there is in animals. A hen is not afraid of what may happen to her chick, does not know all the diseases that may befall it, and does not know all those remedies with which people imagine that they can save from illness and death. And for a hen her young are not a source of torment. She does for them what it is natural and pleasurable for her to do; her young ones are a pleasure to her. When a chick falls ill her duties are quite definite: she warms and feeds it. And doing this she knows that she is doing all that is necessary. If her chick dies she does not ask herself why it died, or where it has gone to; she cackles for a while, and then leaves off and goes on living as before. But for our unfortunate women, my wife among them, it was not so. Not to mention illnesses and how to cure them, she was always hearing and reading from all sides endless rules for the rearing and educating of children, which were continually being superseded by others. This is the way to feed a child: feed it in this way, on such a thing; no, not on such a thing, but in this way; clothes, drinks, baths, putting to bed, walking, fresh air, – for all these things we, especially she, heard of new rules every week, just as if children had only begun to be born into the world since yesterday. And if a child that had not been fed or bathed in the right way or at the right time fell ill, it appeared that we were to blame for not having done what we ought.

'That was so while they were well. It was a torment even then. But if one of them happened to fall ill, it was all up: a regular hell! It is supposed that illness can be cured and that there is a science about it, and people – doctors – who know about it. Ah, but not all of them know – only the very best. When a child is ill one must get hold of the very best one, the one who saves, and then the child is saved; but if you don't get that doctor, or if you don't live in the place where that doctor lives, the child is lost. This was not a creed peculiar to her, it is the creed of all the women of our class, and she heard nothing else from all sides. Catherine Seménovna lost two children because Iván Zakhárych was not called in in time, but Iván Zakhárych saved Mary Ivánovna's eldest girl, and the Petróvs moved in time to various hotels by the doctor's advice, and the children remained alive; but if they had not been segregated the children would have died. Another who had a delicate child moved south by the doctor's advice and saved the child. How can she help being tortured and agitated all the time, when the lives of the children for whom she has an animal attachment depend on her finding out in time what Iván Zakhárych will say! But what Iván Zakhárych will say nobody knows, and he himself least of all, for he is well aware that he knows nothing and therefore cannot be of any use, but just shuffles about at random so that people should not cease to believe that he knows something or other. You see, had she been wholly an animal she would not have suffered so, and if she had been quite a human being she would have had faith in God and would have said and thought, as a believer does: "The Lord gave and the Lord hath taken away. One can't escape from God."

'Our whole life with the children, for my wife and consequently for me, was not a joy but a torment. How could she help torturing herself? She tortured herself incessantly. Sometimes when we had just made peace after some scene of jealousy, or simply after a quarrel, and thought we should be able to live, to read, and to think a little, we had no sooner settled down to some occupation than the news came that Vásya was being sick, or Másha showed symptoms of dysentery, or Andrúsha had a rash, and there was an end to peace, it was not life any more. Where was one to drive to? For what doctor? How isolate the child? And then it's a case of enemas, temperatures, medicines, and doctors. Hardly is that over before something else begins. We had no regular settled family life but only, as I have already said, continual escapes from imaginary and real dangers. It is like that in most families nowadays you know, but in my family it was especially acute. My wife was a child-loving and a credulous woman.

'So the presence of children not only failed to improve our life but poisoned it. Besides, the children were a new cause of dissension. As soon as we had children they became the means and the object of our discord, and more often the older they grew. They were not only the object of discord but the weapons of our strife. We used our children, as it were, to fight one another with. Each of us had a favourite weapon among them for our strife. I used to fight her chiefly through Vásya, the eldest boy, and she me through Lisa. Besides that, as they grew older and their characters became defined, it came about that they grew into allies whom each of us tried to draw to his or her side. They, poor things, suffered terribly from this, but we, with our incessant warfare, had no time to think of that. The girl was my ally, and the eldest boy, who resembled his mother and was her favourite, was often hateful to me.

17

'Well, and so we lived.[33] Our relations to one another grew more and more hostile and at last reached a stage where it was not disagreement that caused hostility but hostility that caused disagreement. Whatever she might say I disagreed with beforehand, and it was just the same with her.

'In the fourth year we both, it seemed, came to the conclusion that we could not understand one another or agree with one another. We no longer tried to bring any dispute to a conclusion. We invariably kept to our own opinions even about the most trivial questions, but especially about the children. As I now recall them the views I maintained were not at all so dear to me that I could not have given them up; but she was of the opposite opinion and to yield meant yielding to her, and that I could not do. It was the same with her. She probably considered herself quite in the right towards me, and as for me I always thought myself a saint towards her. When we were alone together we were doomed almost to silence, or to conversations such as I am convinced animals can carry on with one another: "What is the time? Time to go to bed. What is today's dinner? Where shall we go? What is there in the papers? Send for the doctor; Másha has a sore throat." We only needed to go a hairbreadth beyond this impossibly limited circle of conversation for irritation to flare up. We had collisions and acrimonious words about the coffee, a tablecloth, a trap, a lead at bridge, all of them things that could not be of any importance to either of us. In me at any rate there often raged a terrible hatred of her. Sometimes I watched her pouring out tea, swinging her leg, lifting a spoon to her mouth, smacking her lips and drawing in some liquid, and I hated her for these things as though they were the worst possible actions. I did not then notice that the periods of anger corresponded quite regularly and exactly to the periods of what we called love. A period of love – then a period of animosity; an energetic period of love, then a long period of animosity; a weaker manifestation of love, and a shorter period of animosity. We did not then understand that this love and animosity were one and the same animal feeling only at opposite poles. To live like that would have been awful had we understood our position; but we neither understood nor saw it. Both salvation and punishment for man lie in the fact that if he lives wrongly he can befog himself so as not to see the misery of his position. And this we did. She tried to forget herself in intense and always hurried occupation with household affairs, busying herself with the arrangements of the house, her own and the children's clothes, their lessons, and their health; while I had my own occupations: wine, my office duties, shooting, and cards. We were both continually occupied, and we both felt that the busier we were the nastier we might be to each other. "It's all very well for you to grimace," I thought, "but you have harassed me all night with your scenes, and I have a meeting on." "It's all very well for you," she not only thought but said, "but I have been awake all night with the baby." Those new theories of hypnotism, psychic diseases, and hysterics are not a simple folly, but a dangerous and repulsive one. Charcot[34] would certainly have said that my wife was hysterical, and that I was abnormal, and he would no doubt have tried to cure me. But there was nothing to cure.

'Thus we lived in a perpetual fog, not seeing the condition we were in. And if what did happen had not happened, I should have gone on living so to old age and should have thought, when dying, that I had led a good life. I should not have realised the abyss of misery and the horrible falsehood in which I wallowed.

'We were like two convicts hating each other and chained together, poisoning one another's lives and trying not to see it. I did not then know that ninety-nine per cent of married people live in a similar hell to the one I was in and that it cannot be otherwise. I did not then know this either about others or about myself.

'It is strange what coincidences there are in regular, or even in irregular, lives! Just when the parents find life together unendurable, it becomes necessary to move to town for the children's education.'

He stopped, and once or twice gave vent to his strange sounds, which were now quite like suppressed sobs. We were approaching a station.

'What is the time?' he asked.

I looked at my watch. It was two o'clock.

'You are not tired?' he asked.

'No, but you are?'

'I am suffocating. Excuse me, I will walk up and down and drink some water.'

He went unsteadily through the carriage. I remained alone thinking over what he had said, and I was so engrossed in thought that I did not notice when he re-entered by the door at the other end of the carriage.

18

'Yes, I keep diverging,' he began. 'I have thought much over it. I now see many things differently and I want to express it.

'Well, so we lived in town. In town a man can live for a hundred years without noticing that he has long been dead and has rotted away. He has no time to take account of himself, he is always occupied. Business affairs, social intercourse, health, art, the children's health and their education. Now one has to receive so-and-so and so-and-so, go to see so-and-so and so-and-so; now one has to go and look at this, and hear this man or that woman. In town, you know, there are at any given moment one or two, or even three, celebrities whom one must on no account miss seeing. Then one has to undergo a treatment oneself or get someone else attended to, then there are teachers, tutors, and governesses, but one's own life is quite empty. Well, so we lived and felt less the painfulness of living together. Besides at first we had splendid occupations, arranging things in a new place, in new quarters; and we were also occupied in going from the town to the country and back to town again.

'We lived so through one winter, and the next there occurred, unnoticed by anyone, an apparently unimportant thing, but the cause of all that happened later.

'She was not well and the doctors told her not to have children, and taught her how to avoid it. To me it was disgusting. I struggled against it, but she with frivolous obstinacy insisted on having her own way and I submitted. The last excuse for our swinish life – children – was then taken away, and live became viler than ever.

'To a peasant, a labouring man, children are necessary; though it is hard for him to feed them, still he needs them, and therefore his marital relations have a justification. But to us who have children, more children are unnecessary; they are an additional care and expense, a further division of property, and a burden. So our swinish life has no justification. We either artificially deprive ourselves of children or regard them as a misfortune, the consequences of carelessness, and that is still worse.

'We have no justification. But we have fallen morally so low that we do not even feel the need of any justification.

'The majority of the present educated world devote themselves to this kind of debauchery without the least qualm of conscience.

'There is indeed nothing that can feel qualms, for conscience in our society is non-existent, unless one can call public opinion and the criminal law a "conscience". In this case neither the one nor the other is infringed: there is no reason to be ashamed of public opinion for everybody acts in the same way – Mary Pávlovna, Iván Zakhárych, and the rest. Why breed paupers or deprive oneself of the possibility of social life? There is no need to fear or be ashamed in face of the criminal law either. Those shameless hussies, or soldiers' wives, throw their babies into ponds or wells, and they of course must be put in prison, but we do it all at the proper time and in a clean way.

'We lived like that for another two years. The means employed by those scoundrel-doctors evidently began to bear fruit; she became physically stouter and handsomer, like the late beauty of summer's end. She felt this and paid attention to her appearance. She developed a provocative kind of beauty which made people restless. She was in the full vigour of a well-fed and excited woman of thirty who is not bearing children. Her appearance disturbed people. When she passed men she attracted their notice. She was like a fresh, well-fed, harnessed horse, whose bridle has been removed. There was no bridle, as is the case with ninety-nine hundredths of our women. And I felt this – and was frightened.'

19

He suddenly rose and sat down close to the window.

'Pardon me,' he muttered and, with his eyes fixed on the window, he remained silent for about three minutes. Then he sighed deeply and moved back to the seat opposite mine. His face was quite changed, his eyes looked pathetic, and his lips puckered strangely, almost as if he were smiling. 'I am rather tired but I will go on with it. We have still plenty of time, it is not dawn yet. Ah, yes,' he began after lighting a cigarette, 'she grew plumper after she stopped having babies, and her malady – that everlasting worry about the children – began to pass . . . at least not actually to pass, but she as it were woke up from an intoxication, came to herself, and saw that there was a whole divine world with its joys which she had forgotten, but a divine world she did not know how to live in and did not at all understand. "I must not miss it! Time is passing and won't come back!" So, I imagine, she thought, or rather felt, nor could she have thought or felt differently: she had been brought up in the belief that there was only one thing in the world worthy of attention – love. She had married and received something of that love, but not nearly what had been promised and was expected. Even that had been accompanied by many disappointments and sufferings, and then this unexpected torment: so many children! The torments exhausted her. And then, thanks to the obliging doctors, she learnt that it is possible to avoid having children. She was very glad, tried it, and became alive again for the one thing she knew – for love. But love with a husband, befouled by jealousy and all kinds of anger, was no longer the thing she wanted. She had visions of some other, clean, new love; at least I thought she had. And she began to look about her as if expecting something. I saw this and could not help feeling anxious. It happened again and again that while talking to me, as usual through other people – that is, telling a third person what she meant for me – she boldly, without remembering that she had expressed the opposite opinion an hour before, declared, though half-jokingly, that a mother's cares are a fraud, and that it is not worth while to devote one's life to children when one is young and can enjoy life. She gave less attention to the children, and less frenziedly than before, but gave more and more attention to herself, to her appearance (though she tried to conceal this), and to her pleasures, even to her accomplishments. She again enthusiastically took to the piano which she had quite abandoned, and it all began from that.'

He turned his weary eyes to the window again but, evidently making an effort, immediately continued once more.

'Yes, that man made his appearance . . . ' he became confused and once or twice made that peculiar sound with his nose.

I could see that it was painful for him to name that man, to recall him, or speak about him. But he made an effort and, as if he had broken the obstacle that hindered him, continued resolutely.

'He was a worthless man in my opinion and according to my estimate. And not because of the significance he acquired in my life but because he really was so. However, the fact that he was a poor sort of fellow only served to show how irresponsible she was. If it had not been he then it would have been another. It had to be!'

Again he paused. 'Yes, he was a musician, a violinist; not a professional, but a semi-professional semi-society man.

'His father, a landowner, was a neighbour of my father's. He had been ruined, and his children – there were three boys – had obtained settled positions; only this one, the youngest, had been handed over to his godmother in Paris. There he was sent to the *Conservatoire* because he had a talent for music, and he came out as a violinist and played at concerts. He was a man . . . ' Having evidently intended to say something bad about him, Pózdnyshev restrained himself and rapidly said: 'Well, I don't really know how he lived, I only know that he returned to Russia that year and appeared in my house.

'With moist almond-shaped eyes, red smiling lips, a small waxed moustache, hair done in the latest fashion, and an insipidly pretty face, he was what women call "not bad looking". His figure was weak though not misshapen, and he had a specially developed posterior, like a woman's, or such as Hottentots are said to have. They too are reported to be musical. Pushing himself as far as possible into familiarity, but sensitive and always ready to yield at the slightest resistance, he maintained his dignity in externals, wore buttoned boots of a special Parisian fashion, bright-coloured ties, and other things foreigners acquire in Paris, which by their noticeable novelty always attract women. There was an affected external gaiety in his manner. That manner, you know, of speaking about everything in allusions and unfinished sentences, as if you knew it all, remembered it, and could complete it yourself.

'It was he with his music who was the cause of it all. You know at the trial the case was put as if it was all caused by jealousy. No such thing, that is, I don't mean "no such thing", it was and yet it was not. At the trial it was decided that I was a wronged husband and that I had killed her while defending my outraged honour (that is the phrase they employ, you know). That is why I was acquitted. I tried to explain matters at the trial but they took it that I was trying to rehabilitate my wife's honour.

'What my wife's relations with that musician may have been has no meaning for me, or for her either. What has a meaning is what I have told you about – my swinishness. The whole thing was an outcome of the terrible abyss between us of which I have told you – that dreadful tension of mutual hatred which made the first excuse sufficient to produce a crisis. The quarrels between us had for some time past become frightful, and were all the more startling because they alternated with similarly intense animal passion.

'If he had not appeared there would have been someone else. If the occasion had not been jealousy it would have been something else. I maintain that all husbands who live as I did, must either live dissolutely, separate, or kill themselves or their wives as I have done. If there is anybody who has not done so, he is a rare exception. Before I ended as I did, I had several times been on the verge of suicide, and she too had repeatedly tried to poison herself.

20

'Well, that is how things were going not long before it happened. We seemed to be living in a state of truce and had no reason to infringe it. Then we chanced to speak about a dog which I said had been awarded a medal at an exhibition. She remarked "Not a medal, but an honourable mention." A dispute ensues. We jump from one subject to another, reproach one another, "Oh, that's nothing new, it's always been like that." "You said . . . " "No, I didn't say so." "Then I am telling lies! . . . " You feel that at any moment that dreadful quarrelling which makes you wish to kill yourself or her will begin. You know it will begin immediately, and fear it like fire and therefore wish to restrain yourself, but your whole being is seized with fury. She being in the same or even a worse condition purposely misinterprets every word you say, giving it a wrong meaning. Her every word is venomous; where she alone knows that I am most sensitive, she stabs. It gets worse and worse. I shout: "Be quiet!" or something of that kind.

'She rushes out of the room and into the nursery. I try to hold her back in order to finish what I was saying, to prove my point, and I seize her by the arm. She pretends that I have hurt her and screams: "Children, your father is striking me!" I shout: "Don't lie!" "But it's not the first time!" she screams, or something like that. The children rush to her. She calms them down. I say, "Don't sham!" She says, "Everything is sham in your eyes, you would kill anyone and say they were shamming. Now I have understood you. That's just what you want!" "Oh, I wish you were dead as a dog!" I shout. I remember how those dreadful words horrified me. I never thought I could utter such dreadful, coarse words, and am surprised that they escaped me. I shout them and rush away into my study and sit down and smoke. I hear her go out into the hall preparing to go away. I ask, "Where are you going to?" She does not reply. "Well, devil take her," I say to myself, and go back to my study and lie down and smoke. A thousand different plans of how to revenge myself on her and get rid of her, and how to improve matters and go on as if nothing had happened, come into my head. I think all that and go on smoking and smoking. I think of running away from her, hiding myself, going to America. I get as far as dreaming of how I shall get rid of her, how splendid that will be, and how I shall unite with another, an admirable woman – quite different. I shall get rid of her either by her dying or by a divorce, and I plan how it is to be done. I notice that I am getting confused and not thinking of what is necessary, and to prevent myself from perceiving that my thoughts are not to the point I go on smoking.

'Life in the house goes on. The governess comes in and asks: "Where is madame? When will she be back?" The footman asks whether he is to serve tea. I go to the dining-room. The children, especially Lisa who already understands, gaze inquiringly and disapprovingly at me. We drink tea in silence. She has still not come back. The evening passes, she has not returned, and two different feelings alternate within me. Anger because she torments me and all the children by her absence which will end by her returning; and fear that she will not return but will do something to herself. I would go to fetch her, but where am I to look for her? At her sister's? But it would be so stupid to go and ask. And it's all the better: if she is bent on tormenting someone, let her torment herself. Besides that is what she is waiting for; and next time it would be worse still. But suppose she is not with her sister but is doing something to herself, or has already done it! It's past ten, past eleven! I don't go to the bedroom – it would be stupid to lie there alone waiting – but I'll not lie down here either. I wish to occupy my mind, to write a letter or to read, but I can't do anything. I sit alone in my study, tortured, angry, and listening. It's three o'clock, four o'clock, and she is not back. Towards morning I fall asleep. I wake up, she has still not come!

'Everything in the house goes on in the usual way, but all are perplexed and look at me inquiringly and reproachfully, considering me to be the cause of it all. And in me the same struggle still continues: anger that she is torturing me, and anxiety for her.

'At about eleven in the morning her sister arrives as her envoy. And the usual talk begins. "She is in a terrible state. What does it all mean?" "After all, nothing has happened." I speak of her impossible character and say that I have not done anything.

' "But, you know, it can't go on like this," says her sister.

' "It's all her doing and not mine," I say. "I won't take the first step. If it means separation, let it be separation."

'My sister-in-law goes away having achieved nothing. I had boldly said that I would not take the first step; but after her departure, when I came out of my study and saw the children piteous and frightened, I was prepared to take the first step. I should be glad to do it, but I don't know how. Again I pace up and down and smoke; at lunch I drink vodka and wine and attain what I unconsciously desire – I no longer see the stupidity and humiliation of my position.

'At about three she comes. When she meets me she does not speak. I imagine that she has submitted, and begin to say that I had been provoked by her reproaches. She, with the same stern expression on her terribly harassed face, says that she has not come for explanations but to fetch the children, because we cannot live together. I begin telling her that the fault is not mine and that she provoked me beyond endurance. She looks severely and solemnly at me and says: "Do not say any more, you will repent it." I tell her that I cannot stand comedies. Then she cries out something I don't catch, and rushes into her room. The key clicks behind her – she has locked herself in. I try the door, but getting no answer, go away angrily. Half an hour later Lisa runs in crying. "What is it? Has anything happened?" "We can't hear mama." We go. I pull at the double doors with all my might. The bolt had not been firmly secured, and the two halves both open. I approach the bed, on which she is lying awkwardly in her petticoats and with a pair of high boots on. An empty opium bottle is on the table. She is brought to herself. Tears follow, and a reconciliation. No, not a reconciliation: in the heart of each there is still the old animosity, with the additional irritation produced by the pain of this quarrel which each attributes to the other. But one must of course finish it all somehow, and life goes on in the old way. And so the same kind of quarrel, and even worse ones, occurred continually: once a week, once a month, or at times every day. It was always the same. Once I had already procured a passport to go abroad – the quarrel had continued for two days. But there was again a partial explanation, a partial reconciliation, and I did not go.

21

'So those were our relations when that man appeared. He arrived in Moscow – his name is Trukhachévski – and came to my house. It was in the morning. I received him. We had once been on familiar terms and he tried to maintain a familiar tone by using non-committal expressions, but I definitely adopted a conventional tone and he at once submitted to it. I disliked him from the first glance. But curiously enough a strange and fatal force led me not to repulse him, not to keep him away, but on the contrary to invite him to the house. After all, what could have been simpler than to converse with him coldly, and say goodbye without introducing him to my wife? But no, as if purposely, I began talking about his playing, and said I had been told he had given up the violin. He replied that, on the contrary, he now played more than ever. He referred to the fact that there had been a time when I myself played. I said I had given it up but that my wife played well. It is an astonishing thing that from the first day, from the first hour of my meeting him, my relations with him were such as they might have been only after all that subsequently happened. There was something strained in them: I noticed every word, every expression he or I used, and attributed importance to them.

'I introduced him to my wife. The conversation immediately turned to music, and he offered to be of use to her by playing with her. My wife was, as usual of late, very elegant, attractive, and disquietingly beautiful. He evidently pleased her at first sight. Besides she was glad that she would have someone to accompany her on a violin, which she was so fond of that she used to engage a violinist from the theatre for the purpose; and her face reflected her pleasure. But catching sight of me she at once understood my feeling and changed her expression, and a game of mutual deception began. I smiled pleasantly to appear as if I liked it. He, looking at my wife as all immoral men look at pretty women, pretended that he was only interested in the subject of the conversation – which no longer interested him at all; while she tried to seem indifferent, though my false smile of jealousy with which she was familiar, and his lustful gaze, evidently excited her. I saw that from their first encounter her eyes were particularly bright and, probably as a result of my jealousy, it seemed as if an electric current had been established between them, evoking as it were an identity of expressions, looks, and smiles. She blushed and he blushed. She smiled and he smiled. We spoke about music, Paris, and all sorts of trifles. Then he rose to go, and stood smilingly, holding his hat against his twitching thigh and looking now at her and now at me, as if in expectation of what we would do. I remember that instant just because at that moment I might not have invited him, and then nothing would have happened. But I glanced at him and at her and said silently to myself, "Don't suppose that I am jealous," "or that I am afraid of you," I added mentally addressing him, and I invited him to come some evening and bring his violin to play with my wife. She glanced at me with surprise, flushed, and as if frightened began to decline, saying that she did not play well enough. This refusal irritated me still more, and I insisted the more on his coming. I remember the curious feeling with which I looked at the back of his head, with the black hair parted in the middle contrasting with the white nape of his neck, as he went out with his peculiar springing gait suggestive of some kind of a bird. I could not conceal from myself that that man's presence tormented me. "It depends on me," I reflected, "to act so as to see nothing more of him. But that would be to admit that I am afraid of him. No, I am not afraid of him; it would be too humiliating," I said to myself. And there in the ante-room, knowing that my wife heard me, I insisted that he should come that evening with his violin. He promised to do so, and left.

'In the evening he brought his violin and they played. But it took a long time to arrange matters – they had not the music they wanted, and my wife could not without preparation play what they had. I was very fond of music and sympathised with their playing, arranging a music-stand for him and turning over the pages. They played a few things, some songs without words, and a little sonata by Mozart. They played splendidly, and he had an exceptionally fine tone. Besides that, he had a refined and elevated taste not at all in correspondence with his character.

'He was of course a much better player than my wife, and he helped her, while at the same time politely praising her playing. He behaved himself very well. My wife seemed interested only in music and was very simple and natural. But though I pretended to be interested in the music I was tormented by jealousy all the evening.

'From the first moment his eyes met my wife's I saw that the animal in each of them, regardless of all conditions of their position and of society, asked, "May I?" and answered, "Oh, yes, certainly." I saw that he had not at all expected to find my wife, a Moscow lady, so attractive, and that he was very pleased. For he had no doubt whatever that she was *willing*. The only crux was whether that unendurable husband could hinder them. Had I been pure I should not have understood this, but, like the majority of men, I had myself regarded women in that way before I married and therefore could read his mind like a manuscript. I was particularly tormented because I saw without doubt that she had no other feeling towards me than a continual irritation only occasionally interrupted by the habitual sensuality; but that this man – by his external refinement and novelty and still more by his undoubtedly great talent for music, by the nearness that comes of playing together, and by the influence music, especially the violin, exercises on impressionable natures – was sure not only to please but certainly and without the least hesitation to conquer, crush, bind her, twist her round his little finger and do whatever he liked with her. I could not help seeing this and I suffered terribly. But for all that, or perhaps on account of it, some force obliged me against my will to be not merely polite but amiable to him. Whether I did it for my wife or for him, to show that I was not afraid of him, or whether I did it to deceive myself – I don't know, but I know that from the first I could not behave naturally with him. In order not to yield to my wish to kill him there and then, I had to make much of him. I gave him expensive wines at supper, went into raptures over his playing, spoke to him with a particularly amiable smile, and invited him to dine and play with my wife again the next Sunday. I told him I would ask a few friends who were fond of music to hear him. And so it ended.'

Greatly agitated, Pózdnyshev changed his position and emitted his peculiar sound.

'It is strange how the presence of that man acted on me,' he began again, with an evident effort to keep calm. 'I come home from the Exhibition a day or two later, enter the ante-room, and suddenly feel something heavy, as if a stone had fallen on my heart, and I cannot understand what it is. It was that passing through the ante-room I noticed something which reminded me of him. I realised what it was only in my study, and went back to the ante-room to make sure. Yes, I was not mistaken, there was his overcoat. A fashionable coat, you know. (Though I did not realise it, I observed everything connected with him with extraordinary attention.) I enquire: sure enough he is there. I pass on to the dancing-room, not through the drawing-room but through the schoolroom. My daughter, Lisa, sits reading a book and the nurse sits with the youngest boy at the table, making a lid of some kind spin round. The door to the dancing-room is shut but I hear the sound of a rhythmic arpeggio and his and her voices. I listen, but cannot make out anything.

'Evidently the sound of the piano is purposely made to drown the sound of their voices, their kisses . . . perhaps. My God! What was aroused in me! Even to think of the beast that then lived in me fills me with horror! My heart suddenly contracted, stopped, and then began to beat like a hammer. My chief feeling, as usual whenever I was enraged, was one of self-pity. "In the presence of the children! of their nurse!" thought I. Probably I looked awful, for Lisa gazed at me with strange eyes. "What am I to do?" I asked myself. "Go in? I can't: heaven only knows what I should do. But neither can I go away." The nurse looked at me as if she understood my position. "But it is impossible not to go in," I said to myself, and I quickly opened the door. He was sitting at the piano playing those arpeggios with his large white upturned fingers. She was standing in the curve of the piano, bending over some open music. She was the first to see or hear, and glanced at me. Whether she was frightened and pretended not to be, or whether she was really not frightened, anyway she did not start or move but only blushed, and that not at once.

' "How glad I am that you have come: we have not decided what to play on Sunday," she said in a tone she would not have used to me had we been alone. This and her using the word "we" of herself and him, filled me with indignation. I greeted him silently.

'He pressed my hand, and at once, with a smile which I thought distinctly ironic, began to explain that he had brought some music to practise for Sunday, but that they disagreed about what to play: a classical but more difficult piece, namely Beethoven's sonata for the violin, or a few little pieces. It was all so simple and natural that there was nothing one could cavil at, yet I felt certain that it was all untrue and that they had agreed how to deceive me.

'One of the most distressing conditions of life for a jealous man (and everyone is jealous in our world) are certain society conventions which allow a man and woman the greatest and most dangerous proximity. You would become a laughing-stock to others if you tried to prevent such nearness at balls, or the nearness of doctors to their women-patients, or of people occupied with art, sculpture, and especially music. A couple are occupied with the noblest of arts, music; this demands a certain nearness, and there is nothing reprehensible in that and only a stupid jealous husband can see anything undesirable in it. Yet everybody knows that it is by means of those very pursuits, especially of music, that the greater part of the adulteries in our society occur. I evidently confused them by the confusion I betrayed: for a long time I could not speak. I was like a bottle held upside down from which the water does not flow because it is too full. I wanted to abuse him and to turn him out, but again felt that I must treat him courteously and amiably. And I did so. I acted as though I approved of it all, and again because of the strange feeling which made me behave to him the more amiably the more his presence distressed me. I told him that I trusted his taste and advised her to do the same. He stayed as long as was necessary to efface the unpleasant impression caused by my sudden entrance – looking frightened and remaining silent – and then left, pretending that it was now decided what to play next day. I was however fully convinced that compared to what interested them the question of what to play was quite indifferent.

'I saw him out to the ante-room with special politeness. (How could one do less than accompany a man who had come to disturb the peace and destroy the happiness of a whole family?) And I pressed his soft white hand with particular warmth.

22

'I did not speak to her all that day – I could not. Nearness to her aroused in me such hatred of her that I was afraid of myself. At dinner in the presence of the children she asked me when I was going away. I had to go next week to the District Meetings of the Zémstvo. I told her the date. She asked whether I did not want anything for the journey. I did not answer but sat silent at table and then went in silence to my study. Latterly she used never to come to my room, especially not at that time of day. I lay in my study filled with anger. Suddenly I heard her familiar step, and the terrible, monstrous idea entered my head that she, like Uriah's wife,[35] wished to conceal the sin she had already committed and that that was why she was coming to me at such an unusual time. "Can she be coming to me?" thought I, listening to her approaching footsteps. "If she is coming here, then I am right," and an inexpressible hatred of her took possession of me. Nearer and nearer came the steps. Is it possible that she won't pass on to the dancing-room? No, the door creaks and in the doorway appears her tall handsome figure, on her face and in her eyes a timid ingratiating look which she tries to hide, but which I see and the meaning of which I know. I almost choked, so long did I hold my breath, and still looking at her I grasped my cigarette-case and began to smoke.

' "Now how can you? One comes to sit with you for a bit, and you begin smoking" – and she sat down close to me on the sofa, leaning against me. I moved away so as not to touch her.

' "I see you are dissatisfied at my wanting to play on Sunday," she said.

' "I am not at all dissatisfied," I said.

' "As if I don't see!"

' "Well, I congratulate you on seeing. But I only see that you behave like a coquette . . . You always find pleasure in all kinds of vileness, but to me it is terrible!"

' "Oh, well, if you are going to scold like a cabman I'll go away."

' "Do, but remember that if you don't value the family honour, I value not you (devil take you) but the honour of the family!"

' "But what is the matter? What?"

' "Go away, for God's sake be off!"

'Whether she pretended not to understand what it was about or really did not understand, at any rate she took offence, grew angry, and did not go away but stood in the middle of the room.

' "You have really become impossible," she began. "You have a character that even an angel could not put up with." And as usual trying to sting me as painfully as possible, she reminded me of my conduct to my sister (an incident when, being exasperated, I said rude things to my sister); she knew I was distressed about it and she stung me just on that spot. "After that, nothing from you will surprise me," she said.

' "Yes! Insult me, humiliate me, disgrace me, and then put the blame on me," I said to myself, and suddenly I was seized by such terrible rage as I had never before experienced.

'For the first time I wished to give physical expression to that rage. I jumped up and went towards her; but just as I jumped up I remember becoming conscious of my rage and asking myself: "Is it right to give way to this feeling?" and at once I answered that it was right, that it would frighten her, and instead of restraining my fury I immediately began inflaming it still further, and was glad it burnt yet more fiercely within me.

' "Be off, or I'll kill you!" I shouted, going up to her and seizing her by the arm. I consciously intensified the anger in my voice as I said this. And I suppose I was terrible, for she was so frightened that she had not even the strength to go away, but only said: "Vásya, what is it? What is the matter with you?"

' "Go!" I roared louder still. "No one but you can drive me to fury. I do not answer for myself!"

'Having given reins to my rage, I revelled in it and wished to do something still more unusual to show the extreme degree of my anger. I felt a terrible desire to beat her, to kill her, but knew that this would not do, and so to give vent to my fury I seized a paperweight from my table, again shouting "Go!" and hurled it to the floor near her. I aimed it very exactly past her. Then she left the room, but stopped at the doorway, and immediately, while she still saw it (I did it so that she might see), I began snatching things from the table – candlesticks and inkstand – and hurling them on the floor still shouting "Go! Get out! I don't answer for myself!" She went away – and I immediately stopped.

'An hour later the nurse came to tell me that my wife was in hysterics. I went to her; she sobbed, laughed, could not speak, and her whole body was convulsed. She was not pretending, but was really ill.

'Towards morning she grew quiet, and we made peace under the influence of the feeling we called love.

'In the morning when, after our reconciliation, I confessed to her that I was jealous of Trukhachévski, she was not at all confused, but laughed most naturally; so strange did the very possibility of an infatuation for such a man seem to her, she said.

' "Could a decent woman have any other feeling for such a man than the pleasure of his music? Why, if you like I am ready never to see him again . . . not even on Sunday, though everybody has been invited. Write and tell him that I am ill, and there's an end of it! Only it is unpleasant that anyone, especially he himself, should imagine that he is dangerous. I am too proud to allow anyone to think that of me!"

'And you know, she was not lying, she believed what she was saying; she hoped by those words to evoke in herself contempt for him and so to defend herself from him, but she did not succeed in doing so. Everything was against her, especially that accursed music. So it all ended, and on the Sunday the guests assembled and they again played together.

23

'I suppose it is hardly necessary to say that I was very vain: if one is not vain there is nothing to live for in our usual way of life. So on that Sunday I arranged the dinner and the musical evening with much care. I bought the provisions myself and invited the guests.

'Towards six the visitors assembled. He came in evening dress with diamond studs that showed bad taste. He behaved in a free and easy manner, answered everything hurriedly with a smile of agreement and understanding, you know, with that peculiar expression which seems to say that all you may do or say is just what he expected. Everything that was not in good taste about him I noticed with particular pleasure, because it ought all to have had the effect of tranquillising me and showing that he was so far beneath my wife that, as she had said, she could not lower herself to his level. I did not now allow myself to be jealous. In the first place I had worried through that torment and needed rest, and secondly I wanted to believe my wife's assurances and did believe them. But though I was not jealous I was nevertheless not natural with either of them, and at dinner and during the first half of the evening before the music began I still followed their movements and looks.

'The dinner was, as dinners are, dull and pretentious. The music began pretty early. Oh, how I remember every detail of that evening! I remember how he brought in his violin, unlocked the case, took off the cover a lady had embroidered for him, drew out the violin, and began tuning it. I remember how my wife sat down at the piano with pretended unconcern, under which I saw that she was trying to conceal great timidity – chiefly as to her own ability – and then the usual A on the piano began, the pizzicato of the violin, and the arrangement of the music. Then I remember how they glanced at one another, turned to look at the audience who were seating themselves, said something to one another, and began. He took the first chords. His face grew serious, stern, and sympathetic, and listening to the sounds he produced, he touched the strings with careful fingers. The piano answered him. The music began . . . '

Pózdnyshev paused and produced his strange sound several times in succession. He tried to speak, but sniffed, and stopped.

'They played Beethoven's Kreutzer Sonata,'[36] he continued. 'Do you know the first presto? You do?' he cried. 'Ugh! Ugh! It is a terrible thing, that sonata. And especially that part. And in general music is a dreadful thing! What is it? I don't understand it. What is music? What does it do? And why does it do what it does? They say music exalts the soul. Nonsense, it is not true! It has an effect, an awful effect – I am speaking of myself – but not of an exalting kind. It has neither an exalting nor a debasing effect but it produces agitation. How can I put it? Music makes me forget myself, my real position; it transports me to some other position not my own. Under the influence of music it seems to me that I feel what I do not really feel, that I understand what I do not understand, that I can do what I cannot do. I explain it by the fact that music acts like yawning, like laughter: I am not sleepy, but I yawn when I see someone yawning; there is nothing for me to laugh at, but I laugh when I hear people laughing.

'Music carries me immediately and directly into the mental condition in which the man was who composed it. My soul merges with his and together with him I pass from one condition into another, but why this happens I don't know. You see, he who wrote, let us say, the Kreutzer Sonata – Beethoven – knew of course why he was in that condition; that condition caused him to do certain actions and therefore that condition had a meaning for him, but for me – none at all. That is why music only agitates and doesn't lead to a conclusion. Well, when a military march is played the soldiers march to the music and the music has achieved its object. A dance is played, I dance and the music has achieved its object. Mass has been sung, I receive Communion, and that music too has reached a conclusion. Otherwise it is only agitating, and what ought to be done in that agitation is lacking. That is why music sometimes acts so dreadfully, so terribly. In China, music is a State affair. And that is as it should be. How can one allow anyone who pleases to hypnotise another, or many others, and do what he likes with them? And especially that this hypnotist should be the first immoral man who turns up?

'It is a terrible instrument in the hands of any chance user! Take that Kreutzer Sonata for instance, how can that first presto be played in a drawing-room among ladies in low-necked dresses? To hear that played, to clap a little, and then to eat ices and talk of the latest scandal? Such things should only be played on certain important significant occasions, and then only when certain actions answering to such music are wanted; play it then and do what the music has moved you to. Otherwise an awakening of energy and feeling unsuited both to the time and the place, to which no outlet is given, cannot but act harmfully. At any rate that piece had a terrible effect on me; it was as if quite new feelings, new possibilities, of which I had till then been unaware, had been revealed to me. "That's how it is: not at all as I used to think and live, but that way," something seemed to say within me. What this new thing was that had been revealed to me I could not explain to myself, but the consciousness of this new condition was very joyous. All those same people, including my wife and him, appeared in a new light.

'After that allegro they played the beautiful, but common and unoriginal, andante with trite variations, and the very weak finale. Then, at the request of the visitors, they played Ernst's Elegy[37] and a few small pieces. They were all good, but they did not produce on me a one-hundredth part of the impression the first piece had. The effect of the first piece formed the background for them all.

'I felt light-hearted and cheerful the whole evening. I had never seen my wife as she was that evening. Those shining eyes, that severe, significant expression while she played, and her melting languor and feeble, pathetic, and blissful smile after they had finished. I saw all that but did not attribute any meaning to it except that she was feeling what I felt, and that to her as to me new feelings, never before experienced, were revealed or, as it were, recalled. The evening ended satisfactorily and the visitors departed.

'Knowing that I had to go away to attend the Zémstvo[38] Meetings two days later, Trukhachévski on leaving said he hoped to repeat the pleasure of that evening when he next came to Moscow. From this I concluded that he did not consider it possible to come to my house during my absence, and this pleased me.

'It turned out that as I should not be back before he left town, we should not see one another again.

'For the first time I pressed his hand with real pleasure, and thanked him for the enjoyment he had given us. In the same way he bade a final farewell to my wife. Their leave-taking seemed to be most natural and proper. Everything was splendid. My wife and I were both very well satisfied with our evening party.

24

'Two days later I left for the Meetings, parting from my wife in the best and most tranquil of moods.

'In the district there was always an enormous amount to do and a quite special life, a special little world of its own. I spent two ten-hour days at the Council. A letter from my wife was brought me on the second day and I read it there and then.

'She wrote about the children, about uncle, about the nurse, about shopping, and among other things she mentioned, as a most natural occurrence, that Trukhachévski had called, brought some music he had promised, and had offered to play again, but that she had refused.

'I did not remember his having promised any music, but thought he had taken leave for good, and I was therefore unpleasantly struck by this. I was however so busy that I had no time to think of it, and it was only in the evening when I had returned to my lodgings that I reread her letter.

'Besides the fact that Trukhachévski had called at my house during my absence, the whole tone of the letter seemed to me unnatural. The mad beast of jealousy began to growl in its kennel and wanted to leap out, but I was afraid of that beast and quickly fastened him in. "What an abominable feeling this jealousy is!" I said to myself. "What could be more natural than what she writes?"

'I went to bed and began thinking about the affairs awaiting me next day. During those Meetings, sleeping in a new place, I usually slept badly, but now I fell asleep very quickly. And as sometimes happens, you know, you feel a kind of electric shock and wake up. So I awoke thinking of her, of my physical love for her, and of Trukhachévski, and of everything being accomplished between them. Horror and rage compressed my heart. But I began to reason with myself. "What nonsense!" said I to myself. "There are no grounds to go on, there is nothing and there has been nothing. How can I so degrade her and myself as to imagine such horrors? He is a sort of hired violinist, known as a worthless fellow, and suddenly an honourable woman, the respected mother of a family, *my* wife . . . What absurdity!" So it seemed to me on the one hand. "How could it help being so?" it seemed on the other. "How could that simplest and most intelligible thing help happening – that for the sake of which I married her, for the sake of which I have been living with her, what alone I wanted of her, and which others including this musician must therefore also want? He is an unmarried man, healthy (I remember how he crunched the gristle of a cutlet and how greedily his red lips clung to the glass of wine), well fed, plump, and not merely unprincipled but evidently making it a principle to accept the pleasures that present themselves. And they have music, that most exquisite voluptuousness of the senses, as a link between them. What then could make him refrain? She? But who is she? She was, and still is, a mystery. I don't know her. I only know her as an animal. And nothing can or should restrain an animal."

'Only then did I remember their faces that evening when, after the Kreutzer Sonata, they played some impassioned little piece, I don't remember by whom, impassioned to the point of obscenity. "How dared I go away?" I asked myself, remembering their faces. Was it not clear that everything had happened between them that evening? Was it not evident already then that there was not only no barrier between them, but that they both, and she chiefly, felt a certain measure of shame after what had happened? I remember her weak, piteous, and beatific smile as she wiped the perspiration from her flushed face when I came up to the piano. Already then they avoided looking at one another, and only at supper when he was pouring out some water for her, they glanced at each other with the vestige of a smile. I now recalled with horror the glance and scarcely perceptible smile I had then caught. "Yes, it is all over," said one voice, and immediately the other voice said something entirely different. "Something has come over you, it can't be that it is so," said that other voice. It felt uncanny lying in the dark and I struck a light, and felt a kind of terror in that little room with its yellow wallpaper. I lit a cigarette and, as always happens when one's thoughts go round and round in a circle of insoluble contradictions, I smoked, taking one cigarette after another in order to befog myself so as not to see those contradictions.

'I did not sleep all night, and at five in the morning, having decided that I could not continue in such a state of tension, I rose, woke the caretaker who attended me and sent him to get horses. I sent a note to the Council saying that I had been recalled to Moscow on urgent business and asking that one of the members should take my place. At eight o'clock I got into my trap and started.'

25

The conductor entered and seeing that our candle had burnt down put it out, without supplying a fresh one. The day was dawning. Pózdnyshev was silent, but sighed deeply all the time the conductor was in the carriage. He continued his story only after the conductor had gone out, and in the semi-darkness of the carriage only the rattle of the windows of the moving carriage and the rhythmic snoring of the clerk could be heard. In the half-light of dawn I could not see Pózdnyshev's face at all, but only heard his voice becoming ever more and more excited and full of suffering.

'I had to travel twenty-four miles by road and eight hours by rail. It was splendid driving. It was frosty autumn weather, bright and sunny. The roads were in that condition when the tyres leave their dark imprint on them, you know. They were smooth, the light brilliant, and the air invigorating. It was pleasant driving in the tarantas.[39] When it grew lighter and I had started I felt easier. Looking at the houses, the fields, and the passers-by, I forgot where I was going. Sometimes I felt that I was simply taking a drive, and that nothing of what was calling me back had taken place. This oblivion was peculiarly enjoyable. When I remembered where I was going to, I said to myself, "We shall see when the time comes; I must not think about it." When we were half-way an incident occurred which detained me and still further distracted my thoughts. The tarantas broke down and had to be repaired. That breakdown had a very important effect, for it caused me to arrive in Moscow at midnight, instead of at seven o'clock as I had expected, and to reach home between twelve and one, as I missed the express and had to travel by an ordinary train. Going to fetch a cart, having the tarantas mended, settling up, tea at the inn, a talk with the innkeeper – all this still further diverted my attention. It was twilight before all was ready and I started again. By night it was even pleasanter driving than during the day. There was a new moon, a slight frost, still good roads, good horses, and a jolly driver, and as I went on I enjoyed it, hardly thinking at all of what lay before me; or perhaps I enjoyed it just because I knew what awaited me and was saying goodbye to the joys of life. But that tranquil mood, that ability to suppress my feelings, ended with my drive. As soon as I entered the train something entirely different began. That eight-hour journey in a railway carriage was something dreadful, which I shall never forget all my life. Whether it was that having taken my seat in the carriage I vividly imagined myself as having already arrived, or that railway travelling has such an exciting effect on people, at any rate from the moment I sat down in the train I could no longer control my imagination, and with extraordinary vividness which inflamed my jealousy it painted incessantly, one after another, pictures of what had gone on in my absence, of how she had been false to me. I burnt with indignation, anger, and a peculiar feeling of intoxication with my own humiliation, as I gazed at those pictures, and I could not tear myself away from them; I could not help looking at them, could not efface them, and could not help evoking them.

'That was not all. The more I gazed at those imaginary pictures the stronger grew my belief in their reality. The vividness with which they presented themselves to me seemed to serve as proof that what I imagined was real. It was as if some devil against my will invented and suggested to me the most terrible reflections. An old conversation I had had with Trukhachévski's brother came to my mind, and in a kind of ecstasy I rent my heart with that conversation, making it refer to Trukhachévski and my wife.

'That had occurred long before, but I recalled it. Trukhachévski's brother, I remember, in reply to a question whether he frequented houses of ill-fame, had said that a decent man would not go to places where there was danger of infection and it was dirty and nasty, since he could always find a decent woman. And now his brother had found my wife! "True, she is not in her first youth, has lost a side-tooth, and there is a slight puffiness about her; but it can't be helped, one has to take advantage of what one can get," I imagined him to be thinking. "Yes, it is condescending of him to take her for his mistress!" I said to myself. "And she is safe . . . " "No, it is impossible!" I thought horror-struck. "There is nothing of the kind, nothing! There are not even any grounds for suspecting such things. Didn't she tell me that the very thought that I could be jealous of him was degrading to her? Yes, but she is lying, she is always lying!" I exclaimed, and everything began anew . . . There were only two other people in the carriage; an old woman and her husband, both very taciturn, and even they got out at one of the stations and I was quite alone. I was like a caged animal: now I jumped up and went to the window, now I began to walk up and down trying to speed the carriage up; but the carriage with all its seats and windows went jolting on in the same way, just as ours does . . . '

Pózdnyshev jumped up, took a few steps, and sat down again.

'Oh, I am afraid, afraid of railway carriages, I am seized with horror. Yes, it is awful!' he continued. 'I said to myself, "I will think of something else. Suppose I think of the innkeeper where I had tea," and there in my mind's eye appears the innkeeper with his long beard and his grandson, a boy of the age of my Vásya. "My Vásya! He will see how the musician kisses his mother. What will happen in his poor soul? But what does she care? She loves" . . . and again the same thing rose up in me. "No, no . . . I will think about the inspection of the District Hospital. Oh, yes, about the patient who complained of the doctor yesterday. The doctor has a moustache like Trukhachévski's. And how impudent he is . . . they both deceived me when he said he was leaving

Moscow," and it began afresh. Everything I thought of had some connection with them. I suffered dreadfully. The chief cause of the suffering was my ignorance, my doubt, and the contradictions within me: my not knowing whether I ought to love or hate her. My suffering was of a strange kind. I felt a hateful consciousness of my humiliation and of his victory, but a terrible hatred for her. "It will not do to put an end to myself and leave her; she must at least suffer to some extent, and at least understand that I have suffered," I said to myself. I got out at every station to divert my mind. At one station I saw some people drinking, and I immediately drank some vodka. Beside me stood a Jew who was also drinking. He began to talk, and to avoid being alone in my carriage I went with him into his dirty third-class carriage reeking with smoke and bespattered with shells of sunflower seeds. There I sat down beside him and he chattered a great deal and told anecdotes. I listened to him, but could not take in what he was saying because I continued to think about my own affairs. He noticed this and demanded my attention. Then I rose and went back to my carriage. "I must think it over," I said to myself. "Is what I suspect true, and is there any reason for me to suffer?" I sat down, wishing to think it over calmly, but immediately, instead of calm reflection, the same thing began again: instead of reflection, pictures and fancies. "How often I have suffered like this," I said to myself (recalling former similar attacks of jealousy), "and afterwards it all ended in nothing. So it will be now perhaps, yes certainly it will. I shall find her calmly asleep, she will wake up, be pleased to see me, and by her words and looks I shall know that there has been nothing and that this is all nonsense. Oh, how good that would be! But no, that has happened too often and won't happen again now," some voice seemed to say; and it began again. Yes, that was where the punishment lay! I wouldn't take a young man to a lock-hospital to knock the hankering after women out of him, but into my soul, to see the devils that were rending it! What was terrible, you know, was that I considered myself to have a complete right to her body as if it were my own, and yet at the same time I felt I could not control that body, that it was not mine and she could dispose of it as she pleased, and that she wanted to dispose of it not as I wished her to. And I could do nothing either to her or to him. He, like Vánka the Steward,[40] could sing a song before the gallows of how he kissed the sugared lips and so forth. And he would triumph. If she has not yet done it but wishes to – and I know that she does wish to – it is still worse; it would be better if she had done it and I knew it, so that there would be an end to this uncertainty. I could not have said what it was I wanted. I wanted her not to desire that which she was bound to desire. It was utter insanity.

26

'At the last station but one, when the conductor had been to collect the tickets, I gathered my things together and went out on to the brake-platform, and the consciousness that the crisis was at hand still further increased my agitation. I felt cold, and my jaw trembled so that my teeth chattered. I automatically left the terminus with the crowd, took a cab, got in, and drove off. I rode looking at the few passers-by, the night-watchmen, and the shadows of my trap thrown by the street lamps, now in front and now behind me, and did not think of anything. When we had gone about half a mile my feet felt cold, and I remembered that I had taken off my woollen stockings in the train and put them in my satchel. "Where is the satchel? Is it here? Yes." And my wicker trunk? I remembered that I had entirely forgotten about my luggage, but finding that I had the luggage-ticket I decided that it was not worth while going back for it, and so continued my way.

'Try now as I will, I cannot recall my state of mind at the time. What did I think? What did I want? I don't know at all. All I remember is a consciousness that something dreadful and very important in my life was imminent. Whether that important event occurred because I thought it would, or whether I had a presentiment of what was to happen, I don't know. It may even be that after what has happened all the foregoing moments have acquired a certain gloom in my mind. I drove up to the front porch. It was past midnight. Some cabmen were waiting in front of the porch expecting, from the fact that there were lights in the windows, to get fares. (The lights were in our flat, in the dancing-room and drawing-room.) Without considering why it was still light in our windows so late, I went upstairs in the same state of expectation of something dreadful, and rang. Egór, a kind, willing, but very stupid footman, opened the door. The first thing my eyes fell on in the hall was a man's cloak hanging on the stand with other outdoor coats. I ought to have been surprised but was not, for I had expected it. "That's it!" I said to myself. When I asked Egór who the visitor was and he named Trukhachévski, I enquired whether there was anyone else. He replied, "Nobody, sir." I remember that he replied in a tone as if he wanted to cheer me and dissipate my doubts of there being anybody else there. "So it is, so it is," I seemed to be saying to myself. "And the children?" "All well, heaven be praised. In bed, long ago."

'I could not breathe, and could not check the trembling of my jaw. "Yes, so it is not as I thought: I used to expect a misfortune but things used to turn out all right and in the usual way. Now it is not as usual, but is all as I pictured to myself. I thought it was only fancy, but here it is, all real. Here it all is . . . !"

'I almost began to sob, but the devil immediately suggested to me: "Cry, be sentimental, and they will get away quietly. You will have no proof and will continue to suffer and doubt all your life." And my self-pity immediately vanished, and a strange sense of joy arose in me, that my torture would now be over, that now I could punish her, could get rid of her, and could vent my anger. And I gave vent to it – I became a beast, a cruel and cunning beast.

' "Don't!" I said to Egór, who was about to go to the drawing-room. "Here is my luggage-ticket, take a cab as quick as you can and go and get my luggage. Go!" He went down the passage to fetch his overcoat. Afraid that he might alarm them, I went as far as his little room and waited while he put on his overcoat. From the drawing-room, beyond another room, one could hear voices and the clatter of knives and plates. They were eating and had not heard the bell. "If only they don't come out now," thought I. Egór put on his overcoat, which had an astrakhan collar, and went out. I locked the door after him and felt creepy when I knew I was alone and must act at once. How, I did not yet know. I only knew that all was now over, that there could be no doubt as to her guilt, and that I should punish her immediately and end my relations with her.

'Previously I had doubted and had thought: "Perhaps after all it's not true, perhaps I am mistaken." But now it was so no longer. It was all irrevocably decided. "Without my knowledge she is alone with him at night! That is a complete disregard of everything! Or worse still: it is intentional boldness and impudence in crime, that the boldness may serve as a sign of innocence. All is clear. There is no doubt." I only feared one thing – their parting hastily, inventing some fresh lie, and thus depriving me of clear evidence and of the possibility of proving the fact. So as to catch them more quickly I went on tiptoe to the dancing-room where they were, not through the drawing-room but through the passage and nurseries.

'In the first nursery slept the boys. In the second nursery the nurse moved and was about to wake, and I imagined to myself what she would think when she knew all; and such pity for myself seized me at that thought that I could not restrain my tears, and not to wake the children I ran on tiptoe into the passage and on into my study, where I fell sobbing on the sofa.

' "I, an honest man, I, the son of my parents, I, who have all my life dreamt of the happiness of married life; I, a man who was never unfaithful to her . . . And now! Five children, and she is embracing a musician because he has red lips!

' "No, she is not a human being. She is a bitch, an abominable bitch! In the next room to her children whom she has all her life pretended to love. And writing to me as she did! Throwing herself so barefacedly on his neck! But what do I know? Perhaps she long ago carried on with the footmen, and so got the children who are considered mine!

' "Tomorrow I should have come back and she would have met me with her fine coiffure, with her elegant waist and her indolent, graceful movements" (I saw all her attractive, hateful face), "and that beast of jealousy would for ever have sat in my heart lacerating it. What will the nurse think? . . . And Egór? And poor little Lisa! She already understands something. Ah, that impudence, those lies! And that animal sensuality which I know so well," I said to myself.

'I tried to get up but could not. My heart was beating so that I could not stand on my feet. "Yes, I shall die of a stroke. She will kill me. That is just what she wants. What is killing to her? But no, that would be too advantageous for her and I will not give her that pleasure. Yes, here I sit while they eat and laugh and . . . Yes, though she was no longer in her first freshness he did not disdain her. For in spite of that she is not bad looking, and above all she is at any rate not dangerous to his precious health. And why did I not throttle her then?" I said to myself, recalling the moment when, the week before, I drove her out of my study and hurled things about. I vividly recalled the state I had then been in; I not only recalled it, but again felt the need to strike and destroy that I had felt then. I remember how I wished to act, and how all considerations except those necessary for action went out of my head. I entered into that condition when an animal or a man, under the influence of physical excitement at a time of danger, acts with precision and deliberation but without losing a moment and always with a single definite aim in view.

'The first thing I did was to take off my boots and, in my socks, approach the sofa, on the wall above which guns and daggers were hung. I took down a curved Damascus dagger that had never been used and was very sharp. I drew it out of its scabbard. I remember the scabbard fell behind the sofa, and I remember thinking "I must find it afterwards or it will get lost." Then I took off my overcoat which I was still wearing, and stepping softly in my socks I went there.

27

'Having crept up stealthily to the door, I suddenly opened it. I remember the expression of their faces. I remember that expression because it gave me a painful pleasure – it was an expression of terror. That was just what I wanted. I shall never forget the look of desperate terror that appeared on both their faces the first instant they saw me. He I think was sitting at the table, but on seeing or hearing me he jumped to his feet and stood with his back to the cupboard. His face expressed nothing but quite unmistakable terror. Her face too expressed terror but there was something else besides. If it had expressed only terror, perhaps what happened might not have happened; but on her face there was, or at any rate so it seemed to me at the first moment, also an expression of regret and annoyance that love's raptures and her happiness with him had been disturbed. It was as if she wanted nothing but that her present happiness should not be interfered with. These expressions remained on their faces but an instant. The look of terror on his changed immediately to one of enquiry: might he, or might he not, begin lying? If he might, he must begin at once; if not, something else would happen. But what? . . . He looked enquiringly at her face. On her face the look of vexation and regret changed as she looked at him (so it seemed to me) to one of solicitude for him.

'For an instant I stood in the doorway holding the dagger behind my back.

'At that moment he smiled, and in a ridiculously indifferent tone remarked: "And we have been having some music."

' "What a surprise!" she began, falling into his tone. But neither of them finished; the same fury I had experienced the week before overcame me. Again I felt that need of destruction, violence, and a transport of rage, and yielded to it. Neither finished what they were saying. That something else began which he had feared and which immediately destroyed all they were saying. I rushed towards her, still hiding the dagger that he might not prevent my striking her in the side under her breast. I selected that spot from the first. Just as I rushed at her he saw it, and – a thing I never expected of him –

seized me by the arm and shouted: "Think what you are doing! . . . Help, someone! . . . "

'I snatched my arm away and rushed at him in silence. His eyes met mine and he suddenly grew as pale as a sheet to his very lips. His eyes flashed in a peculiar way, and – what again I had not expected – he darted under the piano and out at the door. I was going to rush after him, but a weight hung on my left arm. It was she. I tried to free myself, but she hung on yet more heavily and would not let me go. This unexpected hindrance, the weight, and her touch which was loathsome to me, inflamed me still more. I felt that I was quite mad and that I must look frightful, and this delighted me. I swung my left arm with all my might, and my elbow hit her straight in the face. She cried out and let go my arm. I wanted to run after him, but remembered that it is ridiculous to run after one's wife's lover in one's socks; and I did not wish to be ridiculous but terrible. In spite of the fearful frenzy I was in, I was all the time aware of the impression I might produce on others, and was even partly guided by that impression. I turned towards her. She fell on the couch, and holding her hand to her bruised eyes, looked at me. Her face showed fear and hatred of me, the enemy, as a rat's does when one lifts the trap in which it has been caught. At any rate I saw nothing in her expression but this fear and hatred of me. It was just the fear and hatred of me which would be evoked by love for another. But still I might perhaps have restrained myself and not done what I did had she remained silent. But she suddenly began to speak and to catch hold of the hand in which I held the dagger.

' "Come to yourself! What are you doing? What is the matter? There has been nothing, nothing, nothing . . . I swear it!"

'I might still have hesitated, but those last words of hers, from which I concluded just the opposite – that everything had happened – called forth a reply. And the reply had to correspond to the temper to which I had brought myself, which continued to increase and had to go on increasing. Fury, too, has its laws.

' "Don't lie, you wretch!" I howled, and seized her arm with my left hand, but she wrenched herself away. Then, still without letting go of the dagger, I seized her by the throat with my left hand, threw her backwards, and began throttling her. What a firm neck it was . . . ! She seized my hand with both hers trying to pull it away from her throat, and as if I had only waited for that, I struck her with all my might with the dagger in the side below the ribs.

'When people say they don't remember what they do in a fit of fury, it is rubbish, falsehood. I remembered everything and did not for a moment lose consciousness of what I was doing. The more frenzied I became the more brightly the light of consciousness burnt in me, so that I could not help knowing everything I did. I knew what I was doing every second. I cannot say that I knew beforehand what I was going to do; but I knew what I was doing when I did it, and even I think a little before, as if to make repentance possible and to be able to tell myself that I could stop. I knew I was hitting below the ribs and that the dagger would enter. At the moment I did it I knew I was doing an awful thing such as I had never done before, which would have terrible consequences. But that consciousness passed like a flash of lightning and the deed immediately followed the consciousness. I realised the action with extraordinary clearness. I felt, and remember, the momentary resistance of her corset and of something else, and then the plunging of the dagger into something soft. She seized the dagger with her hands, and cut them, but could not hold it back.

'For a long time afterwards, in prison when the moral change had taken place in me, I thought of that moment, recalled what I could of it, and considered it. I remembered that for an instant, only an instant, before the action I had a terrible consciousness that I was killing, had killed, a defenceless woman, my wife! I remember the horror of that consciousness and conclude from that, and even dimly remember, that having plunged the dagger in I pulled it out immediately, trying to remedy what had been done and to stop it. I stood for a second motionless waiting to see what would happen, and whether it could be remedied.

'She jumped to her feet and screamed: "Nurse! He has killed me."

'Having heard the noise the nurse was standing by the door. I continued to stand waiting, and not believing the truth. But the blood rushed from under her corset. Only then did I understand that it could not be remedied, and I immediately decided that it was not necessary it should be, that I had done what I wanted and had to do. I waited till she fell down, and the nurse, crying "Good God!" ran to her, and only then did I throw away the dagger and leave the room.

' "I must not be excited; I must know what I am doing," I said to myself without looking at her and at the nurse. The nurse was screaming – calling for the maid. I went down the passage, sent the maid, and went into my study. "What am I to do now?" I asked myself, and immediately realised what it must be. On entering the study I went straight to the wall, took down a revolver and examined it – it was loaded – I put it on the table. Then I picked up the scabbard from behind the sofa and sat down there.

'I sat thus for a long time. I did not think of anything or call anything to mind. I heard the sounds of bustling outside. I heard someone drive up, then someone else. Then I heard and saw Egór bring into the room my wicker trunk he had fetched. As if anyone wanted that!

' "Have you heard what has happened?" I asked. "Tell the yard-porter to inform the police." He did not reply, and went away. I rose, locked the door, got out my cigarettes and matches and began to smoke. I had not finished the cigarette before sleep overpowered me. I must have slept for a couple of hours. I remember dreaming that she and I were friendly together, that we had quarrelled but were making it up, there was something rather in the way, but we were friends. I was awakened by someone knocking at the door. "That is the police!" I thought, waking up. "I have committed murder, I think. But perhaps it is *she*, and nothing has happened." There was again a knock at the door. I did not answer, but was trying to solve the question whether it had happened or not. Yes, it had! I remembered the resistance of the corset and the plunging in of the dagger, and a cold shiver ran down my back. "Yes, it has. Yes, and now I must do away with myself too," I thought. But I thought this knowing that I should *not* kill myself. Still I got up and took the revolver in my hand. But it is strange: I remember how I had many times been near suicide, how even that day on the railway it had seemed easy, easy just because I thought how it would stagger her – now I was not only unable to kill myself but even to think of it. "Why should I do it?" I asked myself, and there was no reply. There was more knocking at the door. "First I must find out who is knocking. There will still be time for this." I put down the revolver and covered it with a newspaper. I went to the door and unlatched it. It was my wife's sister, a kindly, stupid widow. "Vásya, what is this?" and her ever ready tears began to flow.

' "What do you want?" I asked rudely. I knew I ought not to be rude to her and had no reason to be, but I could think of no other tone to adopt.

' "Vásya, she is dying! Iván Zakhárych says so." Iván Zakhárych was her doctor and adviser.

' "Is he here?" I asked, and all my animosity against her surged up again. "Well, what of it?"

' "Vásya, go to her. Oh, how terrible it is!" said she.

' "Shall I go to her?" I asked myself, and immediately decided that

I must go to her. Probably it is always done, when a husband has killed his wife, as I had – he must certainly go to her. "If that is what is done, then I must go," I said to myself. "If necessary I shall always have time," I reflected, referring to the shooting of myself, and I went to her. "Now we shall have phrases, grimaces, but I will not yield to them," I thought. "Wait," I said to her sister, "it is silly without boots, let me at least put on slippers."

28

'Wonderful to say, when I left my study and went through the familiar rooms, the hope that nothing had happened again awoke in me; but the smell of that doctor's nastiness – iodoform and carbolic – took me aback. "No, it had happened." Going down the passage past the nursery I saw little Lisa. She looked at me with frightened eyes. It even seemed to me that all the five children were there and all looked at me. I approached the door, and the maid opened it from inside for me and passed out. The first thing that caught my eye was her light-grey dress thrown on a chair and all stained black with blood. She was lying on one of the twin beds (on mine because it was easier to get at), with her knees raised. She lay in a very sloping position supported by pillows, with her dressing jacket unfastened. Something had been put on the wound. There was a heavy smell of iodoform in the room. What struck me first and most of all was her swollen and bruised face, blue on part of the nose and under the eyes. This was the result of the blow with my elbow when she had tried to hold me back. There was nothing beautiful about her, but something repulsive as it seemed to me. I stopped on the threshold. "Go up to her, do," said her sister. "Yes, no doubt she wants to confess," I thought. "Shall I forgive her? Yes, she is dying and may be forgiven," I thought, trying to be magnanimous. I went up close to her. She raised her eyes to me with difficulty, one of them was black, and with an effort said falteringly: ' "You've got your way, killed . . . " and through the look of suffering and even the nearness of death her face had the old expression of cold animal hatred that I knew so well. "I shan't . . . let you have . . . the children, all the same . . . She" (her sister) "will take . . . "

'Of what to me was the most important matter, her guilt, her faithlessness, she seemed to consider it beneath her to speak.

' "Yes, look and admire what you have done," she said looking towards the door, and she sobbed. In the doorway stood her sister with the children. "Yes, see what you have done."

'I looked at the children and at her bruised disfigured face, and for the first time I forgot myself, my rights, my pride, and for the first time saw a human being in her. And so insignificant did all that had offended me, all my jealousy, appear, and so important what I had done, that I wished to fall with my face to her hand, and say: "Forgive me," but dared not do so.

'She lay silent with her eyes closed, evidently too weak to say more. Then her disfigured face trembled and puckered. She pushed me feebly away.

' "Why did it all happen? Why?"

' "Forgive me," I said.

' "Forgive! That's all rubbish! the devil . . . Only not to die! . . . " she cried, raising herself, and her glittering eyes were bent on me. "Yes, you have had your way! . . . I hate you! Ah! Ah!" she cried, evidently already in delirium and frightened at something. "Shoot! I'm not afraid! . . . Only kill everyone . . . ! He has gone . . . ! Gone . . . "

'After that the delirium continued all the time. She did not recognise anyone. She died towards noon that same day. Before that they had taken me to the police-station and from there to prison. There, during the eleven months I remained awaiting trial, I examined myself and my past, and understood it. I began to understand it on the third day: on the third day they took me *there* . . . '

He was going on but, unable to repress his sobs, he stopped. When he recovered himself he continued: 'I only began to understand when I saw her in her coffin . . . '

He gave a sob, but immediately continued hurriedly: 'Only when I saw her dead face did I understand all that I had done. I realised that I, I, had killed her; that it was my doing that she, living, moving, warm, had now become motionless, waxen, and cold, and that this could never, anywhere, or by any means, be remedied. He who has not lived through it cannot understand . . . Ugh! Ugh! Ugh! . . . ' he cried several times and then was silent.

We sat in silence a long while. He kept sobbing and trembling as he sat opposite me without speaking. His face had grown narrow and elongated and his mouth seemed to stretch right across it.

'Yes,' he suddenly said. 'Had I then known what I know now, everything would have been different. Nothing would have induced me to marry her . . . I should not have married at all.'

Again we remained silent for a long time.

'Well, forgive me . . . ' He turned away from me and lay down on the seat, covering himself up with his plaid. At the station where I had to get out (it was at eight o'clock in the morning) I went up to him to say goodbye. Whether he was asleep or only pretended to be, at any rate he did not move. I touched him with my hand. He uncovered his face, and I could see he had not been asleep.

'Goodbye,' I said, holding out my hand. He gave me his and smiled slightly, but so piteously that I felt ready to weep.

'Yes, forgive me . . . ' he said, repeating the same words with which he had concluded his story.

Afterword by the Author*

I have received, and still continue to receive, numbers of letters from persons who are perfect strangers to me, asking me to state in plain and simple language my own views on the subject handled in the story entitled 'The Kreutzer Sonata'. With this request I shall now endeavour to comply.

My views on the question may be succinctly stated as follows: Without entering into details, it will be generally admitted that I am accurate in saying that many people condone in young men a course of conduct with regard to the other sex which is incompatible with strict morality, and that this dissoluteness is pardoned generally. Both parents and the government, in consequence of this view, may be said to wink at profligacy, and even in the last resource to encourage its practice. I am of opinion that this is not right.

It is not possible that the health of one class should necessitate the ruin of another, and, in consequence, it is our first duty to turn a deaf ear to such an essential immoral doctrine, no matter how strongly society may have established or law protected it. Moreover, it needs to be fully recognised that men are rightly to be held responsible for the consequences of their own acts, and that these are no longer to be visited on the woman alone. It follows from this that it is the duty of men who do not wish to lead a life of infamy to practice such continence in respect to all woman as they would were the female society in which they move made up exclusively of their own mothers and sisters.

---

* For readers interested in seeing how Tolstoy developed his views on sex and marriage we have added the text of his later Afterword to 'The Kreutzer Sonata' in the contemporary translation by B. J. Tucker (Boston, 1890).

A more rational mode of life should be adopted which would include abstinence from all alcoholic drinks, from excess in eating and from flesh meat, on the one hand, and recourse to physical labour on the other. I am not speaking of gymnastics, or of any of those occupations which may be fitly described as playing at work; I mean the genuine toil that fatigues. No one need go far in search of proofs that this kind of abstemious living is not merely possible, but far less hurtful to health than excess. Hundreds of instances are known to every one. This is my first contention.

In the second place, I think that of late years, through various reasons which I need not enter, but among which the above-mentioned laxity of opinion in society and the frequent idealisation of the subject in current literature and painting may be mentioned, conjugal infidelity has become more common and is considered less reprehensible. I am of opinion that this is not right. The origin of the evil is twofold. It is due, in the first place, to a natural instinct, and, in the second, to the elevation of this instinct to a place to which it does not rightly belong. This being so, the evil can only be remedied by effecting a change in the views now in vogue about 'falling in love' and all that this term implies, by educating men and women at home through family influence and example, and abroad by means of healthy public opinion, to practice that abstinence which morality and Christianity alike enjoin. This is my second contention.

In the third place I am of opinion that another consequence of the false light in which 'falling in love', and what it leads to, are viewed in our society, is that the birth of children has lost its pristine significance, and that modern marriages are conceived less and less from the point of view of the family. I am of opinion that this is not right. This is my third contention.

In the fourth place, I am of opinion that the children (who in our society are considered an obstacle to enjoyment – an unlucky accident, as it were) are educated not with a view to the problem which they will be one day called on to face and to solve, but solely with an eye to the pleasure which they may be made to yield to their parents. The consequence is, that the children of human beings are brought up for all the world like the young of animals, the chief care of their parents being not to train them to such work as is worthy of men and women, but to increase their weight, or add a cubit to their stature, to make them spruce, sleek, well fed, and comely. They rig them out in all manner of fantastic costumes, wash them, over-feed them, and refuse to make them work. If the children of the lower orders differ in this last respect from those of the well-to-do classes, the difference is merely formal; they work from sheer necessity, and not because their parents recognise work as a duty. And in over-fed children, as in over-fed animals, sensuality is engendered unnaturally early.

Fashionable dress today, the course of reading, plays, music, dances, luscious food, all the elements of our modern life, in a word, from the pictures on the little boxes of sweetmeats up to the novel, the tale, and the poem, contribute to fan this sensuality into a strong, consuming flame, with the result that sexual vices and diseases have come to be the normal conditions of the period of tender youth, and often continue into the riper age of full-blown manhood. And I am of opinion that this is not right.

It is high time it ceased. The children of human beings should not be brought up as if they were animals; and we should set up as the object and strive to maintain as the result of our labours something better and nobler than a well-dressed body. This is my fourth contention.

In the fifth place, I am of opinion that, owing to the exaggerated and erroneous significance attributed by our society to love and to the idealised states that accompany and succeed it, the best energies of our men and women are drawn forth and exhausted during the most promising period of life; those of the men in the work of looking for, choosing, and winning the most desirable objects of love, for which purpose lying and fraud are held to be quite excusable; those of the women and girls in alluring men and decoying them into liaisons or marriage by the most questionable means conceivable, as an instance of which the present fashions in evening dress may be cited. I am of opinion that this is not right.

The truth is, that the whole affair has been exalted by poets and romancers to an undue importance, and that love in its various developments is not a fitting object to consume the best energies of men. People set it before them and strive after it, because their view of life is as vulgar and brutish as is that other conception frequently met with in the lower stages of development, which sees in luscious and abundant food an end worthy of man's best efforts. Now, this is not right and should not be done. And, in order to avoid doing it, it is only needful to realise the fact that whatever truly deserves to be held up as a worthy object of man's striving and working, whether it be the service of humanity, of one's country, of science, of art, not to speak of the service of God, is far above and beyond the sphere of personal enjoyment. Hence, it follows that not only to form a liaison, but even to contract marriage, is, from a Christian point of view, not a progress, but a fall. Love, and all the states that accompany and follow it, however we may try in prose and verse to prove the contrary, never do and never can facilitate the attainment of an aim worthy of men, but always make it more difficult. This is my fifth contention.

How about the human race? If we admit that celibacy is better and nobler than marriage, evidently the human race will come to an end. But, if the logical conclusion of the argument is that the human race will become extinct, the whole reasoning is wrong.

To that I reply that the argument is not mine; I did not invent it. That it is incumbent on mankind so to strive, and that celibacy is preferable to marriage, are truths revealed by Christ nineteen hundred years ago, set forth in our catechisms, and professed by us as followers of Christ.

Chastity and celibacy, it is urged, cannot constitute the ideal of humanity, because chastity would annihilate the race which strove to realise it, and humanity cannot set up as its ideal its own annihilation. It may be pointed out in reply that only that is a true ideal, which, being unattainable, admits of infinite gradation in degrees of proximity. Such is the Christian ideal of the founding of God's kingdom, the union of all living creatures by the bonds of love. The conception of its attainment is incompatible with the conception of the movement of life. What kind of life could subsist if all living creatures were joined together by the bonds of love? None. Our conception of life is inseparably bound up with the conception of a continual striving after an unattainable ideal.

But even if we suppose the Christian ideal of perfect chastity realised, what then? We should merely find ourselves face to face on the one hand with the familiar teaching of religion, one of whose dogmas is that the world will have an end; and on the other of so-called science, which informs us that the sun is gradually losing its heat, the result of which will in time be the extinction of the human race.

Now there is not and cannot be such an institution as Christian marriage, just as there cannot be such a thing as a Christian liturgy (Matthew 4:5–12; John 4:21), nor Christian teachers, nor church fathers (Matthew 23:8–10), nor Christian armies, Christian law courts, nor Christian States. This is what was always taught and believed by true Christians of the first and following centuries. A Christian's ideal is not marriage, but love for God and for his neighbour. Consequently in the eyes of a Christian relations in marriage not only do not constitute a lawful, right, and happy state, as our society and our churches maintain, but, on the contrary, are always a fall.

Such a thing as Christian marriage never was and never could be. Christ did not marry, nor did he establish marriage; neither did his disciples marry. But if Christian marriage cannot exist, there is such a thing as a Christian view of marriage. And this is how it may be formulated: A Christian (and by this term I understand not those who call themselves Christians merely because they were baptised and still receive the sacrament once a year, but those whose lives are shaped and regulated by the teachings of Christ), I say, cannot view the marriage relation otherwise than as a deviation from the doctrine of Christ – as a sin. This is clearly laid down in Matthew 5:28, and the ceremony called Christian marriage does not alter its character one jot. A Christian will never, therefore, desire marriage, but will always avoid it.

If the light of truth dawns upon a Christian when he is already married, or if, being a Christian, from weakness he enters into marital relations with the ceremonies of the church, or without them, he has no other alternative than to abide with his wife (and the wife with her husband, if it is she who is a Christian) and to aspire together with her to free themselves of their sin. This is the Christian view of marriage; and there cannot be any other for a man who honestly endeavours to shape his life in accordance with the teachings of Christ.

To very many persons the thoughts I have uttered here and in 'The Kreutzer Sonata' will seem strange, vague, even contradictory. They certainly do contradict, not each other, but the whole tenor of our lives, and involuntarily a doubt arises, 'on which side is truth – on the side of the thoughts which seem true and well-founded, or on the side of the lives of others and myself?' I, too, was weighed down by that same doubt when writing 'The Kreutzer Sonata'. I had not the faintest presentiment that the train of thought I had started would lead me whither it did. I was terrified by my own conclusion, and I was at first disposed to reject it, but it was impossible not to hearken to the voice of my reason and my conscience. And so, strange though they may appear to many, opposed as they undoubtedly are to the trend and tenor of our lives, and incompatible though they may prove with what I have heretofore thought and uttered, I have no choice but to accept them. 'But man is weak,' people will object. 'His task should be regulated by his strength.'

This is tantamount to saying, 'My hand is weak. I cannot draw a straight line – that is, a line which will be the shortest line between two given points – and so, in order to make it more easy for myself, I, intending to draw a straight, will choose for my model a crooked line.'

The weaker my hand, the greater the need that my model should be perfect.

THE DEVIL

*But I say unto you, that everyone that looketh on a woman to lust
after her hath committed adultery with her already in his heart.*

*And if thy right eye causeth thee to stumble, pluck it out, and
cast it from thee: for it is profitable for thee that one of thy
members should perish, and not thy whole body be cast into hell.*

*And if thy right hand causeth thee to stumble, cut if off, and cast
it from thee: for it is profitable for thee that one of thy members
should perish, and not thy whole body go into hell.*

Matthew 5:28–30

I

A BRILLIANT CAREER lay before Eugène Irténev. He had everything
necessary to attain it: an admirable education at home, high
honours when he graduated in law at Petersburg University, and
connections in the highest society through his recently deceased
father; he had also already begun service in one of the Ministries
under the protection of the Minister. Moreover he had a fortune;
even a large one, though insecure. His father had lived abroad and
in Petersburg, allowing his sons, Eugène and Andrew (who was
older than Eugène and in the Horse Guards), six thousand rubles a
year each, while he himself and his wife spent a great deal. He only
used to visit his estate for a couple of months in summer and did not
concern himself with its direction, entrusting it all to an unscrupu-
lous manager who also failed to attend to it, but in whom he had
complete confidence.

After the father's death, when the brothers began to divide the
property, so many debts were discovered that their lawyer even
advised them to refuse the inheritance and retain only an estate left
them by their grandmother, which was valued at a hundred
thousand rubles. But a neighbouring landed-proprietor who had
done business with old Irténev, that is to say, who had promissory
notes from him and had come to Petersburg on that account, said
that in spite of the debts they could straighten out affairs so as to
retain a large fortune (it would only be necessary to sell the forest
and some outlying land, retaining the rich Semënov estate with
four thousand desyatins[41] of black earth, the sugar factory, and two
hundred desyatins of water-meadows) if one devoted oneself to the

management of the estate, settled there, and farmed it wisely and economically.

And so, having visited the estate in spring (his father had died in Lent), Eugène looked into everything, resolved to retire from the Civil Service, settle in the country with his mother, and undertake the management with the object of preserving the main estate. He arranged with his brother, with whom he was very friendly, that he would pay him either four thousand rubles a-year, or a lump sum of eighty thousand, for which Andrew would hand over to him his share of the inheritance.

So he arranged matters and, having settled down with his mother in the big house, began managing the estate eagerly, yet cautiously.

It is generally supposed that Conservatives are usually old people, and that those in favour of change are the young. That is not quite correct. Usually Conservatives are young people: those who want to live but who do not think about how to live, and have not time to think, and therefore take as a model for themselves a way of life that they have seen.

Thus it was with Eugène. Having settled in the village, his aim and ideal was to restore the form of life that had existed, not in his father's time – his father had been a bad manager – but in his grandfather's. And now he tried to resurrect the general spirit of his grandfather's life – in the house, the garden, and in the estate management – of course with changes suited to the times – everything on a large scale – good order, method, and everybody satisfied. But to do this entailed much work. It was necessary to meet the demands of the creditors and the banks, and for that purpose to sell some land and arrange renewals of credit. It was also necessary to get money to carry on (partly by farming out land, and partly by hiring labour) the immense operations on the Semënov estate, with its four hundred desyatins of ploughland and its sugar factory, and to deal with the garden so that it should not seem to be neglected or in decay.

There was much work to do, but Eugène had plenty of strength – physical and mental. He was twenty-six, of medium height, strongly built, with muscles developed by gymnastics. He was full-blooded and his whole neck was very red, his teeth and lips were bright, and his hair soft and curly though not thick. His only physical defect was short-sightedness, which he had himself developed by using spectacles, so that he could not now do without a pince-nez, which had already formed a line on the bridge of his nose.

Such he was physically. For his spiritual portrait it might be said that the better people knew him the better they liked him. His mother had always loved him more than anyone else, and now after her husband's death she concentrated on him not only her whole affection but her whole life. Nor was it only his mother who so loved him. All his comrades at the high school and the university not merely liked him very much, but respected him. He had this effect on all who met him. It was impossible not to believe what he said, impossible to suspect any deception or falseness in one who had such an open, honest face and in particular such eyes.

In general his personality helped him much in his affairs. A creditor who would have refused another trusted him. The clerk, the village Elder, or a peasant, who would have played a dirty trick and cheated someone else, forgot to deceive under the pleasant impression of intercourse with this kindly, agreeable, and above all candid man.

It was the end of May. Eugène had somehow managed in town to get the vacant land freed from the mortgage, so as to sell it to a merchant, and had borrowed money from that same merchant to replenish his stock, that is to say, to procure horses, bulls, and carts, and in particular to begin to build a necessary farmhouse. The matter had been arranged. The timber was being carted, the carpenters were already at work, and manure for the estate was being brought on eighty carts, but everything still hung by a thread.

2

Amid these cares something came about which though unimportant tormented Eugène at the time. As a young man he had lived as all healthy young men live, that is, he had had relations with women of various kinds. He was not a libertine but neither, as he himself said, was he a monk. He only turned to this, however, in so far as was necessary for physical health and to have his mind free, as he used to say. This had begun when he was sixteen and had gone on satisfactorily – in the sense that he had never given himself up to debauchery, never once been infatuated, and had never contracted a disease. At first he had had a seamstress in Petersburg, then she got spoilt and he made other arrangements, and that side of his affairs was so well secured that it did not trouble him.

But now he was living in the country for the second month and did not at all know what he was to do. Compulsory self-restraint was beginning to have a bad effect on him.

Must he really go to town for that purpose? And where to? How?

That was the only thing that disturbed him; but as he was convinced that the thing was necessary and that he needed it, it really became a necessity, and he felt that he was not free and that his eyes involuntarily followed every young woman.

He did not approve of having relations with a married woman or a maid in his own village. He knew by report that both his father and grandfather had been quite different in this matter from other landowners of that time. At home they had never had any entanglements with peasant women, and he had decided that he would not do so either; but afterwards, feeling himself ever more and more under compulsion and imagining with horror what might happen to him in the neighbouring country town, and reflecting on the fact that the days of serfdom were now over, he decided that it might be done on the spot. Only it must be done so that no one should know of it, and not for the sake of debauchery but merely for health's sake – as he said to himself. And when he had decided this he became still more restless. When talking to the village Elder, the peasants, or the carpenters, he involuntarily brought the conversation round to women, and when it turned to women he kept it on that theme. He noticed the women more and more.

3

To settle the matter in his own mind was one thing but to carry it out was another. To approach a woman himself was impossible. Which one? Where? It must be done through someone else, but to whom should he speak about it?

He happened to go into a watchman's hut in the forest to get a drink of water. The watchman had been his father's huntsman, and Eugène Ivánich chatted with him, and the man began telling some strange tales of hunting sprees. It occurred to Eugène Ivánich that it would be convenient to arrange matters in this hut, or in the wood, only he did not know how to manage it and whether old Daniel would undertake the arrangement. 'Perhaps he will be horrified at such a proposal and I shall have disgraced myself, but perhaps he will agree to it quite simply.' So he thought while listening to Daniel's stories. Daniel was telling how once when they had been stopping at the hut of the sexton's wife in an outlying field, he had brought a woman for Fëdor Zakhárich Pryánishnikov.

'It will be all right,' thought Eugène.

'Your father, may the kingdom of heaven be his, did not go in for nonsense of that kind.'

'It won't do,' thought Eugène. But to test the matter he said: 'How was it you engaged on such bad things?'

'But what was there bad in it? She was glad, and Fëdor Zakhárich was satisfied, very satisfied. I got a ruble. Why, what was he to do? He too is a lively limb apparently, and drinks wine.'

'Yes, I may speak,' thought Eugène, and at once proceeded to do so.

'And do you know, Daniel, I don't know how to endure it' – he felt himself going scarlet.

Daniel smiled.

'I am not a monk – I have been accustomed to it.'

He felt that what he was saying was stupid, but was glad to see that Daniel approved.

'Why of course, you should have told me long ago. It can all be arranged,' said he: 'only tell me which one you want.'

'Oh, it is really all the same to me. Of course not an ugly one, and she must be healthy.'

'I understand!' said Daniel briefly. He reflected.

'Ah! There is a tasty morsel,' he began. Again Eugène went red. 'A tasty morsel. See here, she was married last autumn,' Daniel whispered – 'and he hasn't been able to do anything. Think what that is worth to one who wants it!'

Eugène even frowned with shame.

'No, no,' he said. 'I don't want that at all. I want, on the contrary' (what could the contrary be?), 'on the contrary I only want that she should be healthy and that there should be as little fuss as possible – a woman whose husband is away in the army or something of that kind.'

'I know. It's Stepanída I must bring you. Her husband is away in town, just the same as a soldier. And she is a fine woman, and clean. You will be satisfied. As it is I was saying to her the other day – you should go, but she . . . '

'Well then, when is it to be?'

'Tomorrow if you like. I shall be going to get some tobacco and I will call in, and at the dinner-hour come here, or to the bath-house behind the kitchen garden. There will be nobody about. Besides after dinner everybody takes a nap.'

'All right then.'

A terrible excitement seized Eugène as he rode home. 'What will happen? What is a peasant woman like? Suppose it turns out that she is hideous, horrible? No, she is handsome,' he told himself, remembering some he had been noticing. 'But what shall I say? What shall I do?'

He was not himself all that day. Next day at noon he went to the forester's hut. Daniel stood at the door and silently and significantly nodded towards the wood. The blood rushed to Eugène's heart, he was conscious of it and went to the kitchen-garden. No one was there. He went to the bath-house – there was no one about, he looked in, came out, and suddenly heard the crackling of a breaking twig. He looked round – and she was standing in the thicket beyond the little ravine. He rushed there across the ravine. There were nettles in it which he had not noticed. They stung him and, losing the pince-nez from his nose, he ran up the slope on the farther side. She stood there, in a white embroidered apron, a red-brown skirt, and a bright red kerchief, barefoot, fresh, firm, and handsome, and smiling shyly.

'There is a path leading round – you should have gone round,' she said. 'I came long ago, ever so long.'

He went up to her and, looking her over, touched her.

A quarter of an hour later they separated; he found his pince-nez, called in to see Daniel, and in reply to his question: 'Are you satisfied, master?' gave him a ruble and went home.

He was satisfied. Only at first had he felt ashamed, then it had passed off. And everything had gone well. The best thing was that he now felt at ease, tranquil and vigorous. As for her, he had not even seen her thoroughly. He remembered that she was clean, fresh, not bad-looking, and simple, without any pretence. 'Whose wife is she?' said he to himself. 'Péchnikov's, Daniel said. What Péchnikov is that? There are two households of that name. Probably she is old Michael's daughter-in-law. Yes, that must be it. His son does live in Moscow. I'll ask Daniel about it sometime.'

From then onward that previously important drawback to country life – enforced self-restraint – was eliminated. Eugène's freedom of mind was no longer disturbed and he was able to attend freely to his affairs.

And the matter Eugène had undertaken was far from easy: before he had time to stop up one hole a new one would unexpectedly show itself, and it sometimes seemed to him that he would not be able to go through with it and that it would end in his having to sell the estate after all, which would mean that all his efforts would be wasted and that he had failed to accomplish what he had undertaken. That prospect disturbed him most of all.

All this time more and more debts of his father's unexpectedly came to light. It was evident that towards the end of his life he had borrowed right and left. At the time of the settlement in May,

Eugène had thought he at last knew everything, but in the middle of the summer he suddenly received a letter from which it appeared that there was still a debt of twelve thousand rubles to the widow Esípova. There was no promissory note, but only an ordinary receipt which his lawyer told him could be disputed. But it did not enter Eugène's head to refuse to pay a debt of his father's merely because the document could be challenged. He only wanted to know for certain whether there had been such a debt.

'Mamma! Who is Kalériya Vladímirovna Esípova?' he asked his mother when they met as usual for dinner.

'Esípova? She was brought up by your grandfather. Why?'

Eugène told his mother about the letter.

'I wonder she is not ashamed to ask for it. Your father gave her so much!'

'But do we owe her this?'

'Well now, how shall I put it? It is not a debt. Papa, out of his unbounded kindness . . . '

'Yes, but did Papa consider it a debt?'

'I cannot say. I don't know. I only know it is hard enough for you without that.'

Eugène saw that Mary Pávlovna did not know what to say, and was as it were sounding him.

'I see from what you say that it must be paid,' said he. 'I will go to see her tomorrow and have a chat, and see if it cannot be deferred.'

'Ah, how sorry I am for you, but you know that will be best. Tell her she must wait,' said Mary Pávlovna, evidently tranquillised and proud of her son's decision.

Eugène's position was particularly hard because his mother, who was living with him, did not at all realise his position. She had been so accustomed all her life long to live extravagantly that she could not even imagine to herself the position her son was in, that is to say, that today or tomorrow matters might shape themselves so that they would have nothing left and he would have to sell everything and live and support his mother on what salary he could earn, which at the very most would be two thousand rubles. She did not understand that they could only save themselves from that position by cutting down expense in everything, and so she could not understand why Eugène was so careful about trifles, in expenditure on gardeners, coachmen, servants – even on food. Also, like most widows, she nourished feelings of devotion to the memory of her departed spouse quite different from those she had felt for him while he lived, and she did not admit the thought that anything the departed had done or arranged could be wrong or could be altered.

Eugène by great efforts managed to keep up the garden and the conservatory with two gardeners, and the stables with two coachmen. And Mary Pávlovna naïvely thought that she was sacrificing herself for her son and doing all a mother could do, by not complaining of the food which the old mancook prepared, of the fact that the paths in the park were not all swept clean, and that instead of footmen they had only a boy.

So, too, concerning this new debt, in which Eugène saw an almost crushing blow to all his undertakings, Mary Pávlovna only saw an incident displaying Eugène's noble nature. Moreover she did not feel much anxiety about Eugène's position, because she was confident that he would make a brilliant marriage which would put everything right. And he could make a very brilliant marriage: she knew a dozen families who would be glad to give their daughters to him. And she wished to arrange the matter as soon as possible.

4

Eugène himself dreamt of marriage, but not in the same way as his mother. The idea of using marriage as a means of putting his affairs in order was repulsive to him. He wished to marry honourably, for love. He observed the girls whom he met and those he knew, and compared himself with them, but no decision had yet been taken. Meanwhile, contrary to his expectations, his relations with Stepanída continued, and even acquired the character of a settled affair. Eugène was so far from debauchery, it was so hard for him secretly to do this thing which he felt to be bad, that he could not arrange these meetings himself and even after the first one hoped not to see Stepanída again; but it turned out that after some time the same restlessness (due he believed to that cause) again overcame him. And his restlessness this time was no longer impersonal, but suggested just those same bright, black eyes, and that deep voice, saying, 'ever so long', that same scent of something fresh and strong, and that same full breast lifting the bib of her apron, and all this in that hazel and maple thicket, bathed in bright sunlight.

Though he felt ashamed he again approached Daniel. And again a rendezvous was fixed for midday in the wood. This time Eugène looked her over more carefully and everything about her seemed attractive. He tried talking to her and asked about her husband. He really was Michael's son and lived as a coachman in Moscow.

'Well, then, how is it you . . . ' Eugène wanted to ask how it was she was untrue to him.

'What about "how is it"?' asked she. Evidently she was clever and quick-witted.

'Well, how is it you come to me?'

'There now,' said she merrily. 'I bet he goes on the spree there. Why shouldn't I?'

Evidently she was putting on an air of sauciness and assurance, and this seemed charming to Eugène. But all the same he did not himself fix a rendezvous with her. Even when she proposed that they should meet without the aid of Daniel, to whom she seemed not very well disposed, he did not consent. He hoped that this meeting would be the last. He liked her. He thought such intercourse was necessary for him and that there was nothing bad about it, but in the depth of his soul there was a stricter judge who did not approve of it and hoped that this would be the last time, or if he did not hope that, at any rate did not wish to participate in arrangements to repeat it another time.

So the whole summer passed, during which they met a dozen times and always by Daniel's help. It happened once that she could not be there because her husband had come home, and Daniel proposed another woman, but Eugène refused with disgust. Then the husband went away and the meetings continued as before, at first through Daniel, but afterwards he simply fixed the time and she came with another woman, Prókhorova – as it would not do for a peasant woman to go about alone.

Once at the very time fixed for the rendezvous a family came to call on Mary Pávlovna, with the very girl she wished Eugène to marry, and it was impossible for Eugène to get away. As soon as he could do so, he went out as though to the threshing-floor, and round by the path to their meeting-place in the wood. She was not there, but at the accustomed spot everything within reach had been broken – the black alder, the hazel-twigs, and even a young maple the thickness of a stake. She had waited, had become excited and angry, and had skittishly left him a remembrance. He waited and waited, and then went to Daniel to ask him to call her for tomorrow. She came and was just as usual.

So the summer passed. The meetings were always arranged in the wood, and only once, when it grew towards autumn, in the shed that stood in her backyard.

It did not enter Eugène's head that these relations of his had any importance for him. About her he did not even think. He gave her money and nothing more. At first he did not know and did not think that the affair was known and that she was envied throughout the village, or that her relations took money from her and encouraged her, and that her conception of any sin in the matter had been quite obliterated by the influence of the money and her family's approval. It seemed to her that if people envied her, then what she was doing was good.

'It is simply necessary for my health,' thought Eugène. 'I grant it is not right, and though no one says anything, everybody, or many people, know of it. The woman who comes with her knows. And once she knows she is sure to have told others. But what's to be done? I am acting badly,' thought Eugène, 'but what's one to do? Anyhow it is not for long.'

What chiefly disturbed Eugène was the thought of the husband. At first for some reason it seemed to him that the husband must be a poor sort, and this as it were partly justified his conduct. But he saw the husband and was struck by his appearance: he was a fine fellow and smartly dressed, in no way a worse man than himself, but surely better. At their next meeting he told her he had seen her husband and had been surprised to see that he was such a fine fellow.

'There's not another man like him in the village,' said she proudly.

This surprised Eugène, and the thought of the husband tormented him still more after that. He happened to be at Daniel's one day and Daniel, having begun chatting, said to him quite openly: 'And Michael asked me the other day: "Is it true that the master is living with my wife?" I said I did not know. Anyway, I said, better with the master than with a peasant.'

'Well, and what did he say?'

'He said: "Wait a bit. I'll get to know and I'll give it her all the same."'

'Yes, if the husband returned to live here I would give her up,' thought Eugène.

But the husband lived in town and for the present their intercourse continued.

'When necessary I will break it off, and there will be nothing left of it,' thought he.

And this seemed to him certain, especially as during the whole summer many different things occupied him very fully: the erection of the new farmhouse, and the harvest, and building, and above all meeting the debts and selling the waste land. All these were affairs that completely absorbed him and on which he spent his thoughts when he lay down and when he got up. All that was real life. His intercourse – he did not even call it connection – with Stepanída he paid no attention to. It is true that when the wish to see her arose it came with such strength that he could think of nothing else. But this did not last long. A meeting was arranged, and he again forgot her for a week or even for a month.

In autumn Eugène often rode to town, and there became friendly with the Ánnenskis. They had a daughter who had just finished the Institute.[42] And then, to Mary Pávlovna's great grief, it happened that Eugène 'cheapened himself,' as she expressed it, by falling in love with Liza Ánnenskaya and proposing to her.

From that time his relations with Stepanída ceased.

5

It is impossible to explain why Eugène chose Liza Ánnenskaya, as it is always impossible to explain why a man chooses this and not that woman. There were many reasons – positive and negative. One reason was that she was not a very rich heiress such as his mother sought for him, another that she was naïve and to be pitied in her relations with her mother, another that she was not a beauty who attracted general attention to herself, and yet she was not bad-looking. But the chief reason was that his acquaintance with her began at the time when he was ripe for marriage. He fell in love because he knew that he would marry.

Liza Ánnenskaya was at first merely pleasing to Eugène, but when he decided to make her his wife his feelings for her became much stronger. He felt that he was in love.

Liza was tall, slender, and long. Everything about her was long; her face, and her nose (not prominently but downwards), and her fingers, and her feet. The colour of her face was very delicate, creamy white and delicately pink; she had long, soft, and curly, light-brown hair, and beautiful eyes, clear, mild, and confiding. Those eyes especially struck Eugène, and when he thought of Liza he always saw those clear, mild, confiding eyes.

Such was she physically; he knew nothing of her spiritually, but only saw those eyes. And those eyes seemed to tell him all he needed to know. The meaning of their expression was this: While still in the Institute, when she was fifteen, Liza used continually to fall in love with all the attractive men she met and was animated and happy only when she was in love. After leaving the Institute she continued to fall in love in just the same way with all the young men she met, and of course fell in love with Eugène as soon as she made his acquaintance. It was this being in love which gave her eyes that particular expression which so captivated Eugène. Already that winter she had been in love with two young men at one and the same time, and blushed and became excited not only when they entered the room but whenever their names were mentioned. But afterwards, when her mother hinted to her that Irténev seemed to have serious intentions, her love for him increased so that she became almost indifferent to the two previous attractions, and when Irténev began to come to their balls and parties and danced with her more than with others and evidently only wished to know whether she loved him, her love for him became painful. She dreamed of him in her sleep and seemed to see him when she was awake in a dark room, and everyone else vanished from her mind. But when he proposed and they were formally engaged, and when they had kissed one another and were a betrothed couple, then she had no thoughts but of him, no desire but to be with him, to love him, and to be loved by him. She was also proud of him and felt emotional about him and herself and her love, and quite melted and felt faint from love of him.

The more he got to know her the more he loved her. He had not at all expected to find such love, and it strengthened his own feeling still more.

6

Towards spring he went to his estate at Semënovskoe to have a look at it and to give directions about the management, and especially about the house which was being done up for his wedding.

Mary Pávlovna was dissatisfied with her son's choice, not only because the match was not as brilliant as it might have been, but also because she did not like Varvára Alexéevna, his future mother-in-law. Whether she was good-natured or not she did not know and could not decide, but that she was not well bred, not *comme il faut* – 'not a lady' as Mary Pávlovna said to herself – she saw from their first acquaintance, and this distressed her; distressed her because she was accustomed to value breeding and knew that Eugène was sensitive to it, and she foresaw that he would suffer much annoyance on this account. But she liked the girl. Liked her chiefly because Eugène did. One could not help loving her, and Mary Pávlovna was quite sincerely ready to do so.

Eugène found his mother contented and in good spirits. She was getting everything straight in the house and preparing to go away herself as soon as he brought his young wife. Eugène persuaded her to stay for the time being, and the future remained undecided.

In the evening after tea Mary Pávlovna played patience as usual. Eugène sat by, helping her. This was the hour of their most intimate talks. Having finished one game and while preparing to begin another, she looked up at him and, with a little hesitation, began thus: 'I wanted to tell you, Jénya – of course I do not know, but in general I wanted to suggest to you – that before your wedding it is absolutely necessary to have finished with all your bachelor affairs so that nothing may disturb either you or your wife. God forbid that it should. You understand me?'

And indeed Eugène at once understood that Mary Pávlovna was hinting at his relations with Stepanída which had ended in the previous autumn, and that she attributed much more importance to those relations than they deserved, as solitary women always do. Eugène blushed, not from shame so much as from vexation that good-natured Mary Pávlovna was bothering – out of affection no doubt, but still was bothering – about matters that were not her business and that she did not and could not understand. He answered that there was nothing that needed concealment, and that he had always conducted himself so that there should be nothing to hinder his marrying.

'Well, dear, that is excellent. Only, Jénya . . . don't be vexed with me,' said Mary Pávlovna, and broke off in confusion.

Eugène saw that she had not finished and had not said what she wanted to. And this was confirmed when a little later she began to tell him how, in his absence, she had been asked to stand godmother at . . . the Péchnikovs.

Eugène flushed again, not with vexation or shame this time, but with some strange consciousness of the importance of what was about to be told him – an involuntary consciousness quite at variance with his conclusions. And what he expected happened. Mary Pávlovna, as if merely by way of conversation, mentioned that this year only boys were being born – evidently a sign of a coming war. Both at the Vásins and the Péchnikovs the young wife had a first child – at each house a boy. Mary Pávlovna wanted to say this casually, but she herself felt ashamed when she saw the colour mount to her son's face and saw him nervously removing, tapping, and replacing his pince-nez and hurriedly lighting a cigarette. She became silent. He too was silent and could not think how to break that silence. So they both understood that they had understood one another.

'Yes, the chief thing is that there should be justice and no favouritism in the village – as under your grandfather.'

'Mamma,' said Eugène suddenly, 'I know why you are saying this. You have no need to be disturbed. My future family-life is so sacred to me that I should not infringe it in any case. And as to what occurred in my bachelor days, that is quite ended. I never formed any union and no one has any claims on me.'

'Well, I am glad,' said his mother. 'I know how noble your feelings are.'

Eugène accepted his mother's words as a tribute due to him, and did not reply.

Next day he drove to town thinking of his fiancée and of anything in the world except of Stepanída. But, as if purposely to remind him, on approaching the church he met people walking and driving back from it. He met old Matvéy with Simon, some lads and girls, and then two women, one elderly, the other, who seemed familiar, smartly dressed and wearing a bright-red kerchief. This woman was walking lightly and boldly, carrying a child in her arms. He came up to them, and the elder woman bowed, stopping in the old-fashioned way, but the young woman with the child only bent her head, and from under the kerchief gleamed familiar, merry, smiling eyes.

Yes, this was she, but all that was over and it was no use looking at her: 'and the child may be mine,' flashed through his mind. No, what nonsense! There was her husband, she used to see him. He did not even consider the matter further, so settled in his mind was it that it had been necessary for his health – he had paid her money and there was no more to be said; there was, there had been, and there could be, no question of any union between them. It was not that he stifled the voice of conscience, no – his conscience simply said nothing to him. And he thought no more about her after the conversation with his mother and this meeting. Nor did he meet her again.

Eugène was married in town the week after Easter, and left at once with his young wife for his country estate. The house had been arranged as usual for a young couple. Mary Pávlovna wished to leave, but Eugène begged her to remain, and Liza still more strongly, and she only moved into a detached wing of the house.

And so a new life began for Eugène.

Y

7

The first year of his marriage was a hard one for Eugène. It was hard because affairs he had managed to put off during the time of his courtship now, after his marriage, all came upon him at once.

To escape from debts was impossible. An outlying part of the estate was sold and the most pressing obligations met, but others remained, and he had no money. The estate yielded a good revenue, but he had had to send payments to his brother and to spend on his own marriage, so that there was no ready money and the factory could not carry on and would have to be closed down. The only way of escape was to use his wife's money; and Liza, having realised her husband's position, insisted on this herself. Eugène agreed, but only on condition that he should give her a mortgage on half his estate, which he did. Of course this was done not for his wife's sake, who felt offended at it, but to appease his mother-in-law.

These affairs with various fluctuations of success and failure helped to poison Eugène's life that first year. Another thing was his wife's ill-health. That same first year in autumn, seven months after their marriage, a misfortune befell Liza. She was driving out to meet her husband on his return from town, and the quiet horse became rather playful and she was frightened and jumped out. Her jump was comparatively fortunate – she might have been caught by the wheel – but she was pregnant, and that same night the pains began and she had a miscarriage from which she was long in recovering. The loss of the expected child and his wife's illness, together with the disorder in his affairs, and above all the presence of his mother-in-law, who arrived as soon as Liza fell ill – all this together made the year still harder for Eugène.

But notwithstanding these difficult circumstances, towards the end of the first year Eugène felt very well. First of all his cherished hope of restoring his fallen fortune and renewing his grandfather's way of life in a new form, was approaching accomplishment, though slowly and with difficulty. There was no longer any question of having to sell the whole estate to meet the debts. The chief estate, though transferred to his wife's name, was saved, and if only the beet crop succeeded and the price kept up, by next year his position of want and stress might be replaced by one of complete prosperity. That was one thing.

Another was that however much he had expected from his wife, he had never expected to find in her what he actually found. He found not what he had expected, but something much better. Raptures of love – though he tried to produce them – did not take place or were very slight, but he discovered something quite different, namely, that he was not merely more cheerful and happier but that it had become easier to live. He did not know why this should be so, but it was.

And it was so because immediately after marriage his wife decided that Eugène Irténev was superior to anyone else in the world: wiser, purer, and nobler than they, and that therefore it was right for everyone to serve him and please him; but that as it was impossible to make everyone do this, she must do it herself to the limit of her strength. And she did; directing all her strength of mind towards learning and guessing what he liked, and then doing just that thing, whatever it was and however difficult it might be.

She had the gift which furnishes the chief delight of intercourse with a loving woman: thanks to her love of her husband she penetrated into his soul. She knew his every state and his every shade of feeling – better it seemed to him than he himself – and she behaved correspondingly and therefore never hurt his feelings, but always lessened his distresses and strengthened his joys. And she understood not only his feelings but also his joys. Things quite foreign to her – concerning the farming, the factory, or the appraisement of others – she immediately understood so that she could not merely converse with him, but could often, as he himself said, be a useful and irreplaceable counsellor. She regarded affairs and people and everything in the world only through his eyes. She loved her mother, but having seen that Eugène disliked his mother-in-law's interference in their life she immediately took her husband's side, and did so with such decision that he had to restrain her.

Besides all this she had very good taste, much tact, and above all she had repose. All that she did, she did unnoticed; only the results of what she did were observable, namely, that always and in everything there was cleanliness, order, and elegance. Liza had at once understood in what her husband's ideal of life consisted, and she tried to attain, and in the arrangement and order of the house did attain, what he wanted. Children it is true were lacking, but there was hope of that also. In winter she went to Petersburg to see a specialist and he assured them that she was quite well and could have children.

And this desire was accomplished. By the end of the year she was again pregnant.

The one thing that threatened, not to say poisoned, their happiness was her jealousy – a jealousy she restrained and did not exhibit, but from which she often suffered. Not only might Eugène not love any other woman – because there was not a woman on earth worthy of him (as to whether she herself was worthy or not she never asked herself) – but not a single woman might therefore dare to love him.

8

This was how they lived: he rose early, as he always had done, and went to see to the farm or the factory where work was going on, or sometimes to the fields. Towards ten o'clock he would come back for his coffee, which they had on the veranda: Mary Pávlovna, an uncle who lived with them, and Liza. After a conversation which was often very animated while they drank their coffee, they dispersed till dinner-time. At two o'clock they dined and then went for a walk or a drive. In the evening when he returned from his office they drank their evening tea and sometimes he read aloud while she worked, or when there were guests they had music or conversation. When he went away on business he wrote to his wife and received letters from her every day. Sometimes she accompanied him, and then they were particularly merry. On his name-day and on hers guests assembled, and it pleased him to see how well she managed to arrange things so that everybody enjoyed coming. He saw and heard that they all admired her – the young, agreeable hostess – and he loved her still more for this.

All went excellently. She bore her pregnancy easily and, though they were afraid, they both began making plans as to how they would bring the child up. The system of education and the arrangements were all decided by Eugène, and her only wish was to carry out his desires obediently. Eugène on his part read up medical works and intended to bring the child up according to all the precepts of science. She of course agreed to everything and made preparations, making warm and also cool 'envelopes',[43] and preparing a cradle. Thus the second year of their marriage arrived and the second spring.

9

It was just before Trinity Sunday. Liza was in her fifth month, and though careful she was still brisk and active. Both his mother and hers were living in the house, but under pretext of watching and safeguarding her only upset her by their tiffs. Eugène was specially engrossed with a new experiment for the cultivation of sugar-beet on a large scale.

Just before Trinity Liza decided that it was necessary to have a thorough house-cleaning as it had not been done since Easter, and she hired two women by the day to help the servants wash the floors and windows, beat the furniture and the carpets, and put covers on them. These women came early in the morning, heated the coppers, and set to work. One of the two was Stepanída, who had just weaned her baby boy and had begged for the job of washing the floors through the office-clerk – whom she now carried on with. She wanted to have a good look at the new mistress. Stepanída was living by herself as formerly, her husband being away, and she was up to tricks as she had formerly been first with old Daniel (who had once caught her taking some logs of firewood), afterwards with the master, and now with the young clerk. She was not concerning herself any longer about her master. 'He has a wife now,' she thought. But it would be good to have a look at the lady and at her establishment: folk said it was well arranged.

Eugène had not seen her since he had met her with the child. Having a baby to attend to she had not been going out to work, and he seldom walked through the village. That morning, on the eve of Trinity Sunday, he got up at five o'clock and rode to the fallow land which was to be sprinkled with phosphates,[44] and had left the house before the women were about, and while they were still engaged lighting the copper fires.

He returned to breakfast merry, contented, and hungry; dismounting from his mare at the gate and handing her over to the gardener. Flicking the high grass with his whip and repeating a phrase he had just uttered, as one often does, he walked towards the house. The phrase was: 'phosphates justify' – what or to whom, he neither knew nor reflected.

They were beating a carpet on the grass. The furniture had been brought out.

'There now! What a house-cleaning Liza has undertaken! ... Phosphates justify ... What a manageress she is! A manageress! Yes, a manageress,' said he to himself, vividly imagining her in her white wrapper and with her smiling joyful face, as it nearly always was when he looked at her. 'Yes, I must change my boots, or else "phosphates justify", that is, smell of manure, and the manageress is in such a condition. Why "in such a condition"? Because a new little Irténev is growing there inside her,' he thought. 'Yes, phosphates justify,' and smiling at his thoughts he put his hand to the door of his room.

But he had not time to push the door before it opened of itself and he came face to face with a woman coming towards him carrying a pail, barefoot and with sleeves turned up high. He stepped aside to let her pass and she too stepped aside, adjusting her kerchief with a wet hand.

'Go on, go on, I won't go in, if you ...' began Eugène and suddenly stopped, recognising her.

She glanced merrily at him with smiling eyes, and pulling down her skirt went out at the door.

'What nonsense! ... It is impossible,' said Eugène to himself, frowning and waving his hand as though to get rid of a fly, displeased at having noticed her. He was vexed that he had noticed her and yet he could not take his eyes from her strong body, swayed by her agile strides, from her bare feet, or from her arms and shoulders, and the pleasing folds of her shirt and the handsome skirt tucked up high above her white calves.

'But why am I looking?' said he to himself, lowering his eyes so as not to see her. 'And anyhow I must go in to get some other boots.' And he turned back to go into his own room, but had not gone five steps before he again glanced round to have another look at her without knowing why or wherefore. She was just going round the corner and also glanced at him.

'Ah, what am I doing!' said he to himself. 'She may think ... It is even certain that she already does think ...'

He entered his damp room. Another woman, an old and skinny one, was there, and was still washing it. Eugène passed on tiptoe across the floor, wet with dirty water, to the wall where his boots stood, and he was about to leave the room when the woman herself went out.

'This one has gone and the other, Stepanída, will come here alone,' someone within him began to reflect.

'My God, what am I thinking of and what am I doing!' He seized his boots and ran out with them into the hall, put them on there, brushed himself, and went out on to the veranda where both the mammas were already drinking coffee. Liza had evidently been expecting him and came on to the veranda through another door at the same time.

'My God! If she, who considers me so honourable, pure, and innocent – if she only knew!' – thought he.

Liza as usual met him with shining face. But today somehow she seemed to him particularly pale, yellow, long, and weak.

During coffee, as often happened, a peculiarly feminine kind of conversation went on which had no logical sequence but which evidently was connected in some way for it went on uninterruptedly.

The two old ladies were pin-pricking one another, and Liza was skilfully manoeuvring between them.

'I am so vexed that we had not finished washing your room before you got back,' she said to her husband. 'But I do so want to get everything arranged.'

'Well, did you sleep well after I got up?'

'Yes, I slept well and I feel well.'

'How can a woman be well in her condition during this intolerable heat, when her windows face the sun,' said Varvára Alexéevna, her mother. 'And they have no venetian-blinds or awnings. I always had awnings.'

'But you know we are in the shade after ten o'clock,' said Mary Pávlovna.

'That's what causes fever; it comes of dampness,' said Varvára Alexéevna, not noticing that what she was saying did not agree with what she had just said. 'My doctor always says that it is impossible to diagnose an illness unless one knows the patient. And he certainly knows, for he is the leading physician and we pay him a hundred rubles a visit. My late husband did not believe in doctors, but he did not grudge me anything.'

'How can a man grudge anything to a woman when perhaps her life and the child's depend . . . '

'Yes, when she has means a wife need not depend on her husband. A good wife submits to her husband,' said Varvára Alexéevna – 'only Liza is too weak after her illness.'

'Oh no, mamma, I feel quite well. But why have they not brought you any boiled cream?'

'I don't want any. I can do with raw cream.'

'I offered some to Varvára Alexéevna, but she declined,' said Mary Pávlovna, as if justifying herself.

'No, I don't want any today.' And as if to terminate an unpleasant conversation and yield magnanimously, Varvára Alexéevna turned to Eugène and said: 'Well, and have you sprinkled the phosphates?'

Liza ran to fetch the cream.

'But I don't want it. I don't want it.'

'Liza, Liza, go gently,' said Mary Pávlovna. 'Such rapid movements do her harm.'

'Nothing does harm if one's mind is at peace,' said Varvára Alexéevna as if referring to something, though she knew that there was nothing her words could refer to.

Liza returned with the cream and Eugène drank his coffee and listened morosely. He was accustomed to these conversations, but today he was particularly annoyed by its lack of sense. He wanted to think over what had happened to him but this chatter disturbed him. Having finished her coffee Varvára Alexéevna went away in a bad humour. Liza, Eugène, and Mary Pávlovna stayed behind, and their conversation was simple and pleasant. But Liza, being sensitive, at once noticed that something was tormenting Eugène, and she asked him whether anything unpleasant had happened. He was not prepared for this question and hesitated a little before replying that there had been nothing. This reply made Liza think all the more. That something was tormenting him, and greatly tormenting, was as evident to her as that a fly had fallen into the milk, yet he would not speak of it. What could it be?

II

After breakfast they all dispersed. Eugène as usual went to his study, but instead of beginning to read or write his letters, he sat smoking one cigarette after another and thinking. He was terribly surprised and disturbed by the unexpected recrudescence within him of the bad feeling from which he had thought himself free since his marriage. Since then he had not once experienced that feeling, either for her – the woman he had known – or for any other woman except his wife. He had often felt glad of this emancipation, and now suddenly a chance meeting, seemingly so unimportant, revealed to him the fact that he was not free. What now tormented him was not that he was yielding to that feeling and desired her – he did not dream of so doing – but that the feeling was awake within him and he had to be on his guard against it. He had no doubt but that he would suppress it.

He had a letter to answer and a paper to write, and sat down at his writing-table and began to work. Having finished it and quite forgotten what had disturbed him, he went out to go to the stables. And again as ill-luck would have it, either by unfortunate chance or intentionally, as soon as he stepped from the porch a red skirt and red kerchief appeared from round the corner, and she went past him swinging her arms and swaying her body. She not only went past him, but on passing him ran, as if playfully, to overtake her fellow-servant.

Again the bright midday, the nettles, the back of Daniel's hut, and in the shade of the plane trees her smiling face biting some leaves, rose in his imagination.

'No, it is impossible to let matters continue so,' he said to himself, and waiting till the women had passed out of sight he went to the office.

It was just the dinner-hour and he hoped to find the steward still there, and so it happened. The steward was just waking up from his after-dinner nap, and stretching himself and yawning was standing in the office, looking at the herdsman who was telling him something.

'Vasíli Nikoláich!' said Eugène to the steward.

'What is your pleasure?'

'I want to speak to you.'

'What is your pleasure?'

'Just finish what you are saying.'

'Aren't you going to bring it in?' said Vasíli Nikoláich to the herdsman.

'It's heavy, Vasíli Nikoláich.'

'What is it?' asked Eugène.

'Why, a cow has calved in the meadow. Well, all right, I'll order them to harness a horse at once. Tell Nicholas Lysúkh to get out the dray cart.'

The herdsman went out.

'Do you know,' began Eugène, flushing and conscious that he was doing so, 'do you know, Vasíli Nikoláich, while I was a bachelor I went off the track a bit . . . You may have heard . . .'

Vasíli Nikoláich, evidently sorry for his master, said with smiling eyes: 'Is it about Stepanída?'

'Why, yes. Look here. Please, please do not engage her to help in the house. You understand, it is very awkward for me . . .'

'Yes, it must have been Ványa the clerk who arranged it.'

'Yes, please . . . and hadn't the rest of the phosphates better be strewn?' said Eugène, to hide his confusion.

'Yes, I am just going to see to it.'

So the matter ended, and Eugène calmed down, hoping that as he had lived for a year without seeing her, so things would go on now. 'Besides, Vasíli Nikoláich will speak to Iván the clerk; Iván will speak to her, and she will understand that I don't want it,' said

Eugène to himself, and he was glad that he had forced himself to
speak to Vasíli Nikoláich, hard as it had been to do so.

'Yes, it is better, much better, than that feeling of doubt, that
feeling of shame.' He shuddered at the mere remembrance of his sin
in thought.

12

The moral effort he had made to overcome his shame and speak to
Vasíli Nikoláich tranquillised Eugène. It seemed to him that the
matter was all over now. Liza at once noticed that he was quite calm,
and even happier than usual. 'No doubt he was upset by our mothers
pin-pricking one another. It really is disagreeable, especially for him
who is so sensitive and noble, always to hear such unfriendly and ill-
mannered insinuations,' thought she.

The next day was Trinity Sunday. It was a beautiful day, and the
peasant women, on their way into the woods to plait wreaths, came,
according to custom, to the landowner's home and began to sing
and dance. Mary Pávlovna and Varvára Alexéevna came out on to
the porch in smart clothes, carrying sunshades, and went up to the
ring of singers. With them, in a jacket of Chinese silk, came out the
uncle, a flabby libertine and drunkard, who was living that summer
with Eugène.

As usual there was a bright, many-coloured ring of young women
and girls, the centre of everything, and around these from different
sides like attendant planets that had detached themselves and were
circling round, went girls hand in hand, rustling in their new print
gowns; young lads giggling and running backwards and forwards
after one another; full-grown lads in dark blue or black coats and
caps and with red shirts, who unceasingly spat out sunflower-seed
shells; and the domestic servants or other outsiders watching the
dance-circle from aside. Both the old ladies went close up to the
ring, and Liza accompanied them in a light blue dress, with light
blue ribbons on her head, and with wide sleeves under which her
long white arms and angular elbows were visible.

Eugène did not wish to come out, but it was ridiculous to hide,
and he too came out on to the porch smoking a cigarette, bowed to
the men and lads, and talked with one of them. The women
meanwhile shouted a dance-song with all their might, snapping
their fingers, clapping their hands, and dancing.

'They are calling for the master,' said a youngster coming up to
Eugène's wife, who had not noticed the call. Liza called Eugène to

look at the dance and at one of the women dancers who particularly pleased her. This was Stepanída. She wore a yellow skirt, a velveteen sleeveless jacket and a silk kerchief, and was broad, energetic, ruddy, and merry. No doubt she danced well. He saw nothing.

'Yes, yes,' he said, removing and replacing his pince-nez. 'Yes, yes,' he repeated. 'So it seems I cannot be rid of her,' he thought.

He did not look at her, fearing her attraction, and just on that account what his passing glance caught of her seemed to him especially attractive. Besides this he saw by her sparkling look that she saw him and saw that he admired her. He stood there as long as propriety demanded, and seeing that Varvára Alexéevna had called her 'my dear' senselessly and insincerely and was talking to her, he turned aside and went away.

He went into the house in order not to see her, but on reaching the upper story he approached the window, without knowing how or why, and as long as the women remained at the porch he stood there and looked and looked at her, feasting his eyes on her.

He ran, while there was no one to see him, and then went with quiet steps on to the veranda, and from there, smoking a cigarette, he passed through the garden as if going for a stroll, and followed the direction she had taken. He had not gone two steps along the alley before he noticed behind the trees a velveteen sleeveless jacket, with a pink and yellow skirt and a red kerchief. She was going somewhere with another woman. 'Where are they going?'

And suddenly a terrible desire scorched him as though a hand were seizing his heart. As if by someone else's wish he looked round and went towards her.

'Eugène Ivánich, Eugène Ivánich! I have come to see your honour,' said a voice behind him, and Eugène, seeing old Samókhin who was digging a well for him, roused himself and turning quickly round went to meet Samókhin. While speaking with him he turned sideways and saw that she and the woman who was with her went down the slope, evidently to the well or making an excuse of the well, and having stopped there a little while ran back to the dance-circle.

13

After talking to Samókhin, Eugène returned to the house as depressed as if he had committed a crime. In the first place she had understood him, believed that he wanted to see her, and desired it herself. Secondly that other woman, Anna Prókhorova, evidently knew of it.

Above all he felt that he was conquered, that he was not master of his own will but that there was another power moving him, that he had been saved only by good fortune, and that if not today then tomorrow or a day later, he would perish all the same.

'Yes, perish,' he did not understand it otherwise: to be unfaithful to his young and loving wife with a peasant woman in the village, in the sight of everyone – what was it but to perish, perish utterly, so that it would be impossible to live? No, something must be done.

'My God, my God! What am I to do? Can it be that I shall perish like this?' said he to himself. 'Is it not possible to do anything? Yet something must be done. Do not think about her' – he ordered himself. 'Do not think!' and immediately he began thinking and seeing her before him, and seeing also the shade of the plane tree.

He remembered having read of a hermit who, to avoid the temptation he felt for a woman on whom he had to lay his hand to heal her, thrust his other hand into a brazier and burnt his fingers. He called that to mind. 'Yes, I am ready to burn my fingers rather than to perish.' He looked round to make sure that there was no one in the room, lit a candle, and put a finger into the flame. 'There, now think about her,' he said to himself ironically. It hurt him and he withdrew his smoke-stained finger, threw away the match, and laughed at himself. What nonsense! That was not what had to be done. But it was necessary to do something, to avoid seeing her – either to go away himself or to send her away. Yes – send her away. Offer her husband money to remove to town or to another village. People would hear of it and would talk about it. Well, what of that? At any rate it was better than this danger. 'Yes, that must be done,' he said to himself, and at that very moment he was looking at her without moving his eyes. 'Where is she going?' he suddenly asked himself. She, it seemed to him, had seen him at the window and now, having glanced at him and taken another woman by the hand, was going towards the garden swinging her arm briskly. Without knowing why or wherefore, merely in accord with what he had been thinking, he went to the office.

Vasíli Nikoláich in holiday costume and with oiled hair was sitting at tea with his wife and a guest who was wearing an oriental kerchief.

'I want a word with you, Vasíli Nikoláich!'

'Please say what you want to. We have finished tea.'

'No. I'd rather you came out with me.'

'Directly; only let me get my cap. Tánya, put out the samovár,' said Vasíli Nikoláich, stepping outside cheerfully.

It seemed to Eugène that Vasíli had been drinking, but what was to be done? It might be all the better – he would sympathise with him in his difficulties the more readily.

'I have come again to speak about that same matter, Vasíli Nikoláich,' said Eugène – 'about that woman.'

'Well, what of her? I told them not to take her again on any account.'

'No, I have been thinking in general, and this is what I wanted to take your advice about. Isn't it possible to get them away, to send the whole family away?'

'Where can they be sent?' said Vasíli, disapprovingly and ironically as it seemed to Eugène.

'Well, I thought of giving them money, or even some land in Koltóvski – so that she should not be here.'

'But how can they be sent away? Where is he to go – torn up from his roots? And why should you do it? What harm can she do you?'

'Ah, Vasíli Nikoláich, you must understand that it would be dreadful for my wife to hear of it.'

'But who will tell her?'

'How can I live with this dread? The whole thing is very painful for me.'

'But really, why should you distress yourself? Whoever stirs up the past – out with his eye! Who is not a sinner before God and to blame before the Tsar, as the saying is?'

'All the same it would be better to get rid of them. Can't you speak to the husband?'

'But it is no use speaking! Eh, Eugène Ivánich, what is the matter with you? It is all past and forgotten. All sorts of things happen. Who is there that would now say anything bad of you? Everybody sees you.'

'But all the same go and have a talk with him.'

'All right, I will speak to him.'

Though he knew that nothing would come of it, this talk somewhat calmed Eugène. Above all, it made him feel that through excitement he had been exaggerating the danger.

Had he gone to meet her by appointment? It was impossible. He had simply gone to stroll in the garden and she had happened to run out at the same time.

14

After dinner that very Trinity Sunday, Liza, while walking from the garden to the meadow, where her husband wanted to show her the clover, took a false step and fell when crossing a little ditch. She fell gently, on her side; but she gave an exclamation, and her husband saw an expression in her face not only of fear but of pain. He was about to help her up, but she motioned him away with her hand.

'No, wait a bit, Eugène,' she said, with a weak smile, and looked up guiltily as it seemed to him. 'My foot only gave way under me.'

'There, I always say,' remarked Varvára Alexéevna, 'can anyone in her condition possibly jump over ditches?'

'But it is all right, mamma. I shall get up directly.' With her husband's help she did get up, but she immediately turned pale, and looked frightened.

'Yes, I am not well!' and she whispered something to her mother.

'Oh, my God, what have you done! I said you ought not to go there,' cried Varvára Alexéevna. 'Wait – I will call the servants. She must not walk. She must be carried!'

'Don't be afraid, Liza, I will carry you,' said Eugène, putting his left arm round her. 'Hold me by the neck. Like that.' And stooping down he put his right arm under her knees and lifted her. He could never afterwards forget the suffering and yet beatific expression of her face.

'I am too heavy for you, dear,' she said with a smile. 'Mamma is running, tell her!' And she bent towards him and kissed him. She evidently wanted her mother to see how he was carrying her.

Eugène shouted to Varvára Alexéevna not to hurry, and that he would carry Liza home. Varvára Alexéevna stopped and began to shout still louder.

'You will drop her, you'll be sure to drop her. You want to destroy her. You have no conscience!'

'But I am carrying her excellently.'

'I do not want to watch you killing my daughter, and I can't.' And she ran round the bend in the alley.

'Never mind, it will pass,' said Liza, smiling.

'Yes. If only it does not have consequences like last time.'

'No. I am not speaking of that. That is all right. I mean mamma. You are tired. Rest a bit.'

But though he found it heavy, Eugène carried his burden proudly and gladly to the house and did not hand her over to the housemaid and the mancook whom Varvára Alexéevna had found and sent to meet them. He carried her to the bedroom and put her on the bed.

'Now go away,' she said, and drawing his hand to her she kissed it. 'Ánnushka and I will manage all right.'

Mary Pávlovna also ran in from her rooms in the wing. They undressed Liza and laid her on the bed. Eugène sat in the drawing-room with a book in his hand, waiting. Varvára Alexéevna went past him with such a reproachfully gloomy air that he felt alarmed.

'Well, how is it?' he asked.

'How is it? What's the good of asking? It is probably what you wanted when you made your wife jump over the ditch.'

'Varvára Alexéevna!' he cried. 'This is impossible. If you want to torment people and to poison their life . . . ' (he wanted to say, 'then go elsewhere to do it,' but restrained himself). 'How is it that it does not hurt you?'

'It is too late now.' And shaking her cap in a triumphant manner she passed out by the door.

The fall had really been a bad one; Liza's foot had twisted awkwardly and there was danger of her having another miscarriage. Everyone knew that there was nothing to be done but that she must just lie quietly, yet all the same they decided to send for a doctor.

'Dear Nikoláy Seménich,' wrote Eugène to the doctor, 'you have always been so kind to us that I hope you will not refuse to come to my wife's assistance. She . . . ' and so on. Having written the letter he went to the stables to arrange about the horses and the carriage. Horses had to be got ready to bring the doctor and others to take him back. When an estate is not run on a large scale, such things cannot be quickly decided but have to be considered. Having arranged it all and dispatched the coachman, it was past nine before he got back to the house. His wife was lying down, and said that she felt perfectly well and had no pain. But Varvára Alexéevna was sitting with a lamp screened from Liza by some sheets of music and knitting a large red coverlet, with a mien that said that after what had happened peace was impossible, but that she at any rate would do her duty no matter what anyone else did.

Eugène noticed this, but, to appear as if he had not done so, tried to assume a cheerful and tranquil air and told how he had chosen the horses and how capitally the mare, Kabúshka, had galloped as left trace-horse in the troyka.[45]

'Yes, of course, it is just the time to exercise the horses when help is needed. Probably the doctor will also be thrown into the ditch,' remarked Varvára Alexéevna, examining her knitting from under her pince-nez and moving it close up to the lamp.

'But you know we had to send one way or other, and I made the best arrangement I could.'

'Yes, I remember very well how your horses galloped with me under the arch of the gateway.' This was a long-standing fancy of hers, and Eugène now was injudicious enough to remark that that was not quite what had happened.

'It is not for nothing that I have always said, and have often remarked to the prince, that it is hardest of all to live with people who are untruthful and insincere. I can endure anything except that.'

'Well, if anyone has to suffer more than another, it is certainly I,' said Eugène. 'But you . . . '

'Yes, it is evident.'

'What?'

'Nothing, I am only counting my stitches.'

Eugène was standing at the time by the bed and Liza was looking at him, and one of her moist hands outside the coverlet caught his hand and pressed it. 'Bear with her for my sake. You know she cannot prevent our loving one another,' was what her look said.

'I won't do so again. It's nothing,' he whispered, and he kissed her damp, long hand and then her affectionate eyes, which closed while he kissed them.

'Can it be the same thing over again?' he asked. 'How are you feeling?'

'I am afraid to say for fear of being mistaken, but I feel that he is alive and will live,' said she, glancing at her stomach.

'Ah, it is dreadful, dreadful to think of.'

Notwithstanding Liza's insistence that he should go away, Eugène spent the night with her, hardly closing an eye and ready to attend on her.

But she passed the night well, and had they not sent for the doctor she would perhaps have got up.

By dinner-time the doctor arrived and of course said that though if the symptoms recurred there might be cause for apprehension, yet actually there were no positive symptoms, but as there were also no contrary indications one might suppose on the one hand that – and on the other hand that . . . And therefore she must lie still, and that 'though I do not like prescribing, yet all the same she should take this mixture and should lie quiet'. Besides this, the doctor gave Varvára Alexéevna a lecture on woman's anatomy, during which

Varvára Alexéevna nodded her head significantly. Having received his fee, as usual into the backmost part of his palm, the doctor drove away and the patient was left to lie in bed for a week.

15

Eugène spent most of his time by his wife's bedside, talking to her, reading to her, and what was hardest of all, enduring without murmur Varvára Alexéevna's attacks, and even contriving to turn these into jokes.

But he could not stay at home all the time. In the first place his wife sent him away, saying that he would fall ill if he always remained with her; and secondly the farming was progressing in a way that demanded his presence at every step. He could not stay at home, but had to be in the fields, in the wood, in the garden, at the threshing-floor; and everywhere he was pursued not merely by the thought but by the vivid image of Stepanída, and he only occasionally forgot her. But that would not have mattered, he could perhaps have mastered his feeling; what was worst of all was that, whereas he had previously lived for months without seeing her, he now continually came across her. She evidently understood that he wished to renew relations with her and tried to come in his way. Nothing was said either by him or by her, and therefore neither he nor she went directly to a rendez-vous, but only sought opportunities of meeting.

The most possible place for them to meet was in the forest, where peasant women went with sacks to collect grass for their cows. Eugène knew this and therefore went there every day. Every day he told himself that he would not go, and every day it ended by his making his way to the forest and, on hearing the sound of voices, standing behind the bushes with sinking heart looking to see if she was there.

Why he wanted to know whether it was she who was there, he did not know. If it had been she and she had been alone, he would not have gone to her – so he believed – he would have run away; but he wanted to see her.

Once he met her. As he was entering the forest she came out of it with two other women, carrying a heavy sack full of grass on her back. A little earlier he would perhaps have met her in the forest. Now, with the other women there, she could not go back to him. But though he realised this impossibility, he stood for a long time behind a hazel-bush, at the risk of attracting the other women's attention. Of course she did not return, but he stayed there a long time. And, great heavens, how delightful his imagination made her appear to him! And this not only once, but five or six times, and each time more intensely. Never had she seemed so attractive, and never had he been so completely in her power.

He felt that he had lost control of himself and had become almost insane. His strictness with himself had not weakened a jot; on the contrary he saw all the abomination of his desire and even of his action, for his going to the wood was an action. He knew that he only need come near her anywhere in the dark, and if possible touch her, and he would yield to his feelings. He knew that it was only shame before people, before her, and no doubt before himself also, that restrained him. And he knew too that he had sought conditions in which that shame would not be apparent – darkness or proximity – in which it would be stifled by animal passion. And therefore he knew that he was a wretched criminal, and despised and hated himself with all his soul. He hated himself because he still had not surrendered: every day he prayed God to strengthen him, to save him from perishing; every day he determined that from today onward he would not take a step to see her, and would forget her. Every day he devised means of delivering himself from this enticement, and he made use of those means.

But it was all in vain.

One of the means was continual occupation; another was intense physical work and fasting; a third was imagining clearly to himself the shame that would fall upon him when everybody knew of it – his wife, his mother-in-law, and the folk around. He did all this and it seemed to him that he was conquering, but midday came – the hour of their former meetings and the hour when he had met her carrying the grass – and he went to the forest. Thus five days of torment passed. He only saw her from a distance, and did not once encounter her.

16

Liza was gradually recovering, she could move about and was only uneasy at the change that had taken place in her husband, which she did not understand.

Varvára Alexéevna had gone away for a while, and the only visitor was Eugène's uncle. Mary Pávlovna was as usual at home.

Eugène was in his semi-insane condition when there came two days of pouring rain, as often happens after thunder in June. The rain stopped all work. They even ceased carting manure on account of the dampness and dirt. The peasants remained at home. The herdsmen wore themselves out with the cattle, and eventually drove them home. The cows and sheep wandered about in the pasture-land and ran loose in the grounds. The peasant women, barefoot and wrapped in shawls, splashing through the mud, rushed about to seek the runaway cows. Streams flowed everywhere along the paths, all the leaves and all the grass were saturated with water, and streams flowed unceasingly from the spouts into the bubbling puddles.

Eugène sat at home with his wife, who was particularly wearisome that day. She questioned Eugène several times as to the cause of his discontent, and he replied with vexation that nothing was the matter. She ceased questioning him but was still distressed.

They were sitting after breakfast in the drawing-room. His uncle for the hundredth time was recounting fabrications about his society acquaintances. Liza was knitting a jacket and sighed, complaining of the weather and of a pain in the small of her back. The uncle advised her to lie down, and asked for vodka for himself. It was terribly dull for Eugène in the house. Everything was weak and dull. He read a book and a magazine, but understood nothing of them.

'I must go out and look at the rasping-machine they brought yesterday,' said he, and got up and went out.

'Take an umbrella with you.'

'Oh, no, I have a leather coat. And I am only going as far as the boiling-room.'

He put on his boots and his leather coat and went to the factory; and he had not gone twenty steps before he met her coming towards him, with her skirts tucked up high above her white calves. She was walking, holding down the shawl in which her head and shoulders were wrapped.

'Where are you going?' said he, not recognising her the first instant. When he recognised her it was already too late. She stopped, smiling, and looked long at him.

'I am looking for a calf. Where are you off to in such weather?' said she, as if she were seeing him every day.

'Come to the shed,' said he suddenly, without knowing how he said it. It was as if someone else had uttered the words.

She bit her shawl, winked, and ran in the direction which led from the garden to the shed, and he continued his path, intending to turn off beyond the lilac-bush and go there too.

'Master,' he heard a voice behind him. 'The mistress is calling you, and wants you to come back for a minute.'

This was Mísha, his manservant.

'My God! This is the second time you have saved me,' thought Eugène, and immediately turned back. His wife reminded him that he had promised to take some medicine at the dinner-hour to a sick woman, and he had better take it with him.

While they were getting the medicine some five minutes elapsed, and then, going away with the medicine, he hesitated to go direct to the shed lest he should be seen from the house, but as soon as he was out of sight he promptly turned and made his way to it. He already saw her in imagination inside the shed smiling gaily. But she was not there, and there was nothing in the shed to show that she had been there.

He was already thinking that she had not come, had not heard or understood his words – he had muttered them through his nose as if afraid of her hearing them – or perhaps she had not wanted to come. 'And why did I imagine that she would rush to me? She has her own husband; it is only I who am such a wretch as to have a wife, and a good one, and to run after another.' Thus he thought sitting in the shed, the thatch of which had a leak and dripped from its straw. 'But how delightful it would be if she did come – alone here in this rain. If only I could embrace her once again, then let happen what may. But I could tell if she has been here by her footprints,' he reflected. He looked at the trodden ground near the shed and at the path overgrown by grass, and the fresh print of bare feet, and even of one that had slipped, was visible. 'Yes, she has been here. Well, now it is settled. Wherever I may see her I shall go straight to her. I will go to her at night.' He sat for a long time in the shed and left it exhausted and crushed. He delivered the medicine, returned home, and lay down in his room to wait for dinner.

17

Before dinner Liza came to him and, still wondering what could be the cause of his discontent, began to say that she was afraid he did not like the idea of her going to Moscow for her confinement, and that she had decided that she would remain at home and on no account go to Moscow. He knew how she feared both her confinement itself and the risk of not having a healthy child, and therefore he could not help being touched at seeing how ready she was to sacrifice everything for his sake. All was so nice, so pleasant, so clean, in the house; and in his soul it was so dirty, despicable, and foul. The whole evening Eugène was tormented by knowing that notwithstanding his sincere repulsion at his own weakness, notwithstanding his firm intention to break off – the same thing would happen again tomorrow.

'No, this is impossible,' he said to himself, walking up and down in his room. 'There must be some remedy for it. My God! What am I to do?'

Someone knocked at the door as foreigners do. He knew this must be his uncle. 'Come in,' he said.

The uncle had come as a self-appointed ambassador from Liza.

'Do you know, I really do notice that there is a change in you,' he said – 'and Liza – I understand how it troubles her. I understand that it must be hard for you to leave all the business you have so excellently started, but *que veux-tu?*[46] I should advise you to go away. It will be more satisfactory both for you and for her. And do you know, I should advise you to go to the Crimea. The climate is beautiful and there is an excellent *accoucheur*[47] there, and you would be just in time for the best of the grape season.'

'Uncle,' Eugène suddenly exclaimed. 'Can you keep a secret? A secret that is terrible to me, a shameful secret.'

'Oh, come – do you really feel any doubt of me?'

'Uncle, you can help me. Not only help, but save me!' said Eugène. And the thought of disclosing his secret to his uncle whom he did not respect, the thought that he would show himself in the worst light and humiliate himself before him, was pleasant. He felt himself to be despicable and guilty, and wished to punish himself.

'Speak, my dear fellow, you know how fond I am of you,' said the uncle, evidently well content that there was a secret and that it was a shameful one, and that it would be communicated to him, and that he could be of use.

'First of all I must tell you that I am a wretch, a good-for-nothing, a scoundrel – a real scoundrel.'

'Now what are you saying . . . ' began his uncle, as if he were offended.

'What! Not a wretch when I – Liza's husband, Liza's! One has only to know her purity, her love – and that I, her husband, want to be untrue to her with a peasant woman!'

'What is this? Why do you want to – you have not been unfaithful to her?'

'Yes, at least just the same as being untrue, for it did not depend on me. I was ready to do so. I was hindered, or else I should . . . now. I do not know what I should have done . . . '

'But please, explain to me . . . '

'Well, it is like this. When I was a bachelor I was stupid enough to have relations with a woman here in our village. That is to say, I used to have meetings with her in the forest, in the field . . . '

'Was she pretty?' asked his uncle.

Eugène frowned at this question, but he was in such need of external help that he made as if he did not hear it, and continued: 'Well, I thought this was just casual and that I should break it off and have done with it. And I did break it off before my marriage. For nearly a year I did not see her or think about her.' It seemed strange to Eugène himself to hear the description of his own condition. 'Then suddenly, I don't myself know why – really one sometimes believes in witchcraft – I saw her, and a worm crept into my heart; and it gnaws. I reproach myself, I understand the full horror of my action, that is to say, of the act I may commit any moment, and yet I myself turn to it, and if I have not committed it, it is only because God preserved me. Yesterday I was on my way to see her when Liza sent for me.'

'What, in the rain?'

'Yes. I am worn out, Uncle, and have decided to confess to you and to ask your help.'

'Yes, of course, it's a bad thing on your own estate. People will get to know. I understand that Liza is weak and that it is necessary to spare her, but why on your own estate?'

Again Eugène tried not to hear what his uncle was saying, and hurried on to the core of the matter.

'Yes, save me from myself. That is what I ask of you. Today I was hindered by chance. But tomorrow or next time no one will hinder me. And she knows now. Don't leave me alone.'

'Yes, all right,' said his uncle – 'but are you really so much in love?'

'Oh, it is not that at all. It is not that, it is some kind of power that has seized me and holds me. I do not know what to do. Perhaps I shall gain strength, and then . . . '

'Well, it turns out as I suggested,' said his uncle. 'Let us be off to the Crimea.'

'Yes, yes, let us go, and meanwhile you will be with me and will talk to me.'

18

The fact that Eugène had confided his secret to his uncle, and still more the sufferings of his conscience and the feeling of shame he experienced after that rainy day, sobered him. It was settled that they would start for Yálta in a week's time. During that week Eugène drove to town to get money for the journey, gave instructions from the house and from the office concerning the management of the estate, again became gay and friendly with his wife, and began to awaken morally.

So without having once seen Stepanída after that rainy day he left with his wife for the Crimea. There he spent an excellent two months. He received so many new impressions that it seemed to him that the past was obliterated from his memory. In the Crimea they met former acquaintances and became particularly friendly with them, and they also made new acquaintances. Life in the Crimea was a continual holiday for Eugène, besides being instructive and beneficial. They became friendly there with the former Marshal of the Nobility of their province, a clever and liberal-minded man who became fond of Eugène and coached him, and attracted him to his Party.

At the end of August Liza gave birth to a beautiful, healthy daughter, and her confinement was unexpectedly easy.

In September they returned home, the four of them, including the baby and its wet-nurse, as Liza was unable to nurse it herself. Eugène returned home entirely free from the former horrors and quite a new and happy man. Having gone through all that a husband goes through when his wife bears a child, he loved her more than ever. His feeling for the child when he took it in his arms was a funny, new, very pleasant and, as it were, a tickling feeling. Another new thing in his life now was that, besides his occupation with the estate, thanks to his acquaintance with Dúmchin (the ex-Marshal) a new interest occupied his mind, that of the Zémstvo[48] – partly an ambitious interest, partly a feeling of duty. In October there was to be a special Assembly, at which he was to be elected. After arriving home he drove once to town and another time to Dúmchin.

Of the torments of his temptation and struggle he had forgotten even to think, and could with difficulty recall them to mind. It seemed to him something like an attack of insanity he had undergone.

To such an extent did he now feel free from it that he was not even afraid to make enquiries on the first occasion when he remained alone with the steward. As he had previously spoken to him about the matter he was not ashamed to ask.

'Well, and is Sídor Péchnikov still away from home?' he enquired.

'Yes, he is still in town.'

'And his wife?'

'Oh, she is a worthless woman. She is now carrying on with Zenóvi. She has gone quite on the loose.'

'Well, that is all right,' thought Eugène. 'How wonderfully indifferent to it I am! How I have changed.'

19

All that Eugène had wished had been realised. He had obtained the property, the factory was working successfully, the beet-crops were excellent, and he expected a large income; his wife had borne a child satisfactorily, his mother-in-law had left, and he had been unanimously elected to the Zémstvo.

He was returning home from town after the election. He had been congratulated and had had to return thanks. He had had dinner and had drunk some five glasses of champagne. Quite new plans of life now presented themselves to him, and he was thinking about these as he drove home. It was the Indian summer: an excellent road and a hot sun. As he approached his home Eugène was thinking of how, as a result of this election, he would occupy among the people the position he had always dreamed of; that is to say, one in which he would be able to serve them not only by production, which gave employment, but also by direct influence. He imagined what his own and the other peasants would think of him in three years' time. 'For instance this one,' he thought, driving just then through the village and glancing at a peasant who with a peasant woman was crossing the street in front of him carrying a full water-tub. They stopped to let his carriage pass. The peasant was old Péchnikov, and the woman was Stepanída. Eugène looked at her, recognised her, and was glad to feel that he remained quite tranquil. She was still as good-looking as ever, but this did not touch him at all. He drove home.

'Well, may we congratulate you?' said his uncle.

'Yes, I was elected.'

'Capital! We must drink to it!'

Next day Eugène drove about to see to the farming which he had been neglecting. At the outlying farmstead a new threshing machine was at work. While watching it Eugène stepped among the women, trying not to take notice of them; but try as he would he once or twice noticed the black eyes and red kerchief of Stepanída, who was carrying away the straw. Once or twice he glanced sideways at her and felt that something was happening, but could not account for it to himself. Only next day, when he again drove to the threshing-floor and spent two hours there quite unnecessarily, without ceasing to caress with his eyes the familiar, handsome figure of the young woman, did he feel that he was lost, irremediably lost. Again those torments! Again all that horror and fear, and there was no saving himself.

What he expected happened to him. The evening of the next day, without knowing how, he found himself at her backyard, by her hay-shed, where in autumn they had once had a meeting. As though having a stroll, he stopped there lighting a cigarette. A neighbouring peasant woman saw him, and as he turned back he heard her say to someone: 'Go, he is waiting for you – on my dying word he is standing there. Go, you fool!'

He saw how a woman – she – ran to the hay-shed; but as a peasant had met him it was no longer possible for him to turn back, and so he went home.

20

When he entered the drawing-room everything seemed strange and unnatural to him. He had risen that morning vigorous, determined to fling it all aside, to forget it and not allow himself to think about it. But without noticing how it occurred he had all the morning not merely not interested himself in the work, but tried to avoid it. What had formerly cheered him and been important was now insignificant. Unconsciously he tried to free himself from business. It seemed to him that he had to do so in order to think and to plan. And he freed himself and remained alone. But as soon as he was alone he began to wander about in the garden and the forest. And all those spots were besmirched in his recollection by memories that gripped him. He felt that he was walking in the garden and pretending to himself that he was thinking out some-thing, but that really he was not thinking out anything, but insanely and unreasonably expecting her; expecting that by some miracle she would be aware that he was expecting her, and would come here at once and go somewhere where no one would see them, or would come at night when there would be no moon, and no one,

THE DEVIL 247

not even she herself, would see – on such a night she would come and he would touch her body . . .

'There now, talking of breaking off when I wish to,' said he to himself. 'Yes, and that is having a clean healthy woman for one's health's sake! No, it seems one can't play with her like that. I thought I had taken her, but it was she who took me; took me and does not let me go. Why, I thought I was free, but I was not free and was deceiving myself when I married. It was all nonsense – fraud. From the time I had her I experienced a new feeling, the real feeling of a husband. Yes, I ought to have lived with her.

'One of two lives is possible for me: that which I began with Liza: service, estate management, the child, and people's respect. If that is life, it is necessary that she, Stepanída, should not be there. She must be sent away, as I said, or destroyed so that she shall not exist. And the other life – is this: For me to take her away from her husband, pay him money, disregard the shame and disgrace, and live with her. But in that case it is necessary that Liza should not exist, nor Mimi [the baby]. No, that is not so, the baby does not matter, but it is necessary that there should be no Liza – that she should go away – that she should know, curse me, and go away. That she should know that I have exchanged her for a peasant woman, that I am a deceiver and a scoundrel! – No, that is too terrible! It is impossible. But it might happen,' he went on thinking – 'it might happen that Liza might fall ill and die. Die, and then everything would be capital.

'Capital! Oh, scoundrel! No, if someone must die it should be Stepanída. If she were to die, how good it would be.

'Yes, that is how men come to poison or kill their wives or lovers. Take a revolver and go and call her, and instead of embracing her, shoot her in the breast and have done with it.

'Really she is – a devil. Simply a devil. She has possessed herself of me against my own will.

'Kill? Yes. There are only two ways out: to kill my wife or her. For it is impossible to live like this.* It is impossible! I must consider the matter and look ahead. If things remain as they are what will happen? I shall again be saying to myself that I do not wish it and that I will throw her off, but it will be merely words; in the evening I shall be at her backyard, and she will know it and will come out. And if people know of it and tell my wife, or if I tell her myself – for I can't lie – I shall not be able to live so. I cannot!

* At this point the alternative ending, printed at the end of the story, begins.

People will know. They will all know – Parásha and the blacksmith. Well, is it possible to live so?

'Impossible! There are only two ways out: to kill my wife, or to kill her. Yes, or else . . . Ah, yes, there is a third way: to kill myself,' said he softly, and suddenly a shudder ran over his skin. 'Yes, kill myself, then I shall not need to kill them.' He became frightened, for he felt that only that way was possible. He had a revolver. 'Shall I really kill myself? It is something I never thought of – how strange it will be . . .'

He returned to his study and at once opened the cupboard where the revolver lay, but before he had taken it out of its case his wife entered the room.

21

He threw a newspaper over the revolver.

'Again the same!' said she aghast when she had looked at him.

'What is the same?'

'The same terrible expression that you had before and would not explain to me. Jénya, dear one, tell me about it. I see that you are suffering. Tell me and you will feel easier. Whatever it may be, it will be better than for you to suffer so. Don't I know that it is nothing bad?'

'You know? While . . .'

'Tell me, tell me, tell me. I won't let you go.'

He smiled a piteous smile.

'Shall I? – No, it is impossible. And there is nothing to tell.'

Perhaps he might have told her, but at that moment the wet-nurse entered to ask if she should go for a walk. Liza went out to dress the baby.

'Then you will tell me? I will be back directly.'

'Yes, perhaps . . .'

She never could forget the piteous smile with which he said this. She went out.

Hurriedly, stealthily like a robber, he seized the revolver and took it out of its case. It was loaded, yes, but long ago, and one cartridge was missing.

'Well, how will it be?' He put it to his temple and hesitated a little, but as soon as he remembered Stepanída – his decision not to see her, his struggle, temptation, fall, and renewed struggle – he shuddered with horror. 'No, this is better,' and he pulled the trigger . . .

When Liza ran into the room – she had only had time to step down from the balcony – he was lying face downwards on the floor: black, warm blood was gushing from the wound, and his corpse was twitching.

There was an inquest. No one could understand or explain the suicide. It never even entered his uncle's head that its cause could be anything in common with the confession Eugène had made to him two months previously.

Varvára Alexéevna assured them that she had always foreseen it. It had been evident from his way of disputing. Neither Liza nor Mary Pávlovna could at all understand why it had happened, but still they did not believe what the doctors said, namely, that he was mentally deranged – a psychopath. They were quite unable to accept this, for they knew he was saner than hundreds of their acquaintances.

And indeed if Eugène Irténev was mentally deranged everyone is in the same case; the most mentally deranged people are certainly those who see in others indications of insanity they do not notice in themselves.

Variation of the conclusion of 'The Devil'

'To kill, yes. There are only two ways out: to kill my wife, or to kill her. For it is impossible to live like this,' said he to himself, and going up to the table he took from it a revolver and, having examined it – one cartridge was wanting – he put it in his trouser pocket.

'My God! What am I doing?' he suddenly exclaimed, and folding his hands he began to pray.

'O God, help me and deliver me! Thou knowest that I do not desire evil, but by myself am powerless. Help me,' said he, making the sign of the cross on his breast before the icon.

'Yes, I can control myself. I will go out, walk about and think things over.'

He went to the entrance-hall, put on his overcoat and went out on to the porch. Unconsciously his steps took him past the garden along the field path to the outlying farmstead. There the threshing machine was still droning and the cries of the driver-lads were heard. He entered the barn. She was there. He saw her at once. She was raking up the corn, and on seeing him she ran briskly and merrily about, with laughing eyes, raking up the scattered corn with agility.

Eugène could not help watching her though he did not wish to do so. He only recollected himself when she was no longer in sight. The clerk informed him that they were now finishing threshing the corn that had been beaten down – that was why it was going slower and the output was less. Eugène went up to the drum, which occasionally gave a knock as sheaves not evenly fed in passed under it, and he asked the clerk if there were many such sheaves of beaten-down corn.

'There will be five cartloads of it.'

'Then look here . . .' began Eugène, but he did not finish the sentence. She had gone close up to the drum and was raking the corn from under it, and she scorched him with her laughing eyes. That look spoke of a merry, careless love between them, of the fact that she knew he wanted her and had come to her shed, and that she as always was ready to live and be merry with him regardless of all conditions or consequences. Eugène felt himself to be in her power but did not wish to yield.

He remembered his prayer and tried to repeat it. He began saying it to himself, but at once felt that it was useless. A single thought now engrossed him entirely: how to arrange a meeting with her so that the others should not notice it.

'If we finish this lot today, are we to start on a fresh stack or leave it till tomorrow?' asked the clerk.

'Yes, yes,' replied Eugène, involuntarily following her to the heap to which with the other women she was raking the corn.

'But can I really not master myself?' said he to himself. 'Have I really perished? O God! But there is no God. There is only a devil. And it is she. She has possessed me. But I won't, I won't! A devil, yes, a devil.'

Again he went up to her, drew the revolver from his pocket and shot her, once, twice, thrice, in the back. She ran a few steps and fell on the heap of corn.

'My God, my God! What is that?' cried the women.

'No, it was not an accident. I killed her on purpose,' cried Eugène. 'Send for the police-officer.'

He went home and went to his study and locked himself in, without speaking to his wife.

'Do not come to me,' he cried to her through the door. 'You will know all about it.'

An hour later he rang, and bade the manservant who answered the bell: 'Go and find out whether Stepanída is alive.'

The servant already knew all about it, and told him she had died an hour ago.

'Well, all right. Now leave me alone. When the police-officer or the magistrate comes, let me know.'

The police-officer and magistrate arrived next morning, and Eugène, having bidden his wife and baby farewell, was taken to prison.

He was tried. It was during the early days of trial by jury, and the verdict was one of temporary insanity, and he was sentenced only to perform church penance.

He had been kept in prison for nine months and was then confined in a monastery for one month.

He had begun to drink while still in prison, continued to do so in the monastery, and returned home an enfeebled, irresponsible drunkard.

Varvára Alexéevna assured them that she had always predicted this. It was, she said, evident from the way he disputed. Neither Liza nor Mary Pávlovna could understand how the affair had happened, but for all that, they did not believe what the doctors said, namely, that he was mentally deranged – a psychopath. They could not accept that, for they knew that he was saner than hundreds of their acquaintances.

And indeed, if Eugène Irténev was mentally deranged when he committed this crime, then everyone is similarly insane. The most mentally deranged people are certainly those who see in others indications of insanity they do not notice in themselves.

NOTES

Family Happiness

1 (p. 6) *sonata quasi una fantasia* This is surely the sonata usually known as the *Moonlight Sonata*, Op. 27, no. 2, in C sharp minor. Although its companion in E flat major also has the superscription *quasi una fantasia*, the former is famous for its opening *adagio*, and fits the story very well.

2 (p. 14) *Schulhoff* Julius Schulhoff (1825–95) was a composer of popular pieces for the piano.

3 (p. 21) *Lieutenant Strelsky . . . Alfred . . . Eleonora* references to the popular Romantic literature of the time

4 (p. 25) *Fast of the Assumption* a two-week fast ending on 28 August

5 (p. 49) *Lermontov* Mikhail Yurevich Lermontov (1814–41) was a Romantic poet and novelist regarded as second only to Pushkin and influenced by him and Byron.

6 (p. 50) *Croesus* a king of Lydia famous in ancient Greek literature for his riches

7 (p. 61) *sign of the cross* a Russian custom designed to protect the child from the evils of the night. Masha's appearance in her ball gown signals her dubious priorities and anticipates similar implied criticism of Anna as a mother in *Anna Karenina*.

8 (p. 63) *Baden* The spa town of Baden-Baden was a particularly favoured resort of the European aristocracy in the nineteenth century.

The Death of Ivan Ilyich

9 (p. 79) *Golovin* Ilyich's surname is derived from the Russian word for head, perhaps signifying that he is deficient in the qualities associated with the heart.

10 (p. 87) *phénix de la famille* 'the prodigy [literally "phoenix"] of the family'

11 (p. 87) *respice finem*   consider the end – a very appropriate motto as the story will show

12 (p. 88) *Il faut que la jeunesse se passe*   The equivalent in English is, 'Youth will have its day.'

13 (p. 89) *comme il faut*   appropriate to his class and status (literally 'just as it should be')

14 (p. 89) *reforms . . . in 1864*   These included the introduction, encouraged by the reforming Tsar Alexander II, of trial by jury.

15 (p. 91) *de gaité de coeur*   out of high spirits

16 (p. 94) *the Empress Marya's institutions*   charitable organisations of which the Tsarina was patron

17 (p. 96) *étagère*   a what-not, i.e. a free-standing piece of furniture consisting of open shelves supported by posts

18 (p. 121) *à la Capoul*   imitating the distinctive hairstyle of Victor Capoul (1839–1924), a much admired tenor of the period, who wore his hair in tight curls rising from the nape of his neck to the top of his head. Tolstoy would undoubtedly have regarded the style as very effeminate.

19 (p. 121) *Sarah Bernhardt*   French actress (1844–1923) famous for her performances in both female and male parts

20 (p. 121) *Adrienne Lecouvreur*   a play by the French dramatists Scribe and Legouve

The Kreutzer Sonata

21 (p. 134) *the second bell*   the third ringing of the station bell would mean that the train's departure was imminent.

22 (p. 136) *tower*   Maude rather oddly uses this as the translation of *terem*, the Russian word for the domestic areas to which Russian women were once confined – very roughly similar to an Oriental harem, but without the polygamy.

23 (p. 138) *Domostroy*   literally 'Home-constructor', an ancient book of instructions on domestic and religious matters

24 (p. 143) *brothels*   These were licensed by the Russian government and subject to medical inspection.

25 (p. 145) *Rigulboche*   a well-known Montparnasse can-can dancer

26 (p. 152) *Sisyphus*   In accounts of the classical Hades, Sisyphus was condemned to spend eternity rolling a giant boulder to the top of a hill, only to have it fall down to the bottom again every time he had nearly succeeded.

27 (p. 154) *Schopenhauers, the Hartmanns, and all the Buddhists as well* proponents of the idea that life on this earth is suffering and that man should seek means to escape from it into annihilation or some higher state of being. The writings of Artur Schopenhauer (1788–1860) were particularly influential. K. R. E. von Hartmann (1842–1906) is also seen as a pessimist about human life, with perhaps less justification.

28 (p. 160) *Wein, Weib und Gesang*   wine, women and song

29 (p. 160) *Venuses and Phrynes*   Venus was of course the Roman goddess of love, Phryne the name of a classical courtesan.

30 (p. 160) *the Trubá and the Grachevka*   streets in Moscow's red-light district

31 (p. 162) *a fine head-dress*   part of the costume provided, according to Maude, by upper-class Russian families for the peasant wet-nurses who were usually employed to relieve rich mothers of the need to breastfeed their children

32 (p. 163) *doctors*   This dislike of doctors is a recurrent theme in these stories.

33 (p. 167) *Well, and so we lived*   In Tolstoy's early unrevised version, circulated as a lithograph, this sentence precedes a long passage which includes the following statement, 'What I chiefly felt was that I was a man, and that a man as I understand it should be master, but that I had fallen under my wife's slipper, as the saying is, and could not manage to escape from under it. What chiefly kept me under her slipper was the children. I wished to get up and assert my authority, but it never came off . . . '

34 (p. 168) *Charcot*   Jean Martin Charcot (1825–93) was a Parisian doctor specialising in mental illness and the use of techniques such as hypnosis to treat hysteria.

35 (p. 180) *Uriah's wife*   In the Bible, Bathsheba, the unfaithful wife of Uriah the Hittite, is the cause of her husband's death. II Samuel, 11:2–7

36 (p. 183) *Beethoven's Kreutzer Sonata*   the Sonata no. 9 in A major, Op. 47, described by Marion Scott (see Bibliography) as opening 'with an introduction and first movement 'on a scale of emotional and executive magnificence unmatched in any other violin sonata' (Scott, p. 240)

37 (p. 185) *Ernst's Elegy*   Heinrich Wilhelm Ernst (1814–65) was a violinist and composer popular at the time.

38 (p. 185) *Zémstvo* local assemblies set up as a stepping stone towards greater democracy in the reign of Alexander II. In fact, the peasant and middle-class members tended to defer to the aristocracy.

39 (p. 188) *tarantas* a type of low carriage with four wheels

40 (p. 190) *Vánka the Steward* the hero of some old Russian ballads. He was hanged for seducing his master's wife.

The Devil

41 (p. 209) *desyatins* measurements of land area equalling 1.09 hectares or 2.9 acres

42 (p. 219) *the Institute* an upper-class boarding school, similar in its aims to a Swiss or English 'finishing school' for young ladies

43 (p. 225) *'envelopes'* small mattresses with an attached coverlet in which babies were carried from place to place.

44 (p. 226) *phosphates* used as fertiliser

45 (p. 236) *troyka* a sleigh on wooden runners drawn by three horses

46 (p. 242) *que veux tu* 'what do you want [to do]'

47 (p. 242) *accoucheur* obstetrician

48 (p. 244) *Zémstvo* see note on *The Kreutzer Sonata*, p. 185